Award-winning author **Jennifer Faye** pens fun contemporary romances. Internationally published, with books translated into more than a dozen languages, she is a two-time winner of the *RT Book Reviews* Reviewers' Choice Award and winner of the CataRomance Reviewers' Choice Award. Now living her dream, she resides with her very patient husband and Writer Kitty. When she's not plotting out her next romance you can find her with a mug of tea and a book. Learn more at jenniferfaye.com

Cathy Gillen Thacker is a married mother of three. She and her husband reside in North Carolina. Her stories have made numerous appearances on bestseller lists, but her best reward is knowing one of her books made someone's day a little brighter. A popular Mills & Boon author, she loves telling passionate stories with happy endings and thinks nothing beats a good romance and a hot cup of tea! Visit her at cathygillenthacker.com for information on her books, recipes and a list of her favourite things.

BOUND BY A RING
AND A SECRET

JENNIFER FAYE

THE TWIN PROPOSAL

CATHY GILLEN THACKER

MILLS & BOON

First Published in Great Britain 2021
by Mills & Boon, an imprint of HarperCollins*Publishers* Ltd
1 London Bridge Street, London, SE1 9GF

www.harpercollins.co.uk

HarperCollins*Publishers*
1st Floor, Watermarque Building,
Ringsend Road, Dublin 4, Ireland

Bound by a Ring and a Secret © 2021 Jennifer F. Stroka
The Twin Proposal © 2021 Cathy Gillen Thacker

ISBN: 978-0-263-29960-1

0421

MIX
Paper from
responsible sources

FSC
www.fsc.org
FSC™ C007454

Printed and bound in Spain
by CPI, Barcelona

BOUND BY A RING
AND A SECRET

JENNIFER FAYE

For Lucas Lee.

Welcome to the world, sweetie!

You are a bundle of heart-warming smiles and contagious giggles.

You light up my life! Love you!

CHAPTER ONE

HOME AGAIN.

Gianna Cappellini didn't smile.

Today, the usual euphoria of returning to the small Italian village of Gemma was lacking. Whereas her home was normally her sanctuary—a place to settle in and unwind—this time it felt different. *She* felt different.

As the hired car moved closer to her destination, she wrung her hands as she stared out the back-seat window. It was a sunny June day without a cloud in the sky. As picturesque Lake Como came into view, she merely sighed in relief.

Her gaze momentarily strayed to her still bare ring finger. Another romance had ended in disaster. Looking back, how could it have ended any other way? She'd wanted so badly to be loved that she'd tried to be someone she wasn't.

It hadn't always been that way. In the beginning, she and Naldo had rebounded into each other after messy break-ups. Naldo had flirted with her and she'd fallen hard for his not-so-original lines. Things turned serious quickly as they talked about their future—him continuing to host his hit television show while she stayed in the background working the camera as she followed him around the world.

And then suddenly he dumped her. There hadn't been so much as a warning or a conversation. Just a simple, *I can't do this anymore. It's over.* And then he'd refused to speak to her. The jerk!

Her rosy glasses fell away as reality bumped hard into her. And she didn't like what she saw. She had been so busy being congenial—so agreeable—with everything he said or did that she barely recognized herself. How did she lose herself? What had happened to all the things that were important to her?

But all that was behind her now—for the most part. To-night, she'd get to sleep in her own comfy bed. Oh, how she'd missed it. There would be no more restless nights in a tent—no more roughing it on uneven ground. She didn't even want to think about all the other luxuries she'd done without in the past several weeks.

And come tomorrow, she'd figure out what came next.

One of those things would be facing her cousin and ex-plaining things. Thankfully, her cousin was the only person she'd confided in about her whirlwind romance and the ex-pected engagement. And even then, she'd kept the details to the bare minimum, not even mentioning his famous name as she hadn't wanted to jinx things before the engagement was made official with a diamond ring.

Now that the relationship had imploded, what would she say to her cousin? *It was just one of those things.* Or the truth: she had the worst luck where men were concerned.

The car dropped her off at the edge of the village, allow-ing her to stop by the market and pick up a few essentials before heading to the villa. She hadn't been home in a little more than a month and during that time she'd used a local real-estate management service to rent out her place. She worked as a camerawoman for a nature channel and she'd come to rely on the extra funds from renting her house. It wasn't ideal but it supplemented her savings. And those savings were what would keep her afloat until her agent found her a new gig.

After picking up cream for her coffee and a few other groceries, she paid and headed for the exit. Taped to the door, she noticed a flyer for Fiorire Botanical Gardens' prestigious annual photography competition. Gianna had always wanted to enter but never had the time. The entry deadline was coming up. She tucked the information in the back of her mind.

She stepped out of the store with a sack of groceries in one hand and her luggage in the other. It was then that she realized in her haste to complete her errands she'd sent the car away and would now have to walk the rest of the way home. Not that it was far—perhaps a fifteen-minute walk, give or take a couple of minutes, depending on how fast she moved. But part of her travel was uphill on a bumpy dirt road. There were only a handful of villas on the dead-end road where she lived. Hers was the last one—

"Gianna?" came a distant voice.

She didn't have to turn around to know who was calling her name. It was her cousin—the one person she'd really hoped to avoid. It wasn't that she didn't love her cousin. In truth, she loved Carla dearly. She was more like a sister than a cousin. But Gianna just wasn't ready to admit that she'd failed at romance. Again.

Pretending she hadn't heard her cousin, she kept moving in the opposite direction. Her steps were sure and quick. She forced herself to hold her head high though the guilt of her actions weighed on her.

She told herself she just needed a little time to settle in and get her bearings. Once she found the right words and was able to say them without feeling like an utter failure, she'd be able to face her rich, beautiful and successful cousin, who had her life totally together, including her pick of successful men. Why couldn't she be more like her? More congenial? More beautiful? More whatever it was that made every man that met Carla immediately fall in love with her?

But none of that mattered anymore. Gianna was done with men. She'd lost herself in one too many relationships—dismissing what was important to her to make them happy—and she wasn't going to let that happen again.

Outside of the village, Gianna lowered her head. She promised herself that she'd make this up to her cousin. With her gaze focused on the ruts that constituted a road, she continued trudging down the desolate lane that was surrounded by lush vegetation and trees. The suitcase's little wheels rolled over the gravel, making a terrible racket. When a wheel got stuck, which happened repeatedly, she gave it a forceful yank.

At the end of the lane was her home; the stately pale pink villa with white trim and a terracotta roof that she'd inherited from her grandmother. Its beauty was timeless. It sat upon a hillside, providing a stunning view of Lake Como.

And what the villa lacked in modern style, it made up for with rustic charm. With seven bedrooms and five bathrooms, it was far too large for one person. And yet Gianna couldn't imagine parting with it. Just like her grandmother, she loved it here.

Woof. Woof.

A medium-sized dog with short light tan fur emerged from the bushes. It rushed into the lane, blocking her.

It stopped.

Gianna stopped. Now what?

Her grip on her luggage handle tightened. Her body tensed. She stared at the dog. He stared back at her. Then, drawing on the knowledge of animals she'd gained from working on nature documentaries, she averted her gaze ever so slightly. She didn't want the dog to misinterpret her staring at him as a sign of aggression.

She searched her memory and was certain she'd never seen this dog before. She wasn't sure if he was friendly or not. But they couldn't just stand here trying not to stare at each other.

"Hi, boy." She forced a smile.

His tail swished back and forth. That was a good sign. The dog approached her. Gianna wasn't sure what she should do, so she did nothing. Her heart continued to pound. As he drew nearer, her palms grew moist. He could probably sense her nervousness from a mile away. And yet his tail kept wagging as he grew closer.

And then he stopped in front of her. He sat down and gazed up at her. It was then that she noticed he had the kindest big brown eyes. She held out her hand to him and his dark nose sniffed it. She proceeded to run her hand over his head. He rubbed against her hand before dancing around in a circle.

It appeared they'd become fast friends. She breathed a sigh of relief. He might be rather big in size but she sensed by his bright eyes and his playful behavior that he wasn't very old.

"Hi, buddy. What are you doing out here?" And then she realized how silly it was asking a dog a question. It wasn't like he could answer her. But it seemed wrong not to speak to him, like she was ignoring him or something. "Do you have a collar?"

She knelt down and continued petting him. There was a depression in his fur as though he normally wore a collar, but there wasn't one there now. Strange.

It was obvious he had a home—a home where he was cared for. His fur was clean and groomed. He was well fed. And he had manners. So that told her somewhere in this world, someone was searching for their four-footed friend. And most likely beside themselves with worry.

She slowly moved her hand to her pocket and then withdrew her phone. She didn't want to make any sudden movements and startle the dog.

Her phone flashed that the battery was low. Hopefully, it'd hold out long enough to take a couple photos.

"I'm just going to take your picture. Hold still."

He did everything but stay still. He sniffed her and then the camera. About the fifth try, she finally had a usable photo that she could post on social media in an attempt to find his human.

Gianna's gaze met the dog's. "Don't worry. We'll get you home. In the meantime, would you like to come home with me?"

She grabbed the handle on her suitcase and then looked at him. "Come on. We'll go to my place and I'll make a few phone calls. We'll get you home in no time."

She started walking because what else was she going to do? He was too big for her to carry. She really hoped he'd follow her. She didn't like the thought of leaving him out here on his own. In a way, she felt responsible for him. She didn't want anything to happen to him.

When she turned back, she found the dog was still sitting in the same spot. This wasn't her problem, she told herself. She should just keep going. The dog probably knew his way home. But then she recalled his missing collar. What did it mean? Had someone dumped him on the side of the road? The thought made her heart sink down to her cute white sandals.

"I have food," she said, hoping he would understand what she was saying. "Food. Are you hungry?"

He cocked his head to the side.

"Come on, boy. I'll feed you."

He got up and strolled over to her. She smiled. Apparently, he liked to eat. Thank goodness food was a universal language. They walked side by side for a bit. Then he ran ahead and she worried he'd run away.

"Puppy! Puppy, come back."

He rounded the corner. With the heavy green vegetation, she wasn't able to see where he'd gone. She tried to run after him, but her luggage got hung in a rut. She had to stop and free it. By then she knew the dog would be long gone. She just hoped nothing happened to him.

When her home finally came into sight, she sighed. She

was beginning to feel like her journey would never end. But at last she was here. She opened the gate and let herself onto the grounds. It was here that she could lick her wounds while figuring out a new plan for her life because aside from losing her almost-fiancé, she'd also quit her job. She had a lot to figure out.

It wasn't until she reached the door that she noticed the dog sitting off to the side. How did he get past the gate? She let go of her luggage and turned to the dog. "How did you know I lived here? Are you psychic or something?"

Woof. Woof-woof.

"Well, I'm not quite sure what you're trying to tell me because I don't speak dog. But since you're here, how about you come inside? I'll see what I can find for you to eat."

She unlocked the door and followed him in. A cursory glance around the spacious living room and then the large modern kitchen told her things were in their appropriate place. She had to admit that renting out her house made her uncomfortable, even if the money was quite good. She loved this place. It held some of her most treasured childhood memories. And she'd be heartbroken if anything ever happened to it.

Woof.

She smiled as she glanced at the dog, who was now sitting by her side as though they'd been together for years. He looked up at her with such warmth in his big brown eyes. What had she done to deserve his trust? And yet here he was sitting next to her, waiting for the food she'd promised him.

She moved to her luggage and the cloth shopping bag she'd draped around the handle. Inside, she had some fresh baked bread, meats and cheeses. Quite honestly, she wasn't sure what dogs were allowed to eat but she couldn't imagine that in a pinch a sandwich would be totally frowned upon. And so that's what she did. She made her new friend a sandwich and one for herself. Her stomach rumbled in anticipation. She hadn't eaten yet that day. She'd been getting by on caffeine, but her stomach was in utter rebellion over its liquid diet.

She was quite tempted to take a bite of her sandwich first, but when she glanced over at those needy eyes, she couldn't resist him. This pup had such a sweet gentle soul.

"Here you go." She held out a quarter of the sandwich.

The dog carefully took it without so much as nipping her. He chewed...and chewed...and chewed...and finally swallowed. She'd been worried he wouldn't like the sandwich, but as he looked at her for more, she realized he'd liked it just fine. She took a bite of her own sandwich. Not bad. The dog started impatiently nudging her elbow with his cold wet nose.

"Okay. Okay. I'm getting it." As she picked up the plate with his sandwich, she said, "You know, now that you're eating me out of house and home, I'll have to go back to the store." She held out the next piece. "Here you go—"

"Hey! What are you doing?"

The boom of the unfamiliar male voice made her jump. The plate slipped from her hand. It crashed to the floor. Little pieces of glass pelted her ankles and feet.

What in the world? Her heart leaped into her throat. She sensed someone standing behind her. What was she to do now?

CHAPTER TWO

THE POUNDING OF her heart echoed in her ears.

An intruder in these parts was quite unheard of. In the village of Gemma, everyone knew your name. That was one of the many charms that convinced Gianna to keep her grandmother's villa. But this man's deep voice was unfamiliar to her. Who was he? And what was he doing in her house?

Gianna had to do something to defend herself. She visually searched for a weapon, finding one on the stove. Her fingers wrapped around the handle of a heavy cast-iron skillet. It could definitely do some damage.

Swinging the pan up over her head, she turned. "You better leave. Now."

The man's dark eyes widened. His gaze moved upward to the heavy pan in her hands. He stood his ground. Then his gaze returned to meet hers.

"I'm not going anywhere."

She didn't know whether to be afraid of him or utterly frustrated. "Then I'm ringing the *polizia*."

"You do realize you'll have to put down the pan before you can phone anyone?" His eyes twinkled with amusement.

She glared at him. This wasn't funny. He was supposed to be intimidated. Not amused.

"Leave. Now." She mustered up her most intimidating voice and gestured toward the door with her head because the pan was too heavy to hold with just one hand.

The man crossed his arms, making his biceps bulge. He didn't so much as budge a millimeter.

He was strikingly tall as she had to crane her neck to

stare into his eyes. His brown hair was a bit longer on top with a little curl. It was a casual look to go with the scruff along his prominent jawline.

A navy T-shirt fit snug across his broad, strong shoulders and clung to his muscular chest. She swallowed hard. She shouldn't be checking him out. Whether he was hot or not, he'd broken into her home.

His phone buzzed. He withdrew it from his pocket, checked the screen and then slipped it back in his pocket.

When her gaze once more met his, there was amusement dancing in his eyes. He'd caught her giving him a brief once-over. She inwardly groaned. That was not good— not good at all.

Still, she couldn't deny that he was quite handsome in that playboy sort of way. Not that she was interested. First, he was an intruder in her house. Second, he was infuriating in the way he didn't take her seriously. And lastly, she was done with men, cute or otherwise.

In an effort to reach for her phone, she tried releasing the pan's handle with one hand, but the weight of the cast iron was too much to hold with just one hand. Maybe she should have spent more time at the gym and less time traipsing around the continent with a sweet-talking man who didn't really care about her and was just biding his time until his ex stepped back into his life.

"I have a dog," she said, glancing down at the stray pup. It was hidden from the man's view by the kitchen island.

The man smiled. "You mean *my* dog?"

His dog?

The man stepped forward. "Tito. Here, boy." Immediately, the dog darted around the kitchen island. The man knelt down to pet the dog. "What are you doing letting a stranger in our house—"

"Your house?"

The man continued talking to the dog as though he

hadn't heard her. "You're supposed to protect the place. Instead, you run off. I've been looking everywhere for you."

The dog whined and then laid down in front of the man. The pup lowered his head to the kitchen floor and then covered his muzzle with his paw.

Inwardly, Gianna was going, *Aww…* But outwardly she wasn't letting down her guard with this man. He had a lot of explaining to do. Like why he'd walked into her house like he owned it.

The man straightened and turned to her. "If you put down the pan, we can discuss the fact that you're in my house."

Her arms slowly lowered, not because she trusted the man, but rather from muscle fatigue. She studied the man's strikingly handsome face, looking for amusement, as though he were making a joke. But the look he gave her was very serious. How could he believe he had any rights to this place? This house had been in her family for generations.

She placed the pan on the countertop. Gianna picked up her phone, finding the battery had finally died. But he didn't have to know that. She held it in her hand as though she were ready to make a call. "Okay. Explain yourself."

His eyes twinkled again as though he found everything about her amusing. Well, the feeling didn't go both ways.

"My name is Dario Marchello."

Why does that name sound familiar? She instinctively knew she should know his name, but she just couldn't place it. The jet lag was causing her mind to be foggy.

"Well, Mr. Marchello, you still haven't said what you're doing here?"

"Call me, Dario. And I've rented the place last month and this month."

Her mouth gaped. That's how she knew the name. He was her renter. A sexy renter at that, but he still had to go.

"And who would you be?"

"Gianna Cappellini. I own this house."

Dario glanced around as though he were looking for someone else. "And you live in this big house all by yourself?"

"Yes, I do," she said proudly. It wasn't until the words were spoken that she realized she was speaking to a stranger. She rushed to add, "But I have family in the area." It was true. "My cousin is on her way here." Sort of true. "She'll be over anytime now." A bit of a stretch. But knowing her cousin, she was sure to visit sooner rather than later. Then, turning the conversation back on him, she asked, "And you rented such a big house just for yourself?"

He nodded. "And Tito."

Enough with the war of words. She had things to do. She glanced down at the tiny pieces of shattered plate all over the floor. "I need to clean this mess up before someone gets hurt."

"I'll help you," he offered.

"Why would you do that?"

"Because I startled you, causing you to drop the plate. For that, I'm sorry."

She was impressed with his manners. For the next several minutes, they worked together, cleaning up the shards while keeping the dog away.

When his phone buzzed again, she said, "If you need to take that—"

"It can wait." His tone was a bit terse, as though he was intent on avoiding whoever was on the other end of that phone call.

Once everything was in order, she turned to him. "Thank you for the help, but I still don't understand what you're doing here."

His dark brows rose. "You're the one that isn't supposed to be here."

And this is where things became rather sticky. "I don't think you understand. Our agreement was for a one-month rental."

"And then I spoke with the property management company to see if it was available for another month. They said it was."

Gianna inwardly groaned. She recalled the management company trying to reach her numerous times, but at the time she'd been in a remote area of France where cell signals were hit or miss. There was one call where words were broken by stretches of silence. Gianna knew they had a question about the house but after repeated tries, she couldn't make out what they were saying. She trusted them, as the company's owner was friends with her extended family, and so she'd said to use their best judgment. Perhaps she shouldn't have been that trusting.

"They were mistaken," she said.

"I have it in writing. And I've already paid."

Hmm…that explained the mysterious increase in her bank account. This was getting complicated. She wanted to offer him money to just go away and leave her alone in her misery but her savings were greatly needed now that she was jobless.

It's not that she'd been planning to quit her job—at least not so suddenly—but rather it became necessary. After all, how do you continue to work with the man you thought you had a future with when he suddenly dumps you for his ex? It was beyond her powers of diplomacy. Space—lots of space—was the only solution. And quite frankly, the allure of sleeping under the stars and being one with nature had long since passed her by.

"I'm sorry for the mix-up," she said. "But I'll give you back the money you paid for the extra month."

Frown lines marred his much too handsome face. "This isn't about the money."

"What's it about, then?"

A muscle in his clean-shaven cheek twitched as he pressed his hands to his lean waist. "I went through the proper process to rent this house for another month. I paid the fee and have the paperwork. I don't see why I should leave."

"But surely there has to be somewhere else for you to go."

He shook his head. "This place is exactly what I need right now. Besides, everything in the area is rented. It's the summer. Families want to get away from the hustle and bustle of the city. And quite frankly, I don't have the time to search for other accommodations when I've already secured this place until the end of the month."

There had to be some sort of compromise. But what?

And so she mentally scrambled for a way to get this man out of her life. If money wasn't going to work, then she'd have to give him what he wanted.

She lifted her gaze to meet his. "Fine. If I can find you similar accommodations nearby, will you move out?"

His phone buzzed again. His dark brows drew together as he checked the caller ID. "I better get this. Excuse me."

She nodded in understanding, even if she was anxious to come to some sort of understanding with him. There was no way he was staying here—with her. Even if there was plenty of room.

Dario had stepped outside to the patio area. He left the door ajar and though she wasn't trying to eavesdrop, as his voice rose in volume, it carried into the kitchen.

She could excuse herself to another part of the house, but this was her home. And he was an unwanted, unwelcome guest. She stood her ground.

"Yes. I got your notes."

A moment of silence passed. "No, I don't know when I'll get back to you. I need some time."

More silence. "Two weeks is impossible. What about six weeks?"

She sure was curious what all the negotiating was about. She sat down on a kitchen stool as she watched Dario pace back and forth along the length of the pool with his dog right behind him.

He raked his fingers through his hair. "Fine. I'll have it back to you by the end of the month." He ended the call.

Gianna turned back to the counter as though she were contemplating eating more of her sandwich, but with her stomach twisted in a knot, it was impossible to eat.

"Everything okay?" The words slipped past her lips before she remembered they weren't friends—not even close.

"It's fine." His tone let her know it was anything but fine. "What were we talking about?"

She really wanted to ask him about the phone conversation that had left him utterly distracted, but as it was none of her business, she let it go. "We were talking about me finding you alternative accommodations."

"Right." He hesitated. "I suppose that would work, but I'd have to approve it first."

The distraction had helped her. At last, she could take a full breath. "Good." A slight smile of triumph pulled at the corners of her lips. "I'll get to work on it. I'll let you know what I find."

"Don't get too excited. There's nothing available. I already looked before I knew this place was available for another month."

The slight lift of the corners of her mouth suddenly dipped into a frown. "Maybe you missed something."

"Maybe." But he didn't sound convinced. "I'll just move my things from the master bedroom to the guesthouse before I go check the fence to see how Tito escaped."

"Oh. Okay." She didn't know how she felt about sharing her place with a total stranger. But at least the guesthouse was completely separate from the main house. A large in-ground pool and patio area separated the two accommodations.

Without another word, he set off toward the master bedroom—her bedroom. He'd been sleeping in her bed. Delicious visions of him in nothing but his boxers slipping between her sheets were suddenly all she could see, and the house started to feel uncomfortably warm.

She stepped outside, hoping a breeze would cool her down. There had to be another place for him to stay because no way were they spending the month together. Not a chance.

CHAPTER THREE

THIS DEVELOPMENT WAS most unwelcome.

Dario Marchello had no desire to share his idyllic get-away. Still, if he had to share it, Gianna was certainly a beautiful housemate. As soon as the thought came to him, he dismissed it. His entire future was on the line. He didn't have time to be distracted.

Nor did he indulge in relationships that lasted more than two weeks. He'd learned that any longer than this and the women he dated started to think of their relationship as a committed one. And nothing could be further from the truth.

It was stamped into his DNA that committed relation-ships don't work. His parents' marriage ended in divorce when he was young. Not only did they give up on each other, but they'd also given up on him and his brother.

His jaw clenched tight as he recalled being dumped on his paternal grandparents as though he and his brother were pets that just didn't work out. He tried not to think about the past. Happy memories were few and far between. It was best to focus on the future.

He made short work of transferring his things to the guesthouse. After which he went in search of Tito's escape path before his beloved dog pulled another disappearing act. It didn't take long to find the hole under the fence and Tito's missing collar. Dario filled in the hole, topping it with some large rocks to deter a repeat performance.

His thoughts drifted back to Gianna and why she was living in this great big villa all alone. What was her story?

The writer in him started crafting different backstories for her, from an orphaned heiress to a young widow. When he realized he was still thinking about Gianna instead of focusing on this agent's notes, he chased images of the mystery woman from his mind.

A couple of hours later, he was still sitting in the patio area, staring at his agent's comments on his laptop. He read them over and over as though they'd suddenly enlighten him as to what to write next. So far it hadn't worked.

When he heard Gianna moving about in the large kitchen, he glanced at his Rolex. It was dinnertime. He should probably do something about that, but first he wanted to write a few words, any words. Otherwise, his entire day would be a waste and that was unacceptable.

He stared at the blinking cursor. He shifted in his chair, not finding a comfortable position. Wondering if anything urgent was needed at the family business, he flipped to his email. Nothing new. What did he expect? He was, after all, on vacation, using the unused days he'd been accruing since joining his grandfather and older brother at Marchello Spices.

He switched the screen back to his manuscript. He once more stared at the blinking cursor. With an exasperated sigh, he closed the laptop and set it aside. He got to his feet and moved toward the kitchen. He rapped his knuckles on the framework of the open French doors. Tito was right beside him.

Gianna jumped. She spun around from where she was peering into the fridge. "You startled me."

Dario cleared his throat. "Sorry. I seem to have a habit of doing that."

Tito rushed over to her. It appeared she'd already won over his dog. She fussed over him and Tito ate it up.

"Thankfully, I didn't have anything in my hands this time." She sent him a tentative smile that didn't quite reach her eyes. "What do you need?"

Need? Well, that would be something she couldn't give

him—more time and the right words to fix his novel. Sooner or later, his older brother would insist he get back to the office. And he couldn't blame him. They weren't raised to sit back and do nothing—even if they were fortunate enough to come from great wealth.

He shook his head. "Nothing."

Her pretty eyes clouded with confusion. "Then what are you doing in here?"

"Oh. Right." What was wrong with him? He wasn't normally stumbling over his words. After all, words were his thing. At least he thought they were, but these revisions were proving otherwise. He swallowed hard. "I was just going to see if I could take you to dinner." When her fine brows rose in surprise and then settled into a line of suspicion, he added, "I meant as a thank-you, you know, for letting me stay here."

"But I didn't say you could stay."

"Oh. Does that mean you found an available rental?" Disappointment assailed him as he'd gotten quite used to this place. There was a peacefulness here that he'd never felt before. And the view of the lake was relaxing—maybe too relaxing.

"Actually, that was something I needed to discuss with you. I, um, called around and there's nothing available."

He struggled not to send her an I-told-you-so smile. And then before she could tell him that he had to move out immediately, he blurted, "I don't mind staying in the guesthouse."

"I don't know."

"Listen, your rental agency ran a background check on me before renting the house to me. I've already paid for the month in advance. And quite honestly, I'm a great tenant. I'm so quiet you won't even know I'm here."

She didn't say anything, as though taking in everything

he'd just said. With each blink of her eyes, it was like she was processing the information he'd given her.

"What is it you're doing here?" she asked.

His immediate response was to give her some flimsy excuse, but he had no reason to hide his actions from her. She was a perfect stranger—someone he'd never see again. "I'm writing a book."

He waited for her shocked response, but she appeared to take his answer in stride—something his family wouldn't do. His grandfather would be horrified to know he preferred writing to working in the family business. His brother would undoubtedly be disappointed. And his grandmother, well, he wasn't sure what her reaction would be.

"That's interesting."

"And this place gives me the privacy I need to finish the book." He couldn't tell if he was swaying her into letting him stay or not.

She seemed to mull over his words. "And you'd be all right in the guesthouse?"

It wasn't as comfy as the main house but it would do. And best of all, his family didn't know where to find him. If he were back at his Verona apartment, his brother would stop by regularly, wondering what he was up to on his time off. His grandfather, who still had one foot in the company, would find excuses for him to come to the office. And his grandmother would expect him for the usual Sunday dinner. But here at the lake, he didn't have to live up to anyone's expectations.

Gianna's rosy lips pursed together as though she were giving the situation serious thought. "Perhaps we could give it a trial period. Say, until the end of the week."

"But that's only two days away."

"Exactly." She smiled as though she'd solved both of their problems.

Did she really think she'd find cause to eject him that

easily? She didn't know him very well. He would win her over. One way or the other. Because he wasn't going back to the city until he finished this book.

"Now about dinner," he said.

"No." She shook her head. "Thank you."

That was the absolute fastest rejection he'd ever received. His ego took a definite hit. And he just couldn't let it go. He had to know what she found so objectionable about him. Was it because he was now her roommate—sort of? Or did she have a boyfriend?

He ignored the sense of disappointment. She most likely had a significant other in her life. After all, she was really cute. And her beauty didn't come from a makeup kit. Hers was all natural, from her blue eyes to her long dark lashes to her pert nose and pouty lips.

With each passing moment, his curiosity grew. "May I ask why?"

"I… I don't want to go into the village."

Relief flooded his system. This too he ignored. "Are you worried your boyfriend will see you with another man?"

"Hardly. He dumped me." Her voice rose with emotion. "That lying, scheming jerk. I don't know why I ever trusted him. I should have known he wasn't over his ex when her name came up frequently. Of course, he said she was in the past, but all along I had this feeling there was more to it. But did I listen to my little voice? Nope. I shoved aside my suspicions and told myself I was being paranoid." She grabbed a pan and placed it on the stove with a loud clang. "I'm the worst judge of men. You know he isn't the first man I almost married. The first time around, I was just out of school. We'd dated for years. I had the ring and the dress. Right before I was to walk down the aisle, he bailed. If I pick them, you can bet your last dollar it won't work out."

Dario stood quietly, trying to keep his mouth from drop-

ping open. First, what guy would dump her? It went beyond her striking face or curvy figure. He didn't know her
well, but he'd observed her sharing her lunch with his dog.
Only someone with a kind heart would do that. And so far
she hadn't ordered him to leave. That said a lot about her.

"I'm sorry." He didn't know what else to say.

She whipped around and stared at him as though she'd
forgotten he was still standing there. "You have nothing to
be sorry about, but my ex does. He cost me not only a relationship but also my job and now I have to face my cousin
and tell her I'm not getting married. Again."

"You were engaged?"

"Well, no. Not exactly. He mentioned it—looking back
it had been way too casual—but I was in love with the idea
of being in love. I wanted—no, I needed—this relationship
to be the right one. And so I told my cousin. I had to tell
someone or I would have burst."

He tried to piece together what he'd learned. "So what
you're saying is that you don't want to go into the village because you're avoiding your cousin, who thinks you're happily engaged. And you're not ready to tell her how things
ended?"

Her gaze met his. "Exactly."

"Isn't she going to figure it out?"

She shrugged. "I suppose. But if it's later, it won't be the
shortest engagement in the history of man."

"I bet there's been shorter." Her narrowed gaze let him
know he wasn't helping the situation. "Okay. We'll eat in."
His gaze moved to the stove where there were now four
empty pans. "It looks like you already have something in
mind."

Her gaze moved to the stove before turning back to him.
Color filled her cheeks. "I don't know why I did that. I
don't cook."

"Oh."

She was full of surprises. He had the feeling living with her for the next month definitely wasn't going to be boring. Far from it. But if he wanted to finish his book, he was going to need to keep his distance because she was a distraction—a beautiful one—but a distraction nonetheless.

"How about I cook?" he suggested. "You know, as a thank-you for letting me stay. I was planning to make spaghetti Bolognese. How does that sound to you?"

"Anything I don't burn sounds good to me." She turned to put the pans away. "I'm sorry."

"For what?"

"I can't believe I dumped all that on you. It wasn't fair. It's just that I've been keeping it all inside for the past two weeks until we finished shooting the segment and now that I'm home, well, I just can't bear to face my cousin. She'll look at me like I'm pathetic. At this point, it would do me in."

"So you told a stranger. No big deal. I won't tell anyone so long as you don't tell anyone that I'm here writing a book."

"You've got yourself a deal."

"Should we shake on it?" It seemed like the natural thing to do.

But when his hand engulfed hers, the jolt of attraction that zinged through his body was not natural. It was extraordinary. He wondered if she could feel it too. What would she say if he were to seal this deal with a kiss? His gaze lingered on her pouty lips. Would she swoon in his arms? The thought definitely appealed to him—

She jerked her hand away. The moment was lost. Was it possible she'd read his mind? Impossible. He couldn't even believe he was having those thoughts about her after he got done reminding himself how important it was for him not to get distracted until his book was submitted.

Her cheeks darkened with color. "I… I should get out of your way." She turned her back to him and then turned around again. "Unless you need my help?"

"I've got it. Thanks."

He set to work and realized Tito was missing. Usually the dog followed him everywhere. He glanced out at the patio and immediately spotted Tito. As if by magnetic attraction, the pup clung to Gianna's side. She knelt down and hugged him. If Dario didn't know better, he'd think she'd stolen his dog.

But it wasn't Tito he was worried about. It was himself. He'd have to keep his distance from Gianna. He didn't think straight when he was around her.

CHAPTER FOUR

WHAT HAD GOTTEN into her?

The following morning, Gianna made herself comfortable on the patio. She was still berating herself. Since when did she tell a total stranger about her personal life? Apparently, starting now. Gianna could still remember the way Dario had looked at her. He must think she'd totally lost her mind. And she couldn't blame him.

At least dinner had gone better. The spaghetti had been cooked to perfection. Not too soft and not too chewy. And the sauce had the perfect balance of spices. If he weren't a writer, she'd suggest he become a chef.

Though she didn't say it because he had been very quiet throughout dinner. As such, she'd done the same. She'd already said more than enough for one day. And after dinner, she'd insisted on cleaning up—alone. It was the least she could do.

Today, her first order of business was calling her agent. As much as she enjoyed being home, she couldn't afford not to work.

The conversation thankfully didn't last long because she didn't want to dwell on why she'd quit her last job. The bad news was that there were no film crew jobs available, but he'd let her know when something opened up.

In the meantime, she needed to get it all together before she saw her cousin. She needed to figure out what to say without breaking down in tears. Because every time she thought of what a fool she'd been, the tears of frustration welled up in her eyes. When would she learn not to be so trusting—

"Good morning." Speaking of being trusting, her unexpected houseguest strolled out to the patio. It was then that she noticed his tousled hair. It looked as though he had run his fingers through it many times that morning.

"Morning? But it's almost lunchtime."

His brows rose. "Is it that late already?"

"It is."

"I guess I got caught up in my work and lost track of time."

"There's coffee in the kitchen if you want some."

"Thanks. That sounds good. I ran out a bit ago and didn't take the time to make more." He paused next to Tito and bent down to scratch behind his ears. "I wondered where you'd gotten off to."

"He came begging for some of my eggs and toast."

"Sorry about that. He is a bit of a beggar."

"With those puppy eyes, it's impossible to say no."

Once Dario had a cup full of coffee, he returned to the patio. He stopped next to a chair at the table. "Mind if I join you?"

"Not at all." She closed her laptop.

"I didn't mean to interrupt your work."

She shook her head. "Trust me. You weren't."

"Are you sure, because I can go back to my room—"

"No. Stay. I wasn't working. Remember? I quit my job."

"Oh, that's right. Sorry. You know it's probably not too late to get it back. Just tell them you quit in the heat of the moment and now you regret it. What is it you do?"

"I'm a camerawoman. I've been working on a nature series." And then she realized the conversation had drifted back to her and her problems. Not a subject she wanted to discuss. "But enough about me. What's it like to write a book?"

He shook his head. "You don't want to hear about that."

"Oh, but I do. I have to admit, I'm quite curious."

"Well, the majority of the time, I'm staring at the wall, hoping for a bit of inspiration to come to me."

"And the rest of the time?"

"I'm typing."

"Typing?" He certainly wasn't one for spilling details without a lot of encouragement. "What are you typing? Your life story?"

"Close." He smiled. "Just joking. I write fiction. Or rather, I've written the book and now I'm going back and fixing it."

"Wow. And that's what you've been doing here for the past month?" When he nodded, she said, "That's very impressive."

"Really?"

"Why do you sound surprised?"

"Because my family would think it's a cute hobby but not practical. They want me to have what they deem a *real job*."

"I'm sorry. I understand. I'm not doing what my family thinks I should be doing either."

"And what's that?"

"Getting married. Having my husband work at the family market so he can one day take over. And let's not forget the grandkids. Not that those aren't great things but I need to figure out what makes me happy before I can make someone else happy."

His gaze searched hers. "And did you do that? Do you know what makes you happy?"

She shrugged. "I thought I did. I loved standing behind a camera and then later editing the scenes."

"And now?"

She shrugged. "I still like being behind a camera but I don't know about the rest. Maybe I've just been on the road for too long, living out of hotels and tents."

"Tents?"

She smiled and nodded. "That surprises you?"

"No." He smiled. "Okay. Yes, it does. I don't know any women who would sleep outside in a tent."

"We roughed it for a lot of the footage. Our meals were heated on a portable grill and we won't even discuss the bathroom and shower arrangements." She shook her head. Though some of her experiences were absolutely amazing, there were other parts she just didn't want to recall.

"And your ex—he was part of the crew?"

"No. Naldo is the host of the documentary."

"Oh. I see."

"So there's no way I can go back to that group, even if I wanted to. And I don't want to—"

"Gianna?" a familiar voice called from a distance.

It was her cousin, Carla. Panic launched Gianna's heart into her throat.

Gianna's first instinct was to hide inside and pretend like she wasn't home. It would be so much easier. But she'd never been one to hide. So she would face her cousin, even though she dreaded the pity that she would inevitably see in Carla's eyes when she heard about Gianna's latest romantic debacle.

And worse yet, Carla would do what Carla always did. She'd try to fix things. She would host parties—parties with lots of single men. There would be guys that were friends with Carla, there would be brothers of friends and every other eligible bachelor she could track down and invite to one of her spectacular events.

But that wasn't for Gianna. She had done the rich bachelor before. It never worked out. If she ever let herself get involved again, it would be with a man who led a simpler life. Her gaze moved across the table to her housemate. It would be someone like Dario.

Not that she was interested in him or anything. In fact, she was shocked that such a thought had crossed her mind.

Her focus right now was to be on herself and what comes next in her life—not on a really sexy tempting man.

Carla stepped into the patio area with a big bright smile on her face. "There you are."

Gianna got to her feet and stepped toward her cousin. Carla approached her and wrapped her in a big warm hug. Gianna reciprocated. And then they gave each other a feathery cheek kiss as they always did when they hadn't seen each other in a while.

Gianna pulled back. "Carla, what are you doing here?"

"Well, I thought I saw you in the village yesterday. I called out to you but you must not have heard me. Anyway, I didn't have time to go after you because I was late for an appointment." Carla lifted her big dark sunglasses and rested them on her head like a hair band as she sent Gianna a bright sunny smile. "And by the time I got home, it was late. I figured you'd be tired after traveling, so I didn't bother you. So here I am now."

"Sorry. I should have called you when I got home but, as you suspected, I had jet lag."

"Where were you this time?"

"France."

Carla's eyes widened. "You do live a very exciting life."

"It's not that exciting." Far from it.

"Oh, but it is. I should go with you sometime."

"I keep telling you that you won't like roughing it in a tent and at times going without a shower or proper bathroom."

Carla's face scrunched up. "That would be unbearable. But I'd still liked to see those beautiful locations you film in person…maybe just for a day trip."

"We'll see." They'd had this conversation many times over the last few years. It never went further than talking.

Carla moved to the side and smiled at Dario. "Hi. I'm Carla Falco, Gianna's cousin."

Dario's eyes momentarily widened. "As in Falco's Fresco Ristorante?"

Carla's smile drooped a bit. "Yes."

Dario got to his feet and stepped around the table. He extended his hand to Carla. "Nice to meet you," he said, like a true gentleman. "I'm Dario Marchello."

Carla took his hand in both of hers as her smile brightened. "It's so nice to finally meet you—"

"Excuse me." An unfamiliar male voice caused all heads to turn. "Dario, you're a hard man to find."

Carla let go of Dario's hand as they all turned at once to their visitor. A tall man approached them. Gianna noticed how her cousin's eyes lit up as she stared at their visitor. Gianna couldn't blame her. This man was definitely good-looking but not quite as handsome as Dario.

The man's gaze moved to Gianna and then paused on her cousin. "Excuse me, ladies. I'm sorry to interrupt."

"Oh, you aren't interrupting." Carla approached him. "I already did that."

The man's smile broadened, showing the dimples in his cheeks, but Gianna noticed that the smile didn't quite reach his dark eyes. The man was not happy about something, but he was working very hard to cover it up. What was up with that?

"I didn't know there was a party." The man's pointed gaze moved to Dario.

Dario crossed his arms, never once flinching from the man's lethal stare. "If there was a party, you wouldn't have been invited as you don't believe in having a good time."

The man's face remained emotionless. "I don't believe in partying when there's work to be done."

Dario stood. "So you came here to monitor my actions?"

"Do I need to?"

Wow! The tension between the two men was positively palpable. Though the stranger had dark hair and was slightly taller than Dario, their similar facial features gave away that they were brothers. Though something told her that their close biological link didn't make either of them happy at the moment.

Hoping to break the tension, Gianna stepped forward and extended her hand. "Welcome. I'm Gianna."

He gave her hand a firm shake. "I'm Franco. Dario's older brother."

Carla stepped forward. "Are you Franco Marchello, as in Marchello Spices?"

He let go of Gianna's hand and then turned to her cousin. "I am." He studied Carla's face for a moment. "Have we met?"

"No. I've just seen your name on some of my father's business correspondence."

"I'm afraid you have the advantage. Who's your father?"

"Carlo Falco."

"Interesting. So if I wanted to talk business—"

"You'd have to speak to my father." Carla's tone held a note of bitterness.

"You two look a lot alike," Gianna said, hoping to change the subject. She knew her cousin was thoroughly annoyed with her father and his archaic thoughts about women in the business world.

"But we don't act alike," Dario said. "How did you find me?"

"It wasn't hard. You're driving a company car, remember? Those are all outfitted with GPS."

Gianna swung around to look at Dario. His lips were pressed together in a formidable line as a muscle in his cheek twitched. She frowned at him, hoping he would lighten up. She wondered if things were always this contentious between these two or if something specific had happened to cause the rift.

"It's so nice to have you here." Carla kept her attention focused on Franco. "Are you staying in the area?"

"Only for the night. I came to talk some sense into my brother." Franco's attention moved to his brother. "What are you doing all the way out here?"

"Don't you know?" Carla asked before she leaned closer to Franco to loudly whisper, "They're engaged."

Gianna's mouth gaped. She looked at Dario, wanting him to know that she had nothing to do with her cousin jumping to such a wild conclusion.

Franco's dark brows drew together as his mouth lowered into a frown. "That's not true."

"But it is," Carla insisted. "I think it was supposed to be a secret until they make a big announcement, but since you're family, I'd have thought for sure your brother would have told you."

"You must be mistaken," Franco said to Carla as his pointed stare met Dario's. "My brother has no intention of getting married."

Carla grinned. "I think Gianna changed his mind."

Dario moved to Gianna's side. He slipped an arm around her waist and pulled her against him. And for just a fraction of a second, she liked being so close to him. It was as if they fit together. In the next heartbeat, reality came crashing in on her.

What in the world? Dario is playing along with this? Has he lost his mind?

"Dario, what are you doing?" she whispered.

Dario's gaze met hers. It was impossible to read his thoughts. "There's no sense hiding it. They were bound to learn about the engagement sooner or later."

Her mouth opened to deny such an engagement existed but Franco beat her to the punch. "So it's true?"

Dario nodded. And then he smiled, much like a Cheshire cat. "It is. Gianna and I are to be married."

"Married?" Franco sent him a skeptical look. "That's rather unexpected." His gaze moved between the two of them. "How long have you known each other?"

What was Dario doing? Heat swirled in Gianna's chest and then rushed up her neck, setting her cheeks aflame. This couldn't be happening. Dario was taking her painful experience of being dumped by her ex for his former girlfriend and using it…for what? Why was he fabricating their relationship for his brother? She wanted to ask him but Carla's curious gaze settled on them, as though she too was waiting to hear the answer.

Dario continued to hold her close as he addressed his brother. "Since when did you become my parent?"

Gianna finally came out of her shock at being called Dario's fiancée and found her voice. "Franco, perhaps you'd like to join us. I have coffee or iced tea?"

The lines between Franco's brows deepened as he continued staring at his brother. "And you feel an engagement is a good enough reason to just leave your work behind and what?" For the first time Franco glanced around at the villa. "Stay here in your love shack?"

Love shack? What? No one talked about her beloved home like that. Those were fighting words. It might not be as fancy as other homes but it had its own charms. Gianna's narrowed gaze settled on Franco. "I'll have you know that this was my grandparents' home. It is no shack."

Franco blinked and glanced at her with a blank look, as though he'd been so focused on his brother that he'd forgotten she was even there.

Dario tightened his hold on her and raised his voice so his brother would hear each and every word that he uttered. "You've just insulted Gianna and her home. You may take verbal swipes at me but never her."

Franco's head lowered ever so slightly. And for a moment, he actually looked contrite. Then his gaze met hers.

"I'm sorry. I didn't mean to slight your home. It looks lovely. Sometimes, well, most of the time my brother tries my patience."

Gianna sent a pleading look to her cousin, who looked utterly amused by the verbal battle being waged in front of them. Just then Tito came and leaned against Gianna's leg as though not sure what he should do now. Gianna finally caught Carla's attention and signaled with her eyes that she needed a little assistance to gain the brothers' attention. Carla nodded in understanding.

"I know," Carla said. "We'll have a private dinner this evening, you know, to celebrate the engagement."

Gianna shook her head. "No. I don't think that's a good idea."

"I'm sorry you feel that way," Franco said. "And it's my fault. I've given you a poor first impression and I apologize." His gaze met Gianna's. "I'm just a bit taken aback that my brother, who hates commitments, would settle down so suddenly."

Carla spoke up, "Maybe if you give my cousin a chance, you'd learn the reason your brother has changed his bachelor ways."

Franco nodded in agreement. He rubbed the back of his neck. "I'd like that." And then his gaze returned to Gianna. "I hope you'll give me another chance."

Gianna felt like the fly caught in the proverbial cobweb. No matter what she decided, she was in trouble. Either she went along with this outlandish ruse that Dario had concocted to obviously annoy his brother or she had to appear foolish and an utter failure in front of her cousin, whose respect meant the world to her.

"I don't know," Gianna said, looking to Dario for some help on getting out of an awkward evening where they'd obviously be found out. There was no way anyone would believe they were lovers. The truth was bound to come out.

"We have no plans," Dario said so nonchalantly that no one would ever suspect he'd spontaneously made up their whole relationship without even so much as consulting her. "Do we Gianna?"

She resisted the urge to glare at him. But when they were alone once more, she had a lot to say to him—a whole lot. He may write fiction but she didn't intend to get caught up in a fictional engagement with him.

"No. We don't."

And so their fate was sealed.

CHAPTER FIVE

HE WASN'T HANDLING this correctly.

Dario had been so caught off guard by his brother's sudden appearance that he'd reached for any excuse to explain his presence at the villa that had nothing to do with his writing. He didn't want his brother's negative thoughts about his pursuit of a writing career to infiltrate his mind. He already had enough of his own doubts about being able to pull off writing book number two.

One-hit wonder.

The taunt flitted through his mind. And his brother and family didn't even know about book one because Dario had insisted on using a pen name: D.J. March. If everyone hated his book, he hadn't wanted to embarrass his family, especially when the family business carried the same name. As shocking as it was, book one had become an international best seller.

He didn't know how the writing of book one could have flowed so easily and yet book two was a start-and-stop endeavor. *Dig deeper.* It's what his agent kept saying after reading a draft of book two. Dario didn't know if there was any deeper he could go.

Still, he shouldn't have dragged Gianna into this mess with him. It was enough that she'd opened her home to him. But pretending to be his fiancée was asking too much of her.

Dario cleared his throat. "I need to say something—"

"We both need to say something," Gianna interrupted. "We don't think the dinner is a good idea." When Carla's eyes widened in surprise, Gianna went on to add, "What I mean to say is we don't want to impose on you both. I'm sure Franco must have plans and Carla, you always have a busy social calendar."

It's not what Dario thought she was going to say. Why did she stop him from setting everyone straight about their relationship? And then a sinking feeling in his gut had him wondering if he'd read Gianna all wrong. Was she some sort of gold digger? Had she recognized the name of their family's company and realized Dario wasn't a struggling writer but an heir to a fortune?

A knot of worry tightened with each breath. His gaze moved to Gianna and he was tempted to say something here and now, but doing that would just confirm his brother's poor impression of him. No, he would wait until they were alone and then he'd sort this out.

Carla waved away any concerns about the impromptu dinner party. "It's no trouble at all. It's the least I can do for my cousin. And it'll just be the four of us as my father is about to leave on a business trip." Carla turned to Franco. "You'll join us, won't you?"

"I'm sure my brother has to get back to the city," Dario interjected, hoping Franco had more pressing matters in the city. "Don't you, Franco?"

"As a matter of fact, I've just completed my business—"

"Business here?" Dario didn't believe him. It was just an excuse to come here and check up on him, just like his brother had been doing most of his life.

Franco nodded. "Believe it or not, I don't have time to chase after you. The family business is at stake."

"You make it sound like it's in trouble. And that would never happen. Grandfather wouldn't stand for it."

"Shows how much you've been around the office lately."

"I haven't been gone that long." Just over a month. How much could happen in four weeks?

"Even when you were there, you weren't there. You're always distracted." Franco's gaze moved to Gianna. "Now

I guess I know what, or should I say whom, had you so distracted."

Gianna pulled out of Dario's hold and stepped toward his brother. "I can assure you that I'm no one's distraction." Her gaze narrowed on his brother. "I don't know you but you are certainly nothing like your brother."

"You mean because I have a solid work ethic—"

"No, because you are rather boorish."

Franco's eyes widened as his mouth opened slightly but no words came out.

Dario smiled. With each passing second, his smile broadened and then his amusement spilled over into laughter. He didn't think there was anyone in this world that could make his brother speechless.

Gianna spun around and nailed him with a sharp stare. "What are you laughing about?"

He quickly contained his amusement. "Nothing. Nothing at all."

He noticed how her blue eyes glittered when she was fired up. And here he thought he was the only one that let his brother get under his skin. Not that his brother was a bad guy—far from it. It's like their father used to say, the brothers mixed like oil and water.

Still, he wanted to know if Gianna had meant to come to his defense. Or if she had done it strictly out of self-defense. But as the question teetered on the tip of his tongue, he bit it back. Now wasn't the time for such probing questions—not with an avid audience.

He turned his attention back to his brother, who had smartly decided to quiet down. A smile pulled ever so slightly at the corners of Dario's lips. Perhaps keeping Gianna around wasn't such a bad idea after all. At least until he finished his book—if that ever happened.

Carla moved to Franco's side. "Perhaps we shouldn't have intruded on their private time."

Franco blinked as though her voice had drawn him from his thoughts. He glanced over at Carla and smiled. "I think you're right." Franco glanced back at Dario and Gianna. "I apologize for my unexpected arrival. Though I did try to call."

He had? Dario pulled his phone from his pocket and glanced at it to find more than two dozen missed calls. As he flipped to the call log, he was relieved to find that only a few were from his brother. A large number were from his agent. And then there were others from his editor at the publishing house. Everyone was getting anxious for the book—the book that he was certain, at this stage, would be an utter disappointment.

"I had my phone muted so it wouldn't interrupt me—" He halted his words. He was about to add while he was writing, but he'd caught himself in time.

"They want to be alone," Carla added as she slipped her hand into the crook of his brother's arm. "Perhaps we should go. We have plenty of time to catch up with them this evening."

His brother checked the time again. "You're right. We should go."

Carla smiled brightly. "Wonderful. I'll see everyone at my villa at seven. Don't be late." When both she and Franco turned to leave, Dario noticed that Carla was still holding onto his brother—who also didn't have time for a relationship. And yet his brother didn't seem to mind Carla's company. Interesting.

"Now, where do you live?" Franco's voice faded as they headed back toward the drive.

The time of reckoning had come. Dario swallowed hard and then turned to face Gianna. "I'm sorry about all that. I had absolutely no idea he'd track me down here."

She turned her back to him as she moved toward the table with Tito by her side. "You don't have to apologize."

"But I do. I dragged you into this—this *fake* relationship—without even asking you." He'd stressed the word fake to see if it'd get a reaction from her. It didn't. Thankfully. Because he wasn't about to let her think anything would ever happen between them.

"As I recall, it was my cousin who got us into this fine mess." She moved to the kitchen, but then quickly returned with her hands full.

They both sat down at the table. Gianna poured them each a glass of freshly squeezed lemonade from the home-grown lemons in her side yard.

Dario raked his fingers through his hair. "Tonight we have to be honest with them and explain the misunderstanding."

Gianna arched a brow. "Are you willing to tell your brother what you're really doing here?"

Dario's lips pressed into a firm line as he shook his head. He needed to keep it a secret from his family for just a little longer—just until he finished these revisions—revisions that just might be the death of him. He just couldn't wrap his mind around what he needed to do to make this book as good—no, better—than the last one.

"Then I propose we make a deal."

He wasn't sure he liked where this was going, but he had to admit she'd spiked his curiosity. "I'm listening."

"How about for the next month we let my cousin and your brother believe we're engaged?"

"I don't know—"

"It'll give you the time you need to finish your book."

That was much as true. "But what will you get out of it?"

"I'd like to be the one to end the relationship."

"And why would you want to do that?"

"So my cousin doesn't pity me and think I can't keep a man—even if it's the truth." Pain showed in her eyes.

Whoever had dumped her was a fool. Sure, he hadn't

known her long but from what he could see she had a kind heart, she defended those she considered her friends and, well, he liked her—though merely as a friend, nothing more.

How could he refuse her request, when it would help him the most? The thought of being dumped, fictional or not, would be a blow to his ego. But it was a price he was willing to pay to make his dream of being a true and honest author and not the one-hit wonder that his agent had mentioned in passing as a possibility.

Dario extended his hand to her. It was already out there when he recalled their prior handshake and how it'd affected him. But surely he'd blown that out of proportion.

Her brow scrunched up. "What are you doing?"

"You wanted to make a deal, right?" When she nodded, he continued, "Then we need to shake on it to make it official."

She hesitated. "News of our engagement won't go any further than the four of us, right?"

"Absolutely. After all, I'm not looking forward to getting dumped publicly."

Her gaze met his as though judging if he was telling the truth or not. Then she placed her soft hand in his. With her blue gaze still holding his, he wrapped his fingers around her hand and gave a slight squeeze.

As he continued to hold her hand a little longer than was necessary, a sense of awareness pulsed up his arm and set his heart beating faster. There it was again—that strong sense of attraction. He suddenly wondered if pretending to be in love with this beautiful woman was going to be harder than he'd ever imagined.

Gianna withdrew her hand and glanced away. Was it possible that she'd sensed his desire where she was concerned? He definitely needed to keep his hands to himself for the next month.

CHAPTER SIX

ONE MONTH.

Well, not quite.

Four entire weeks.

Twenty-eight very long days.

No matter which way Gianna phrased it, it still sounded like forever. What exactly had she gotten herself into?

As Gianna dressed for dinner that evening, her stomach shivered with nerves. What had she been thinking to perpetuate this preposterous notion that she and Dario were in love? After all, they hardly knew each other.

The breath caught in her throat. There was no way they were going to get through this dinner without the two people closest to them figuring out that this was one big charade.

In the next breath, she realized she couldn't just blurt out at dinner that it was all a lie. Then her cousin would know how foolish she'd been to fall for someone she worked with—someone who'd just broken up with someone else—and that she'd rebounded straight into a fake relationship. Even to her own ears, it sounded pathetic. Maybe there was a way they could pull off this fake engagement. After all, it was only dinner.

Gianna moved faster. After showering, styling her shoulder-length hair and applying a modest amount of makeup, she only had to pick out a dress. How hard could that be?

Her first choice was a little black dress. After all, it was her go-to outfit. But as she held it in front of her, she frowned. There was absolutely nothing summery about it.

And the color was all wrong to celebrate a new love and engagement.

Gianna dug to the back of her closet where she had some summer dresses she'd bought at an end-of-the-season sale. There was a sky blue one, an aqua one and a white one. Each had a different cut. One by one, she held them in front of her, turning this way and that way in front of the mirror. It was so hard to choose. But a traditional bride's color was white so that's the one she chose.

With the dress on, she slipped on some heels and rushed out to the pool area and headed straight for the guesthouse. The door was open as usual, but she didn't want to intrude. Instead, she stood outside and knocked on the wood trim. "Dario, we need to go. Are you almost ready?"

"I've been ready for some time." The voice came from behind her.

She turned to find Dario sitting in a chair in the shadows with Tito lying next to him. "Why didn't you say something when you saw me rush across the patio?"

He shrugged. "You seemed to be in such a hurry that I was curious what was up."

"And so you sat quietly watching."

"Something like that." He glanced at his Rolex, which looked strikingly similar to his brother's. "But you know we still have a good fifteen minutes until we have to leave."

She sat down at the table. "We have a problem."

His expression turned serious. "Are you thinking of backing out of our deal? Because we did shake on it."

"No. Well, not exactly."

His brow crinkled with worry lines. "What exactly is it?"

"They're going to figure out that we're not a couple."

"What makes you think that? They were certainly eager enough to believe it earlier."

"But that was different. We weren't sitting down at dinner, carrying on a conversation. And they weren't asking us questions. They'll quickly figure out we don't know the first thing about each other." She clenched her hands together to keep from nervously fidgeting with her teardrop pearl pendant.

"Ah, but that's not quite true."

"It isn't?"

He smiled and shook his head. "I know your most painful secret and you happen to know my most prized wish. And those are two things that no one else knows about us."

Heat crept into her cheeks. "But you know my secret because I had an embarrassing meltdown in front of you."

"Doesn't matter how you told me. The fact is you did tell me."

"And you only told me about your book because you were trying to convince me to let you stay here."

"Again, the circumstances don't matter."

She frowned at him. "Has anyone ever told you that you can be quite contrary?"

"No. But I bet if you mention it to my brother that he'll agree with you." Dario sent her a charming smile that made her stomach dip, and for a moment, she forgot her worries.

She smiled. "You know I think you're right about that one."

"So what would you like to know about me before we go to dinner?" He once more checked the time. "You have precisely eleven minutes to learn my life story."

"That isn't much time."

He averted his eyes. "There really isn't that much to know."

She had the feeling there was a whole lot to know, but he wasn't anxious to pry open the closed door and reveal his skeletons. She couldn't blame him. She wasn't so anxious herself. "Maybe we could just start with the little things."

"Such as?"

"Your favorite color? Your birthday? Where did you go to school? You know, those sorts of things that every fiancée should know about their partner."

His favorite color was blue whereas hers was purple. He was four years older than her. And he attended college in the States like she'd done. The difference was that he'd earned a business degree on the East Coast while she'd gone to film school on the West Coast.

The more they talked the more she could see the possibility of them being real friends and not just temporary housemates. But they didn't have long to talk and so no deep dark secrets were revealed by either of them. And she wondered what he had to hide. Surely, it couldn't be as bad as her romantic past.

A candlelit dinner for four.

A terrace that overlooked Lake Como.

Boy. Girl. Boy. Girl. It was really rather cozy.

A gentle breeze brushed over Gianna's bare arms, easing the warmth from the slowly sinking sun. She'd moved the food around her plate more than she'd eaten it. The truth was her stomach was tied up in a big knot.

"Let's see the ring," Carla said with excitement.

Gianna stared down at her bare ring finger. She wasn't sure how to explain the absence of a ring.

Dario spoke up. "She doesn't have it."

"You didn't buy your fiancée a ring before asking her to marry you?" Franco frowned at him.

Gianna jumped to Dario's defense. "Of course, he did. It's just that it's too big and kept falling off. We have to get it sized."

"So how did you two meet?" Carla's gaze moved between the two of them.

Gianna's body tensed. This was the question she'd been expecting and the absolute last question she wanted to answer. It was part of the reason she'd been unusually talkative that evening, hoping to divert attention away from them. Gianna's gaze moved to Dario. He stared blankly back at her. *Oh, no. He's going to be no help.*

Gianna turned back to her cousin. "You don't want to hear that story. It's boring."

"I highly doubt that." Carla's eyes zeroed in on her with intense interest. Her cousin was a romantic at heart. "I definitely want to hear the details. Did he sweep you right off your feet?"

Gianna felt cornered. She knew what her cousin was like when she was on to something. She wouldn't let up until she got the details. Panic sent her heart racing.

"We met here in Gemma." Gianna's mind scrambled for details that eluded her.

"That's right," Dario chimed in. His gaze caught and held hers. "It was a nice weekend and I needed to get away from the city."

"And I was between shoots so I was home. I was walking home from the village when this dog came strolling down the road toward me." Gianna continued staring into Dario's warm brown eyes. "He seemed so sweet and lost."

"Tito was leading me toward my future," Dario said and for the briefest second, Gianna wanted to believe him. "He'd gotten away from me when we were walking down by the lake."

"But he found me and followed me home." Gianna smiled as she recalled her first meeting with Tito.

"But how in the world did Dario find you both?" Carla's voice drew Gianna from her thoughts.

She glanced over to find Carla with her chin propped

up by the palm of her hand as she ate up each word they were dishing up. Gianna chanced a glance at Franco. He was leaning back in his chair with his arms crossed. His dark eyes didn't betray his thoughts. She could only hope he was buying what they were selling.

Dario reached out, placing his hand over hers. The warmth of his touch caused her heart to beat faster. And when her gaze once more met his, her stomach fluttered.

He smiled broadly, showing off his adorable dimples. "That's where serendipity played a part. Because I obviously wasn't leaving without Tito."

"And I needed to find his owner."

"So Gianna called me. As soon as I heard her voice, I knew there was something special about her."

Gianna smiled. "You did not."

"I did." He said the words so earnestly that even she wanted to believe him. "I asked her to meet me at a small café here in the village. And as soon as I saw her, I was a goner."

Heat swirled in her chest and rushed up her neck, setting her cheeks aflame. He was saying all the words she'd longed for a man to say to her. And in the moment, she wanted it all to be true.

And then he leaned toward her. *What is he doing?* He kept moving closer, all the while his thumb stroked the back of her hand. Her heart beat erratically.

Was he—was he going to kiss her? Her heart leaped into her throat. Anticipation thrummed in her veins. As his lips hovered over hers, her eyes fluttered shut.

He pressed his mouth to hers. Time stood still. Reality slipped away as they encompassed this alternate universe where they allowed themselves to enjoy the kiss that had been inevitable since their first meeting.

She savored the firm press of his mouth to hers—the gentle touch of his fingers over hers. This kiss shouldn't be this good—this stirring. She was over men. She was focusing solely on her career. But would it hurt to savor this very brief moment? A moan swelled in her throat. She tamped it down.

And then he pulled back. A huge smile lit up his handsome face and made his brown eyes sparkle in the candlelight. He gave her hand a squeeze before releasing it. What did that squeeze mean? Was he trying to tell her something? Had the kiss affected him as much as it had her? Her pulse was still racing.

As he turned to say something to his brother, Gianna blinked. She resisted the urge to run a finger over her tingling lips. Had that really happened? Had he kissed her like a lover?

Oh, yes, he had. But it was all just a show. That was it. Nothing more. Right? Because neither one of them were into relationships. And the more she got to know him, the more she liked him—as a friend.

And then she remembered how quickly her last relationship had started for all the wrong reasons. She wasn't about to repeat that mistake. Her heart slowed its pace. She wouldn't let herself get drawn in. Not again.

With that in mind, she swallowed hard before turning her attention back to the conversation at hand. What were they discussing? She had totally lost track of what was being said.

"I admit I had my doubts about the two of you," Franco said, "but no one can fake a kiss like that one."

"I agree," Carla said. "You two were made for each other."

"Can you do us a favor?" Gianna asked. "Can you keep the engagement to yourselves for a little while? We wanted to get the ring sized before we started telling people."

Both Carla and Franco seemed a bit surprised by the request, but they agreed.

The conversation moved to talk about Franco wanting Dario to return to the office to cover for him. Dario refused to leave. He said he would handle whatever came up remotely. And Gianna was left trying to pretend that the kiss had never happened. Someone should be filming this because she certainly deserved an award for her acting skills.

CHAPTER SEVEN

COCKTAILS. CHECK.

Dinner. Check.

Kiss. Double-check.

Dario smiled as he and Gianna got ready to leave. The truth was that he'd actually enjoyed himself tonight. He hadn't relaxed around his brother in a very long time. And it was all thanks to Gianna. She'd made it possible to see his brother as a friend again. He knew it wouldn't last, but he was grateful for the evening.

And then there was that kiss. He wouldn't mind repeating it. It had been much sweeter than the tiramisu they'd had for dessert. And so much more addictive.

But he knew the danger in getting drawn in by someone. His mother was on her third—he paused to think about it— yes, her third marriage. She was still hoping someone else could make her happy. It never worked out.

Secretly, he thought his mother was still hung up on their father. But that was a lost cause. His father couldn't commit to living in one place for a year much less commit to a relationship. It just wasn't in his DNA.

And Dario believed he was a lot like his father. He looked like him—so everyone said—and he couldn't commit to anything, be it the family business or a relationship. At least he'd recognized this early on, before destroying the lives of a devoted wife and two adoring kids.

Still, he would continue to play the part of Gianna's fiancé so long as they both realized it was all fiction, including the kiss—especially the kiss. This would soon be over. He would hopefully move on with his publishing dreams and Gianna would move on to working for a new television show, leaving no lingering strings between them.

Carla smiled. "That was a lovely evening. We'll have to do this again."

Dario struggled not to smile. He was home free. Their little charade had worked. By the time he saw his brother again, hopefully his revisions would be complete and approved by both his agent and editor. Oh, and his sudden engagement would have ended as suddenly as it had begun. Other than his brother and Gianna's cousin, no one would know about their ever so brief engagement.

"What are you smiling about?" Franco looked directly at him.

He was smiling? He supposed he was as he felt rather proud of himself. Still, he didn't want his brother pushing for the source of his pleasure. He schooled his face into a nonchalant expression. "I didn't realize I was smiling."

"Mind sharing what has made you so happy?"

Carla patted Franco's arm. "He's in love. What more is there to say?"

Franco sighed before nodding in agreement. Dario could sense his brother wasn't as on board with this engagement as he'd like people to think. Did it bother Franco that Gianna didn't run in the same circles as their family? What else could he object to? Gianna was beautiful, friendly and fun to be around.

Franco turned to Dario. "It'd be helpful if you were back at the office while I'm out of town."

So that's what was eating at his brother. He was relieved it had nothing to do with Gianna.

Dario shook his head. He was standing firm about not returning to the office until he'd completed his book.

"I'm sorry," Gianna spoke up. "He promised he'd help me with a special project."

Everyone's gazes turned in her direction. Dario had to

wonder what she was up to this time. They hadn't discussed any special project, had they? He searched his memory. No, they hadn't. He wouldn't forget something like that.

"Special project," Carla said, "That sounds interesting."

Franco cleared his throat. "What sort of special project?"

Dario's thoughts echoed the words of his brother. What did she have in mind for him? Whatever she'd come up with, he hoped it was just a story to get him off the hook as far as going back to the office because he had to stay focused on the book.

"You know how I told you I'm a camerawoman?" When Franco nodded, she continued. "Well, I'm also into still life photography. There's a photography competition coming up and I plan to enter it."

She did? This was news to Dario. Although, just about everything about her was news to him. Still, there was something about the conviction in her voice and the gleam in her eyes that told him this was more than just a cover story to help him out. She was quite serious about entering.

Franco's brow arched. "The one at the Botanical Gardens?"

Gianna smiled and nodded. "The very one."

"What will be your focus?"

She continued to smile as she shook her head. "I can't tell you that. After all, I don't want anyone to steal my idea."

Franco nodded. "Understood. I suppose I should be going. I have a number of phone calls to return when I get back to my room and I have to hit the road early in the morning."

"It was so nice meeting you," Gianna said. "I hope we get to meet again."

"Of course we will. You're marrying my brother."

Color bloomed in Gianna's cheeks. "Of course. What I meant to say is that I hope we see each other soon."

"We will."

"We will?" Dario asked, wondering if his brother was planning another impromptu visit.

"Yes." Franco's gaze met his. "Have you forgotten Nonno and Nonna's anniversary party?"

He had.

"No, I haven't. But I can't recall what day they selected for the dinner."

"Oh. It's no longer just a dinner. It's going to be a full-fledged party that lasts all weekend."

"Sounds very impressive," Gianna said.

"It definitely will be. This is their sixtieth wedding anniversary. It'll be a chance for you to meet the extended family." Franco gave his brother a brief hug. When Gianna held her hand out to him, he smiled. He ignored her offer of a handshake and instead hugged her too—just like she was family. He paused in front of Carla, took her hand and kissed the back of it. "Thank you for such a lovely evening. Now, I really must go."

"I'm sorry everyone has to leave so soon," Carla said. "I suppose we all must be responsible adults. Although, wouldn't it be fun for once to party the night away and sleep until lunchtime like when we were kids?"

They all agreed before making their way to the driveway.

Dario opened the car door for Gianna. Once he climbed in the driver's seat, he started the car and off they drove into the dusky evening.

"That went better than I thought it would go," he said. "Other than your cousin, we should be in the clear."

"You don't think your brother will be back to check up on us?"

He shook his head while keeping his gaze on the road as they passed through the village. Many of the locals were still out and about enjoying the summer evening. "No. My brother has one focus—the business. It's the only reason he was here. He wanted me back in the office. The thing is, I don't feel needed there. My grandfather, who is supposed to be retiring, still stays involved. Sure, I'm a Marchello and I can sign the checks but, well, I want to contribute something unique to this world—something that's solely me." He slowed to a stop at an intersection. He glanced over at her. "Is that wrong?"

"No. Not at all. And I guess in a way that's what I'm doing behind the camera. Even though I'm portraying someone or something else, it's still my perspective that frames the footage."

For the first time ever, he felt as though he'd just gained an ally. He smiled. "Thanks."

"For what? I didn't do anything."

"You did more than you think." He checked the intersection and then proceeded toward home—his temporary home.

The evening had gone much better than he'd expected and it was just early enough that he would be able to get some more writing done. But he didn't know what to write—not yet. And the thought of staring at a blank page soured his good mood.

"What's wrong?" Gianna's voice drew him from his troubling thoughts.

"What did you say?"

"You were frowning. You know you don't have to lie to me. You can admit if you hated the evening."

He shook his head as his thoughts rewound back to the moment of their kiss. He shouldn't have done it. At first, he had thought of it to get his brother off his back with his little quips, but then as he'd turned to Gianna and his gaze had settled on her glossy lips, he'd forgotten all about his brother. His focus had been solely on her. She was beautiful. He'd thought that the first time he'd met her and since then he'd come to find that her beauty started on the inside and worked its way out.

So when it came to kissing her, he couldn't resist. The idea had tempted and teased him until he had to know what it'd be like to feel her shimmery lips pressed to his. His imagined kiss had been good, but it was nothing compared to the real thing.

It was for that very reason that it couldn't happen again. Gianna wasn't one to be trifled with as she'd already had her heart broken. And he couldn't offer her the things that were important to her: love, commitment, marriage and a family.

Just the thought of being trapped in a relationship knotted him up on the inside. It was best to forget the playacting and get back to being housemates. Nothing more.

"Trust me, I wasn't frowning about the evening. I thought that it went well. So much better than I ever would have imagined."

"Then what's bothering you?"

He sighed. He hadn't intended to get into this with her. But after the bond they'd formed by covering for each other, he couldn't just brush her off now. "I was thinking about my book."

"And it made you frown?"

He nodded. "It needs changes and I'm struggling with them. It's why I needed the extra month here at the villa. I need to get it revised and submitted before I head back to the city and get distracted with business."

"And it's not going well?"

"I'm stuck. There's something missing from the book and I just can't figure out what it is. I didn't have this problem with *The Rise of Lavar*."

"That's your book?" When he nodded, she said, "I loved it! I had no idea you wrote it."

His face grew warm. "You don't have to say that."

"I mean it. I lost sleep reading it. It was a real page-turner."

She was the first person to say that to him, aside from his agent and editor. It felt really good.

"I can't believe you read my book."

"I was hoping there'd be a second book."

"I'm hoping the same thing."

"I'm sorry you're having problems with it, but you'll figure it out."

He pulled to a stop in the driveway in front of the villa. He turned off the engine and then turned to her. "I wouldn't be so certain. I have a deadline at the end of the month. One way or another, I have to turn in what I have and take my chances with the publisher."

"They won't reject it."

His brows rose. "You sound awfully confident. You haven't even read it."

She smiled. "If it's anything like the first book, it'll be another best seller."

He was still having a hard time believing she'd chosen his book to read out of the millions of books available. "Did you really read it?"

"Since you seem to have a hard time believing it, I'll prove it." She dashed out of the car and made her way into the house.

He followed her. All the while, he was smiling. She really liked his writing before she even knew who he was. His chest puffed up ever so slightly and his chin rose a notch. He had to finish this rewrite—if not for himself, then for Gianna. His first official fan. That sounded so strange to him.

She met up with him on the patio and held up a paper-back copy of the book. "See. I told you I read it. And if you still don't believe me, look at the bent spine. There might even be a coffee stain or two."

He continued to smile as he accepted the well-read book. "And you really liked it?" He just had to be certain. For some reason, her opinion really mattered to him. "You're not just saying it to be nice to me? Not that you have a reason to be nice to me—"

"Stop." She smiled at him. "Yes, I'm being totally serious. I loved the book. You made the world of Lavar so real. I could see it all in my mind."

"You could?" The problem with being a writer in hiding was that you never got to talk to people face-to-face about your work. And agents and editors don't count. But Gianna was neither. She was just a reader—a reader whose opinion mattered a lot to him.

She laughed. "You aren't very good at taking compliments, are you?"

He shrugged. He wasn't used to receiving them.

"You did a wonderful job with the descriptions. And the hero's journey to becoming the head of the Lavarians was impressive. I didn't see the end coming."

"Neither did I. It sort of wrote itself."

"Really?"

He nodded. "I had a loose outline but then the characters took over and told their own story."

"That must have been exciting. I love surprises." The smile slipped from her face. "Well, most surprises. The good kind. Not the I'm-dumping-you-and-going-back-to-my-ex kind."

He felt bad for her. "I wouldn't like that surprise either."

They continued to discuss his book. And he surprised himself by being so open about it. The things he thought really worked in the book, the things he'd wished he thought to include and the parts that just didn't come across the way he wanted them to. But overall, he was very happy with the final result.

"The thing about this second book is my agent says it isn't different enough from the first."

"I'm sorry. I wish I could help."

"Thanks. I keep thinking of what to change but so far none of it works. It just feels off, if you know what I mean. Like it's being forced."

"If you want, I could read it and see if I have any ideas." She waggled her brows as though enticing him to agree.

He couldn't help but laugh. "If I didn't know better, I'd think you were just finding an excuse to read the next book before anyone else."

"Would that be so bad?"

"No. But I don't want to disappoint you."

"You won't."

"That's what you say now but you haven't read the book yet."

"So let me." She clasped her hands together and sent him a pleading look. "Please. All this talk about it has me dying to know what happens next."

He was torn. Part of him said that an unbiased opinion would be helpful. But the other part of him didn't want Gianna disappointed with his book—with him. If she hated it, there would be an awkwardness between them. He didn't want that to happen. He was just getting used to their friendship.

He was about to turn her down when he recalled how much she'd helped him with his brother and given him this month to revisit the book. He couldn't afford to squander the time. And she was truly offering to help him without asking for anything in return. He would be a fool to turn her down.

"Okay," he said. "Do you prefer print or digital?"

Her face lit up like a kid's on Christmas morning. "Digital because I'm going to be taking it to bed with me."

Suddenly, he was disappointed to know it was just his book she was taking to bed. As soon as the thought came to him, he dismissed it. He couldn't let that one impulsive kiss distract him into thinking they'd ever share more. Even if the thought was tempting… So deliciously tempting.

It couldn't happen because he refused to hurt her. And he would eventually. Of that he was certain.

"Dario?" Gianna waved her hand in front of his face. "Hey, where did you go?"

"To bed." Suddenly, his face felt warm, and when she sent him a puzzled look, he swallowed hard and said, "I mean it's time to go to bed." As an after-thought, he added, "Alone." He got to his feet and started for the guesthouse. He called out over his shoulder, "I'll send you the file."

"But you don't even have my email address."

He stopped and smothered a groan. The last thing he needed was to spend more time with her. The longer he was around her, the more his thoughts drifted into dangerous territory. Still, he couldn't ignore her.

He turned back to her. "Sorry. I forgot."

"I'll just jot it down for you." Without waiting for him to respond, she rushed into the main house. A minute later, she returned with a bright orange slip of paper. She held it out to him. "Here you go."

When he went to take it from her, their fingers touched. A now familiar electric current rushed up his arm and then down his spine. His whole body was awakened.

His gaze met hers. He forgot what he'd been about to say. His heart pounded so loud that he was certain she could hear it.

He should look away. He should move. He should do something. Anything.

And then his gaze dipped to her lips. They shimmered in the moonlight. It was as though they were tempting him—teasing him. After all, it wouldn't be their first kiss. What would it hurt to follow that seemingly innocent kiss with another one—one with more heat, more passion and more desire?

Gianna yanked back her hand. "I better make a cup of tea to take to bed."

He just stood there wordlessly because his brain and mouth were at a total disconnect. He watched the gentle sway of her hips as she walked away. His mouth grew dry. He swallowed hard. It was all he could do not to go after her.

It wasn't until she disappeared around a corner that the spell was broken. He blinked and turned away. What in the world had happened there? It was though she'd bewitched him with just the touch of her hand. But that was impossible. He may write fantasy but that didn't mean he believed in it. Still, something kept happening between them. He just wasn't prepared to analyze it. They were friends. Nothing more.

CHAPTER EIGHT

BUZZ-BUZZ.

Gianna groaned. Her eyelids lifted a fraction to check the caller ID. She didn't recognize it. The brightness of the sun had her eyelids slamming back shut. The darkness welcomed her. She was so tired and sleep felt so good. Just a little longer...

Buzz-buzz.

She groaned again but this time she opened one eye to see the bright sunshine streaming in through the window. To be that bright out, it had to mean she'd slept in. Her other eye fluttered open. When she rolled over, her e-reader slipped from her chest and clattered to the floor.

Gianna groaned once more. She hoped this wasn't an omen of what was to come this day. Lucky for her, she'd bought a protective cover for it. She must have fallen asleep while reading. She picked it up and then placed it next to the bed. That's when she noticed her bedside lamp was still on.

She'd been so caught up in reading Dario's book last night that she hadn't wanted to stop, even when her eyes had grown heavy. She grabbed her e-reader and opened it. She was only 48 percent of the way through the book and she couldn't wait to finish it. But first she had work to do.

In her free time, she'd been adding photos to a stock image site. It didn't make her a lot of money, but now that she'd quit her job, every little bit helped. She liked to do nature scenes. And she'd been hoping to capture the sunrise over Lake Como, but she'd totally missed it that day.

Still, there was a meadow not far from her house and it had the most beautiful wildflowers every year. She was hoping they were in full bloom. She'd been serious the other night about entering the photography competition. And once she snapped some photos, she'd come back here and continue reading.

In no time, she was dressed and ready to go. Her first stop was her office in the back of the house. She turned on her computer and then brought up the website for the photography competition. The deadline to enter was tomorrow night. She filled out the form and paid the staggering entry fee.

She printed out the instructions. She noted two dates on her digital calendar. The first date was when the prints had to be received. The second date was the day of judging. It was at the end of the month. She told herself she had plenty of time to come up with the winning entry, but she felt rushed. However, she always did like a challenge.

She shut down her computer and rushed to the kitchen. She grabbed some fruit, bread and cheese, and placed it all in her backpack. Armed with her camera, she headed out past the pool.

Woof. Woof.

With his tail wagging, Tito rushed up to her. A smile pulled at her lips as she bent down to pet him. "What are you up to this morning?"

Woof.

"I'm not sure what you want." She glanced around for Dario, but he appeared to be inside the guesthouse, probably working on his revisions. "I'm sorry, Tito. But I have to go."

She gave him a final pat and started to walk away. He proceeded to follow her. She stopped and he stopped. She smiled as he gazed up at her with those big brown eyes.

"You can't come with me. Dario will miss you." She supposed she would have to be a little firmer with him. She lowered her voice, hoping it sounded more commanding. "Stay."

Tito lowered his head and whined as though he didn't know what he'd done wrong. It pulled on her heartstrings.

She knelt down and hugged him. "I'm sorry. Maybe next time."

She started toward the back of the property. When she paused to look over her shoulder, Tito was a few steps behind her. He stopped and then looked at the ground.

A big smile pulled at her lips. If Tito didn't already belong to Dario, she'd adopt him. He was such a sweetie. What would it hurt to take him with her?

She backtracked. "Okay, we'll check with Dario and see if he'll let you go with me. Would you like that?"

Woof.

"Aw…see, I know what you're saying this time."

At the guesthouse, she rapped her knuckles on the door. "Dario?"

"Coming." There were some shuffling sounds, a crash and a mutter. Then the door opened. "Sorry. I ran into the corner of the table. But don't worry. Nothing is broken. The table I mean, not me."

She continued to smile as she took in his disheveled appearance. His hair was once again mussed. There were shadows under his eyes as though he hadn't slept much last night either. And there was scruff along his jawline.

He cleared his throat. "Are you here to talk about the book?"

She had been hoping to avoid him until she'd had a chance to finish reading it. "The book, um, no."

His dark brows drew together as disappointment clouded his eyes. "That bad?"

"Oh, no. That isn't what I meant. I guess I'm a slow reader but there's no way I could read it all last night." She thought of ditching her plans for the day and reading the rest of his book. As soon as the thought came to her, she realized that's what her former self would do. But this new her had to stay focused on her future. "I really liked what I read—"

"You did?"

She smiled and nodded. "You're a very talented writer."

"So then you don't think it needs massive revisions?"

"I... I didn't say that."

"Then you agree with my agent that something big is missing."

"I didn't say that either." She could see the worry written all over his face. "I just need to finish reading the book before I share my thoughts."

"Okay. You know you don't have to finish reading it if you don't want to."

"I know. But I really have to see how it ends. Anyway, I didn't mean to keep you," she said. "I just wanted to know if it'd be all right if I took Tito for a walk."

Tito moved to her side and sat down. And then he leaned his body against her leg.

"Looks like you totally won him over," Dario said.

"It's more like the other way around. I can't tell you how much food he's mooched from me with those big brown eyes. I don't know how you can resist him."

"I can't. That's why it's fine if he wants to go with you. By the way, where are you going?"

"For a hike. I want to take some photos. I know of this meadow not far away that has the most colorful wildflowers." And then a thought came to her. "Would you like to go with us?"

Dario raked his fingers through his hair. "I'm not exactly dressed to go out."

"Trust me. Where we're going, no one will see you. Unless you're worried about some wildlife wondering if you're one of them."

"Hey." He sent her a sheepish look. "Am I that bad?"

"Let's just say you look like you've been up all night."

"Not all night but a good portion of it. And how about you?"

She knew what he was asking. He wanted to know if she'd stayed up last night reading his book. "I was up very late. That's why I'm getting such a late start on the day."

"It's only a little past eight."

"Exactly. I like to be up with the sun."

He dramatically rolled his eyes. "You're starting to sound like my brother now."

She pressed a hand to her chest. "I'm wounded." She sent him a teasing smile. "Do I really sound that bad?"

"Maybe not that bad." Dario smiled for the first time that morning. "Give me a second to brush my teeth and make myself presentable. And I need to grab Tito's leash." He didn't wait for her response as he rushed back inside.

She turned back to Tito. "Looks like we're all going for a walk. If I didn't know better, I'd think that's what you had in mind all along."

Why had she offered to take Dario with them? It wasn't like they had to spend more time together. Their one night of engaged bliss was over. Carla was busy proving to her father that she was more than capable of taking over the family business. And Franco was out of the country. The charade was over. So why had she suggested spending the day with Dario?

He shouldn't be here.

He should be working.

And yet, Dario couldn't bring himself to turn around and go home. He told himself it was the sunshine and fresh air that had him feeling totally revived, and it had nothing to do with Gianna's presence—with her glowing smile and the pleasant lilt of her voice.

They walked a bit. All the while, Tito was pulling on his retractable leash. The pup was eager to smell everything.

Meanwhile, Gianna had grown quiet, lost in her own world, leaving him to his own meandering thoughts. Then she'd suddenly stop. She'd study something in the distance. He'd tried peering over her shoulder to find out what was so interesting. Each time he did it, he didn't see anything special. To him, it all appeared just to be some dirt, foliage or trees.

However, Gianna had amazing sight. Where he'd see nothing but an old log, she'd see a log with green moss and a white butterfly. And when she showed him a preview of the photo, he was in awe.

"You're really good at this photography stuff."

"Thanks. It's a hobby."

"A hobby? You should make it your occupation. I can envision those prints ending up on peoples' walls." He intended to buy some for his apartment if she made them available.

Her cheeks pinkened. "You don't have to say that."

"But it's the truth. Those are at least as good as the prints in your house."

Her gaze searched his. "You really think so?"

"I do. Trust me. I'm a Marchello. We are raised to be honest."

She smiled at him. "Except in the case of our engagement?"

"Okay. So there are exceptions. But I was serious. Those prints at the house are really good. Did you take them?"

"No. My grandmother was a photographer. I guess that's how I got caught up in it."

"But instead you spend most of your time filming documentaries?"

She nodded. "I like that too. I've been to some amazing places like the Himalayas, the Australian Outback and the Amazon."

His eyes widened. "That's some résumé. What's next?"

"I don't know." Her gaze lowered. "I broke a rule and mixed business with pleasure. And there was no way I could continue to work with my ex. My agent is searching for a new position and in the meantime, I sell stock images on the side while I prepare for the competition."

"I meant with your personal life." His gaze dipped to her lips—one of the reasons he hadn't gotten much sleep the night before. "Will you dump me for some good-looking guy?"

She laughed. A soft melodious sound. It was something that put him at ease. It made him forget that their romantic relationship was no more real that the characters in his book. And yet, he couldn't turn away from her. He was totally and completely drawn in.

"Go ahead and admit it," he coaxed. "I'm the best boyfriend ever."

Her eyes sparkled with amusement. "Yes, you are. Because you're not real."

He feigned a scowl. "I am too."

She was still smiling and now she was shaking her head. "No, you're not."

"I am and I can prove it." Without giving thought to his actions and instead totally living in the moment, he leaned toward her.

She pressed a hand to his chest and attempted to step back. "Dario…"

Gianna started to fall. He reached out to her in the nick of time, drawing her to him. Her soft curves pressed firmly against him.

"What in the world?" She looked down.

He did the same. It appeared while they were having a war of words, Tito was busy walking in a circle, ensnaring them with his leash. And now Tito was sitting with his back to them as though saying I got you two together, now you have to do the rest.

"We have to get untangled," Gianna said.

"Do we?"

Her gaze swung around and met his. "What are you saying?"

He continued to hold her in his arms, not because she needed the support but rather because he liked the way she felt there. He stared deep into her eyes. And when he spoke, his voice came out much deeper than normal. "Isn't it obvious?"

Her pouty lips opened but no words came out. She pressed them back together, but her eyes darkened with desire. A lopsided smile tugged at the corner of his mouth. He wasn't in this alone. What would it hurt to revisit that kiss from last night?

He needed to know if she was as sweet as he remembered. It'd taken every bit of willpower for him to restrain himself in front of his brother and her cousin. But out here, in the middle of nowhere, there was only Tito to watch them. And right now, his dog had given them a moment of privacy. And Dario intended to take full advantage of it.

His head lowered. He heard her inhale a quick breath. He was certain Gianna was about to rebuff his advance. But then his lips met hers. She didn't move, as though stunned by the action. It surely couldn't be that surprising.

They may not be a real couple—an engaged couple— but there were sparks and chemistry flaring between them. And if he didn't prove to himself that it was all flash with no substance, he'd never be able to concentrate on his revisions—revisions that still had him baffled.

But right now, as his lips moved over Gianna's, he wasn't confused. He knew exactly what he wanted—more of her. His worries about his book slipped to the back of his mind.

As the kiss deepened, he pulled her closer to him. Her hands landed on his chest. The heat of her touch radiated through his shirt and set his skin afire.

Her mouth opened to him, letting him delve inside. Instead of proving that he'd made too much of the kiss at dinner, he realized the real thing was so much more enticing—so much hotter.

Her fingers slipped up over his shoulders and wrapped around the back of his neck. She pulled him closer. The blood pounded in his veins. He'd never shared a kiss like this before. It was so addictive—

Woof. Woof-woof.

And then there was a jerk on the leash. Their lips parted. Tito continued to bark and pull on the leash. In the distance was a hare. It paused to look at Tito and then it hopped off into the green foliage. Tito continued to bark and yank on the leash.

It took Dario a moment to come back to his senses. He leaned over and grabbed hold of the leash. "Stop." When the dog didn't listen, he gave a quick tug on the leash as he raised his voice. "Tito, no."

The dog quieted and sat down but he kept his gaze focused on the last place he'd seen the hare.

The easiest thing would be to release Tito from his leash until they unwound themselves, but he knew as soon as the dog was off the leash that he'd hightail it after the hare. Dario had no intention of spending the rest of the day searching for his dog. Plus, untangling the leash gave him something to do besides face Gianna and her inevitable questions.

But he soon realized that untangling them was awkward to say the least. There was a lot of, *Sorry. Excuse me. Watch out.* Heat rushed to his face. He wasn't sure about Gianna's reaction because he hadn't worked up the nerve to look her in the face.

That kiss had been a mistake. But it had been the most tantalizing mistake. And it hadn't done what he'd hoped it would do—get her out of his system. Instead, he wanted her now more than ever. What had he done?

CHAPTER NINE

THIS WAS GOING to be a good day.

Gianna smiled and stretched. As she tossed back the sheet, she realized it'd been a long time since she woke up with a smile on her face. And it felt good.

Only now was she able to acknowledge how unhappy she'd been while seeing Naldo. In the past, she'd always made excuses for her unhappiness. Was it possible that she'd known all along that her relationship with Naldo wasn't what it should be? Was she so eager to prove to herself and others that she could keep a man in her life that she'd blinded herself to what was in front of her face?

And what about Dario? What was up with him kissing her? Not to mention her kissing him back.

She would never admit that when he'd kissed her it was like she was floating above the earth. Or how she'd replayed that kiss over and over in her mind. No, she couldn't admit any of that because it had been a mistake. Just like all the other relationships in her life. The only person she could count on was herself. And she'd do well to remember that going forward.

She sat up and threw her legs over the edge of the bed. The best thing she could do for herself was focus on her photography. As much as she loved motion pictures, there was something about catching that special singular moment on film. And that's what she planned to do today.

She headed for the shower. It didn't take her long to rush through her morning routine, especially since she wasn't doing anything special with her hair. Once her bangs were styled, she threw the rest of her still damp hair up in a messy bun. It wasn't like anyone would notice, considering she planned to spend the day in her office.

In the kitchen, she was greeted by Tito. She knelt down and fussed over him. "Good morning." She glanced around, finding they were alone. "You know, I should be mad at you." The pup looked at her with those big innocent eyes. "Don't give me that. You know what you did—"

Woof. Woof-woof.

She loved how Tito always acted as though he knew what she was saying. He didn't understand her, did he? She shrugged. It was more fun to pretend as though he could talk back to her.

"I see how it is. You're going to act all innocent." The dog cocked his head to the side as she continued to talk. "You wrapped us up in your leash on purpose. But it isn't going to work. Dario isn't any more into me than I am into him."

Woof!

"So if you promise not to do it again, I guess I'll let it slide this time." She held her hand out to him. "Let's shake on it."

Tito hesitated and she was starting to think he didn't understand what she wanted him to do. Then the pup placed his paw in her hand and they shook.

"Very well, then." She straightened. "Looks like you're on your own this morning. Are you hungry?"

Woof.

"How did I already know that answer?" Still, she glanced around for Dario but he was nowhere to be seen. She reached for some dog treats she'd picked up in the village the prior evening.

"Don't tell your dad I gave you these."

Tito munched them down, and then without a sound, he turned and went to lie down in the open doorway.

Gianna yawned. She'd finished reading Dario's book

somewhere in the wee hours of the morning. Part of her was anxious to let him know her thoughts, but the other part of her was hesitant. She knew he was really nervous about the book and she didn't know how he'd take some of what she had to say.

Still, she'd promised to tell him what she thought and she couldn't very well back out now. He'd read something negative into her unwillingness to discuss the book. She'd just have to say what she had on her mind and hope he found it helpful.

She opened the fridge, searching for a meal they could share. She grabbed some meat, cheese, bread and fruit. In no time, she had a light brunch put together. A friendly way to lead into their serious conversation.

Balancing the tray in one hand, she moved to the patio. Dario was already seated at the table. He was hunched over his laptop. His fingers were tap-tap-tapping on the keyboard. She wanted to know what he was writing but she didn't dare disturb him.

Maybe he figured out how to fix the story and she could just keep her thoughts to herself. Could she be that lucky? She already knew the answer to that question. Luck was not on her side. Not when it came to men.

As though he could sense her standing there, looking at him, Dario's fingers paused and hovered over the keyboard. He turned his head and his gaze met hers. She couldn't tell what he was thinking because it was though a wall had gone up between them, blocking her out.

It was the kiss—it'd made a mess of things. Why hadn't she turned away? She knew why but she refused to let her thoughts go there.

"Let me just finish typing this sentence—" he glanced back down at his laptop "—and I'll get out of your way."

"There's no need to leave." She moved to the table and placed her tray in the middle. "I made enough to share."

His head lifted. Surprise flashed in his eyes. "You did?"

"Unless you'd rather be alone so you can continue working. If so, I can eat inside."

He pressed a few keys and then closed his laptop. "Don't go. After all, this is your place."

She wasn't sure how to take that. Did he want her to stay? Or was he just being polite? It was so hard to tell. And this was another reason that kiss shouldn't have happened. Now she was nervous around him. She had no idea what to say or do. And so she stood there next to the chair, unsure if she should pick up the tray and move on or if she should sit down and join him.

Deciding he was there first, and it would be best if she just moved on, she reached for the tray. At the same time, Dario stood with his laptop in hand. When she straightened, their gazes met. Heat rushed to her cheeks.

His gaze immediately dipped to the food. "We both don't have to leave. You should stay and enjoy the beautiful day. And that food looks really good."

"We…we could both stay." Her insides shivered with nerves as she waited for him to reject her offer. "There's plenty of food to share."

He didn't say anything at first. But then his gaze once again met hers and a hint of a smile pulled at his lips. "That sounds like a good idea. Thank you."

And so they both took a seat. This was awkward, even more so than their first meeting. And that was saying a lot. She had to say something, anything to ease the tension.

"About yesterday…" they said in unison.

They both grew quiet. Their gazes met and held a little longer than was necessary, but just long enough to set Gianna's heart racing. She licked her dry lips.

"I…" They both spoke again. This was getting ridiculous.

She pressed her lips together. Was he trying to say the same thing as her? That yesterday was a mistake?

"Go ahead," he said, "please say what's on your mind."

By now, her palms were damp and her mouth was dry. Why was this so difficult? After all, it wasn't like they'd spent the night together and woke up in the morning regretting their impulsive actions.

It had just been one simple kiss. Okay, maybe it hadn't exactly been simple. There may have been some steam included. Okay a lot of steam and pent-up desires.

And no, technically, it hadn't been their first kiss. There had been that kiss in front of her cousin and his brother. But it wasn't like either of them intended there to be a third kiss. That was quite out of the question.

His gaze prompted her to speak. She swallowed hard and hoped with all her might that when she spoke her voice didn't betray her nervousness. "I just wanted to say that yesterday shouldn't have happened." She glanced over at him, hoping he'd help her out. "It…it was an accident."

His brows rose high on his forehead. "It was an accident that our lips landed on each other?"

"No. I mean…uh, you know what I mean."

"Actually, I don't know."

She huffed. "It was an accident with the leash. Neither one of us was, you know, paying attention."

Was that amusement twinkling in his eyes? "And that's when your lips accidentally landed on mine?"

"No!" Heat gathered in her chest, rushed up her neck and set her whole face aflame. "I… I mean yes."

Now he outwardly smiled at her as he leaned back in his chair, enjoying her discomfort. He crossed his arms and studied her. "So which is it? Yes? Or no?"

"Stop it. You know that kiss shouldn't have happened. It was a mistake."

"So now it's a mistake, not an accident?" His smile broadened.

She glared at him. What did he find so amusing about this conversation? "Dario, stop. This isn't funny."

He sobered up enough to subdue his smile. "It's okay. We can pretend you didn't kiss me."

"What?" Surely, she hadn't heard him clearly. "I did not. You kissed me."

"Did I?" He arched his brows. "I guess if that's how you want to remember it—"

"I don't want to remember it! At. All." She jumped to her feet. She was done amusing him. "If you aren't going to take this seriously, I'm leaving."

She'd just turned to walk away when he said, "Gianna, wait."

She paused but she didn't turn around. She wasn't going to say another word because she knew he was going to turn it around on her.

"Please come back to the table."

She still didn't move, except to cross her arms. And she'd just started to think he was different than the other men who'd passed through her life. "I think it's best we stay away from each other."

A chair scraped over the patio tiles. The sound of footsteps grew closer. She wanted to walk away before he reached her, but her pride kept her standing in the same spot.

When he came to a stop in front of her, there was no hint of amusement in his eyes. "Gianna, I'm sorry. I shouldn't have given you a hard time."

"Then why did you?"

"I don't know." He raked his fingers through his hair. "I guess I was nervous about what happened. I didn't know what to say to you."

She frowned at him. "And so you thought you'd turn it all around on me and make it seem like the kiss was all my idea?"

He shrugged. "I didn't really think about what I was saying. I was just trying to lighten the mood. I guess I failed."

"You guess you failed?"

"Okay. I did fail." He got that sheepish look on his face similar to Tito's pouty look. "I'm sorry."

"About?" She wasn't letting him off the hook that easily.

"About giving you a hard time. About not apologizing sooner. About kissing you."

"So you admit it?"

"Didn't you just hear me?"

"I mean that you kissed me." Her gaze met and held his. She ignored the way it made her heart kick up its thump-thumping.

"How about we agree that we kissed each other?" His gaze searched hers.

She'd spent all night thinking that he'd kissed her. Was it possible she might have leaned into him? Had they met in the middle?

And quite honestly, did it even matter? He was willing to meet her halfway now. But could they move beyond it? She wanted to believe they could.

She nodded. "Agreed. Can we also agree to forget it happened and never discuss it again?"

"Sounds like a plan." He sent her a hesitant smile. "Now how about we eat some of the delicious food you prepared?"

She'd totally forgotten about the meal. "Um, sure. That sounds good."

Woof. Woof.

Dario ran a hand over Tito's head. "What are you so excited for? Do you think we're going to share the food with you?"

Woof. Woof.

"Don't let him fool you," she said. "He already begged me for a treat."

Dario turned back to the dog. "Is that true?"

Tito whined as though he were trying to speak.

Gianna couldn't help but smile. As she did, she realized the tension that had been crackling in the air had lifted. Their relationship was different since the kiss, but if they both tried, the rest of their time together didn't have to be painfully awkward.

At least they no longer had to pretend they were in love. She was certain that playing lovers was what had prompted that kiss. Yes, that was definitely it. Thankfully, they were back to being just friends. Nothing more.

CHAPTER TEN

HE DREADED WHAT was coming next. The discussion about his book. If she loved it, wouldn't she have said something by now?

Dario popped a grape in his mouth. He hadn't eaten much. As hard as he'd tried to put Gianna at ease about the kiss, he was still hung up on it.

He'd kissed many women in his lifetime but none of them had rocked his world like Gianna had done. But he didn't do relationships. He couldn't let himself count on someone else for his happiness, the way his mother did—man after man.

But now, as they finished eating, Dario needed to think of anything but that kiss. He chanced a glance Gianna's way as she took a sip of fresh squeezed lemonade. What did she think of his book? The question hovered on the tip of his tongue. He held back. What if she hated it? Or what if she liked it but was upset with him for hassling her about the kiss and said she didn't like it out of spite?

He halted his nervous thoughts. He knew Gianna well enough to know she wasn't a spiteful person. She was kind and caring. She went out of her way for people—especially him. So why was he hesitating?

"I finished reading your book," Gianna said, as though she'd been reading his thoughts.

He swallowed hard. "You did?"

She nodded. "That's why I slept in again this morning."

He tried to read her face to figure out whether she'd liked the book or not. But her expression wasn't giving anything away. "And what did you think?"

"I didn't want to put it down."

He smiled. "So you agree with me that it doesn't need anything else and I should submit it to my editor as is?"

She didn't say anything for a moment. The longer she was quiet, the more he lost hope that he'd nailed the book.

"Gianna?"

"I love your writing. You have a way with descriptions. They're so vivid."

He appreciated her compliment but he knew she was avoiding the main issue. "But is there something important missing from the book?"

She drew in a visible breath. Her gaze avoided his. "I'm not an editor or agent. My opinion shouldn't matter."

He knew she was skirting the answer. "Gianna, please, just say it."

Her gaze met his. Sympathy emanated from her eyes. "I just didn't feel the same growth in the hero as I did in the first book."

It was more definitive than what his agent had given him. But he just didn't get it. "It's not the same," he said. "Ator isn't going to grow the way he did in the first book. He was just a child in the beginning of that book and he grew through the chapters, coming into his legacy as leader of the Lavar."

"I understand that. But there's still something missing—"

"There's a lot to the book. There's a new threat to the Lavarians. And there's a threat within his own ranks."

"I know and that part is really good." She hesitated, as though she were going to say more but then changed her mind.

It was hard hearing that other people didn't see his book the way he did. There was a point where he hadn't thought he'd ever finish the book and the fact he had, well, it was a major miracle. Then he'd gone over it and over it, layering in emotions and descriptions. He'd poured hundreds of hours into that manuscript.

He just didn't think he had anything else to add. There were a ton of action scenes. There were victories and some defeats for the hero. There was uncertainty of whether he would or wouldn't succeed in his mission. What else could the book need?

"What if you had something about his personal life in there?" she asked.

"It's all personal to him. Ator's whole life is on the line." Dario knew he was being contrary. He didn't mean to be, but if he didn't defend his book, who would?

Still, there was that little voice in the back of his head that warned he might very well be missing something important. What if he was too stubborn to see his book's imperfections? He wanted his book to be the very best it could be.

It was about far more than the money he would receive if the publisher accepted the book. After all, he was a Marchello—he had a trust fund that he couldn't spend in a lifetime. His connection to this book went so much deeper. He could envision the scenes in his mind. He'd really connected with the characters and he wanted to share them with his readers.

But according to his agent and now Gianna, he hadn't dug deep enough into the hero. That hurt because he'd thought he'd done a really good job with Ator. But he knew if it wasn't good enough, the editor might not even bother to give him revisions. He might just outright reject the manuscript and ask for the advance back. In the publishing world, there were no guarantees.

"Okay." He couldn't believe what he was about to say. "Tell me what you think is missing."

"I told you, I'm no literary professional."

"True. But you're a reader. And you said you really liked the first book, so I trust you."

"I loved the first book. And I think this book could be even better."

"If I wrote what?"

She shrugged. "Ator needs someone close to him."

"He has his best friend, who leads up the strike team."

"Yes, but his best friend answers to him. And when it comes down to it, he backs off when they argue, as you would expect. He needs someone he has no control over. Someone who isn't afraid to speak their mind."

"Someone like you?"

"Someone like me?" She shook her head. "You're joking right?"

Was he? He wasn't even sure why he'd said it. "Well, you aren't afraid to speak your mind. You're willing to tell me what you think without backing down."

"Am I that bad?"

"No. That isn't what I mean." He paused to give her idea some thought. Maybe she was onto something. Because there was definitely something in the heated wordplay between them earlier and maybe a little sexual tension— okay a lot of the latter. Not that he would admit it to her or anyone else.

"What are you thinking?" Her voice interrupted his thoughts.

The truth was he didn't like where his thoughts were going. Not at all. Because thinking about his attraction to Gianna would only make their current arrangement more complicated.

He shook his head, chasing the thought from his mind. "Nothing. It won't work."

"What won't work? Giving him a girlfriend?"

His jaw tightened. "I don't write romance. No way. I'm not doing it."

Gianna planted her hands on her hips as her fine brows

drew together into a firm line. "What exactly are you saying?"

"That I don't write that sappy, emotional stuff."

Her mouth gaped.

"Why are you looking at me like that? That romance stuff is for women. I write fantasy and action."

"You mean all that macho stuff?"

He shrugged again. "Guys don't want to read all that mushy stuff."

"Really? Are you sure?"

He frowned at her. He didn't want to write about matters of the heart. It was way outside his wheelhouse. "I'm not doing it."

She shrugged. "Okay." There was a tone to her voice he couldn't quite place, like she thought he was making a big mistake. "It was just a suggestion."

"That stuff is okay for other people to write but not me."

"You mean, it's okay for women to write romance but not a big tough guy like you."

"No." He raked his fingers through his hair. "That isn't what I mean."

"Oh, wait. Are you saying you don't believe in love?"

This time he was the one who shrugged and looked away. "Something like that." When she didn't say anything, he chanced a glance her way. "What?"

"Nothing."

"Oh, you're thinking something. Just say it."

Gianna shook her head. When her gaze met his, there was sympathy radiating from her eyes. "I shouldn't have pushed so hard. I'm sorry—"

"Don't."

"Don't, what?" The sympathy was still there in her eyes. "I'm just trying to apologize."

"No. You feel sorry for me. And I don't want your sympathy. I don't need it." Why did she think because he didn't believe in love that he should be pitied? He was fine without it. He didn't need it.

"You know, I understand what it's like to get your heart broken. I'm sorry it happened to you too."

He held up his palms. "Whoa! You have this all wrong. No one hurt me." It wasn't exactly true. "No one had to hurt me for me not to believe in true love."

Her gaze narrowed in on him. "So you truly believe that two people can't live happily-ever-after?"

"That's a fairy tale. And fairy tales aren't true." She frowned as she considered his answer. He cleared his throat. "You disagree?"

"Actually, I was wondering if that was my problem. Maybe I've been wanting the illusion of something that doesn't exist outside of books and movies."

He'd never gotten this response before. Any time he'd mentioned his disbelief in true love, he'd always come up against strong opposition. But Gianna was different. A smile tugged at the corner of his lips. Then he noticed the shattered and disillusioned look in Gianna's eyes. She wanted true love to exist, which quite frankly surprised him after her last disastrous relationship.

He tilted his head ever so slightly to the side as he continued to study her. "You seem disappointed to think that true love might not exist. Why?" When her eyes widened with confusion, he further explained his train of thought. "I mean, you've had some bad luck where love is concerned, and yet, you still seem to want to know that it's out there. Why would you want to risk being hurt again?"

"Why wouldn't I?"

"I don't know. That's what I'm asking you."

She frowned at him. "Wait. You're serious. You've really never been in love?"

He shook his head and glanced away. He didn't deserve or need her feeling sorry for him. Was it so hard to believe he was fine on his own? Needing someone was a weakness. His mother had that weakness, moving from man to man to man. He wouldn't be weak like her. He just wouldn't.

Gianna's inquisitive stare searched him for answers. He didn't owe her any explanations. There was absolutely no reason to drag his messy family history into this conversation. Why did everyone seem to think it was strange that he didn't believe in fantasies? Like someone was really going to stick with him through thick and thin. He might write fantasies but he didn't believe they'd come true.

When things got tough, the door was the way to go. It's what his father did when Dario was young. Apparently, a family of four was more than his father was willing to deal with. And after he was gone, everything else just fell apart. Love wasn't worth all that pain—not when it didn't last.

When he glanced back at Gianna, she was still staring at him as though trying to dissect what had happened to him to stop him from believing in true love. "Stop it."

"Stop, what?"

"Looking at me like…like I'm broken. I'm not."

Her eyes widened. "You think you're broken?"

"I didn't say that. I mean, I did…" He rubbed the tense muscles in the back of his neck and groaned in frustration. "I don't want to discuss this anymore."

Buzz. Buzz.

He welcomed the interruption and withdrew his phone from his pocket. "It's my grandmother. She rarely calls me. I should get it."

Gianna nodded just as her phone went off. She checked the caller ID: Vera Cappellini. "It's my mother."

He had a feeling their simultaneous calls weren't a coincidence. He moved toward the other side of the patio to give Gianna some privacy.

"Nonna, what's wrong?"

"Is that any way to greet your grandmother?"

"I'm sorry. I'm just not used to you calling me." He sensed she had something important on her mind and was just working up to saying it. "What did you want to discuss?"

"I thought perhaps you had something to tell me."

A cold sense of dread came over him. He should have known his brother wouldn't keep news of his engagement to himself.

Dario swallowed hard. "Regarding what?"

His grandmother sighed. "I heard you got engaged. I thought I'd hear news like that directly from you."

Dario's gaze immediately sought out Gianna. As she talked, she waved her hand about. She only did that when she was worked up.

He overheard her say, "I'm sorry, Mamma. I should have called you right away." She paused and then said, "Yes, I'm engaged."

"Dario, are you still there?" His grandmother's voice drew back his attention.

"Yes, Nonna. I'm here."

Thanks to his brother and her cousin, their secret engagement wasn't so secret any longer. This wasn't good. Not good at all.

It was as if his life kept getting increasingly intertwined with Gianna's. Before his grandmother hung up, she made sure he knew to bring Gianna to their anniversary weekend—because a single dinner just wasn't enough. And they were just dying to meet his fiancée...

CHAPTER ELEVEN

HER WORLD FELT as though it were spinning off its axis.

Gianna felt bad about letting her mouth run amuck yesterday while talking to Dario. She'd only meant to help with the book and somehow it had spun out of control. She didn't care what he said—someone had hurt him deeply and left painful scars. Her heart ached for him.

She'd always known love growing up. In fact, she sometimes thought her parents had loved her too much. It was part of the reason she'd decided to move to Lake Como. She needed some distance from her parents in order to make her own mistakes without them interfering, in their well-meaning ways, and trying to fix everything for her.

She didn't like to make mistakes—in fact, they were downright awful—but she liked to think she'd learned from each of hers. Perhaps she still had a lot of learning to do.

The second thing to go wrong yesterday was finding out that her parents knew she was engaged. Her mother had been so happy and that made Gianna feel that much worse. Still, she'd made a promise to Dario. And as far as her parents were concerned, the damage was done. Even her father was excited. They were anxious to meet her fiancé.

After both Dario and Gianna had finished speaking with their respective families, neither had been in the mood to speak to the other. Their little fib had taken wings and grown. Now it felt as though everyone knew—everyone that mattered. They'd each gone their separate ways to deal with their guilt in their own way.

She'd decided one thing last night. Though she still believed in true love, she wasn't so sure it was for everyone. She'd also realized that you can't create it just because it's what you thought you wanted—as she'd learned the hard way—and if it came, it would come in its own time.

She needed to make things right with Dario. She made her way out to the patio area, fully expecting him to be seated at the table with his fingers moving rapidly over the keyboard while Tito laid by his side, but he wasn't there.

Her gaze moved to the French doors of the guesthouse. She was surprised to find them closed. Usually they were wide open, letting the gentle breeze rush through, just like she did with the doors of the main house. Was it possible he'd kept them closed because he was mad at her?

No. Surely not. Yes, she'd pushed him about putting some romance into his book and perhaps she'd taken it too far when she'd made it personal, but was he really going to avoid her for the rest of the month?

She moved across the patio and rapped her knuckles on the door. "Dario? Are you in there?"

Woof! Woof-woof!

Well, Tito was definitely in there. And she knew Dario didn't like to go anywhere without him. Actually, they were rather cute together. Dario might think he was immune to love, but she'd seen the way he looked at his dog and there was a deep and abiding love between them. So what if it wasn't a romantic love. The way she saw it, if he was capable of caring that much for an animal, he could also care deeply for a human—if he'd just let himself. Not that she was applying for the position or anything. It was merely an observation.

The door swung open. Dario stood there with his hair going every direction, which she'd come to learn was what happened when he was hard at work. His eyes were a bit bloodshot with shadows beneath them. And his clothes, well, they were the same ones he'd had on yesterday. Was it more than writing that had him looking so disheveled?

"Dario, are you all right?"

He seemed distracted, as though he were lost in his thoughts. "What?"

"I asked if you're feeling all right."

"I'm fine. Did you need something? Because I have to be going."

"No. Not really." She should apologize for pushing him yesterday, but she struggled for the right words. "I, uh…"

"Okay, then. I'll talk to you later." And with that, the door closed.

What in the world had just happened? Her lips pressed into a firm line that slowly sunk down into a frown. That had not gone at all like she'd planned.

Her stubborn streak kicked in. Who was he to shut the door in her face? She wasn't walking away until she'd said what she'd walked over here to say.

She tightened her hand and knocked firmly on the door again. This time she didn't call out. She knew he was in there and he knew she was waiting to speak to him.

It took a minute. A very long minute. Then the door swung open. His handsome face was marred with frown lines. So he wasn't happy to see her again. So be it.

"This won't take long," she said.

"That's good. I need to get back."

To what? His dog? The television? What was it that had him so distracted? And then she thought of his book and the revisions. Could that be what had him so distracted? The thought lightened her mood.

"I just came to say that I'm sorry I pushed you so hard about…" Her voice trailed off as suddenly she felt very uncomfortable about bringing up the *L* word with him. Yesterday, it had just rolled out as a part of a bigger conversation. Today, however, there was no conversation. In fact, Dario kept his hand on the door as though he couldn't wait to shut it. "Anyway, I'm sorry if things were said that shouldn't have been."

He shrugged. "It's fine. Is that all?"

Really? That's all he was going to say? She was beginning to dislike the word *fine*. Well, if he didn't want to talk to her, then she had other things to do.

"Yes, that's all." She turned and walked away.

The door closed behind her.

She had to admit, if only to herself, that her pride was stung. Something had shifted between them after those heart-pounding, toe-curling kisses. She wasn't going to fool herself into thinking they were in love. Been there. Done that. This thing with Dario felt so different from anything she'd ever experienced.

But somewhere along the way she'd thought that they'd formed a solid friendship. After all, she'd told him more about her current life than her cousin—her best friend. And yet, it all came to an abrupt end when she'd challenged his disbelief in true love.

She grabbed her backpack and slung her camera around her neck. She was off. And she didn't know when she'd be back. Not that Dario would miss her or anything.

His fingers pounded on the keyboard.

His thoughts came so rapidly that his fingers couldn't keep up.

Dario didn't know how many hours he'd been sitting with his laptop in hand. His fingers ached from the lengthy typing. His neck was stiff from leaning over his screen. Every other muscle protested from his lack of movement. And yet, he continued to write.

He'd started in bed when he couldn't sleep. He'd made notes and written down random thoughts of how a romance thread could play a part in the book.

At first, he didn't want it to play a very big part. After all, this was a fantasy/action book. It wasn't some heartfelt, tearful paperback. He didn't want to lose the oomph!

And he had to stay true to his hero's macho attitude. But maybe, just maybe, there was a way to add the element. It would make everyone happy. He hoped.

In his mind, he played out scenario after scenario, but none felt right. His hero, Ator, didn't believe he deserved a personal life. His life was dedicated to the preservation of the civilization of Lavar. So that meant whomever Ator got involved with, it would be such a fierce love that even the hero would not be able to ignore it.

As Dario thought about this romance, he noticed how his thoughts kept slipping back to Gianna. She was a force unlike any other he'd ever known. While other women were more inclined to be agreeable with him—well, as long as they thought they had a chance to snare one of the rich and eligible Marchello brothers—Gianna didn't care about impressing him. She spoke her mind. And that impressed him. His hero needed a heroine like Gianna—up front and in his face when she thought he was messing things up.

At first, Dario tried using one of Ator's household staff for a love interest, but it didn't take him long to realize she was no match for the hero. The ideal woman needed to be the hero's equal. Just as Gianna was his equal in smarts and matters of the heart. She might talk a big game about true love, but he knew she was just as leery of it as he was.

And so he kept writing. Note after note. Thought after thought. Never deleting anything because he never knew what idea he might need in the future.

He couldn't let himself get distracted with phone calls, emails or even his gorgeous housemate. If he lost his train of thought, he feared it wouldn't come back.

It had happened to him before. He'd be onto a new thread in a book and the phone would ring. By the time he got off the phone, he'd lost his rhythm. Trying to climb back inside the thoughts of a character was not as easy as it seemed. Sometimes the hero's thoughts flowed and other times it was a process of pulling out one word at a time at a snail's pace.

Because at last he had it—the perfect subplot. The heroine's name was Sefinna, a high-ranking soldier in the enemy forces.

The first time they meet, it's in battle. Instead of killing her, he spares her life. Her culture says that she now owes him her life—but not her army's secrets.

Like moths to a flame, they are drawn to each other. They fight their feelings—but for how long? If they were to act on their feelings and it was uncovered, it would mean the death of both of them.

Dario liked the subplot. He really did. But he also kept telling himself he would fix things with Gianna in a little bit. By the time he was ready for a break, it was late. She had probably already called it a night. He noticed she liked to go to bed early so she could rise before the sun, whereas he was more of a night owl.

But now that he'd reached a point in his writing that he was comfortable taking a break, he stepped onto the patio. He was surprised to find Gianna had just gotten out of the pool. She finished drying off and then wrapped a towel around herself. When she turned and spotted him, she jumped.

"Sorry," he said. "I didn't mean to startle you."

"Well, the pool is all yours." She started toward the main house.

"Gianna, wait." He approached her.

She stopped and turned. "It's late and I'm tired."

"This won't take long. I just want to say I'm sorry for being so abrupt earlier."

"You mean yesterday?"

Yesterday? Had it been that long ago? His sleep-deprived brain realized she must be right. "Yes. I've been working on some ideas to fix the book and I guess I got a bit obsessed."

Her gaze searched his face. "When's the last time you slept?"

"It's been a while. But I promise you when the book is sold, you'll be the first person to read it."

"Get some rest. We can talk tomorrow." She turned and went into the house.

Tito followed her. Even his dog had abandoned him. He wanted to call out to Gianna and ask her to sit with him for a while. He missed her company.

He remained quiet as he stood all alone. Being alone was what he wanted, right? He didn't need anyone. Needing someone made you vulnerable. His mind flashed back to him as a child, watching his mother drive away, leaving him and his brother behind.

He slammed the door on the painful memory. He was okay on his own. He turned and headed for the guesthouse. If he needed company, he had the characters in his book.

CHAPTER TWELVE

THE NEXT FEW DAYS, Gianna split her time between taking photos while on nature walks and working in her office. She'd taken a lot more pictures since she'd been home than she imagined possible. But the weather was too nice to be stuck inside all day.

She thought about grabbing her camera, her tripod and going off on one of her nature walks. Her entry for the photo competition was due soon and she still didn't think she had a winner out of the hundreds of photos she'd taken so far. She pulled her latest batch of photos up on her extra-large monitor. There were some good ones, but for one reason or another, she rejected them all. None of them had what it took to stand out in the crowd.

Just then her phone rang. It was her agent. He had a lead on a new assignment for her. It was another nature show with a different host. This time she'd be in Alaska.

She knew the area was beautiful but the idea of roughing it didn't appeal to her. At least that's what she told herself was the reason she wasn't anxious to leave Lake Como. It certainly had nothing to do with her sleep-deprived, grumpy housemate. Nothing at all.

She told her agent she'd think about it. He said she had some time. Production didn't start for a couple of months.

Maybe what she needed was a break. She headed to the kitchen to pack some food, but passing by the open doors, she noticed Dario working on the patio. His posture was rigid as he leaned over his laptop, rereading what he'd written. Then he blew out a breath and slouched back in the chair. His fingers raked through his hair. It didn't look like the writing was going well.

She thought about going out and speaking with him. Things between them had been rocky lately. She'd like to fix it. However, it needed to be more than a brief conversation. Perhaps he needed to get away from this place too—away from his computer—away from the stress of work.

A little later, Gianna emerged from the house in jean shorts, a pink blouse and one of her grandmother's hats. Her grandmother had had an obsession with hats. Once in a while, Gianna would wear one. Today, she'd chosen a big straw hat with a white bow and pink flowers. It was more than a retro fashion statement. It would help protect her from the sunshine because where they were going there wouldn't be any shade.

Dario glanced up from his laptop. "Don't you look cute?"

She smiled and curtsied. "Why thank you."

He chuckled. "You're in a good mood. I take it things are going well with your photography business?"

She shrugged. "I guess you could say that. But it's not really a business. Right now, it's more of a hobby. But my agent called with a job offer."

"Is that a good thing?"

"I don't know. It'd mean living out of a duffel bag again."

"Then turn it down."

"It's not that easy. I need money to pay the bills." Though she could honestly say she wasn't jumping at the offer. The more time she spent in Gemma, the more she wanted to stay here.

"Your photography could be a business, if you wanted."

It was though he could read her mind. "I've dreamed about opening a little shop to sell my prints, but it would take all my savings and I'm just not sure anyone would be interested in my work. After all, I'm a nobody in the photography world."

"I think you should do it, if it'll make you happy. I can

guarantee you'll have one client. Me. I think you're amazingly talented."

Her face grew warm. "Thank you. But that's something to ponder another day. Right now, I have other plans."

"Are you off to take more photos?"

"Not today. I thought we'd have an outing."

"We? As in you and me?" When she nodded, he said, "Thanks. But I don't think so. I have too much work to do here."

"Really? Because it looks to me like you're stuck."

"That obvious?"

She nodded.

He frowned. "I'll get it. I… I just have to keep working on it."

She approached him. "Or maybe you need to give your mind a break."

"I don't have time for a break. My deadline for these revisions is almost here."

"All the more reason for you to relax." Sensing he was going to refuse her again, she added, "I may not be a writer, but I can't imagine you can just force your imagination to cooperate out of pure will."

"Sadly, you're right. It doesn't work that way. The harder I search for the next words, the harder they are to find."

She closed his laptop. "Come with me."

"Gianna…really I can't. You know how important this book is to me."

"I promise if you come with me now, I'll leave you alone the rest of the day."

"Where are we going?"

"To lunch." She held up her grandmother's picnic basket.

"So now you're bribing me?"

She smiled. "I don't know. Is it working?"

When he blew out a sigh, she knew she'd won. "Yes, it is. Lead the way. Come on, Tito."

Her smile faltered. "About that. I don't think Tito will appreciate this particular outing."

"He wouldn't?" Dario looked confused and a bit disappointed. "Where exactly are we going?"

"Someplace an excitable puppy shouldn't be." She turned to Tito. "I'm sorry, fella. Maybe next time."

Once Tito was situated in the guesthouse, they set off on their adventure. Gianna just hoped he liked her surprise. She'd find out soon enough.

Sailing.

Dario couldn't believe he was sitting in a rowboat of all things. He quite honestly had never gone rowing before. Sure, he'd been on luxury yachts numerous times, as well as cruise ships, but never a modest rowboat. He wasn't sure what to make of it.

His gaze moved to Gianna, who smiled as she looked out over the tranquil water. After he'd insisted on doing the rowing, Gianna used her camera to take some photos of him, of the water and of the mountains in the background. She seemed to be enjoying herself. And he had to admit the physical activity was doing him some good, as well. He didn't feel nearly as stiff and utterly stressed.

"So do you approve of your surprise?" she asked.

"I do. I've never done this before." He glanced around at the shoreline. "It gives me a whole new perspective on the area from here."

Gianna let go of her camera, letting it dangle from the strap around her neck. "Your parents didn't do things like this when you were young?"

He shook his head. "My family was very different from yours. Even from a young age, there were a lot of expectations as far as doing well in school to being at the top of sports. There wasn't much time to have fun."

"You mean your mother and father didn't let you be normal kids?"

He had opened Pandora's box and now he didn't know how to close it. And to his surprise, he wasn't even sure he wanted to close it. As he'd come to learn, Gianna was easy to talk to, and though she didn't always agree with him, she made him see things from a different perspective.

Not that he wanted to think about his dysfunctional family, but he felt as though he owed her the truth. After all, she'd agreed to portray herself as his fake fiancée when there wasn't much in it for her. Who did something like that?

A gentle breeze rushed over him, soothing his frazzled nerves. But prying open the rusty door to the past wasn't easy. He didn't talk about it. Ever. Even as a young child, he'd learned how to swiftly change the subject. These days, he had it down to a fine art.

He shook his head. "You don't want to hear about my messed-up family."

"Messed up? Does this have something to do with why you never mention your mother or father?"

He nodded.

When she spoke, her voice was soft. "Why is that?"

There was shame in his past—in the Marchellos' past—that no one in his family spoke of. Not even amongst themselves. The things he knew of his parents he'd pieced together bit by bit over the course of his lifetime.

He stared out over the water. "From what I gather, my parents were forced together."

"You mean as in an arranged marriage?"

He shook his head. "Not exactly. Their families knew each other. They moved in the same circles. There were expectations from the time they were young children. From what I gathered, they dated in school. They broke up at some point and then much later, with pressure from their families, they got back together and married."

"I feel bad for them. That's a lot of pressure to put on kids."

Dario continued. If he didn't get it out now, he wouldn't later. "Soon, my brother came along. My father was working in the family business under my grandfather's guidance, which is no easy task. Don't get me wrong, I love my grandfather. But he can be difficult. Anyway, I was born a couple of years later and apparently it was too much for their marriage. My father bailed. He up and quit his job, his family, everyone."

Dario still remembered the day. He'd been young, only five or so. But his parents had a really loud argument. His father packed a few things and was out the door. That was the day Dario's world changed forever.

"I'm so sorry you went through that, but at least you had your mother."

He shrugged off her sympathy. "She stuck it out for a year or so. By then she was divorced and on the hunt for husband number two."

"What happened to you and your brother?"

"My mother deposited us on my grandparents' doorstep. It was just supposed to be for the summer, but she never came back to take us home."

Tears started to well up in Gianna's eyes. "That's the saddest thing I think I've ever heard."

He shrugged off her sympathy. "It's fine. We're fine." They weren't. Not really. But dwelling on it helped no one. "It's all in the past."

"Is it?" she asked. "Do you ever see your parents?"

"Over the years, they've drifted in and out of our lives. The last time I saw my mother, she was on her second or was it her third husband? It's hard to keep track."

"And your father?"

"He's pretty much a nomad, moving from place to place. He never remarried. I think he had enough of it the first time around."

"At least you have your grandparents."

"True. But they are cool and distant from each other. They don't argue, at least not in front of my brother and me, but they've never been affectionate in front of us either."

"Oh. No wonder you don't believe in love."

Dario gripped the oars and resumed rowing. He needed something to do to avoid seeing the sympathy in her eyes. It made him feel like that small helpless child once more—it was a feeling he never wanted to experience again.

"My grandparents raised my brother and me. Franco was always anxious to join the family business. It was dictated that I would join him at the helm when the time came. The only problem was that no one asked me if it's what I wanted.

"I went to college and when I graduated, I worked my way up through the business like my father and brother had done. I'm good at what I do. The only problem is I don't like it. I wish I did. I feel guilty for rejecting what my family has built up over generations."

"You shouldn't feel guilty. You can't control where your interests lie. If you feel guilty, then I'll have to feel guilty about not staying and helping with my parents' market or marrying someone who would one day take it over."

His gaze met hers. "Sounds like we're in the same boat."

"Literally." She smiled at her joke.

He smiled too. It was nice to know that finally someone understood him. Once, he'd tried to talk to his brother about their parents. Franco said he understood what he was feeling, but Dario knew his business-driven brother never really understood.

Dario paused the rowing. "I've been a reader all my life. It's what got me through the breakup of my family and everything else. The older I got, the more I read until

I had a library of paperbacks. Fantasy books were always my favorite."

"I like to read romance, but I think you already figured that out."

He nodded. "I noticed them on the bookcases in the living room."

"So how did you get started writing?"

He shook his head. "That part's really boring."

"No, it isn't." She looked at him expectantly. "I'd love to hear it, if you're willing to share."

"One evening, I came home from work and I decided to try and write a book. I'd taken creative writing in college but that was a lot different than writing a complete book. My first attempt was a disaster. So I delved deeper into the writing world. To my surprise, there really is a world of writers who live online. Though the writer's world spans the globe, thanks to the internet, it's actually a pretty small community."

"It seems like you can find most anything on the internet these days. I just joined a group of photographers. They talk about all the new equipment out there and how it compares to the older stuff. I listen but I haven't ventured into any of the discussions."

"I understand. It took me a while to speak up. An online acquaintance guided me to online classes for writers. Little by little, I figured out where I'd gone wrong. It took a long time for me to finish writing my first book as my work in the family business includes a lot of overtime and business dinners. I still have that story somewhere on my laptop."

"That's exciting. You could publish it too."

He shook his head. "I don't think so. I made a lot of mistakes with it. *The Rise of Lavar* is my second book.

"It took me almost two years until I finished it. I was certain it was going to be a best seller. It was so much better than my first attempt. After all, I'd poured my heart and soul into it. I sent it off to an agent. The agent replied immediately with good news and bad news. First, they liked my voice. But second, the book was much too long with way too much description. So I started making the story a lot leaner. It's harder figuring out what to cut than it sounds. I sent the revised manuscript back to the agent. He passed. The next agent passed. And so it went, agent after agent. I was just about to give up when an agent finally took an interest in my book. It took a while to find the right publisher and well, you know the rest of it."

"Yes, I do. Now I can say I knew you when."

He laughed out loud. "You make it sound like I'll be famous."

"You are famous."

"No, I'm not." He didn't feel famous, even though his book had sold close to a million copies around the world and there was even a fan club started online. "I'm just me."

"You can't ever give up on your dream."

This was his chance to speak up and help her. "I won't give up on my dream, if you won't give up on yours."

"What dream is that?"

"I see you with your camera. You're rarely without it. I wouldn't be surprised if you sleep with it—"

"I'm not that bad…am I?"

He smiled and nodded. "I see the way your face lights up when you find something to photograph. It makes you happy."

"Working on a film crew makes me happy too."

"Does it really? Do you get out of bed before the sun so you can shoot the sunrise?"

"I do…but only because my alarm goes off and I know if I'm not where I'm supposed to be on time that a lot of people are going to get upset with me."

"See. I was right. It's not the same."

She sighed. "Okay. You're right. I like photography better. But I don't know if I can make a living doing it."

"You won't know unless you try." He glanced down at the picnic basket. "Now how about we eat? I'm starved."

He'd never been so close to a person. Gianna didn't reject him because of his dysfunctional family or call him crazy because he didn't want to be a part of his family's successful business and bring home an enormous paycheck. She liked him just the way he was without wanting him to change.

He'd kiss her right now if he thought he could pull it off without tipping over the boat. The idea teased and tempted him. What was life without a few risks? He let go of the oars and went to stand—the boat tilted to the side.

"What are you doing?" Gianna frowned at him. "Stop moving."

He settled back on the seat. "Sorry. I was going to, um… help with lunch."

"I've got it. Sit still. My idea of fun isn't swimming to shore."

And so the moment had passed. He'd missed the perfect moment to feel her lips beneath his. He knew it was for the best, even if it didn't feel like it. After all, relationships didn't work out. But Gianna was making him wish they could be the exception.

CHAPTER THIRTEEN

THE LITTLE WHITE cursor hovered over the send button.

Days had passed in a coffee-driven blur. One day had turned into two. And before he knew it, nearly two weeks had flown by. He'd never written with such passion. Gianna had made sure he stopped to eat, but otherwise she'd given him the space to finish the revisions.

And now the moment of truth was upon him. He'd completed the book almost a week early. It was all thanks to Gianna and her constant encouragement. No matter what, she continued to believe in him.

The cursor continued to hover over the send button. Why was he hesitating? He'd done his best work. Hadn't he?

His heart raced as doubt crept into his thoughts. Mentally, he went over his manuscript one last time. Was the new story thread carried through the entire story? Yes. Had he left any plot threads dangling? He didn't think so. But with one hundred and fifty thousand words, it was easy to miss something.

In the next thought, he realized he was overthinking things. After all, this wasn't the final draft of the book—far from it. He still had time to fix anything he'd missed. Plus there would be a number of eyes that read over it before it went to press—well, that's if it went to press. He sure hoped it would, but there were no guarantees.

He'd read on an online forum how the book market could change suddenly. What was hot one day wasn't hot the next day. In the past year, since his first book was released, had the wave of reader excitement for his characters passed him by? He sure hoped not.

Was there anything else he could add to the book at this

point to make it better? He didn't think so. So there was nothing else to do… He pressed Send.

Euphoria rushed through his system. At this particular moment, he didn't care if anyone liked it or not. The point was that he'd finished the second book in the series. It had a beginning, a middle and an end. What more could anyone ask for?

Then again, there was one more thing.

He'd come up with the best hook for the end of the book. When Ator and Sefinna give in to their desires, there's a creek of a floorboard outside the door. Has their secret been found out? Will they pay the ultimate price for their love?

He smiled. Readers would have to stay tuned for the next book. At this point, he had no idea where they went from there. He'd figure it out another day.

Needing someone to celebrate with him, he glanced over at Tito, who had dragged his dog bed out onto the patio. He was now stretched out in it, sleeping.

"Hey, boy, guess what?"

Tito pried one eye open.

"I finished my book. Isn't that great?"

He didn't get so much as a wag of the dog's tail. Tito closed his eye, yawned and rolled over. So much for being his man's best friend.

Dario's thoughts turned to Gianna. Without her, none of this would have happened. Tonight, they were going to live it up. After all, she'd put up with him living much like a zombie these past few weeks.

He closed his laptop and jumped up from the patio table. "Gianna!" He started toward the main house. Where was she? He didn't recall her leaving, but he realized that sometimes he got lost in his thoughts and missed what was right in front of him.

"Gianna? Are you here?"

"In here," she called from the back of her house.

He followed her voice to the room that she'd converted into her office. Her desk faced the window so she could look out over the lush hillside. He couldn't blame her. It was an amazing view. But her back was to him so he wasn't able to read her expression.

"Hey, are you busy?" He really hoped she'd say she wasn't.

"I am. What do you need?"

It wasn't fair for him to drag her away from her work just because he'd finished his own. After all, she'd given him plenty of room while he'd finished his book.

"Ah…" He hesitated. "It's nothing. I'll talk to you later." A bit deflated, he turned and walked away.

Gianna being busy shouldn't douse his mood. He'd accomplished something big—something he hadn't been sure he'd be able to do. But celebrating alone didn't appeal to him. He could walk into the village. There would be plenty of people there, but the thought of celebrating with a bunch of strangers didn't appeal to him either.

There was only one person he wanted to celebrate with—Gianna. He noticed as more and more time passed that he really looked forward to spending time with her. There was something special about her—something down-to-earth.

When she was upset with him, it showed. When she wanted to have a good time, it wasn't to get all dressed up and go into the city to be seen. Instead, Gianna liked to watch a movie or take a walk in nature. She was so very different from the women he dated. And yet, when she did have to go out and be seen, she knew how to dress up and present herself as if she were a movie star.

But a little voice inside him said that this was nothing more than an infatuation. True love did not exist. All he had to do was look at his grandparents and parents. His grandparents tolerated each other but he never saw any real affection between them. And then his parents, well, they were the very definition of dysfunctional. So much so that not only did their marriage fail but they were also barely present in either of their sons' lives.

He didn't want a loveless marriage. The thought of barely speaking to Gianna and merely passing her in the hallway made him sad. Or worse, fighting with her daily like his parents had done would be agony.

It was best to keep his distance from relationships. It'd worked for him so far. But he knew Gianna had somehow breached the walls he'd put up around his heart. He felt something for her—something he'd never felt for anyone else. But he wasn't ready or willing to examine those emotions too closely.

"Dario, sorry about that. I was in the middle of uploading some photos to a website." Gianna strolled out to the patio. "What did you need?"

"I hit Send."

Her eyes widened. "On your book?"

His mood lifted and he smiled. "Yes. It's finally gone."

"That's awesome." She rushed over to him. At first, he wasn't sure what she was planning to do but then she threw her arms around him and hugged him tight. "I'm so proud of you."

His arms snaked their way around her slender waist. He enjoyed holding her close. They fit together like two pieces of a puzzle. He turned his head toward the curve of her neck. It was so very tempting to press a kiss upon that soft skin, but mustering up all his self-restraint, he resisted the urge. He didn't want to ruin their closeness.

Instead, he breathed in her sweet floral scent. He inhaled again, deeper this time, impressing the memory of the addictive scent upon his mind. It would have to be enough for now.

And then she pulled away much too soon. In fact, if it were up to him, he'd never let her go. Wait. Had he really just thought that?

He quickly dismissed the idea. He was getting way ahead of himself. He didn't do long-term relationships. He didn't do commitments. And he certainly didn't do love. He just had to keep reminding himself of that.

He blamed all this emotional stuff on his book. He'd been thinking too long about how to make his hero fall in love. That was it. His brain was still in writing mode. Nothing to worry about. All he needed was a bit of time alone to get his head screwed on straight.

Gianna's eyes sparkled with excitement. She looked so beautiful. There was this funny feeling in his chest, a sensation he'd never experienced before. It warmed him from the inside out.

"We have to go celebrate," she insisted.

He didn't want her to feel obligated to go out of her way for him. He shook his head. "You've already done enough."

"Nonsense. This is huge!" Her voice was filled with genuine excitement. "I know, we'll drive into the city. We'll make it a huge affair."

He couldn't help but smile at the way she was making such a big deal out of his accomplishment. And though he'd originally wanted to jump in the car and go paint up the town, the thought no longer appealed to him. It was enough to celebrate this moment with Gianna. Her excitement was all he needed.

"Thank you," he said. "I really appreciate the thought, but it's getting late and that's a long drive. We'd never be able to get there and back today. And there's Tito to consider."

The smile fell from her face as she considered his words. "I know what we'll do." Her eyes lit up. "It's not as fancy as the city but it's something." Her hands started to move as she talked, emphasizing her words. "After all, we have to do something. This is huge. You worked so hard—"

"Slow down." He reached out, taking her expressive hands into his own. "What is it you have in mind?"

"Dinner in the village."

He was surprised by her suggestions. "Are you sure? I know you've been avoiding it as much as possible lately."

Her gaze lowered. "You noticed that, huh?"

"I did. I've felt really bad about it. I'm sorry our arrangement put you in such an awkward position with your family."

Her gaze rose to meet his. "It's not your fault. I agreed to this."

"But you regret it?"

She shrugged. She wouldn't say it but he knew she regretted the charade. To his surprise, he didn't. He'd really enjoyed their fake relationship.

"You don't have to worry," he said. "It's over."

Her confused gaze rose to meet his. "What?"

"Our engagement ended when I hit Send."

Her expressive eyes widened. "But what about your grandparents' anniversary party? They're expecting both of us."

"I'll just tell them we broke up."

Her lips pursed together as though considering his suggestion. "I don't know."

"I thought you'd be anxious to end this charade. Are you saying you changed your mind? Do you like being engaged to me? I mean, I know what a catch I am." He sent her a teasing smile, but there was a part of him that was serious.

"Don't you wish—" she said quickly. "No. It's just that I worry about ruining this event for them."

"You think they'll be upset by the current status of my love life?"

She shrugged. "I don't know them but you do. Do they worry about you?"

For the longest time, he thought his grandparents were only worried about his future in the family business. But he'd noticed how excited his grandmother had become upon the news of his engagement. She was even talking about wedding plans. At the time, the thought of walking down the aisle had sent cold chills down his spine, but now it wasn't sounding nearly as intimidating...so long as it was Gianna by his side. The thought startled him. Were his thoughts being influenced by more than just his writing?

"Well, my grandmother was excited to meet your family at the party and start the wedding plans."

"My family! She contacted them?"

"It appears my brother gave my grandmother Carla's contact information and from there she was able to reach your parents. She personally invited them. I thought you knew."

"No, I didn't know." She frowned. "Now we have no choice but to stay together until after the party."

"Are you all right with that?"

Her hesitant gaze met his. "Are you?"

He smiled broadly. "I think a few more days as your adoring fiancé won't be a hardship."

"Adoring, huh?"

Heat flashed over his face. "Must just be the writer in me coming out."

"Uh-huh." She started to walk away.

"Where are you going?"

"To get ready for dinner. I have to look good for my adoring fiancé." And with that, she disappeared down the hallway.

He had a feeling she wasn't going to let him forget his choice of words. Not that he regretted them. Gianna was very special. And he did adore her, but that was a long way from love. Wasn't it? After all, look what had happened to his parents.

Candlelight.

Champagne.

And romantic music.

It had been quite a dinner. Gianna smiled as they strolled back to the villa beneath the bright moonlight. All evening, Dario had played the perfect gentleman. He'd been attentive, entertaining and plied her with compliments. She had to keep reminding herself that it wasn't a real date. Or was it?

This evening was like a dream—one of the dreams she had at night when Dario played a role of being much more than a roommate. She thought of pinching herself to make sure she hadn't nodded off and dreamed up this romantic evening. But her hand was neatly tucked in the crook of his arm and she had no desire to break their physical connection.

"Did you have a good evening?" Dario's deep voice broke into her wayward thoughts.

"It was wonderful. Thank you. But it was your big evening. Did you enjoy it?"

"I've never had such an amazing evening. The food was out of this world. The atmosphere was relaxing. And I was with the most gorgeous woman."

So this was a date. A real date. Her smile broadened. She thought of mentioning it, but she couldn't bring herself to vocalize her thoughts. What if Dario didn't feel the same way? What if it ruined this incredible evening? It was best to keep the thought to herself.

She wanted to squeeze as many happy moments into the short time they had left. The thought dampened her mood, but she quickly brushed it aside. They had tonight and she wasn't ready for it to end. There had to be a way to extend it.

When they reached the house, the ground lights lit up the patio area. The pool lights beckoned to her. She led them to the edge of the pool.

It was a warm evening with barely a breeze. Her heated body would welcome the cool water over her skin, and if Dario was to join her, all the better.

"Why don't we take a dip?" She hoped he'd be agreeable.

"First, I have something to ask you." He turned to her. "I've been meaning to do this all evening but I never found the right moment."

Her heart fluttered in her chest. What was he up to?

And then he knelt down on one knee.

"Dario, what are you doing?" Her heart leaped into her throat.

He pulled a blue velvet box from his pocket and held it out to her. "I'm asking you to be my fake fiancée."

The *fake* part put a damper on her excitement. He was playing a part, but oh, my, what a part. Just the thought that it could have been real was enough to send her heart racing.

"Go ahead. Take it." He moved the box closer to her.

She pressed a hand to her chest. Her fingertips could feel the pounding of her heart. "But...but I can't."

He sent her a reassuring smile. "Yes, you can. It's a gift."

"A gift?" She was confused. "You mean it's not—you know—"

"A diamond ring?"

She nodded, not trusting her voice.

"Why don't you look inside and see?"

Well, it wouldn't hurt just to look. She cautiously reached for the box. All the while, her heart raced. Why was she getting so worked up? The proposal wasn't real.

He chuckled. "Go ahead. It won't bite."

She took the box and, in that moment, she was jealous of the woman that would one day receive a real engagement ring from Dario. Because as much as Dario tried to convince himself that true love didn't exist, she knew one day when he least expected it, he'd fall head over heels in love. And the woman he loved would be the luckiest woman in the world.

Suddenly, her stomach soured. The thought of him sharing a similar moment with another woman made her sad.

"Hey." Dario's voice drew her from her thoughts. He was now standing next to her. When she gazed into his eyes, she saw concern. "It's okay. If you don't like it, we can exchange it."

It took her a moment to realize what he was talking about. She glanced back at the unopened box. She pried the lid back to reveal a large pink stone surrounded by small diamond solitaires.

"It's gorgeous," she said, unable to take her eyes off the stunning piece of jewelry. "Is that a sapphire?"

"It's actually a pink diamond."

Her mouth gaped. It took a moment for her to realize the magnitude of this gift. She turned an accusing gaze his way. "You told me it wasn't a diamond ring."

"Well, um, it's not a traditional diamond ring."

"There's a difference?"

He sent her a sheepish smile. "If I'd have said it was a diamond ring, would you have opened it?"

"No. Absolutely not." A diamond ring shouldn't be a prop for a fake relationship. A diamond ring meant eternal love that could make it through the fires that life threw at a couple. It wasn't a trivial piece of jewelry.

His brows rose. "You seem mighty certain of that. I mean, don't all women love diamonds?"

"I don't know about all women, but this one thinks a diamond ring should come with love and the promise of forever."

The color drained from his face. "I see. Well, will a heartfelt thank-you be enough?"

She closed the box and handed it back to him. "Dario, take it back. It's way too much."

His hand closed over hers. His touch was gentle and warm. She loved the way his skin felt against hers. She lifted her gaze to meet his. She meant to say something but as their gazes held, the words vanished from her mind.

His gaze dipped to her lips. Her heart raced as he drew her hand closer until it was pressed to his solid chest. She naturally stepped closer.

When he spoke, his voice was low and full of desire. "You do know I want to kiss you, don't you?"

She gave a slight nod as his gaze continued to hold hers.

With his free hand, he reached out to her. The backs of his fingers brushed lightly over her cheek. "And you realize this is a mistake?"

She once more attempted to speak but the words got clogged in her throat. Instead, she nodded once more.

He lowered his head just as she lifted up on her tiptoes. Their lips pressed to each other. She had waited so long for this moment—the feel of his touch. It was so much better than the memory that kept her awake at night.

His arms wrapped around her like steel bands, anchoring her to him. She released the ring box into his hand and then pressed both hands to his chest. Her fingers worked their way slowly up toward his broad shoulders, taking in all the contours of his muscles. He was the full package—brains and brawn.

But then he pulled back. Uncertainty showed in his eyes. She liked that he didn't automatically assume they'd be spending the night together, though she knew that's where this evening was headed. She just didn't want to rush things. This was too good not to be savored.

Because when Dario went back to his life and she was once more sleeping in a tent while working with a new film crew, she wanted to have the memories to look back on. She knew there would never be another man in her life like Dario.

He stepped back. He raked his fingers through his hair. "We should probably stop there."

"Really? Are you sure?" At that moment, she was feeling daring. She slipped a strap of her summer dress down over her shoulder.

Desire flared in his dark eyes. "Gianna, what are you doing?"

"What do you think I'm doing?"

"I… I don't know."

His avid interest drove her onward. She slipped the other strap down over her shoulder. "It's awfully hot out here." It was no lie. When he looked at her like that, it set her body afire. "Don't you think?"

He nodded but no words were spoken.

She smiled. She reached behind her and released the zipper. Her dress swished to the ground. The breath caught in her lungs. Had she gone too far?

She stood there in her black halter bra, her matching lacy boy shorts and a pair of high heels. She'd never done anything like this before. Her heart pounded as her palms grew moist. She had absolutely no idea what Dario's reaction would be. She knew how she wanted him to react, but right now his wide-eyed stare said she'd surprised both of them.

And then he smiled. A big ole smile lit up his whole face.

She smiled too, enjoying having his full attention. She just had to keep up this act a little longer and then she'd make a grand exit. Because standing here in her underwear, which, granted, provided more covering than her bikini, was still a bit—okay, a lot—nerve-racking.

She resisted the urge to rush as she kicked off her heels. She'd never played a seductress before and she was finding it so much fun. She stepped closer to him, as though she were going to have her way with him, but then she dove into the pool.

When she emerged and swiped the water from her face, she found Dario standing at the pool's edge with a confused look upon his face.

"The water's nice," she said, "why don't you join me?"

She didn't have to ask twice. He stripped down to his boxers and dove in. He swam up to her. "You are a tease."

"Am I?" She grinned at him.

When he reached out to her, she swam away. When he sent her another confused look, she said, "Half of the fun is the chase."

A knowing smile lit up his face. Then he took off after her. He caught her hand here and her leg there. Each time she escaped. She had a feeling he was intentionally letting her get away.

All the while, her pulse raced with excitement. She knew what was at the end of the chase, an amazing night wrapped in his arms.

When she finally emerged at the end of the pool, where they'd first dove in, she let him catch up to her. Playing cat and mouse was fine for a time, but she was in the mood to be caught now.

He snaked an arm around her waist and pulled her close. "You can't get away now."

"I don't want to get away now." Her fingertip followed a drop of water as it slid down his bare chest.

"I wasn't sure before but now I know for certain you're a tease."

She shook her head. "Am not. If I were, I wouldn't have

waited here for you to catch up to me." She slid her arms up around his neck and then raised her legs, wrapping them around his waist. "It seems to me you're the one that has been caught."

He moaned. "You can catch me anytime you want."

And then he claimed her lips once more. There was fire in his kiss—a driving desire that she met with a need of her own. She may not be his real fiancée, but just for tonight, they'd pretend.

CHAPTER FOURTEEN

THE BIG DAY had arrived.

They were getting an early start as there was so much to do. Gianna was so nervous that she could barely eat more than some bread. Her stomach was tied up in knots. She wasn't sure which made her more nervous: the awards at the photography competition and living up to her grandmother's legacy or meeting Dario's entire family for the first time. Both were quite daunting events.

But she knew those weren't the only reasons she was so worked up that morning. There was also the tiny thing about her sleeping with Dario. Just the mere thought of their intimate time together sent her heart racing and made her face burning hot.

Even though their time together was coming to a close after the weekend with both of their families, they'd agreed to have an amicable, very mature breakup.

Although it didn't feel like things were ending. It felt like something new was just beginning. Was that possible? Did Dario feel the same way? Or was she just blowing last night's seduction out of proportion?

Dario appeared before her in dark jeans, a light blue button-up and a blue blazer with dark sunglasses resting on top of his head. He looked like he'd just stepped off a fashion runway. And then her gaze settled on his lips. Oh, those lips...

"You look beautiful." His voice interrupted the beginning of her fantasy.

"Thank you." Heat swirled in her chest and rushed up to engulf her cheeks. She glanced down, hoping he wouldn't see her blush. But then she decided to get the hard part over with. She lifted her chin slightly, enough to meet his gaze. "About last night—"

"We can talk about it later. Right now, we have a competition to get you too." He didn't act any different after their night together. "Are you ready to go?"

"I just have to grab my purse. What about my things for the weekend?" She had a bag with her makeup and other essentials. There was also a garment bag with her dress. Another bag contained her shoes. And then one special surprise for Dario, but he wouldn't get it until later. "Are we going straight from the Botanical Gardens to Verona?"

He glanced at all her things and smiled. "Leave them. We can't take Tito to the Botanical Gardens so we'll get them when we pick him up."

"Okay. I'm ready. I guess."

"You guess." He approached her and gazed into her eyes. "What are you worried about?"

"That I'm making a fool of myself. I don't know why I ever thought I was as good a photographer as my grandmother. She had a special talent when it came to capturing specific moments on film. She won this competition many times."

"And you have the same talent."

"How would you know? I didn't even let you see my entry. What if it's pedestrian?"

"Pedestrian? Really? We're going with the big words now?"

She shook her head. "You know what I mean. What if the photo is uninspiring?"

"I know what the word means. I just can't believe you're doubting yourself."

"Well, you've been doubting yourself about the book and I know for a fact you're a talented author."

He smiled. "Touché. Now let's go or I'm leaving you

here. I'm dying to see your entry since you wouldn't give me a sneak peek. I know it's going to be amazing."

She smiled at his enthusiasm. He made her feel so much better. If she failed at the competition, at least she wouldn't be there alone. There was something very comforting about having Dario by her side. It was as if they'd always been together.

He truly was excited for her.

The ferry ride to Fiorire Island in the southern portion of Lake Como seemed to take forever, even though it was quite a short ride. But Dario was anxious to see Gianna's entry. He'd seen some of her other work—the pieces she said weren't her best. If that hadn't been her best, he couldn't imagine how amazing her entry must be.

He reached out and took her hand as they made their way up the walk to the stately villa nestled in the middle of the colorful and fragrant botanical garden. Once at the door, he had to release her hand in order to purchase their tickets. And then they were given a guide that Gianna immediately started to scan. His chance of holding her hand once more had slipped away.

He focused on reading the brochure. It spoke of the history of the small island. The massive building they were standing in had once been a villa for royalty. Late in the twentieth century the small private island had been donated to a historical preservation group.

For exactly two weeks each year, the museum removed their normal exhibits in order to display the prestigious entries for the international photography competition. Today, the place was packed with visitors.

"Let's just cut to your section," Dario suggested.

She shook her head. "We should just stay in line. We'll get there."

He shifted his weight from one foot to the other. The

advantage of being tall was being able to see over a crowd. There were a lot people ahead of them, all following between the two red velvet ropes. This was going to take forever.

"Don't you want to know how you did?" he asked.

"Of course, I do. But I'd also like to see some of the other entries."

"We could come back another time to see them."

She frowned at him. He quieted down. He hadn't realized just how truly excited he was for her until they'd arrived. All this time she'd been cheering him on with his book and now it was his turn to cheer her on.

He worried that if for some unexpected reason she didn't do well with the competition, she wouldn't pursue her gift as a photographer. And that worried him. He'd seen over the past weeks how it excited her. Something that made you want to get out of bed before the sun was a true passion, in his way of thinking. It's the way he felt about his writing. He didn't want to see her lose that passion.

The line slowly crept forward. Gianna pointed out different aspects of the photos and tried to explain to him about the various lens and filters that were used, but most of it went over his head.

They continued moving. He wasn't even sure what category she'd entered. Gianna had kept everything very hush-hush. She said she didn't want to do anything to jinx herself. He didn't believe in that stuff, but he hadn't argued. And then they approached the section for plants.

"This is it," Gianna whispered as she clasped her hands together.

"You've got this."

They stepped into the room where people were pointing and whispering, as people do in a museum. His gaze moved around the wall, trying to figure out which photo was Gianna's. He had to admit that all the entries were impressive, some more so than others.

"There it is." She pointed halfway around the room.

This time he didn't ask her permission, he simply grabbed her hand, lifted the velvet rope and cut through the center of the room.

"What are you doing?" Gianna looked panicked.

"Sir, you have to follow the line," a security guard said.

"But you don't understand, that's my girlfriend's print on the wall." It wasn't until the words were spoken that he realized he'd publicly called Gianna his girlfriend. And he had no desire to take it back. "And we've been waiting forever to see it."

The guard was a nice young man. "Okay. But just this once. Which one is it?"

Gianna pointed to what looked something like a reddish-orange daisy with a violet center. They couldn't see the whole thing as there were people in front of it, pointing and nodding. But from the distance, Dario couldn't see an award. His heart sunk. Was it possible she hadn't placed in the competition?

He started to think of all the things he could say to boost her up should the worst happen. After all, this was her first competition. And these were just one set of judges. What did they know?

Gianna tightened her grip on his hand. He glanced at her to see what she wanted, but her attention was solely focused on the wall hanging.

And then the people moved on, giving them full view of the print. They stepped closer. The next people in line were excited to know that Gianna was the photographer. They welcomed them to get in line in front of them.

Beside the print was a little shelf with a crystal frame and inside was a small plaque with the competition's name, the year, Gianna's name and the word *WINNER*.

"You did it!" Dario didn't care if he'd announced it too loud.

She turned to him with tears of joy in her eyes. "My grandmother would be so happy."

He leaned over and kissed her. He hadn't put any thought into it. It happened naturally as though they'd been doing it for years. And when she kissed him back, his heart swelled.

When he pulled back, he said, "I'm so proud of you."

"Thank you." She sniffled and swiped away the tears that had spilled onto her cheeks.

"You don't have to leave home for work if you don't want to. This can be the beginning of your photography business."

Excitement glittered in her eyes. "You think so?"

"I always believed you can do whatever you set your mind to."

This time, she lifted up on her tiptoes and gave him a quick kiss.

When she pulled away, he took a closer look at the winning entry. The red and oranges of the daisy-like petals were vibrant and the morning dew sparkled. The flower was the central focus of the piece, but in the background, rays of sunshine showered down upon the flower, making it practically glow. And there was a drop of dew falling from the flower. It was small but when he focused in on it, he noticed that within the droplet was a tiny mirror image of the flower. He was certain there were other amazing details that his untrained eyes were missing, but to him the piece was perfection.

When he turned to say something to Gianna, he found her surrounded by people congratulating her and asking for her business card. She said she didn't have any with her. It looked like she needed to print some because she was going into business. His smile broadened.

Her fans wanted to purchase her work. And he couldn't

have been happier for her. Gianna had found her passion and he knew she would be successful at it. Best of all, she was glowing with happiness.

Part one of the day had been an utter success.

Part two was quite likely to be the opposite.

Gianna's stomach shivered with nerves as Dario, Tito and herself stepped into his grandparents' home, which was even larger and grander than the museum on Fiorire Island. She glanced down, noticing the slight tremor in her hands. What in the world was she getting so worked up for? It wasn't even like they were a real couple. Okay, so maybe things had gotten a little out of control—or rather a whole lot out of delicious control last night. She smiled as she recalled waking up in Dario's arms.

She leaned closer to Dario and whispered, "They're going to hate me."

He glanced over at her. In his eyes, she saw calm reassurance. "It doesn't matter what they think because to me, you're the best. And if they can't see that, it's their loss."

His kind words filled her heart until it was overflowing. How exactly had this very thoughtful and sweet man avoided a commitment all this time? Because from what she could see, aside from his endless hours hiding away writing, he was amazing. Any woman would be lucky to have him in her life.

Her gaze dipped. The burn of jealousy started in the pit of her stomach as she imagined the willowy figure of the smiling woman who would one day stand here with him and meet his grandparents as his real and dearly loved fiancée.

Dario placed a finger beneath her chin and lifted until their gazes met. "Stop worrying. I'll be right here beside you the whole time."

Their gazes held longer than necessary. She found a sense of peace in his presence and his reassuring words.

But as she stared deeper into his eyes, she saw something else. Desire.

Her heart thump-thumped. In that moment, she forgot they were standing in the grand foyer of his grandparents' villa. For the moment, there was just him and her. The pounding of her heart drowned out her worries. The tip of her tongue swiped over her dry lips. His eyes dilated as he watched her. And she reveled in the fact that she could turn him on so quickly.

His head lowered as hers lifted. Their lips met in the middle. He pulled her snugly into his arms. She reached up, wrapping her arms around his neck and lacing her fingers together before drawing him closer.

Why did this feel so right? It shouldn't be that way. After all, they weren't a real couple. But then again, none of her relationships had been like this one. Maybe that had been her problem—

Someone cleared their throat.

They sprang apart. Heat engulfed her whole face. When she glanced over to see an older couple approaching them, she wanted to melt into the marble floor. What had she been thinking? Oh, yes, how much she wanted to kiss Dario over and over again. Talk about bad timing.

Dario reached for her hand, taking it in his. With his other hand, he tugged on Tito's leash, drawing him close. Dario then gave Gianna a firm but reassuring squeeze. She naturally leaned into his side, enjoying the feel of his muscled arm pressed up against her. It felt natural, as though they'd done it many times.

It wasn't until his grandmother's eyes momentarily widened that she realized exactly what she'd done. She straightened, but Dario didn't release his hold on her hand. He kept his fingers wrapped securely around hers. Originally, she'd thought he'd done it to comfort her, but now she wondered if he too needed some support while facing his grandparents.

"Dario, it's about time you came home." His grandmother's face was devoid of emotion until she caught sight of Tito. A distinct frown marred her face. She pointed at Tito. "What's he doing here?"

"I don't have anyone to watch him for the weekend. Tito stays or we go."

His grandmother's pointed stare met his. After a moment, she said, "He can stay so long as he behaves."

"He will." Dario looked down at Tito who was sitting next to him. "You're a good boy, right?"

Woof.

Everyone smiled except his grandparents. Gianna couldn't help but think how strange this cool and aloof greeting was between Dario and his grandparents. Her family was quite the opposite. They were loud and boisterous. Hugs and kisses were exchanged both coming and going.

His grandfather frowned. "You haven't been at the office."

"It's good to see you both." Dario did his best to sound upbeat. "I've missed you."

At last, his grandmother cracked a slight smile. "It's so good to have you home. You've been gone too long." His grandmother's gaze moved to Gianna.

Dario cleared his throat. "Nonna and Nonno, I'd like to introduce you to Gianna Cappellini." He gripped her hand tighter, as though he were nervous. "She's an award-winning photographer. And she's my fiancée." He paused to flash her a big smile. "Gianna, these are my grandparents, Giuseppe and Rosmunda Marchello."

When the older woman held out a hand to her, Gianna thought she meant to shake hands, but the woman grasped her hand and pulled her forward. Gianna reluctantly let go of her grip on Dario's hand and now she felt adrift. What was his grandmother up to?

"Let me have a look at you," his grandmother said. She looked her up and down.

Then her gaze moved between Gianna and Dario. "I think you two will make adorable children together."

"Nonna!" Dario's face filled with color.

Gianna couldn't help but smile. She hadn't considered kids before but with his height and good looks, she believed his grandmother was onto something. Not that they were going to have children now or ever. But the horrified look on his face had Gianna smothering a laugh.

His grandmother scoffed at his reaction. "Honestly, you'd think I'd said something that surprised you. It's only natural you two will have a child."

"Nonna, I don't think now is the time to discuss this." Dario's tone was soft but firm.

"What is your name?" his grandfather asked.

She swallowed. "Gianna."

He shook his head. "I mean your family's name."

"Cappellini."

His gray brows drew together and then he turned to his wife. "Do we know any Cappellinis?"

The woman paused as though to give the question due consideration. "I don't believe we do."

His grandfather turned back to her. "What areas are your parents involved?"

Maybe it was the loud pounding of her heart or her racing pulse but she didn't understand the question. She glanced at Dario for clarification.

Thankfully, he was paying attention. "He wants to know what your parents do for a living."

Well, why didn't he just say that to begin with? She smiled at the older gentleman. "My father owns a market and my mother runs the office for him."

"A market?" his grandfather said, as though he hadn't heard her correctly.

She forced a smile to her lips and nodded. Her family may not be nearly as impressive as the Marchellos but Gianna was proud of her parents. She went on to explain that it was the largest market in their village and how it had been there for close to thirty years. Her father had no intention of retiring. He loved the daily interaction with the community.

His grandfather didn't utter a single acknowledgment to her but rather turned to Dario. "We need to speak."

Gianna felt the sting of an unspoken insult. She didn't live up to his grandfather's expectations. She tried to tell herself it didn't matter as they weren't truly engaged anyway, but it didn't ease the pain that dug at her. The sooner this weekend was over, the better.

"It'll have to wait," Dario's grandmother said. "We need to discuss the wedding plans."

At least his grandmother wasn't opposed to their relationship. It helped ease Gianna's discomfort.

"Nonna," Dario said, "this weekend isn't supposed to be about our engagement. It's about you and Nonno."

"Nonsense. There's enough time for both." His grandmother's eyes lit up and the slight smile lifted into a full one that lit up her whole face. "Now, if we could just find your brother a wife."

"Don't waste your time," Dario said. "He's married to his work."

"Thankfully, someone is," his grandfather grumped. "If it were up to you, there wouldn't be any business."

She glanced at Dario to find his shoulders rigid and his face drawn. His lips were pressed in a firm line as a muscle in his cheek twitched. She sensed he was fighting to hold back a heated response. Suddenly, Gianna didn't feel so bad that his grandfather found her and her family so unworthy of a Marchello. No one lived up to the older man's expectations.

Still, she couldn't just stand by and let his grandfather put down Dario. "Your grandson has worked very hard over the past month."

"Humph!" The man crossed his arms as his gaze narrowed on her. "Like you would know anything about it."

Dario glanced at her and gave a firm shake of his head. He must have thought she was about to spill his secret about his writing. She would never do that to him.

She turned back to his grandfather, who was scowling. It appeared he wasn't used to people standing up to him. Well, he better get used to it because she didn't back down when someone she cared about was being attacked.

"I know your grandson worked remotely. He had his business phone forwarded to his cell phone and he was on his laptop at all hours dealing with whatever came up at the office while his brother was away."

His grandfather's brows rose and then he turned to his grandson. "Is this true?"

Dario nodded. "Everything is under control."

"And you'll be back in the office on Monday?"

Gianna knew that was the very last place Dario wanted to be. She didn't understand why he didn't just tell them that he was a best-selling author. Why would he hide something like that? She was so proud of him that she was about to burst.

"Yes, Nonno. I'll be there."

"Good." His grandfather turned and walked away.

"Now we can get started," Nonna said.

"Can we do it later?" Dario asked. "I promised Gianna I'd show her around."

His grandmother hesitated and then nodded. "Go. Have a good time. Dinner will be promptly at seven and we will be having guests."

Dario showed her to the upstairs. They stopped outside a

guest room. Just then the door swung open. A maid stepped into the hallway. Her eyes widened upon spotting them.

Gianna's gaze lowered to her luggage, which was in the maid's hands. "Where are you taking my things?"

"I was told to move them to Mr. Marchello's suite. Is that not right?"

Gianna looked at him for help. She had no idea what to say. Now that their engagement was known, it was expected that they'd share a room—a bed. Heat crept into her cheeks.

As the maid waited for instructions, Dario said, "Yes, that's right. Thank you."

The young woman smiled and nodded before she rushed off. They followed her to a room at the end of the hallway. They told the maid they'd take care of hanging their own things.

Gianna couldn't believe she was in Dario's inner sanctum—the place where he'd grown up. She didn't know what she'd been expecting. It certainly wasn't the sparsely decorated light taupe walls with landscape portraits. This was a boy's room?

Her gaze moved to the two dressers. There was a framed photo of a football team. She drew near and picked it up. "Which one is you?"

He pointed to the boy in the center with the ball in his hands. She noticed he was smiling for the camera.

"You were a cute kid." She returned the photo to where she'd found it.

She turned and found large wooden bookcases, each shelf crammed with books—some standing and some lying on their sides. There was no room left on any of the shelves.

"You weren't kidding about your love of reading."

"That's not all of them. Just my favorites." He cleared his throat. "I'm sorry about all of this."

She turned her attention back to him. "Is your family always that way?"

He shrugged. "Pretty much."

"Why didn't you just tell them about your writing?"

"I will. When the time is right."

She had a feeling that was just an excuse. "When will that be?"

He lowered his voice to a very soft whisper. "As soon as book two is sold."

"Won't that be a while?"

"I don't know." His face was marred with worry lines. "They were really anxious for it so they might read it right away. But I don't know if they'll like it. It's so different from the first book."

"Relax." She sent him a reassuring smile. "It's a good thing that it's different. Trust me."

"You didn't read it after the revisions."

"But I know you have crazy skills with words. I have faith that you wrote a fantastic book." She moved forward and gave him a hug. "I'm so proud of you."

His arms wrapped around her, pulling her a little closer. The action felt so natural, as though they did it all the time. And she was very tempted to lift her face and claim his lips, so they could pick up where they'd left off before.

But that wasn't what they were here to do. Their one-night fling was over. They were here to put on a show just until his grandparents' big celebration weekend was over. Then they too would be over. The thought left a heaviness in her chest.

Before things got out of control again, she withdrew from his arms. "I should get freshened up." She hesitated. "I guess I should have asked before—how many times will we be expected to dress for an event?"

"Tonight. Tomorrow afternoon and then again in the evening. The same for Saturday. And then Sunday just for the afternoon."

"Oh." She mentally calculated what she had in her wardrobe. "I didn't bring enough dresses to wear."

"Don't worry. We can get whatever you need in the city. I'm going to take Tito for a quick walk. Do you need anything before I go?"

She shook her head.

"I'll be back shortly." With Tito next to him, Dario headed for the door.

Gianna took the time alone to figure out where to put the surprise she'd brought for him. She looked in the closet, but found it too empty. He'd spot it immediately. There also wasn't enough room behind either dresser. She settled for placing it under the bed. What were the chances he'd look under there?

CHAPTER FIFTEEN

ALONE AT LAST.

Dario was quickly realizing how soon his time with Gianna would end. The whole month had gone by much too fast. But now that the book was complete, he didn't have a reason to return to Gemma with her. At least not yet...

If he'd had any doubts about how well suited they were for each other, their night together had been the final deciding factor. It was though they'd been made for each other.

With one of the household staff looking after Tito, Dario was free to show Gianna around his old haunts. As they strolled through Verona, he glanced down at their clasped hands. She was still wearing his ring. He smiled. He still had time to turn this all around—a chance to show her that not all men were like her ex. After all, she'd taught Dario that true love exists in books; maybe it existed in real life too.

"You know you really don't have to do this." Gianna's voice drew him from his thoughts.

"Do what?"

"Spend your afternoon showing me around. I'm sure you have plenty of other things you'd rather be doing."

"You mean like being closed up in the study with my grandfather going over inventory reports or ad campaigns and sales figures." He shook his head. "I'd much rather be out here in the sunshine, showing you my city."

She glanced at him. Their gazes connected and held for a second too long before she turned her head. "And a beautiful city it is."

"But you haven't seen much of it yet." He kept walking

to a bustling market spot. "This is Piazza delle Erbe, otherwise known as the Square of Herbs."

She glanced around the picturesque town square surrounded by historic buildings—oh, the stories they could tell if they could speak. The piazza was overlooked by a tall clock tower. And in the center of the square was a beautiful fountain. And surrounding it were shops and cozy cafés. Gianna was anxious to visit each storefront, tented vendor and restaurant. She wanted to take it all in.

But Dario was headed for the center of the square where tented booths were being visited by a large number of leisurely customers. Young and old alike visited the square. It was vibrant and yet somehow homey. Like her village in the south of Italy. It wasn't until she left it that she realized how much she loved it.

Gianna listened to the hubbub of conversation as she inhaled the delicious aromas drifting into the square from the surrounding restaurants. She couldn't stop smiling as they continued to walk.

Some people had cloth bags hung from their arms stuffed full of their wonderful finds. Others had woven baskets full of fruits and vegetables. There was hardly a soul that hadn't found something to buy.

Dario stopped and bought them each a refreshment. Her dry throat welcomed the sweet drink. They moved about the square, slowly walking from stand to stand, inspecting all the abundant produce. Other people were standing off to the side, talking amongst themselves, smiling and laughing. It was definitely a welcoming place. A place to meet up with old friends and to make new ones.

"I like it here," she said, "It's like bringing a bit of the village life into the big city."

He nodded in agreement. "This is a very special spot for my family."

"Because you sell spices?"

He nodded. "This square is where my great-grandfather started Marchello Spices. He'd bring his herbs to market and people would rave about them. Every week he'd sell out. And as his business grew, he incorporated in more spices and herbs."

She walked with Dario among the vendors, admiring their fresh fruit and vegetables. And then she came to a stop in front of the Marchello Spices stand. She turned to him. "You still keep a stand here, even though your company is so big?"

He smiled and nodded. "My grandfather thought it was foolish and a waste of time and money, but my brother and I disagreed. We thought we should hold on to our heritage and always remember where we started."

She smiled at him. "I think it's wonderful that you retain a bit of your past. Heritage is important."

"Is that why you moved into your grandmother's home and followed in her footsteps with photography?"

She'd never really thought of it that way. "I don't know if I was trying to take after her as much as photography is just a part of me. I feel most comfortable behind the lens of a camera. Framing out snippets of life that tell a story excites me. And as for her house, well, I've loved it there since I was a kid and we'd go to visit. It's just so peaceful."

He smiled at her. "I have to agree with you. I might need to come back and visit when I write my next book."

Hope swelled in her chest. She told herself it was the hope that he'd continue writing and not the hope that he'd come spend more time with her. "You said when not if. Does that mean you'll keep writing?"

He nodded. "Even if my current submission doesn't sell—"

"It will."

His brows lifted in surprise at her outburst but then he smiled. "Even so, I just can't imagine my life without writing. It's now a part of me. It's something I look forward to each day. And when I'm not writing, I'm thinking about writing or plotting out the next scene in my head."

"That sounds so exciting."

"Exciting and exhausting because sometimes there's no turning off my imagination until I sit down and write out some notes so I don't forget what I came up with."

Gianna stepped up to the Marchello stand where there were so many spices and herbs to choose from. The truth was that she'd grown up with Marchello spices in her parents' kitchen. The red, green and white labels were a staple, but what she didn't realize was how extensive Marchello's inventory was until now.

"What are you doing?" Dario asked.

"What does it look like? I'm shopping."

"But you don't have to buy those things just because they're ours."

"I'm not. But there are some things here that I've never seen in the store."

He nodded in understanding. "That's because the stores will only take the main staples of our collection—the big sellers. We used to be able to let the consumers try the products before buying them."

"How was that?"

"They used to be in restaurants where guests could choose from a caddy of different spices to add to their pasta. And they even sold containers of them."

"Wait. I remember now. They were in Carla's family's restaurants."

He nodded. "Until eleven years ago."

"What happened then?"

"I don't know all the details, but Carlo Falco and my grandfather used to be friends. They'd play cards together. Something happened and they've never spoken since."

"I'm sorry that happened."

"So am I. When Franco and I took over the company five years ago, we tried getting our products back in Falco's Fresco Ristorante but Carla's father wouldn't hear of it. When our grandfather found out what we were up to, he got so irate that I thought he was going to have a heart attack. That's when I started taking my writing seriously. Tensions were so high in the family that I needed a way to escape, if you will."

"I feel the same way about my photography. There's just something about being one-on-one with nature."

"What about human subjects?"

She shrugged. "It's okay if I just randomly snap a photo here or there."

"Like you did when I was writing?"

"Exactly. The candid, unposed images are what I like. But I'm not one to open a studio and deal with people regularly." She shook her head. "That's definitely not for me. What about you and your company? What will you do with the spices that don't make it into the stores?"

"Well, we do sell the full line of spices and herbs online, but the sales aren't sustainable. And if the company doesn't find a more reliable, hands-on approach to selling those specialty items, I'm afraid we'll have to cease their production."

Gianna reached in her bag and pulled out the bottle of specially mixed herbs she'd just purchased. "This was my favorite when I was a kid."

"It's one that will be cut from production. I'm sorry."

She frowned as she put it back in her purse. "Maybe I should go back and get more."

When she turned around, he reached out, placing a hand on her arm. He smiled and shook his head. "Relax. You can still get it online. And we're not making those dreadful decisions just yet. My brother is spending a great deal of time traveling and meeting with other restaurant owners to get the more select items in front of customers."

"I hope he's successful."

"I do too. But Falco's Fresco Ristorante is the biggest and most successful chain in the country. If only we could figure out what caused the rift between the two men, maybe we could patch things up and get back to business."

"I'd help you if I could, but this is the first I'm hearing of it." Gianna's phone buzzed. "Sorry. It's Carla."

"Not a problem." He continued browsing the stands while she moved off to the side to take the call.

"Hi. What's going on?"

"I just got to the city. Are you at Dario's grandparents' estate?"

"Actually, I'm in the city. I need to find a couple of dresses—"

"Say no more. We can meet for a late lunch and then I can take you to my favorite shops."

Carla gave her the address of the café and then rushed off the phone.

Gianna returned to Dario, who just finished a brief conversation with an older gentleman. "Sorry about that."

"No problem. It gave me a chance to say hello to some old friends. Is everything okay?"

"Yes. Carla wants to meet up for lunch and then go shopping. I hope you don't mind."

"Not at all. My grandfather wants to have a talk. He appeared to have something serious on his mind. I should go back and do that now before the festivities begin."

"Oh, you don't want to join us for lunch?" She wasn't ready to see him go, not yet.

"I'll just eat back at the villa. I can drop you off on my way."

She shook her head. "I looked it up on my phone. It's not far from here and it's such a beautiful day, I'd like to walk. I hope things go well with your grandfather."

He nodded in agreement. "If you need me, I'm just a phone call away."

They parted there in the piazza. She was disappointed they hadn't gotten to explore more of Verona together. She immediately told herself that they'd do it another time. And in the next breath, she remembered there wouldn't be another time. Their time together was almost over and the thought weighed heavy on her heart.

CHAPTER SIXTEEN

SHE MISSED DARIO ALREADY.

It was silly. But it was true.

The walk to the café had been just what she'd needed before meeting up with her cousin. Because today she was going to confess her secret. She just couldn't let Carla find out with everyone else that her engagement had all been a sham.

But first, Gianna decided to focus on something positive. "I have some news."

"You set a wedding date?"

She smiled and shook her head. "I won the photography contest at the Fiorire Botanical Gardens."

"Congratulations! I'm so happy for you." Carla studied her. "Why aren't you more excited about the win?"

"I'm happy." Gianna reached for a tall glass of tea. "I'm just tired, I guess."

"Oh, my!" Carla's face lit up. "You got the ring. Let me see."

Gianna had momentarily forgotten that she was wearing it. Dario had placed it on her finger at some point during their night together. And now she didn't have the heart to take it off. The ring was just so beautiful. And Dario had insisted there was a no-return policy, so he was stuck with it unless she accepted it as a token of his greatest appreciation for all she'd done to help make his dreams come true.

As she held the ring out for Carla, Gianna admired it too. It may not have come with a promise of eternal love but it had come with what she hoped was an abiding friendship and maybe a little more.

"Wow! That's some ring." Carla sent her a knowing

smile over the small café table. "Why didn't you bring him to lunch? I'd have loved to see him again."

"I didn't want to pressure him. He had an important meeting."

"I bet he would have dropped everything for you. I've seen the way he looks at you. He's crazy about you."

It had been on the tip of her tongue to ask him, but she'd stood her ground and resisted her urge. One night together did not make a couple. But then she realized that she hadn't fessed up to her cousin about her fake engagement. And the guilt weighed on her. With the light lunch complete, now was the time to fess up.

"What is it?" Carla prompted.

Gianna's hesitant gaze met her cousin's. "There's something I need to tell you."

And now that she was saying the words, she wondered if she was going to mess up another relationship in her life. After all, there was no guarantee that her cousin was going to forgive her.

Carla's smile faltered. "Oh, no. Did something happen with you and Dario? Please say it isn't so." When Gianna didn't immediately respond, Carla said, "Gianna? You're starting to worry me."

Gianna drew in a deep breath but it did absolutely nothing to calm her racing heart. She never should have gone along with the fake engagement. She could just add it to her growing list of regrets.

"Oh, no." Carla's eyes displayed her concern. "Whatever it is, you two can fix it. He loves you. After all, look at that engagement ring he gave you."

"That's just it. It's not an engagement ring."

"What? I don't understand." Carla rested her elbows on the table and leaned forward. "Are you trying to say that you two have broken up?"

"It's worse than that."

"What could be worse?"

It took all her resolve to tilt her chin upward ever so slightly, just enough to meet her cousin's worried gaze. "We were never truly engaged."

"What?" Carla leaned back in her chair as though the air had just gone out of her. "But what about the ring?"

"It…it's a thank-you gift. Nothing more."

"You mean this whole time when you said you were getting married, it was lie."

Gianna wanted to turn away from the hurt emanating from her cousin's eyes, but she wouldn't let herself off that easy. She kept meeting her cousin's gaze. "In the beginning, it wasn't a lie."

"So you were engaged to Dario? For real?"

She shook her head. "It was another guy. We worked together. It was a whirlwind romance. I should have known it all moved too quickly, but he was so sweet, so convinced that everything would work out just the way it was supposed to. And I guess in a way it has."

"This guy, he was someone that traveled with you from the jungles of Africa to the icy cold Antarctica?"

She nodded. "He was the host of the series."

Carla's mouth formed an O.

"He'd just broken up with someone and so had I. At first, we were just there for each other, bolstering each other through the painful aftermath. I think in part it was a case of proximity. We shared the same campsites and all of our meals. Let me tell you, there aren't many people out in the wilderness to speak to."

"I can only imagine. So you were really into him?"

She nodded. "At least I thought I was. We had so much in common. And we seemed to want the same things in the future."

"Seemed to?"

Gianna glanced down at the red-and-white-check tablecloth. "I have this bad habit of letting myself get caught up in someone else's life and aligning my desires with theirs. And once we're apart, I realize how skewed my thinking has become."

"Why did you two break up? Did you figure out he was a jerk?"

Gianna shook her head. "He went back to his ex."

"Definitely a jerk! You must be so mad at him."

"I was in the beginning. I was furious. But then I realized it was for the best. I was so tired of living out of a duffel bag and sleeping on the hard ground. I've been running away from home long enough. I thought there was no reason to be here, if I didn't have anyone to share my life with."

"And now?"

"Now, I know that to be truly happy, I have to make a life for myself."

"So why did you let me go on about you and Dario being engaged. And then I got Franco to believe it. Wait. Does he know you two aren't really together?" Color rushed to Carla's cheeks as her thoughts turned to Franco. "He must think I'm such a dolt. I just went on and on about what a great couple you two make—"

"Relax. He still thinks we're engaged."

Carla sighed. "That's good. Not about him not knowing the truth, but that he doesn't think I'm totally clueless. And there's your parents. I might have let it slip…"

"It's okay. I plan to talk to them when they arrive for the party. I didn't feel right about doing it on the phone."

"I was so certain you two were in love. Are you? In love, that is?"

"No!" The rushed answer only made the awkward moment that much more uncomfortable. This time it was Gianna's turn to have heat rush to her cheeks. "Definitely not."

Carla arched a fine penciled brow. "Are you sure about that?"

"Positive!" Again with the too-quick answer.

"He really is a looker," Carla said.

But two could play at this game. "So is his brother, Franco. I noticed how you were looking at him."

Carla glanced away as she fidgeted with her discarded linen napkin. "There's nothing there. He was far too anxious to fly away on business."

"But he will be at his grandparents' anniversary party—"

"Stop." Carla pursed her lips as though choosing her next words carefully. "We were talking about you, not me."

So Carla had been attracted to Franco. Interesting. Very interesting. Gianna wondered what it'd take to get those two together. But as soon as the thought came to her, she dismissed it. From the little she knew of Franco, he was much too intense for her cousin.

Gianna fidgeted with her discarded napkin. "Anyway, I just wanted to say I am sorry for not correcting you when you assumed Dario was my fiancé."

"Why didn't you correct me?"

Gianna shrugged again. Finding words were hard for her. She didn't want to say the wrong thing and make this harder for her cousin to forgive her. She was her best friend in the whole world. Then her thoughts shifted to Dario. He had suddenly become her closest friend. She'd told things to him that she hadn't even told Carla. What was she going to do without him in her life?

"Gianna?" Carla waved a hand in front of her to gain her attention. "Why did you keep up the charade?"

"Because I didn't want to look like a two-time failure. I am so pathetic when it comes to relationships."

"No, you're not. Those men just didn't know how great you are. If they did, they'd have never let you go." Carla leaned forward with sympathy in her eyes. "Speaking of which, I know this great guy—"

"No. Stop." Gianna waved off her cousin. "I don't need a pity date."

"But you don't understand. He's a really great guy. Trust me, you'll love him."

"No, I won't. Because I'm not going to meet him. This is why I didn't tell you that my engagement was off. I didn't want you to feel sorry for me and then try to fix it. I don't need to be fixed."

Carla sat back. She was quiet for a moment, as though digesting this latest problem. "There has to be something I can do."

"Just be my friend."

"But I hate the thought of you being so miserable."

"I'm not."

"You're not?"

Gianna thought about it for a moment and then quite honestly said, "No, I'm not."

At least not yet. But when the day came, and it would very quickly, when she parted ways with Dario and Tito, she would miss them both dearly. But that was then and this was now.

"I just need you to keep this to yourself for a little longer. We're going to tell our families after the party. We don't want to cause any drama before the big event."

"I won't say a word. Because it might just give you both time to realize what you have is real. It might not have started that way, but every time you talk about him, you light up. You're in love with him. And it appears you're the last one to know."

Gianna shook her head, chasing away her cousin's words. She refused to accept them. Because if Carla was right, then she'd just set herself up to be hurt again.

Was that a frown?

Dario drew closer to Gianna as she stood in front of

a full-length mirror in their suite of rooms at his grand-parent's villa. Oh, yes, that was most definitely a frown.

He stepped up behind her as she held up a satin hanger holding a white dress with bright flowers splashed across the material.

"Is that the dress you got this afternoon with your cousin?"

"It's one of them."

"I like it, but you don't seem to like it."

Gianna sighed as she lowered the dress. "It's not the clothes." When she turned quickly, her side brushed against him. He instinctively reached out to her, to keep her from losing her balance. When her gaze met his, there was attraction in her eyes. "It...it's this. It's us. Everyone thinks we're something we're not." Then she pointed to the bed where Tito was lying. "What are we going to do about tonight?"

"I was thinking eventually we'd sleep." He knew what she meant, but he wasn't so sure why she was blowing this development out of proportion.

She frowned at him. "And where will I sleep?"

"I figured next to me—"

She lightly slapped his arm. "Dario, get serious."

"I am. Why are you acting like it's our first time sharing a bed?"

Color bloomed in her cheeks. "Because this is different."

"It doesn't have to be."

Her gaze searched his. "What are you saying?"

"Do you want our relationship to be real?"

Her eyes widened. And then, as though realizing he was still touching her, she stepped back. "That wasn't our agreement."

"Forget our agreement. I shouldn't have suggested it in the first place. What do you want when this weekend is over?"

She shook her head. "You don't know what you're asking."

"Then explain it to me."

"I'm a disaster when it comes to relationships."

"Gianna, that's not true. It takes two to start a relationship and it takes two to end one."

"Not always. I let myself get ahead of things. I set high expectations—too high for anyone to meet."

He sighed. "You haven't done that with me."

"Haven't I?" She gazed deeply into his eyes. "I've been pushing you to finish your book."

"And I have done that. After tomorrow night, I plan to tell my family that I'm walking away from the family business once and for all. It's all my brother's from now on."

"Are you doing that because it's what you really want? Or are you doing it because I talked you into it?"

"You didn't talk me into anything." Where was she getting this stuff from? And why wasn't she hearing him?

"I did. I push for what I think is the right thing whether it's for me or someone I care about. I just keep pushing and pushing."

Wait. Did she just say that she cared about him? It certainly sounded like it. He smiled.

It was at that moment that Gianna turned around. "What are you smiling about? Everything is a disaster."

"Everything is good. Really good." Maybe she just needed a moment to calm down. "I'll meet you downstairs. I need to take Tito for a walk."

Gianna nodded as she turned back to the mirror. She picked up a soft pink dress. It was simple yet elegant. But it worked for Gianna because she didn't need a dress to make a statement. She could do that all by herself.

As he walked away, he was certain that whatever dress she chose for the evening would be just fine. And he hoped her case of nerves would subside. He didn't want to leave her alone at this moment but he couldn't risk Tito having an accident. His grandmother was already unhappy about having a big dog in her house.

Later Dario had a surprise for Gianna. He was returning to Gemma. He hoped when she heard his news that it would put her worries to rest. Because he was anxious to see just where a real relationship would lead them.

CHAPTER SEVENTEEN

IT WAS QUITE a crowd.

All friends and acquaintances of Dario's family.

Gianna's stomach shivered with nerves. She shouldn't be here. She shouldn't be pretending she was something she wasn't.

She glanced down at her white flowery dress and hoped it looked all right. Carla and the saleswoman at the boutique had assured her that it was just perfect on her. Still, she wrung her hands together.

She continued to gaze down from the second-floor balcony, taking in all the smartly dressed people that had arrived for the party. In the living room, someone was playing the grand piano. It was an upbeat tune. She'd overheard that later in the evening there would be a famous singer. The name escaped her but it should be quite a show.

Just then Sergio and Vera Cappellini passed through the open front doors. A big smile lifted Gianna's lips. Her parents had really shown up. She'd told them they didn't need to bother, but they'd insisted it would be rude not to attend and they were very interested in meeting Dario.

Gianna rushed down the stairs to greet them. But trying to move through the throng of people in the foyer was harder to do than she'd ever imagined. It took a lot of "Excuse me…" and "Pardon me…" until she reached them.

"Hi." She smiled and then hugged each of them. "It's so good to see you both."

"You look stunning." Her mother wore a mauve dress that Gianna recalled seeing her wear for one of her cousin's weddings. "I hope this is dressy enough. I don't want to embarrass you."

"Mamma, you look beautiful." And she meant it.

"Thank you, sweetie." Her mother beamed.

"See," her father said, "I told you the same thing and you didn't believe me."

Her mother looked lovingly at her father. "That's because you always say it, even when I'm in my pajamas with my hair going every which way."

He smiled at her. "That's because it's when you look the cutest." He leaned over and gave her mother a quick kiss. "I love you."

"I love you too."

Gianna loudly cleared her throat. "Should I leave you two lovebirds alone?"

"Of course not," her mother said. "You should know by now that your father is a flirt."

"Only with you," he corrected.

"I have some exciting news." Gianna told her parents about winning the competition.

After a bunch of congratulations and another round of hugs, her mother said, "Now where is the ring?"

Gianna lifted her hand to show her mother the glittery ring. Guilt settled on her. She needed to explain to her parents about her relationship with Dario, but with people bumping into them as they moved around the crowded room, there was no privacy.

"Wow!" Her mother took her hand to have a closer look. "That's a huge stone."

Heat filled Gianna's cheeks. She didn't deserve the ring. It wasn't like Dario was really going to marry her. Although things had changed after they'd slept together, had they changed that much? They hadn't finished their conversation. What did Dario want?

"Congratulations, honey." Her mother hugged her again. Then she turned to Gianna's father. "Go ahead. Congratulate your daughter."

Gianna knew this was hard on her father. She'd always been a daddy's girl. "It's okay."

"No, it isn't," her father said. He hugged her. "He better be a really great guy and treat you right or he has to deal with me."

When they pulled apart, Gianna said with utter honesty, "He's a great guy. And I'm positive you'll like him." She stood up on her tiptoes and looked around for Dario. And then she spotted him heading directly for her. She immediately smiled. "Here he comes."

When Dario finally made it to their little group, introductions were made. The men shook hands. She could tell her father was holding out on making his judgement until he knew Dario better, but her mother immediately enveloped Dario in a big hug.

This first meeting had gone so well that Gianna wished it were the real thing. Dario was the first man in her life that her parents had really taken to. What were they going to think when she told them the truth?

"We have to talk later," she said to her mother.

"Is something wrong?"

"No. It's just that I haven't seen you in a while and we need to catch up."

Her mother smiled. "You've got it, but it looks like you're needed elsewhere. Don't worry. We'll be fine on our own."

Gianna walked with Dario around the room, meeting guests. Other than their immediate families, she knew no one at this party. And there were so many names being bandied about that she couldn't remember any of them. So she smiled and made light conversation, avoiding using names at all costs.

Was this what it'd be like to be Dario's fiancée? Would she be expected to host parties? Would she have time to be the fiancée he needed and still pursue her own career?

Or would she do what she always did and sacrifice what was important to her to make Dario happy?

Tonight was the night.

After all the guests had left, Dario intended to come clean to his family about his relationship with Gianna. He was done making excuses to put it off. And after all that, he would tell Gianna about his growing feelings for her.

He couldn't believe how much she'd changed his life in just a few very special weeks. She had worked her magic not only with his book but also with him. She showed him that love didn't have to hurt. It could be a good thing—a great thing. And he had no idea how to thank her—

"There you are, dear." His mother walked up to him with a big smile painted on her face. Her hand, with a giant rock on it, clutched the arm of an older gentleman. By the looks of the man, he was about his grandfather's age.

"Mother," Dario said in greeting. He didn't have much to say to her. Their relationship was about as distant as one could have and still refer to it as a relationship. "I didn't know you were invited."

She gave a short little laugh. "Why, of course, darling. After all, I am still family."

Dario coughed over that one. He made a point of sipping his drink as though to clear his throat. She wasn't family. Maybe she had been when he was born, but not for most of his life. And that choice had been hers—all hers.

"Where's Roger?" Dario asked about her third husband.

She frowned at him. "You mean Robert?"

Roger? Robert? It was close. It wasn't like he'd met the man more than once in passing. "Yes, him."

"We're no longer together," she said softly. "Fernando and I got married last month."

So she was on to husband number four. Dario didn't really care. He'd given up caring about what she did years ago. Still, he shook hands with the man.

One parent down, one to go. He craned his neck, checking the busy room for his father, but didn't see him anywhere. Dario didn't like to be caught off guard.

"If you're looking for your father, he couldn't make it. Last I heard, he was hiking up some mountain or some such thing."

Dario didn't know which shocked him more, that his mother knew his father's whereabouts or that his father had taken up hiking.

"Oh, there you are." Gianna joined him. "Your grandmother sent me to find you."

He noticed his mother eyeing up Gianna. She wanted an introduction, but he didn't intend to give her one. It wasn't like she was truly his mother—a mother that cared about him—a mother who was involved in his life.

He was about to excuse himself and walk away when his mother said, "And who would you be?"

Gianna smiled. "I'm Dario's fiancée."

His mother's heavily painted eyes widened. She turned to him. "You're getting married?"

She said it so loud that all the people around him turned. Dario inwardly groaned. Now not only his family but also all their friends knew about the engagement. And the longer he was around his mother, the more he remembered why he didn't want to get engaged or married for that matter.

But it was too late to undo it now. People started to approach both him and Gianna. They shook their hands, asked for the wedding date, of which they had no answer, and then wished them well.

When there was a break in well-wishers, Dario turned to Gianna. "I'm so sorry about this."

"Me too. I never should have said anything to that woman about us being engaged."

"That was my mother."

Gianna's lips formed an O. Her eyes were full of questions, none of which she vocalized.

He leaned in close to her and said softly, "We'll tell our families after the party. They can get the word out to their friends."

"Sir." One of the wait staff approached them. "There's a gentleman here to see you."

Dario was confused. "Is he one of the guests?"

"No sir. He's waiting in the foyer." The waiter walked away.

Gianna looked at him. "Who do you think it is?"

He shrugged. "I'm not expecting anyone special. Let's go see."

He wasn't going to leave her in the living room to greet all these well-meaning guests on her own. Taking her hand in his, he headed for the door. He wasn't the only one. Both of his grandparents were headed that way. What was going on?

When he stepped into the foyer, his gaze connected with his agent, Ronaldo. What was he doing here?

His grandparents approached Dario. His grandfather asked, "Do you know this person?"

"Uh…yes, I do."

Ronaldo rushed over to him. "I'm so sorry to interrupt but this is just too big to text or say over the phone."

For a moment, Dario forgot they had an audience. "What did they say?"

"They loved the book. They thought the addition of the love story was brilliant. And the fact they are enemies ratcheted up the tension. We have a meeting with them next week to finalize the contract. Congratulations." They shook hands.

"Thank you." Dario turned to Gianna. "This is all thanks

to you. I don't know how I'll ever thank you but I'll think of a way."

"What's going on?" his grandfather's sharp voice cut through Dario's excited haze. "What's this about a book?"

His grandmother elbowed his grandfather. "Quiet down and maybe he'll tell us."

Dario glanced around to see that they were not alone. His brother had finally arrived and was wearing a frown on his face. His mother had a similar expression. Her latest husband, Dario had already forgotten his name, looked utterly confused. Carla was also there. She smiled brightly at him. At least someone was happy for him.

He glanced over at Gianna. Her smile filled him with a calming warmth that started on the inside and worked its way out. The time had come to fill his family in on his secret.

CHAPTER EIGHTEEN

SHE WAS SO happy for him.

Gianna couldn't stop smiling. And as she glanced around at his family, she couldn't understand why they weren't also happy for him. He'd worked so hard for this moment. But they didn't know that part yet.

When he sent her a hesitant look, she nodded at him to go ahead and tell everyone how his dream had come true.

She wanted to shrink away to the back of the crowd. After all, this was Dario's big moment, not hers. But as she started to walk away, he reached out for her hand and drew her back to his side. If he could face his family and reveal his amazing secret, she could stand there and be his biggest supporter.

"We're waiting," Franco called out.

Dario cleaned his throat. "I've been living what I'd guess you'd call a double life."

"A what?" his grandmother asked.

"For the past two years, I've been spending my days at the office but my evenings and weekends I've spent writing."

Gianna smiled and nodded as though to attest to all his hard work. Still none of his family smiled.

"Oh," his grandmother said, "you have a hobby. That's nice, dear. Everyone needs one of those."

"Not a hobby, Nonna. It's my career."

His grandfather muttered something under his breath and shook his head.

Franco spoke up. "You surely don't think you can make it writing one book? Who's going to buy it? You're a nobody."

That was when his agent spoke up. "He's not a nobody. He's D.J. March."

This drew everyone's attention. Franco's face scrunched up in confusion. "You're trying to tell us you're a famous author?"

"He is," Gianna spoke up, hoping to stir up some excitement in his family. "It's how we met." Oops. She wasn't supposed to say that. She was so excited that the words slipped past her lips unchecked.

"Why didn't you tell us?" his grandmother asked.

"Because… I wasn't sure what I wanted to do with my life." Dario turned his gaze to Gianna. "Well, that's not quite true. I wasn't sure I had what it takes to make writing a lifelong career."

His grandmother looked at him with caring eyes. "And now you know that it's what you want to do?"

"It is. Gianna helped me figure it out."

"Ah, this is a waste of time," his grandfather spat out.

"I agree," Dario's mother said. "The family business is worth a fortune. Why would you walk away from it?"

Gianna wanted to answer this for him. She couldn't believe his family was treating him this way. But she knew Dario had to do this on his own.

Dario cleared his throat. "I'm walking away because Franco is the rightful heir to the family business. He's the oldest and he has worked the hardest to see that it flourishes. My heart just isn't in it, not like his."

The two brothers' gazes connected for just a moment and she sensed some sort of understanding had silently flowed between them. Franco looked relieved.

His grandfather stepped forward. "So you're just going to sit around writing books for the rest of your life?"

Dario shrugged. "If I'm lucky enough."

Ronaldo moved next to Dario. "Trust me. Dario has a bright future ahead of him. I didn't get a chance to tell you the best part. There's a bidding war for the movie rights to your first book."

Dario didn't say a word for a moment. Gianna couldn't blame him. It was a lot to take in. They were making a movie based on his book. His characters would be brought to life for all the world to see. She was so proud of him.

"That's amazing."

Dario smiled.

"Pretty cool, huh?" Ronaldo grinned. "We've got to get you packed and on the road. The publisher wants you attending book signings and conferences promoting the first book. They really want a big build up for the release of book two. And then they'll want your input with the script for the movie, so plan on a trip to Hollywood."

Gianna grew quiet as she listened to how Dario's world was about to change. She was so very happy for him, but as reality settled in, she was sad for herself. Because after years of living out of a suitcase, she was ready to settle down in Gemma and sleep in her own comfy bed each night.

And then there was Dario. His career was just taking off and he would be on the go. Here, there and everywhere. His fans would want to meet him, take pictures with him and her gut told her that his second book would be an even a bigger hit than the first. And she wouldn't do anything to hold him back.

Franco stepped forward. "So this is what you've been working on while you were at Lake Como?"

Dario nodded. "Yes, and to buy myself the time I needed away from the business to write, I let you all believe that we're engaged. But that's not true."

"What?" It was a collective shocked response.

"You mean you're not getting married?" his grandmother's gaze narrowed as it moved between the two of them.

Gianna remained silent. This was not the way she would have handled it. And it was then that she noticed her parents had joined the group. Her mother looked devastated and her father looked angry. She felt awful.

"No." Dario shook his head. "We're not. It was all a charade."

Those words were like an arrow to her heart. He seemed to dismiss everything they'd shared these past few weeks as nothing important. Now that all his dreams were coming true, she felt dismissed, like yesterday's news.

"I'm sorry for that," Dario said. "We never planned on it working out this way. One thing led to another and then one person knew, then two people knew and then it all got out of hand."

"So it's all over?" her father asked. "The ring was just for show?"

"The ring is a gift." Dario glanced at her but Gianna couldn't quite meet his gaze. "I hope Gianna will keep it."

She couldn't listen to this anymore. Dario was acting like they were strangers—mere acquaintances. And it was then that she realized she'd fallen in love with him. She was such a fool. He was her third and final fiancé. She was done with romance.

She turned and started toward the front door. She was leaving, even if she had to walk. She just couldn't stand here and listen to Dario talk about them like they'd never shared any of those special moments. Maybe the engagement was fake but she didn't think the rest of it had been.

She could hear her father continuing to drill Dario with questions. Good. It would give her time to get away. She disappeared into the crowd as it appeared everyone had moved from the living room to the foyer to find out what was going on.

She kept her head down as she slowly made it to the door. At last, she stepped out into the evening air. For the first time since Dario told the world they were fakes, she could breath. But her eyes stung with unshed tears.

She blinked them away. She couldn't cry for a relationship that had never existed—because it had clearly never been real in Dario's mind or heart.

She kept walking. She didn't have a destination in mind. She supposed that eventually she'd have to return to the grand villa as her things were still there, but not yet.

"Gianna! Wait."

She knew that voice. It was Dario. What was he doing out here? Why was he following her?

She kept walking at the same pace. She wasn't going to stop. She didn't want to talk to him. There was nothing left to say—he'd said it all.

"Gianna?" He reached out, touching her upper arm. "Didn't you hear me?"

"I just needed some air."

"Can you stop so we can talk?"

"I don't think there's anything left to say."

He stepped in front of her, blocking her way. "Gianna, what's the matter? I thought we agreed that we were going to tell everyone the truth. I mean, I know it wasn't exactly the right time, but it just all came out."

She averted her gaze. She didn't want him to read her emotions. "It's fine. Everything is fine."

"If everything is fine, you wouldn't be out here. Alone. Talk to me."

"I don't have anything to say." And then she realized she never got a chance to congratulate him on his big accomplishment. This time, she lifted her gaze to meet his. "Congratulations on your book sale and movie deal. I knew you could do it."

"Thank you. But I know that's not what has you upset."

"Why do you keep saying that I'm upset? I'm fine. Everything is out in the open and now we can get on with our lives."

"What if I said that I didn't want to get on with my life, not without you?"

Her heart skipped a beat. What was he saying?

In the next heartbeat, she realized that no matter what he said, they weren't destined to be together. He had to go off and chase his dream. She couldn't hold him back—no matter how much it hurt her. He deserved to ride his rising star as far as it'd take him.

And she'd finally figured out what made her truly happy—her photography. She was done reinventing herself to fit into a man's life. She had to follow her own dream.

"Stop," she said. And then she did the one thing she knew she had to do to end things once and for all. "We got caught up in an act, but it's over now. You have a big publishing career to enjoy and another book to write because I can't get enough of Lavar and Ator." Then she slipped the ring from her finger. She placed it in his hand and wrapped his fingers around it. "Take it."

"But it's yours."

She shook her head. Her heart felt as though it were cracking in two. "It's best we end things here. I have to go."

She turned back toward his grandparents' villa. She had to get her things and go. Being around Dario was too painful. She was going to miss him for a long, long time. But she took solace in knowing he'd be happy.

CHAPTER NINETEEN

HOME AGAIN.

Gianna didn't smile.

Today, life felt as though it were playing a bit of déjà vu with her. The last time she'd returned from a trip, she'd thought she was at her lowest point. It had been the end of another relationship and the end of a prestigious job. This time, she'd returned the winner of a prestigious competition and her relationship hadn't actually ended because it'd never really existed. However, she felt so much lower.

The truth was she'd lost the man she loved.

Even thought she'd done the walking, it didn't hurt any less. Tears welled up in her eyes. She blinked them back. She refused to dissolve into a fit of tears. Again. This was for the best—for both them. But at the moment, it sure didn't feel like it.

One day faded into two. Dario called every day and left messages for her to call him. She deleted those messages before she caved into her desire to phone him just to hear his voice again. She knew it would just make matters worse.

Knock-knock.

She wasn't expecting anyone. Maybe if she just sat there quietly, they'd go away. Because there was absolutely no one she wanted to talk to—

"Gianna! I know you're in there." Carla's voice echoed through the door. "I'm coming in."

The door creaked open. Gianna admonished herself for never locking the door. But this was Gemma where crime just didn't happen.

Carla stepped into the living room. Worry showed in

her eyes. "I've been trying to call you." She rushed over and sat down on the couch next to her. "Are you all right?"

"I'm fine." Her wavering voice said she was anything but.

"Why did you leave so suddenly?"

"Once the truth about the engagement was out, I was no longer needed."

"Dario looked devastated after you left. He quickly disappeared."

Gianna met her cousin's gaze. "You know we were never really a couple."

"The only people that believe that are you and Dario. Everyone else could see what you two couldn't or wouldn't accept—that you're crazy in love with each other. Otherwise, why would you be sitting in here with the blinds drawn, staring blindly at the television?" Carla focused on the television. "What are you watching?"

"I have no idea." She hadn't even realized the television was still on. Gianna grabbed the remote and turned it off.

Gianna needed to talk to someone—to have Carla understand her actions—to convince herself that she'd done the right thing. "I can't hold him back. It wouldn't be fair. And in the end, I think he'd come to resent me. And I just couldn't stand for that to happen."

"Maybe it doesn't have to be either-or. Maybe there's a compromise."

"It won't work. I'd rather think of what might have been if the timing had been different."

"Are you sure you want to settle for what-if instead of what-is?"

Did her cousin have a point? Was she just hiding behind excuses of why they couldn't be together because she was afraid that if she really gave them a chance—if she admitted her feelings for Dario—that she'd get hurt again? Was he worth taking that big leap of faith?

* * *

He didn't want to be here.

He didn't want to be around people—unless their name was Gianna Cappellini.

And yet his brother had shown up at his apartment door and insisted he go with him to Sunday dinner at their grandparents. He said his grandfather had a big announcement and they both had to be there. And Franco wasn't leaving without him.

Reluctantly, Dario had taken a quick shower and put on a fresh suit because his grandparents insisted on dressing for dinner. Tito whined about being left behind, but he knew how his grandmother felt about having the dog in the house. It was better this way and he certainly didn't expect to be gone long.

When they arrived, his grandmother insisted that business wait until after dinner. Dario was so caught up in his own troubles that he didn't think too much about what his grandfather had to say. All Dario could think about was Gianna's retreating back as she left him—saying they didn't belong together. How could she say that?

They got along great. She made him smile and he thought he did the same for her. She made him reach for his dreams, no matter how hard it had been for him. She opened his eyes to love and that it didn't always have to be disastrous like his parents or cold and distant like his grandparents.

Love could be fun. It could be warm. And it could be fiery. But most of all, it meant spending time with your best friend—the person you could talk to about anything. At least he'd thought Gianna had become his best friend. Had he only been seeing what he'd wanted to see?

And then there was Tito, who had barely eaten since Gianna's departure. Even his dog was down in the dumps without her around. How did you explain to a pup that the woman he loved to follow around and beg treats from would no longer be a part of his life? Dario didn't have the words because he didn't know how to explain it to himself. One moment, things were fine, and in the next moment, it was over. She was gone.

"Dario?" His brother waved at him. "Nonna was speaking to you."

Dario blinked and turned to his grandmother. "Sorry. What did you say?"

"You haven't eaten. Are you feeling all right?"

He glanced down at his plate, finding that he'd moved the food around but he hadn't eaten a thing. He had absolutely no appetite.

He glanced around at the other plates, finding they'd finished eating. Good. It was almost time for him to leave. Just a little bit longer.

"Now that dinner is over," his grandfather began, "Dario, I know you were excited the other night and you said things you didn't mean—"

"I meant everything I said. I quit." Dario had been expecting some pushback from his grandfather. "I'm not turning my back on the business. And if there comes a time when I'm needed to step in, I'll do it. But for now, Franco can run the business. He's good at it and he likes it."

"And what?" his grandfather said. "You're going to just write books?"

"Yes." And he wasn't going to feel guilty about his choice. It was right for him. And it was right for Franco to have control of the company.

"This is about that woman." His grandfather frowned. "She talked you into quitting."

Dario's body tensed. How dare his grandfather blame any of this on Gianna. It took all his self-restraint to keep his voice calm and level. "Her name is Gianna. She is the kindest, most thoughtful woman. And she didn't talk me into anything. She helped me see what makes me the happiest."

His grandfather sighed as he leaned back in his chair. "Well, when things don't work out the way you planned, just remember that I warned you."

Dario shoulders tensed. It was time to go before he said something he'd regret. He pushed his chair back from the table and then stood. "I have to go."

"I didn't make my announcement," his grandfather said. "It might change your mind about walking away from the business."

His gaze connected with his brother's, who nodded for him to sit down. Dario subdued a groan of frustration and sat once more. As soon as his grandfather had his say, he was out of there.

His grandfather leaned forward, resting his elbows on the table. "I've been going over the books with the accountants. And I know you two were anxious to expand the line of products, but the online sales just aren't enough to sustain the extra products. I'm afraid we'll have to cut them back."

Dario's gaze moved to his brother, seeing how his face had creased with a frown. This is what they'd been worried about. It's what they'd been working to stop from happening, but seeing as their grandfather hadn't signed over full control to them, he still had the final say.

"At least give Franco more time to line up some stores or restaurants to carry the lines," Dario said, hating the thought of all their hard work of finding the right spices and organic herbs just going to waste. They both believed in the products. And so would the consumers as soon as they tried them. But to do that, they had to be readily for sale.

His grandfather turned on him. His brows were drawn together in a firm line. "Why would you care? Remember, you quit."

"It doesn't mean I don't care about the future of the company. Franco and I have worked hard to bring back some of the past products."

His grandfather stood. "You have no say."

"But I do." Franco also stood. "You can't do this. I'm working on getting bigger exposure for our lesser-known products."

Their grandfather crossed his arms. "It'd have to be a very good plan—"

"It is. I'm going to get them back in the Falco Ristorantes—"

"You can't do that!"

"Wait and see." Franco's gaze challenged their grandfather.

"You…you can't. That man's nothing but a cheat. I refuse to do business with him."

"Who?" Both brothers spoke at once.

"Carlo Falco is not to be trusted." Their grandfather's face was red with anger.

Dario couldn't remember the last time his grandfather got this worked up. What was Nonno talking about? And why was this the first time he was hearing about Carlo Falco being disreputable?

"Giuseppe, I can't believe you."

Everyone's attention turned to Nonna. Her narrowed gaze was laser focused on her husband. The tension in the room was so charged that it practically crackled.

"You don't understand—"

"I understand just fine," their grandmother said. "You've been gambling again. And after you swore to me that you were done playing cards—"

"But I did quit. This was a long time ago. If you don't believe me, just ask the boys how long ago our products were removed from the Falco restaurants."

Both Dario and Franco assured their grandmother that

it'd been years since the deal with the Falco's had fallen through. But they'd both been under the impression that it'd been a business decision—not a personal one. *Nonno was a gambler? Wow!* Dario wondered what else he didn't know about his grandparents.

Their grandfather's gaze moved to Franco. "You have six months to increase the profit margin, otherwise I'm stepping back in as acting president and I will make any changes necessary."

The men glared at each other. Tensions had never been this high in the family. And though Dario felt bad for his brother, he was glad he was out of it. His grandfather's constant interference was just too much.

"Enough!" their grandmother said. "I won't stand for anymore of this. Now sit. Dessert will be here shortly."

Dario glanced down at the table, finding the dinner dishes had been cleared from the table during the argument. Dario turned to his grandmother. "I'm going to go."

"Please don't go so soon," she said. "We see you so rarely."

"Let him go," his grandfather said. "He didn't even touch his dinner."

"That's because he's in love." Nonna sent Dario a sympathetic smile. "You should go to Gianna and work things out."

Dario shook his head. "It won't do any good. She said we're over."

"She might have said it but I don't think she meant it. I saw the way she looked at you. She's a woman in love." Nonna's eyes widened as though she'd thought of something. "Stay here. I'll be right back."

Dario didn't want to stay, but he had a soft spot for his grandmother. She wasn't overly affectionate but he knew without a doubt that she loved him and his brother. While she was gone, fresh fruit and some gelato were served. His favorites. He took a bite but it didn't appeal to him.

Nonna quickly returned. "Here you go."

He accepted the small jeweler's box from her. "What is it?"

"It's something I've been holding for you for a very long time. Open it."

He did as she asked. Inside was a diamond ring. It was beautiful in a simplistic way.

"It belonged to your great-grandmother, my mother." She turned to Franco. "Don't worry. I have a ring saved for you too."

"I won't be needing it," Franco said firmly.

Their grandmother sent him a knowing smile. "Trust me. Love will find you when you least expect it." While Franco shook his head, Nonna turned her attention back to Dario. "I've been waiting until you found the right woman to give it to you. Gianna is the right one for you. I knew it as soon as I saw the two of you together."

He knew his grandmother was trying to help but this was just making it harder on him. He closed the box and slid it across the table toward her. "I can't take it."

"Sure you can."

"But I already gave Gianna a ring—a much larger ring—and she rejected it and me."

"Maybe it wasn't the right ring with the right proposal."

Was that it? His grandmother was a wise woman. But could a diamond ring—this family heirloom—change her mind? He honestly didn't know.

"And there's one more thing," his grandmother said. She moved to the doorway and then reached into the hallway. "The maid found this under your bed when they were cleaning your old room. I thought it might be important."

When she held out a large rectangular-shaped package covered with heavy brown wrapping paper, he realized it was the same kind he'd noticed in Gianna's office. And then he saw his name scrolled across the front in Gianna's very distinctive handwriting.

He ripped off the paper, finding one of her prints inside with a note taped to it.

This should be the winning photo.
Too bad there wasn't a category to enter it.
But it is the photo from my heart.
Love, Gianna

"What is it?" his grandmother asked.

"Yes, show us," his brother said.

"Just wait." Dario removed the taped note from the front of the picture.

He gazed at the silhouette of him and Tito walking down a shady wooded path. His back was to the camera, which was the reason he couldn't remember her taking this photo, and he was glancing down at Tito at the same time Tito was glancing up at him. In the background, there was a break in the trees where the sunshine gleamed down. It was a very striking photo. He absolutely loved it.

And it appeared just as he needed a sign. He knew what to do now—follow his heart—straight back to Gemma. There was a woman there that he was madly in love with. Now he just needed to convince her that they belonged together.

CHAPTER TWENTY

THIS JUST HAD to work.

Dario had spent all of Sunday evening staring at the modest diamond ring his grandmother had given him. If a big splashy ring wouldn't sway Gianna's decision, would a smaller ring make any difference?

And then he'd recalled his grandmother's words about the right ring with the right proposal. It was true that he'd never really proposed. Not exactly.

He remembered how marriage had ended with his parents. They not only got rid of each other but also their children. He'd be lying if he didn't fear the same thing might happen to him.

Perhaps that's why he'd skirted around the subject of marriage—why he hadn't laid his heart on the line. The thought of being rejected once more by someone he loved was devastating.

But now that he'd officially stepped away from the family business, he knew his fictional characters wouldn't be enough company. No one, real or fictional, could replace Gianna.

He thought of Ator and how he'd risked his realm in order to be with Sefinna—the enemy. If he could write about people taking big risks for love, why couldn't he do the same thing?

First thing Monday morning, he started to put his plan in motion. He was going to show Gianna that they belonged together. Because they were stronger together—they were happier together—they were their best together. He believed that with all his heart.

By Wednesday, his plan was in full motion. He had enlisted a little help from Carla. If anyone knew Gianna's likes and dislikes, it was her cousin. He hadn't filled her in on his whole plan though, just a piece of it.

At noon on Wednesday, he parked his car in Gemma. Tito was anxious to get out and stretch his legs and so Dario decided to walk the rest of the way to Gianna's villa. He just hoped she was home.

Tito knew the way and the closer they got to the villa, the faster the dog moved. And then when the villa came into sight, Tito took off at a run with his tail swishing back and forth. This was the happiest he'd seen his dog in days. It appeared he wasn't the only one who had missed her.

"Tito! Come back. Tito."

The dog didn't slow down.

Well, this wasn't exactly how he'd envisioned their meeting, but then again, maybe Tito would soften her up for him. After all, not even Gianna could deny her fondness for his dog.

Woof! Woof-woof!

Tito raced up to the closed door that was normally open. Dario now worried that she really wasn't home and he'd have to wait even longer to speak to her. *Please say it isn't so.* He willed her to be home.

Tito jumped at the door as he continued barking and putting up such a fuss that no one could miss it. If Gianna was home, she would open the door.

And she did.

Dario's heart soared at the sight of her. He stopped walking and merely took in her beauty. It felt like a lifetime since he'd last seen her. Oh, how he'd missed her.

Tito's tail moved in a blur. He jumped up, his front paws landing on her chest as he leaned in and licked Gianna's cheek. Gianna hugged him and fussed over him, making Dario jealous that he couldn't switch places with his dog.

Go, Tito! He smiled at his silly dog.

And then her gaze swung around, searching for him. When she spotted him, the smile faded from her face. Oh, no. That wasn't good at all.

He started walking again. Much faster this time. He didn't want to give her a chance to slip away behind a closed door. To his relief, she stayed where she was and continued to fuss over Tito, who ate up every sweet, crooning word she sent his way.

"What are you doing here?" Gianna asked as she straightened.

"Technically, I can still be here." He'd use any excuse to speak to her. "Remember our rental agreement?"

She crossed her arms. "And did you forget it ends today?"

"True enough." Not exactly the greeting he'd hoped for, but she hadn't slammed the door in his face so he'd take it. It took him a moment to remember his excuse to come see her. He reached for the box under his arm. "I promised you this."

Her puzzled gaze moved to the box. "What is it?"

"Here, take it."

She was hesitant but eventually took it from him. She untied the twine from the white box and then lifted the lid. "Your book."

"I told you that once it was sold, you'd be the first one to read it."

"I...uh, thank you. But you didn't have to bring it all this way."

"Actually, I did. I have something I want you to see." He hadn't even gotten all the words out before she started to shake her head. "Please come with me."

"Dario, it's not a good idea. It's best just to leave things as is."

"I disagree."

She frowned. "We've been through all this and it's been decided."

"No. You decided. I didn't. Just give me a few minutes of your time, and if you still want me to go, you won't have to see me again."

She sighed. "You aren't going to leave until I agree, are you?"

Woof-woof!

Gianna looked at Tito and smiled. "Figures you'd be on his side." She turned back to Dario. "Okay. Let's go." It was then that she got a puzzled look on her face. "Where's your car?"

"In the village. Tito wanted to stretch his legs. He doesn't get as much exercise now that we're back in the city."

She turned back to Tito. "You poor baby. You should make Dario walk you more."

When she turned to put the book in the house, Dario said, "Bring it."

Her fine brows scrunched together. "What for?"

"You'll see."

And then they started to walk toward the village. Dario knew he still had a shot with her, but he didn't let his hopes get too high. There was still a chance she didn't feel as deeply for him as he did her.

What was he up to?

Gianna wasn't so sure what made her decide to go with him. She didn't even know where they were headed, because as soon as they'd reached the village, they climbed in Dario's car and he started driving. Destination unknown. He was certainly acting very mysterious.

She told herself to stick to her decision for each of them to go their separate ways. But with each passing kilometer, her resolve weakened.

She chanced a glance his way. While his attention was on traffic, she took in his handsome face. Her heart beat faster. Her gaze zeroed in on his lips. She missed his kisses.

Those kisses that weren't supposed to mean anything—that were supposed to be just for show—they meant everything to her. She would cherish them forever—

Dario turned in her direction. She jerked her attention to the road ahead. Her heart raced. Did he know she'd been staring at him? Heat swirled in her chest and rushed to her cheeks. Why exactly had she agreed to this little adventure?

As they entered Como, she let herself become distracted with the sights. Como was a city whereas Gemma was just a small village. They were very different in size and energy. Where Gemma was laidback, Como was lively.

Dario pulled to a stop in front of some small shops. Tourists with their hands full of shopping bags made their way along the walk. Gianna had absolutely no idea what they were doing here.

"Dario, what are you up to?"

He was currently attaching a leash to Tito's collar. "I'll show you." He and Tito rounded the front of the car and met her on the sidewalk. "Don't forget the book."

Was he serious? What did he plan, a book reading? Wasn't that usually only done with published books? She wasn't quite sure since she'd never attended a book reading. Still, she did as he asked.

When she straightened, he said, "Right this way."

They walked a short distance before coming to a stop in front of a vacant shop. Dario unlocked the door, stepped inside and flipped on the lights.

"What do you think?" he asked.

"Is this yours?" She was confused. It certainly didn't look like the type of place where he'd want to write his books.

"No." He turned to her. "This is yours, if you want it."

"What? I… I don't understand."

He smiled at her, making her stomach dip. "Maybe you should open the box in your arms and start to read."

Now she was really confused. He wanted her to read his book now? "I don't think we have time for me to read it now."

He continued to smile. "Trust me. Just start reading."

And so she opened the box. The book was printed out on white printer paper. The top sheet was the cover page with *The Clash of Lavar* by D.J. March. The next page was the copyright page. But it was the third page that harnessed her full attention. It was the dedication page.

> *To the most amazing woman I've ever known.*
> *You've shown me that true love really does exist.*
> *I love you now and always.*
> *Will you marry me?*

Her mouth gaped as her heart pitter-pattered. Her gaze rose to meet his. He reached in his pocket and removed a black velvet ring box. He opened it and held it out to her as he knelt down on one knee.

"I'm sorry I let you walk away. It was a huge mistake. My life isn't the same without you in it."

Her eyes misted over with tears of joy. Was this really happening? She felt as though she were having an out-of-body experience.

"I love you, Gianna, with all my heart. And I know if we try, we can find a way to be together while we both chase our own dreams."

The happy tears spilled onto her cheeks as she pressed a shaky hand to her lips.

"Gianna Cappellini, will you do me the honor of being my wife?"

Every reason why they wouldn't work faded away. In his eyes, she found the courage to follow her heart. "Yes. Yes, I will."

He stood and slipped the ring on her finger. He gazed

deep into her eyes as he swiped the tears from her cheeks. And then he pressed his lips to hers.

She didn't know how long they stood there in each other's arms. However long it was, it wasn't nearly long enough. When he pulled back, he lost his balance. She reached out to steady him.

It was then that they realized Tito had given them his blessing. He'd once again wrapped them up in his leash. They both smiled as they unwound themselves.

Gianna still had one more question. "I don't understand about this shop."

"It's my wedding gift to you. You've been talking about opening a gallery and I thought you'd like it."

"Like it? I love it." She glanced all around, imagining her prints on the walls. "But if I'm here and you're traveling the world promoting your book—"

"Trust me. We'll make it work. After all, we can hire help and I don't plan to do a lot of traveling. I'll have a beautiful wife to cherish." Tito barked, causing them to laugh. "And a pup to play with. Not to mention my next book to write."

"And I might go with you now and then. I can take pictures while you visit with your fans."

He laughed. "I'm telling you, I'm not famous. I'll be known as the husband of the famous photographer."

"As long as we're together, it'll all work out." And for the first time, she let herself believe it. Together, they could do anything.

EPILOGUE

Several weeks later, Fiorire Botanical Gardens,
Lake Como

RINGS WERE EXCHANGED.

And there wasn't a dry eye in the lush garden.

Okay. So maybe it was just Carla's eyes that were damp. She swiped at them. True love had won out over everything. She was so happy for her cousin and Dario.

That's the way it should always be—marrying for love. However, Carla's father was nagging her to settle down and marry. Her father wouldn't care if love was involved, so long as she married a man fit to run the family business. But she'd set him straight. If—a big if—she married, it'd be on her own timetable.

And that thought was like a bone that stuck in her throat. She'd given up striking out on her own when her mother had died. She'd focused on her education and delved into learning everything there was to know about Falco's Fresco Ristorante. She had worked her way up through the company until she felt ready to stand in for her father, but he wouldn't hear of it.

She was supposed to have been born a boy. Finding out he had a daughter instead of the longed-for son had been a big blow for her father. Still, she'd been named after him, but nothing she did convinced him that she could be a strong, reliable heir—all because she was a female.

Even when he had his heart attack a couple of months ago, he'd argued with her but she'd done what needed to be done. She'd made the day-to-day decisions. She'd kept the business on track. And she'd closed a few big deals. Still, it wasn't enough for her father.

"You may kiss the bride." The minister's voice drew her back to the service.

"Aw..." Carla smothered her reaction.

And then Gianna turned to her, her eyes shimmering with happiness. She didn't have to say anything. The joy was written all over her face. And Carla couldn't be happier for her. If any two people deserved to get their happily-ever-after, they did.

Carla handed over the bouquet of purple lilies and white roses and Gianna turned back to her new husband, slipping her hand in the crook of his arm.

"Ladies and gentlemen, I'd like to introduce for the first time, Mr. and Mrs. Dario Marchello."

The string quartet started to play the recessional as the newlyweds made their way down the aisle. When they were halfway down, Carla's gaze moved to the best man.

When their gazes met, her heart picked up its pace as heat warmed her cheeks. What was wrong with her? It wasn't like she was into Franco. As she'd come to learn, he was just like her father—always thinking about business. The last thing she wanted to do was play second fiddle to a business. And she wasn't even looking for a man in her life right now—she had other priorities.

Still, as she slipped her hand in the crook of his strong arm, she had to admit that she didn't mind having him next to her. They paused for the camera and then continued down the aisle.

As they passed by her father, he glowered at her. She wondered what had elicited such a response from him. Was he still disgruntled that she'd used her own judgment over a matter at the office instead of doing as he'd demanded—even if her decision had saved the company both money and jobs? Or was it perhaps her escort that he didn't care for?

"I guess you're next," Franco said, drawing her from her thoughts.

"Next?"

"You know, getting married."

Once they were out of the way of the next couple, she turned to him. "I'm not sure what you're getting at but I have no plans to get married anytime soon."

"Really?" He arched a disbelieving brow.

What did he know that she didn't? Had there been some erroneous rumor in the paper? They were always making up headlines.

"What have you heard?"

"Your father was overheard saying you would be married by the end of the year."

"He what?" Her brain was still trying to process this bit of information. "Whoever said that is mistaken."

Franco shook his head. "I don't think so. I overheard him myself and he was very matter-of-fact."

She pressed her lips firmly together, holding back her heated words. Her father had been difficult with his need to dictate her life even before his heart attack, but since his recovery, he was utterly impossible. And this explained the solid string of business dinners that he'd insisted she accompany him to—always with an unattached business-man within her age range.

She frowned. "He shouldn't have said that."

Franco held up his hands innocently. "Don't kill the messenger. I thought you knew what he was up to."

She sighed. Franco was right. He had nothing to do with her father and his misguided plans. She knew the heart attack had shaken him up, but this was going too far. "I should have known, but I've been distracted lately with his failing health—something he doesn't worry enough about."

"I'm sure he's just worried about you, about what will happen to you if something happens to him. How is he doing?"

She resisted the urge to shrug. "According to him, he's just fine. According to everyone else, including his doctors, he needs to slow down."

"I'm sorry to hear that. So you're running the business now?"

She nodded. "For now, I am." She caught sight of the bride. "I really need to go."

"Maybe later we could talk a little business."

"Uh…maybe. Now's not really the time." She pasted on a big smile as she moved toward her cousin. "You make the most beautiful bride."

"Thank you. Maybe you'll be next." Gianna waggled her fine brows as she teased her.

"Don't you start too. It appears my father is intent on finding me a husband."

"Really?" When Carla nodded, Gianna continued. "He told you this?"

"Worse. Franco just informed me."

"He wants you to marry Franco—"

"Shh…" Heat rushed up Carla's neck and set her cheeks aflame. "Don't let anyone hear you say that, especially your new husband."

"Well? Does he?"

"No," she said quickly, putting an end to that thought. At least she didn't think her father would have such a preposterous thought in mind. Would he?

Her father could be quite manipulative when he wanted to be. She just needed to outsmart him and show him that she was fine on her own. She didn't need him or anyone arranging her marriage. She refused to be told what she should and shouldn't do.

These weren't the olden days where a woman needed a man. She would do fine on her own, both in business and personally. But first, she had to find a way to convince her father that he could trust her with his beloved company.

* * * * *

THE TWIN PROPOSAL

CATHY GILLEN THACKER

*"Why not?" He let his gaze dart knowingly over her face.

"You still have a lot to learn about men."

Abruptly, Mackenzie fell silent, aware that she knew as much as he did about him.

Their almost twenty-year friendship had become complicated enough, after she had become Griff's phy-sical adviser. To make matters worse, she didn't want to complicate things, but to her dismay to be a distraction to everyone in his present job at..... She didn't know that and now see his now-fluctuation to open the document when his colleagues were beginning to view their ties in...*

She with a delivery of one of her Special Occasions signs, realizing. He..... from one another thing. She motioned for Griff to go on and climbed behind the wheel. Unable to help but adore how his friendships...

Chapter One

"**Y**ou want us to be roommates?" Mackenzie Lockhart echoed in shock, transferring a pink-and-white Guess What the Stork Just Delivered? sign from her garage into the back of her pickup truck, while Bliss, her Bernese mountain dog, watched from inside the vehicle.

His expensive charcoal suit his only defense against the chilly March evening, Griff Montgomery headed over to assist her. As always, the ruggedly handsome Fort Worth attorney had stayed late at work. And, as always, he had volunteered to help Mackenzie with a delivery and setup when she found herself unexpectedly shorthanded.

He came closer, inundating her with his brisk sandalwood and leather scent. Then, loosening his tie another notch, he flashed her a slow, disarming smile as he pushed back the edges of his jacket with his big hands, revealing a sinewy chest and taut, muscular abs. His six-foot-four-inch frame dwarfed her five feet seven inches.

"Why not?" He let his gaze drift curiously over her face. "You know moving in together makes sense…"

Actually, Mackenzie thought, drawing an uneven breath, it did and it didn't.

Their almost twenty-year friendship had become complicated enough when she had become Griff's plus-one at all his law firm functions. And while she didn't mind accompanying him to work events so he wouldn't have to scrounge up an actual date—something he swore he did not have the time or inclination to do—she *did* mind how his colleagues were beginning to view their constant companionship.

But with a delivery of one of her Special Occasion Signs pending, that was a discussion for another time.

She motioned for Griff to get in and climbed behind the wheel. Unable to help but note how his long legs and broad-shouldered frame filled up the roomy interior of her Ford F-150, she turned on the ignition and paused to look at his profile. Alone, none of his features were that remarkable. The same could be said for his short, cropped chestnut-brown hair. But together, with his strong brow, intent amber eyes, straight nose, square jaw and firm masculine lips, she found the man to be heart-stoppingly attractive.

Not that he had ever noticed her in a similar way. From the time they had first met, when she had been ten, and Griff fourteen, he had taken on the role of a protective older brother slash friend. Nothing more. Nothing less. Which was why—despite her initial wild crush on him—it was a good thing she had never allowed herself to think of Griff in any other way, either.

And yet for a moment, as his suggestion hung in the air between them, Mackenzie lost herself in the compelling seductiveness of his gaze.

But she couldn't go there. Couldn't let herself wish for the impossible, any more than she had been able to let herself wish for her parents to still be alive, after they died when she was just a child.

Sometimes things just were what they were. You had to accept that. Move on.

Griff lifted a brow in silent inquiry, as he continued to await her reply.

She swallowed around the sudden dryness of her throat. *Friends. We're just friends.* "We talked about this the last time I lost a rental," she reminded him. Mackenzie had brushed it off then for a very good reason. She didn't want to get her hopes up that things might change, only to end up with crushed expectations and a broken heart in the end. After all, she'd had one failed engagement. Did she really want another embarrassment?

He nodded, his lips tightening at the memory. "Exactly. The previous three times you leased a house, you fixed the property up to such a degree that the owners decided to put them on the market at year's end, which then left you and Bliss homeless, and scrambling to find another rental."

Mackenzie shrugged and put the truck in Reverse, backing out of the driveway. She knew she could avoid this hassle by doing what he had and purchasing a place. As Griff had pointed out on more than one occasion, she had the credit history to qualify for a mortgage and money for a down payment squirreled away. But something always held her back. "I don't mind moving every year." It kept her from getting tied down to any one place or getting too attached. Or financially stuck in the same city as Griff if the unimaginable happened and he did eventually marry and settle down here.

She sighed. Watching him find happiness with another

woman had been hard enough the previous two times, even when she had known the relationships were flawed and would never last.

But she couldn't imagine how painful it would be for her if his relationship with someone else were exactly right.

Griff shook his head at her in mute disapproval. "Well, you should mind having to move that often." For him, a stable home address meant a stable life.

Mackenzie paused at the stop sign and checked the directions. "Just because you've lived in the same downtown loft since you graduated from law school doesn't mean everyone else should do the same. I like change. I like turning something ugly into something attractive. And then," she said, smiling victoriously before he could interrupt, "there is the way I'm able to negotiate drastically reduced rents in exchange for all the updates I make, which in turn gives me more money to spend on expanding Special Occasion Signs."

The business that was her baby, and the key to her stability. Or at least as much as she realistically expected to find in this life.

"I understand the need for as much financial security as possible," Griff said soothingly.

Like her, he'd been orphaned as a child and had ended up alone in the foster care system.

Yet, unlike her, he had never been adopted.

So now, while she and her seven siblings had Carol and Robert Lockhart as parents, as well as a big extended family of in-laws and nieces and nephews that they could depend on, Griff still had no one.

Except for her. Oh, and Bliss, too, since he loved her big ole pup as much as she did. And Joe Carson, his beloved mentor slash managing partner, who worked with him at the big successful law firm in downtown Fort Worth. Not to mention Joe's incredibly kind wife, Alice…

"But comfort should play into it, too," Griff continued, breaking into her thoughts.

Mackenzie envisioned his spacious abode. Although she and Bliss hung out there when her and Griff's busy schedules aligned, which wasn't as often as she would have liked, she still couldn't imagine living in the midst of all that concrete and brick. She needed a front porch and sunshine. Grass. Shady tree-lined streets. And, of course, a workshop for SOS…

"Besides, where would I make my signs if I didn't have a garage and backyard? Bliss and I can't live in your loft." She parked in front of the home where she'd be displaying the celebratory announcement. At 11:00 p.m., the windows were dark. The residential street quiet. Lit only by the corner streetlamp, and the full moon shining in the velvety black Texas sky above.

She got out quietly. Griff followed suit, while Bliss sat patiently in the truck, watching and waiting.

He met her at the tailgate, which he unlatched and let down. "That's just it." His low, gruff voice radiated through her body. "I won't be there, either." He reached into the bed to pull the pieces of the sign forward. "I'm going to be renting a home for the next year while my entire building and my condo unit undergo major renovation."

Griff paused to hand her the bundle of stakes that would hold the signage in place. It was his turn to regard her with a triumphant smile. "So I figured as long as I'm looking for a place and you're looking for a place…" He hefted the large plywood pieces onto the ground. "Why not save some money and rent together? Especially since I found one with a large fenced-in yard, a two-car garage and an adjacent carriage house that would make a perfect studio for you."

They walked side by side across the grass. It wasn't the first time she had leaned on her best friend, or helped him out, either. Yet it felt different tonight. As if they were on the precipice of something *more*. Which was crazy since he had never shown the slightest bit of romantic interest in her. She set down the bundle of long metal stakes. "Does it take large dogs?"

"Yep." He handed her the first plywood section. "The backyard is big and shady. Bliss would love it." Mackenzie positioned the Guess What the Stork Just Delivered? cutout center-right on the front lawn. Then placed the big pink-and-white Stork, with a diaper-wrapped baby in its beak, in the middle. After that, she set about arranging the It's a Girl! sign. Several moments passed before she finally stepped back to regard the three sections critically, to ensure they were where she wanted them. Imagining the new parents' surprise and delight when they arrived home from the hospital the next afternoon, she smiled with satisfaction, then turned back to Griff. "So what's the monthly fee?"

He told her.

Mackenzie calculated silently. "So, nearly twice what I'm paying now," she said unhappily. Griff threaded the long metal stakes through the holders on the back of the painted plywood cutouts. Then pushed them into the ground to secure them. "Except I'd be paying half of that. So it would end up being the same for you, and a little less for me."

Satisfied all was well, Mackenzie took a photo of the announcement, texted it to the grandparent who had ordered it for the happy couple, then walked with Griff back to her truck, where Bliss continued to wait. She reached into the back seat to stroke her pet's silky head. "When is this place available?"

"Immediately," he replied.

Well, that would help, Mackenzie thought. Although she had never minded moving, she hated worrying about where she and Bliss were going to live next.

Affable as ever, Griff continued, "The tenant moved out yesterday. I've got the lockbox code. It's only about ten minutes from here. We can look at it right now if you want."

She was tempted. Yet bitter experience had taught her not to be reckless. Especially in matters of the heart. She climbed back behind the wheel. "How did you find out about it?"

Griff relaxed in the passenger seat beside her. "It's owned by one of my law firm's clients." His gaze shifted over her before returning to her eyes. "So, what do you say?" he asked. "Are you in?"

Mackenzie hesitated. "I'll look at it." But only because it could be hard to find a rental with a fenced backyard that would allow pets. Especially on such short notice.

They started with the most important part—the backyard, because Griff knew if that didn't work for Bliss, Mackenzie would have no interest in seeing the rest.

Fortunately, the entire half-acre property was lit with motion-detector lights. So they were able to snap a leash on her collar, get Bliss out of the truck and take her straight inside the fence.

The Bernese mountain dog stayed close to Mackenzie's side, stopping at the edge of the brick patio, gazing around. The backyard was spacious, the interior of the six-foot wood privacy fence rimmed with overgrown landscape shrubbery, some with flowers. What kind, Griff didn't know.

Not that it mattered to him.

He was just happy to see a sturdy hammock strung between the big live oak and pecan trees, and the expanse of thick green grass.

And adjacent to the main home, the long narrow carriage house. Which would make a perfect work space for Mackenzie. But at the moment, she seemed focused on the domestic side of things.

"It's got a covered patio for my outdoor furniture." Mackenzie pointed out the place where the cushion glider and matching chairs would go.

Griff watched Bliss tilt her head back to look up at her owner. He could have sworn the dog was smiling, as she rubbed her furry head across Mackenzie's thigh. She knelt to take her pet's beautiful face in her hands.

Mackenzie had gotten Bliss as an eight-week-old puppy. In the two years since, they had formed a tight, unshakable bond. One Griff envied. "What do you think, girl? Want to look around?" She unsnapped the leash from her collar and gestured broadly. "You can go explore."

Tail wagging, Bliss set off.

Mackenzie turned back to him.

As always, he was amazed how pulled together she could still manage to look after what had been a very long day. Mackenzie's fair skin was flawless, her high, sculpted cheeks flushed pink, her long-lashed, sea-blue eyes alert. His gaze drifted upward, lingering over her wavy butterscotch blond hair, which was held away from her face with pretty gold clips. She was dressed in a long-sleeved white T-shirt, and a medium blue fleece bearing her business logo. Lower, dark rinse jeans hugged her slender waist and hips. Comfortable shearling-lined boots encased her feet.

"So," Mackenzie murmured softly, tilting her face up to his. "What is really going on here? Why do you suddenly want a roommate after spending the last decade on your own?"

Good question. One he wasn't sure he wanted to answer.

"And why are you interested in living in a residential area of Fort Worth instead of downtown? When I know there have to be plenty of other city apartments to rent."

There were.

"So what gives?" Mackenzie persisted.

He could see she was not going to relent unless he told her the truth. And since he really did want this to work... "I figured as long as I have to make a change, I might as well make a *real* change."

Bliss buried her face in fragrant white blossoms, sniffing intensely.

Meanwhile, Mackenzie kept her eyes on his. "In what sense?"

"I'm tired of trading one concrete jungle for another at the end of every day." Able to see she wasn't quite buying it, he shrugged, confessing, "I thought it might be fun to have a yard to kick back in, instead of a community rooftop." The way a lot of his coworkers did.

"And?" she prodded, guessing there was more.

He grinned, not too proud to admit, "And spend more time hanging out with my two best friends."

Understanding she was being talked about, Bliss trotted over to him and pressed up against his leg. He glanced down fondly and petted her head.

Affection gleaming in her pretty sea-blue eyes, Mackenzie surveyed them both. "You still want a dog, don't you?"

Aware he'd been talking about taking the leap for a couple of years now, Griff met her steady, empathetic gaze. "Yeah, but it's not practical, given how much I'm at work. But I could help you with Bliss when I am home. Walk her. Play ball with her. Cuddle on the sofa..."

She paused to let his words settle around her. "So it's really my dog you want to bunk with."

Her droll tone lit an answering fire in him. "Now, Mack, I wouldn't go so far as to say that," he teased.

She sighed and sent a glance heavenward, seeming, to his relief, more amused than annoyed. "I would. But don't worry." She patted his biceps amiably. "I'm not offended. I'd choose Bliss over you, too."

He chuckled. "Ha ha."

She pushed her lips into a mischievous moue that was more kissable than she realized.

Not about to go *there*, especially if they were going to be living together, he forced himself to be businesslike again. "Want to look around inside first? Or check out the carriage house slash studio?"

She turned serious. "The interior of the home."

He went around front to open up the lockbox, then let her and Bliss in through the back door, switching on overhead lamps as he went.

Mackenzie frowned in disapproval. It was easy to see why. "This is kind of a wreck," she said, as they waded through the trash-littered floors.

Too late, he realized he should have waited another day or two to bring her to see the place. He squinted at Mackenzie and soothed her with a commiserating smile. "Yeah, I know." When he stepped near enough, he caught a whiff of her orange blossom fragrance. "Did I mention the last tenants were evicted?"

"With good reason, it would appear." She snapped the leash back on Bliss and kept her from nosing through a fast food bag.

"A junk hauler is coming in tomorrow to clear all this out." Griff walked with her through the downstairs. "And then it's going to be professionally cleaned."

"I'll just pretend that's already been done then."

She studied the traditional floor plan. The rooms were laid out just as they had been when it had been built in the early seventies. Foyer, formal living and dining room in the front of the house. Kitchen, tiny breakfast nook, laundry–mud room and cozy little family room with fire-place at the rear.

And the "pièce de résistance"?

The ugly-carpeted staircase in the foyer.

Sensing she needed more persuading, Griff said, "We can make whatever changes we want. As with your pre-vious leases, the labor is on us, but the materials can be deducted from the monthly rent as long as we have re-ceipts."

Mackenzie regarded their surroundings with an art-ist's eye. "Do we have to get permission on the colors and so on?"

"He trusts us."

She lifted her eyebrows. "Just like that?"

"Well… I might have showed him some photos of your previous rentals, once you were done with them."

"Ah. So he's looking for a bargain renovation."

Griff chuckled, thinking maybe this change was ex-actly what he needed. To keep him from feeling so bored and restless. One thing was for sure: sharing space with Mackenzie and Bliss would never be dull. He shrugged.

"Actually, it's a married couple who relocated to Montana. And, as far as good deals go, aren't we looking for the same thing?"

Their eyes met and held, the energy between them crackling with undefined emotion. "What's upstairs?"

He had no frigging idea. He eased a hand beneath her elbow. "Let's go and see."

They mounted the stairs to the second floor of the Georgian, Bliss sticking close to their sides. The master bedroom was to the left. Mackenzie poked her head in. "No en-suite bath," she noted, her gaze roving the outdated wallpaper.

"But plenty of closet space," Griff pointed out. One walk in, another with shelves and shoe racks.

"True." Mackenzie smiled.

"And there is a master bathroom right next door to that," he added.

"Except you have to go out into the upstairs hallway to access it."

A few steps maybe. "Too far to walk?" he teased.

She frowned. "I was thinking about privacy."

The thought of her in various states of undress was more intriguing than it should have been. Determined to keep them strictly pals, he snapped his fingers in feigned disappointment. "No walking around naked then."

"Ha! You wish!" She slanted him a look, letting him know once again she was not in the least bit attracted to him. Which was good. Being physically drawn to each other would have ruined their friendship. And made it impossible for him to remain a self-appointed big brother in her life.

Mackenzie drew a bolstering breath that lifted the soft feminine curves of her breasts, and walked on down the hall. There was another full bath and a bedroom to the left, two bedrooms to the right. The one closest to the master was by far the largest. "We could both have a bedroom, and a bath, and an office upstairs," he pointed out.

Her lips curved upward in a tantalizing smile. Clearly, she liked that idea. "Which one were you thinking of taking?"

He nodded toward the one in the middle of the home. "I would leave you the master—being the gentleman that I am."

With a huff, Bliss lay down in the center of the hall.

"You wouldn't want to flip for it?" she asked.

No. he wanted her to be happy. And two closets would make her happy. "Nope," he said. "Besides, you'll need the extra floor space for your yoga."

Her chin jerked up. "Actually, I haven't done that in quite a while."

Really? You couldn't tell that by looking at her. Her slender body was as lithe and fit as ever.

"No time," she said. "But you still run," she recollected.

Aware he was hoping to get Bliss to do that with him sometimes, he nodded. "It's the best way to work off stress." And he had a lot of that with his work as a property lawyer who specialized in eminent domain cases. His gaze moved over her silky-soft lips before returning to focus on the tumult in her eyes. "Want to see the carriage house?"

"I do."

They walked across the backyard patio and the patch of weeds and grass to the long narrow building. "How large is it?"

"Six hundred square feet."

He opened the door on a large single room that was

dusty and filled with crap. She propped her hands on her hips. "What's all this?"

"Stuff from previous renters. It can all go tomorrow when the junk haulers come."

She looked around, considering. "It has a tiny bathroom and shower."

While she saw that as a plus, he did not. He poked his head into the miniscule room, too, beside hers. "Can one person even stand in that?"

She turned her head sideways, sizing him up. They were close enough to kiss. Had they been into that. "Maybe not someone with broad shoulders who is also over six feet three inches tall," she said.

He chuckled. They eased out of the room and back into their own personal space. She wet her lips, still thinking. "There's also room for a fridge, another sink and a hot plate, too."

He hoped she wasn't suggesting she live out here? The idea was for them to be pals, under the same roof, not simply sharing a yard. Tamping down his emotions, he asked casually, "You want to cook out here?"

She shrugged, her feisty independence wrapping around her like an invisible force field. "If I'm super busy, sure. Besides, it's not like the appliances over there—" Mackenzie pointed to the main house "—were all that great. I mean, I haven't seen olive-green appliances and orange wallpaper anywhere since photos from the 1980s."

"I'll work on that," Griff promised. How hard could it be to take off wallpaper anyway? They could also hire someone to do it.

She turned to study him, the same critical way she had just been looking over their surroundings. "You really want this to work, don't you?" she asked.

He nodded. Figuring as long as they were being honest… "But you're wary. Why?"

Worry clouding her expression, she admitted thickly, "Probably because of what happened the last and only other time I lived with a guy."

"Scott."

"Skip," she corrected.

"You were going to marry him."

"Until I realized the only thing he really wanted was a maid and a personal assistant." She sobered. "I don't ever want to be in that position again. Where I feel like what I can do for someone means more to them than I do."

Griff clenched his jaw. He had wanted to punch out her ex then; the feeling was the same now. Where had the jerk gotten off, treating her that way? he wondered furiously.

Determined to keep her from focusing on past hurt, he pointed out dryly, "Well, you'll be safe here, Mack. Because I would never ask you to pick up my dry cleaning. Or shine my shoes."

She tilted her head, as if to say, *I know that.* "Stop joking. I'm serious. If we do this, we have to be like ships that pass in the night. I mean, no coordinating our daily schedules or planning meals around each other. We just go on like normal, and if we happen to be hungry at the same time and want to order pizza, we can, but we don't have to do everything together if we don't want to."

"Gee. Sugarcoat it, why don't you, Mack?"

"You know what I mean," she insisted.

He sobered, too, aware that no guy had gotten past the barricades around her heart in quite a while. Although he wasn't sure why that should bother him so much. It wasn't as if he were trying to make a move on her. "I promise. But can we also agree that…ah…we won't engage in any romantic dalliances around each other?" The thought of finding her with another guy was like a punch to the solar plexus. "Because that would be uncomfortable."

She exhaled in relief. "Agreed." She lifted a delicate palm. "If we want to hook up with someone we'll have to go elsewhere."

He nodded and shoved his hands in the pockets of his suit pants. "Not that you'll have to worry about that anytime soon when it comes to me."

Her answering smile was quick and sexy. "Still haven't found anyone else you want to date?" she said.

"Nope." He zeroed in on her long-lashed blue eyes, figuring as long as she knew his status he should know hers. "You?"

She shook her head. "Too busy."

That was good, he thought. They had enough on their agendas for the moment, managing their mutual moves, and setting up space together. "Back to this place... We've got forty-eight hours before they list it on the rental market. So, if we want it, we need to let them know, put down a deposit and sign a lease by tomorrow."

"What do you think, Bliss?" she asked, while her mountain dog wagged her tail between them. The canine's happiness was clear. "I want it," she said firmly, looking Griff in the eye.

Masculine satisfaction roared through him. "So do I," he admitted gruffly. Grinning, they bumped fists and triumphantly held each other's glance. "Looks like we're going to be roommates, after all," he said.

Chapter Two

"Wow. Don't you look…different," Luanne, Mackenzie's college-age employee, said, catching sight of her as she walked into the commercial storage unit. Her husband Lenny nodded in agreement.

Mackenzie smiled at the couple fondly. The newlyweds worked twenty hours a week for her, putting up and taking down signs.

"I have to go downtown to meet Griff and sign the lease for our new place," Mackenzie explained, handing over their to-do list.

Carson, Hale, Shelton and Strickland was a pretty fancy place. She didn't want to embarrass Griff. Hence, gone were the paint-splattered jeans, loose-fitting denim work shirt and sneakers she'd had on earlier. In their place were a formfitting turquoise dress, white cotton jacket and heels suitable for a downtown law office.

The TCU students exchanged speculative grins.

"We're just friends," Mackenzie repeated.

Eyes widened. "Mmm-hmm." They obviously didn't believe it.

Mackenzie opened the tailgate on her truck and pushed on. "Do you two think you can handle all the deliveries and pickups this weekend? I'm set to move on Saturday and Sunday. But…if you need my help, I can put some of it off for a few days."

"We've got it." Lenny lifted the newly painted signs from the truck bed and set them in the back of his own van.

"You just concentrate on getting yourself and Bliss settled in the new place." Already on task, Luanne pointed out the next bunch to be loaded.

Knowing the young couple had yet to let her down, Mackenzie headed out. Traffic was light for a Thursday afternoon. Because it was close to 5:00 p.m.—closing time for many workplaces—she had no trouble finding a space in the parking garage.

Still, she was full of the jitters as she made her way down the concrete sidewalks, and up to the second highest floor of the Fort Worth high-rise. Was she making a mistake by moving in with Griff? Would familiarity breed contempt…and ruin their long-standing friendship? She had to face it. She had no idea if he liked his toothpaste cap on, or off… Not that it mattered, since they definitely would *not* be sharing a bathroom.

"Griff is still with a client," the receptionist told her.

"Not a problem," managing partner Joe Carson said, coming toward her, his footsteps echoing on the marble floors. Tall and lanky, with cropped salt-and-pepper hair, he was both affable and intimidating. Rimless glasses covered his assessing eyes. "I'll entertain Mackenzie until he's finished."

She released the breath she barely knew she'd been holding.

"So how have you been?" Joe asked, as he took her by the elbow.

"Really good."

"Glad to hear it." Joe led her down a long hall, into another elevator and up one floor into the spacious utopia where the senior partners worked and entertained clients.

Mackenzie had toured the plush offices during company parties, as Griff's guest. But she had never been invited to come in and sit. "You really don't have to entertain me," she said. The last thing she wanted to do was inconvenience the older attorney.

"Actually, I've been wanting to talk to you privately," Joe replied solemnly. He inclined his head at one of the straight-backed chairs in front of his desk.

Feeling a little like she had just been called to the principal's office, Mackenzie sat dutifully, tucking her skirt in around her knees. "About?"

Joe crossed one ankle over the other and leaned against the front of his desk. "I understand the two of you are moving in together. Does this mean you're serious? Thinking about marriage or getting engaged? Or just want a trial run?"

Wow, he was being direct! "Aren't these questions you should be asking Griff?" She kept her tone as casual as possible.

He acquiesced with a nod. "Already have." His look sobered all the more. "I wanted to hear what you have to say."

Mackenzie's heart thudded in her chest. She hadn't felt this off-kilter since she had met her first set of foster parents. And she'd had the then fourteen-year-old Griff to ease the way.

"Why?" she asked, figuring if Joe could be blunt she could, too.

"Griff is not just my mentee. He's like a son to me. I want him to be happy."

Her spine stiffened. She and Griff had nothing to hide. "So do I."

Joe surveyed her thoughtfully. "I also think he deserves to be surrounded by a big, loving family, and would make a great dad…"

Mackenzie agreed whole-heartedly. Griff would make a fantastic father someday! Not that he seemed headed in that direction anytime soon…

Joe Carson frowned before continuing affably, "But he's not getting any younger. So, if kids are going to be in the picture, he's got to get going on that."

It seemed that Griff's mentor was intimating that she was getting in the way of that! Mackenzie flushed. Sincerely, she admitted, "I want that for him, too." It sucked that he had been raised by a single mom and orphaned at age twelve, and been without legit family ties ever since.

Joe studied her. "So…you're not the hold up then?"

Not in the sense that she was refusing to marry Griff or have kids with him, no. But not sure how to actually answer that without revealing information her best friend would not want disclosed, Mackenzie folded her arms in front of her. "What does any of this have to do with Griff's job here?" she asked crisply.

"If Griff is going to have the kind of high-powered career he wants, he's going to need a lot of love and support in his personal life."

Mackenzie guessed where this was going. "And by that you mean married?" Instead of just living together.

Joe paused. "Not necessarily."

"Then…?" She regarded him in confusion.

"To become a senior partner, you have to show evidence of an ability to commit. To give something or someone your all, through thick and thin."

The way people did when they exchanged marriage vows, Mackenzie thought.

"Or in other words, this isn't a firm that expects to be a revolving door for associates," Joe continued. "We consider all one hundred and fifty of our employees to be family, and we take care of them as such. In return, we expect the same kind of loyalty."

She took a bolstering breath. "Why would you think Griff couldn't give you that?"

Joe inclined his head. "In the last ten years, he was serious about a woman, twice. Once in law school, once in the years after. Yet when it came time to commit, he shied away. Now... He's been bringing you to firm functions for the last three years. But instead of putting a ring on your finger, he's announced the two of you are going to be sharing space. And the way he put his announcement, I have to tell you," Joe continued, looking gravely concerned now, "it didn't sound all that romantic a proposition."

That was because it wasn't, Mackenzie thought.

His brow furrowed. "Which makes me wonder if the presumably 'casual' relationship the two of you are in is a good or a bad thing."

It wasn't the first time this had been said to her. Mackenzie's family was of the "fish or cut bait" line of thinking, too.

But that was because they didn't understand what she and Griff had concluded about themselves—that marriage wasn't necessarily going to be the key to their individual happiness—career success was.

Joe moved away from his desk. "Let me show you something."

He led the way out of his office and down the hall, past several closed doors with engraved gold nameplates, to an empty office. Although smaller than Joe's, it too had a glorious view of the city. "This is where our new senior partner will sit," Joe said.

"It's big." Four times the size of Griff's eight-by-ten-foot office on the floor below.

"It also comes with a heavy responsibility. Senior partners are expected to bring in a lot of new business and clients. That means a lot of wining, dining and persuading. They also have to assign and oversee work done by the junior partners, associates and paralegals on their team. When they do go to court, or settlement talks, they are first chair. Not second. That's a lot of work and a lot of pressure."

Enough to give her hives. Which was why she wasn't a big-time lawyer, rapidly on her way up the career ladder. She promised firmly, "Griff is up to it."

"He will still need someone on the home front, to have his back. To be there at the end of a rough week and accompany him to all of the firm's business and social events. Traditionally, that's been a spouse, but the support system could also be a large close extended family, who lives nearby."

Mackenzie felt an arrow to her heart. "Except Griff doesn't have that," she said sadly, mourning the unfairness of it all. He should have been adopted after he had been orphaned, same as her.

"Right. And since he has no family, it makes it more important than ever that he have someone he can count on." Joe looked at her sternly.

Not for the first time, Mackenzie realized she was in

a position to give Griff the kind of steady support he had given her when she had first entered the foster care system. "I will make sure Griff gets whatever he wants or needs," she promised Joe. Just the way he always did the same for her. After all, what else were best friends for? "I will always be there for him," she stressed, meaning it with all her heart.

Joe sized her up. "Then maybe it's time you demonstrated an ability to move on from the casual relationship and really commit, too."

"What was that all about?" Griff asked a few minutes later, looking handsome as ever in his suit and tie. He shut the door to his compact office where the lease sat front and center on his desk.

Mackenzie was still wrestling with her guilt. Had Joe been right? Was their friendship standing in the way of Griff getting what he wanted and deserved in this life?

Trying not to think how much he had done for her over the years, and how little she had done for him in comparison, Mackenzie drew an enervating breath.

Of course, it hadn't been her fault in the beginning. Four years older than her, he'd been the one with the experience. The one to show her how to survive in foster care when she'd been cruelly orphaned and unexpectedly separated from all seven of her siblings for a little over two years. She wouldn't have survived the heart-wrenching experience without him. Had he not stepped in to be her friend and self-appointed protector.

"Did Joe say something to you?"

She forced a smile, quipped, "Besides asking me when I was going to make an honest man of you?"

Looking chagrined, Griff swore softly to himself. "He really said that?"

Mackenzie tilted her head in sassy acknowledgment. "Ah. More or less. And he had a point. You do deserve a lot, and our moving in together could get in the way of that."

"Our moving in together isn't getting in the way of *anything*," Griff said brusquely.

He handed her the lease for their new rental.

Mackenzie sat with her hand poised over the pages. For both of their sakes, she forced herself to continue, "I think Joe really wants you to be married."

Griff scoffed and tugged at the knot of his tie. "To you, maybe."

Feeling less ready to sign the lease than ever, she set the pen down. "He said that to you?" Just now, she'd gotten the feeling that Joe *didn't* approve of her because she wasn't stampeding his mentee to the altar.

Griff's lips thinned. "Let's just say he thinks I would be a fool to let you get away or be romanced by someone else. Because I didn't act fast enough in presenting you with a ring and a marriage proposal."

"What did he say to you about us moving in together?"

Griff braced his hands on his waist and sized her up with a glance. "Honestly?"

Without warning, Mackenzie's heart began to pound. "Yes."

His broad shoulders flexing, Griff exhaled. "He doesn't approve."

Mackenzie picked up the pen and turned it end over end. There had always been a lot about Griff she hadn't quite understood, and that feeling was amplified now. Mostly because he kept his deepest feelings to himself. "Is that going to hurt your chances for senior partner?"

Back in matter-of-fact attorney mode, he pointed out the places where she had to sign. No less determined to go through with their plan to bunk together. "It will hurt my chances of being invited to The Heart of Texas retreat the first weekend in April," he admitted smoothly. He waited while she scanned the document and added her signature. "Although I wasn't likely to be invited without a spouse or a fiancée anyway. And without attending that…"

Mackenzie guessed, "There's no way you'll make senior partner this time around?"

Inscrutable emotion came and went in his mesmerizing amber eyes. "Probably not. Although there is always a first time for everything, and they could still invite me to attend the event solo."

He had certainly earned it, Mackenzie thought fiercely, thinking of the thousands of hours he had put into his work at the firm over the last decade. Still… "Wouldn't that be uncomfortable for you? Since it's all couples stuff?"

Briefly, his expression turned brooding. He turned away. "It wouldn't be the first time I've been the odd man out."

Also true. Her heart aching for him, she recalled the adoption fairs they'd both had to attend while in the foster care system. She'd eventually gotten chosen by Carol and Robert Lockhart, and reunited with her other orphaned siblings. But Griff had never been chosen. He'd shrugged off the rejection. People wanted little kids. He was too big. Too old. Too independent to want to adapt to someone else's family system anyway.

But it had still hurt back then.

And she sensed it still hurt now.

She got out her checkbook to pay her half of the security deposit and first month's rent. "How many are in the running for this senior partner position?"

Griff found his checkbook, too. "Three."

"Anyone have an edge?"

"Well," he said with a grimace, "the other two are both married."

She groaned.

Griff nodded, sharing in the frustration. "I know," he said softly. "But it's not the end of the world." He looked out the window, growing emotionally distant again. "I've been thinking about starting my own firm anyway."

She thought about him leaving the only professional home he had ever known. Leaving Joe. Who was the closest thing to a father figure that Griff had. "You'd really do that?" she asked, her heart going out to him.

He shrugged. "It depends on how much I can earn and save, between now and then, and how much profit I could get out of my condo, if I sell it once the renovations are done. But—" Griff's features tightened "—if it were the only way to move up. Yeah. Sure, I would."

But he didn't seem to *want* to do that, Mackenzie noted. And knowing firsthand how hard it had been to get her own business up and running, she wouldn't advise anyone to take such a big leap unless they were all in. In every way.

He handed her a piece of paper with the amounts written on it.

Determined to help him come up with a way to stay at *Carson, Hale, Shelton and Strickland*, she wrote out both checks. Then asked, "When will there be another opening for a promotion?"

Griff paced his small cubicle office restlessly. "Unless someone retires or resigns unexpectedly, which isn't likely, three years."

No wonder Joe had said Griff wasn't getting any younger. He'd be thirty-seven by then, and she'd be thirty-three. That was a long time for him to sit, cooling his heels. For something that might not come in the end anyway if he were not married.

Their fingers brushed momentarily as she handed him the checks. Skin tingling, and trying not to think about what it would be like if he ever *really* touched her, she asked, "Could you go somewhere else? Like another big or even midsize firm?"

"I could try."

"But?"

Griff strode toward the window. The illumination from the setting sun caught the faint shimmer of copper in his chestnut hair. "It would be unlikely for me to be recruited as a senior partner without already being one here for at least a few years. So I'd have to prove myself all over again. And they'd have their own ideas about what is needed to move up in their hierarchy." He flattened his lips into a grim line. "Meanwhile, I'd be expected to try to convince as many of my current clients as possible to make the move with me, so I'd be burning all my bridges here..."

Mackenzie let out a tremulous breath. "Joe would be angry and hurt."

"Yes."

And Griff clearly didn't want that.

She sighed. "He didn't come right out and say it to me, but Joe really wants you to get this promotion." Griff nodded and Mackenzie pushed on, her frustration mounting as quickly as her empathy. "The worst thing is, you'd probably get it right now, if you were married."

He smiled the way he always did when she jumped fiercely to his defense. "That's kind of a moot point," he told her quietly. "But...you're right. If I do want to stay here to make my mark in the legal world, maybe I do need to change my mind about that."

He'd been saying since his last breakup that marriage wasn't for him, and Mackenzie understood. Because she didn't think it was in the cards for her, either.

"How do you propose to make that happen?" she asked, adding impulsively, "Especially if you're living with me and Bliss."

He shrugged, unconcerned. "Leave it to the professionals, I guess."

Professionals? Mackenzie flushed.

He chided her with a look. "Get your mind out of the gutter, Mack. I'm referring to matchmakers who specialize in finding guys like me an executive wife."

The thought of Griff with another woman was like a punch to her gut. It had been hard enough when he had been dating those other two women, and he'd been seriously emotionally involved with them. Something like this would not only *not* involve love of any kind, even the familial type she shared with him, but the union would be based solely on the money and status he'd accrued.

She stared at him. "Tell me you're joking," she pleaded.

His expression said he was not. He kept his eyes locked with hers, loosened the knot of his tie. "I'm thinking outside the box here, Mack. And if it's the only way to get ahead…"

Although he seemed completely at ease with the notion, Mackenzie couldn't imagine him marrying someone who did not have his best interests at heart, and any woman who married him for financial gain would definitely not want what was best for him!

She pushed to her feet and watched as he undid the first two buttons on his shirt. "It's not." She would not let it be!

He disagreed with a lift of his brow. "Joe wouldn't have pulled you aside and talked to you and tried to get you on board with this scenario if he didn't think that to succeed here, I am going to have to prove my ability to commit to the rest of the senior partners, and get married."

"Well, you can't hire someone to find you a wife! Not when your colleagues already think you're involved with me, and have been for the last three years. Because then you'd look less stable than ever."

Griff rubbed a hand beneath his jaw. "I suppose you're right. I hadn't considered that…"

"Did you consider what they'd think when you told everyone we were moving in together?"

Another shrug, this one even more offhand. "I didn't think they'd care, not in this day and age."

Nor had she, really.

He squinted at her, considering. "What did your folks think?"

"Um, I haven't told them."

He did a double take. "Really."

She waved off his concern. "Well, they're a little old-fashioned in some ways." A lot, actually.

"*Are* you going to tell them?" he prodded.

"Eventually."

He edged closer, his brisk, masculine fragrance washing over her. "When?"

"I don't know! It doesn't matter."

He regarded her speculatively, once again understanding her all too well. "Doesn't it?"

"You're the one with the problems that need to be solved," she grumbled irritably, ignoring the warmth of his body so close to hers. "And that means we're…

I mean, *you're*…stuck sharing an address with me unless you want to back out of our deal."

His mouth quirked in masculine satisfaction. "No. I'm not doing that. I want to be with you and Bliss."

She wanted to be with him, too. More so than she had planned on. And yet… "I never would have agreed to this if I had thought it was going to hurt you," she admitted.

He brushed off her concern with customary ease. "It's just a title."

"And a big bump in salary and reward for all your hard work thus far," she corrected.

His handsome jaw took on that stubborn tilt she knew so well. "Listen, Mack, if I don't get it now there is always next time. Or maybe not. But in any event, I can be happy on less." He flashed a rueful grin. "It's not like I've ever had everything I want anyway. No one does."

True, but… Her heart ached for him. "You've had less than most." Her voice came out just above a whisper.

For a second, he looked touched by her worry. Then his expression shuttered, and he pretended to play the violin with comic intensity.

She hated it when he made jokes when they were really opening up to each other. "I'm serious, Griff!" She caught him by the biceps and stopped his miming. His muscles swelled beneath her fingertips. She kept her eyes on his. "It hurts me to see you get less than you deserve!"

He tensed. Stepped away from her. "Again, that's not your problem, Mack."

Which was, ironically, the same thing he'd said to her all those years ago when she'd lamented the lack of interest potential adoptive parents had in him. Then, she'd been just a kid herself and been unable to help him be more successful in the adoption fairs. But now… Maybe there was something she could do! "If you were able to quickly get married before the partners decide on who they are going to promote..."

He cut her off with a lift of his palm. "I thought we agreed hiring a matchmaker wasn't a viable option now that you and I are moving in together."

And it still wasn't, Mackenzie thought, as inspiration hit with lightning speed. She smiled at him triumphantly, knowing their dilemma had just been solved. "You're not going to need one, Griff. Not when you have *me*."

His brow furrowed. "Don't even think about trying to fix me up with someone," he warned.

It was her turn to behave in comic fashion. Determined to keep this situation as casual and practical as it needed to be, she splayed her hand across her heart and batted her lashes at him. "Not even little ole me?" she teased in her best Southern belle fashion.

He grinned, amused. "As...?"

Still hamming it up, she indulged in a sweeping curtsey. "The aforementioned roommate and potential bride. In name only, of course," she added hastily, at his shock.

Sobering, she continued with quiet deliberation, "Not that anyone else would ever know that."

Still looking completely stunned, but not exactly averse to the idea, she realized in relief, he sat down. "You're proposing a marriage of convenience," he concluded in a low husky drawl.

"I don't see that we have any other choice. You and I are going to be living together. Your managing partner doesn't approve with our one foot out the door approach. But Joe made it pretty clear he *would* approve of you getting married to me. So, since we're already really good friends, and planning to share a house anyway, why not take it one step further and make it legal?"

He regarded her in awe. "You're seriously proposing?" he rasped, his voice thick with emotion.

She seriously was. Sitting down opposite him, she crossed her legs at the knee. "I want to help you obtain that promotion. And be there for you while you make the transition to senior partner." The way he needed her to be. Even if he didn't realize it yet.

Griff's gaze drifted over her face, his eyes holding hers for a long, discomfiting moment. "What happens if we get married, and then I don't get offered the senior partner slot, after all?"

He seemed to be asking if she would be disappointed in him. Regret what they'd done. The answer? Hell no!

Mackenzie drew a deep breath. With effort, she kept herself from doing what she really wanted to do, which was take him all the way in her arms and hug him close. "Well, then we would both know we'd given it our best effort. The point is, Griff, you have always helped me when I've been uncertain or felt out of my depth, or just needed a good friend by my side. And I'm tired of doing more taking than giving in our relationship." Tired of feeling guilty about it, too. When she had so much in terms of family, and he had so little. She lifted her chin. "So…how about this one time…you let me help you?"

To Mackenzie's disappointment, for a long moment, Griff didn't say anything at all. Instead, he shoved his hand through his hair. Stood. Ripped his tie all the way off. Began to pace. "I feel like I'd be taking advantage," he growled finally.

Ignoring the fluttering in her middle, she trod closer. "You wouldn't be," she promised firmly. "Unless—" she felt a momentary twinge of panic, as the next thought hit "—we're not talking about sex, are we?"

Another pause. This one even harder to read. His gaze

drifted over her leisurely before returning to her face. "Not unless you *want* to talk about sex."

"No." She felt herself flush bright red. "I mean if... No."

"Okay." Griff exhaled slowly, his expression still inscrutable, then he adapted the expression he always wore when talking business. He dropped into his desk chair, deep frown lines bracketing his mouth. "But you understand that if we're going to do this, then we still have to make it look as genuine as we can, in every conceivable way."

She leaned against the front of his desk, facing him. "Meaning act like we're husband and wife."

Their thighs were nearly touching. "And love each other."

She peered at him closely. "Well, we *do* love each other, just...not in that way."

He rocked back in his chair, his long legs stretched out in front of him, looking sexy as all get-out. "True."

Another silence fell. She could see him thinking. Calculating. The way he always did when he was about to leap into something.

He gazed at her. Then stood, towering over her once again. "So how do you want to handle this? Get a diamond ring, then announce our engagement?"

"Honestly?" Mackenzie let out a slow breath.

He nodded, encouraging her to go on.

"I think we should just get hitched."

Chapter Three

"Are you sure this is what you want to do?" Griff asked Mackenzie early Friday afternoon. He cast a skeptical eye at J.P. Randall's Bait & Tackle Shop in the rural Texas county where she had spent the second half of her childhood. The one-story white building was halfway between Lake Laramie and town, and a popular stop for tourists and locals alike.

The sign next to the door said: Bait, fresh and frozen for sale. Groceries, beer, coolers and ice available. Spare tires repaired. Wedding licenses issued. Ceremonies performed.

She told herself it was the unexpected heat of the spring day making her sweat. "If we're going to elope in Laramie, this is where it has to be."

He lifted a skeptical brow.

Mackenzie ignored the heat of awareness rising up between them and forced herself to return his level gaze. "It's sort of a tradition for the young and reckless."

He chuckled, his eyes lighting up with customary good humor. "Is that what we are?" he teased. "Young and reckless?"

Mackenzie inhaled the scent of man, and an abundance of green spring grass and wildflowers from the fields around them. Knowing she had her hands full just getting through the legalities ahead, Mackenzie promised silkily, "Guaranteed, we will be deemed that when word gets out what we've done."

Gathering her courage around her, she strode to the door.

The bell chimed as they entered the half-century old convenience shop. A lanky twentysomething man with spiky red hair stood behind the counter. He turned down the Darius Rucker song playing on the sound system and extended his hand. "J.P. Randall the fourth. What can I do for you?"

Looking calm as could be, Griff introduced himself then said, "We want to get married."

"Right now, if possible," Mackenzie added, her heart beginning to race wildly in her chest.

"No problem. Do you have rings?" J.P. asked.

Griff clamped a hand over her shoulders and drew her close to his side. Without warning, she began to tingle all over.

"We've got them as well as the license." He produced it from his pocket. They'd attained it earlier in the week, from the county clerk in Fort Worth. And that, at least, had been a very businesslike transaction.

J.P. studied the license. "You passed the seventy-two hours requirement, so that means you're good to go!" Taking in the two of them, he grinned. Then picked up his cell phone and texted. "My wife, Sheila, can be our witness."

J.P. waved them to the back of the store as a pretty, pregnant, dark-haired young woman joined them. Sheila stepped over to the intercom control system. "What kind of music do y'all want?" she asked. "We've got Elvis Presley's 'Love Me Tender.' The traditional 'Here Comes the Bride.' And Dierks Bentley's 'Breathe You In.'"

"Dierks Bentley," they said in unison.

Grinning, Sheila confessed shyly, "J.P. and I got married to that, too..."

Oh, dear. This was beginning to feel a little too romantic! "Now what do you want to do about the vows?" J.P. asked, pulling out some worn typed pages.

"What are the choices?" Mackenzie responded, suddenly in a hurry to get this over with.

J.P. cleared his throat. "The traditional. I take thee, so and so..."

"Or," Sheila suggested wistfully, "you could both recite the E. E. Cummings poem, 'I Carry Your Heart With Me.'"

"Oh," Mackenzie said before she could stop herself, "I love that poem!"

Griff, never one for poetry, looked perplexed. "Want to use it?"

Suddenly feeling on the verge of tears she couldn't explain and definitely did not want, Mackenzie shook her head. "Um, no."

"It's so romantic!" Sheila looked disappointed.

Exactly the problem. This wasn't a traditional union. Merely a path for Griff to get the opportunities and the future he deserved. She had to remember that. "What else is there?" she asked.

"Well," J.P. boasted proudly. "I wrote some modern ones."

"We'll use those," Mackenzie decided.

J.P. looked at Griff who had yet to weigh in.

Ever the diligent attorney, he reminded her, "You haven't even read them yet."

Mackenzie waved off his caution. "I'm sure they will be perfect for the occasion."

J.P. beamed. He handed one page to Griff, another copy to Mackenzie, with the instructions, "Look at your beloved and then read the first stanza."

Mackenzie smiled. In a real hurry now to get this over with, she looked back down, reciting even as she read, "'What is mine is mine, what is yours is yours, what is ours is ours.'" Oh, Lord. It was all she could do not to laugh. J.P. didn't know how on target he was!

The young man pointed to Griff who was surprisingly poker-faced, if one discounted the new sparkle of amusement in his eyes.

"Your turn," J.P. ordered.

Griff did the same, his low, sexy voice sending a shiver up her spine. And causing another to quiver low in her belly.

"Now the next paragraph," J.P. said solemnly.

Doing her best to hang on to her composure, Mackenzie wet her lips. "'Yesterday was really great, today is even better, and tomorrow will be even more—'" she paused momentarily to inhale a deep breath "'—delightful.'"

With a frown, J.P. interrupted. "I know that's the wrong last word, but I haven't found the right one yet. But feel free to substitute if you want."

Feeling the sooner this was over the better, Mackenzie brushed off the opportunity. "It's fine."

"Now for the rings," J.P. stated officially. "You put them on each other." He looked at them and waited.

Griff frowned. "We don't say anything while we do it?"

"No." The young man cocked his head at them. "It's self-explanatory." He motioned for them to continue.

Griff stepped closer, deliberately invading her space. Aware that she had never been more attracted to him than she was at that very moment, Mackenzie slid the ring on Griff. His palm felt big and rough and warm in hers. So warm and masculine in fact she felt her knees go weak.

He looked her up and down with lazy male confidence. Never breaking eye contact, he took her hand in his and slid the wedding band over her finger. The touch of his hand brushing her skin was even more unbearably sensual.

Heart pounding, legs trembling, Mackenzie started to step back, but Griff caught her palm in his and held on tight.

"Yeah," J.P. said, gazing on approvingly, "you can't forget that."

"Forget what?" Mackenzie started to say.

Then Griff's lips were locked on hers in an overwhelmingly deep, seductive kiss that took her breath away. He clasped her head between his hands, lazily and possessively extending the embrace. And, in return, she melted against him, completely caught up in the warm, minty taste of his mouth, the unhurried pressure of his lips and the liquid stroking of his tongue. The hardness of his chest pressed against the softness of her breasts, and lower still, he was even harder. Demonstrating how much he wanted her. Her pulse increased at the realization, while inside her own desire swirled and caught flame.

She had always dreamed it could be like this, but never really imagined it would. Even if it was all for show...

Mackenzie was dizzy as their kiss came to an end. Griff looked just as stunned.

"You-all are *awesome*," J.P. said, when they finally drew apart.

Mackenzie's knees were shaking. The rest of her was hot and aching.

"That kiss was just so romantic!" Sheila swooned. She held up her phone. "Can I take your picture and put it up on the board and maybe on our social media page?"

J.P. enthused, "We're really trying to grow our wedding business." He pointed to the other photos of happy couples.

Griff shrugged. Mackenzie knew what he was thinking. The chances of any of his coworkers ever coming out this way were nil. Ditto them seeing the bait and tackle shop's social media page. Unless Griff told them where they had tied the knot, and she knew he would not.

She gave her permission. Reluctantly, Griff nodded, too. "But can you wait an hour to post it until I've had a chance to tell my parents that we eloped?" Mackenzie asked, beginning to feel nervous again. "I wouldn't want them to hear it from anyone else."

Actually, if truth be told, she would rather them not know this at all. But Griff had insisted if they were going to do this it had to be as real as possible. And that meant fessing up to her folks.

"Well, *that* was an adventure," Griff remarked fifteen minutes later, when they got back in his Porsche, newly hitched, goodie bag courtesy of J.P. and Sheila in tow.

"Wasn't it?" Mackenzie retorted lightly, surprised to

realize she felt just a tiny bit married to the man beside her. Which was ridiculous. Since this was a favor to her very close guy friend, that was all.

Because Griff seemed to expect her to say more, Mackenzie rambled on nervously. "The only thing that would have made it more memorable was if Bliss had been here with us." But she was being boarded at her favorite doggy day care for the weekend, while they took care of the wedding first, and then their mutual moves.

Griff grinned, his affection for her pet apparent. "You've got a point there. We could have made her the ring bearer and flower girl simultaneously."

Mackenzie laughed at the thought, her tension easing.

Griff glanced down at the silver gift bag with the logo WEDDINGS BY J.P. on it. "What's in the goodie bag?"

"Good question." Mackenzie untied the ribbon closure and peered inside. "A tiny bottle of prosecco and a couple of clear plastic cups shaped like champagne flutes, some protein bars and a couple of energy drinks. And er—" she felt the heat in her cheeks rise "—um...*other*... honeymoon essentials," she finished in a low, strangled tone.

"Like what?" he asked, perplexed.

Too embarrassed to identify them, she merely handed him the bag. He steered to the side of the otherwise empty country road, braked and looked inside the bag.

As he caught sight of the condoms, lubricants and other scented lotions, he said, "Oh." His eyebrows lifted in surprise. "Wow."

"Yeah." Mackenzie snatched the bag back. She stuffed it in the floor well, next to her feet. "Suffice it to say, let's *not* let my parents see that."

Big hands still on the steering wheel, Griff tilted his head. "Think they'd be shocked?"

"I don't know." *And I don't want to find out*, Mackenzie thought, falling silent, as she turned her attention to the scenery.

Griff found it ironic, since he had been the one to teach Mackenzie how to keep her guard up when she had first landed in foster care, that there were times like now when all he wanted to do was bring those same walls crashing down. To find out what was really going on behind her deliberately cheerful demeanor. 'Cause he could have sworn, when they were saying their vows, that her emotions were all over the map.

Just as his were starting to be...

Which was strange, because this was a business deal, born out of friendship, just like their decision to share space.

But figuring they had other issues to figure out now, like how they were going to announce what they had just done, to his boss and her family, he asked, "Are you planning to call your parents?"

"No. I told them to expect me at the ranch and that I'd be bringing you with me. So when we get to the next four-way stop, you're going to want to take a left and get on the highway that leads out to their ranch."

Griff inhaled the scent of her perfume. "You sure you don't want to give them a heads-up first?"

"Nope."

He wasn't sure that was smart.

She waved an airy hand. "As long as they don't know the real reason behind our nuptials, I am sure they will be fine with it. Since they want all of their kids to be married anyway."

But would her folks want her hitched to *him*? Griff wondered as a long-held uncertainty rose up to haunt him.

* * *

Twenty-five minutes later, they reached the entrance to the Circle L Ranch. Split-rail fences lined the long drive up to the main house. The sprawling, two-story white stone abode sported a light charcoal roof and cedar shutters, and had a western farmhouse vibe that perfectly suited the renowned ten-thousand-acre cattle ranch. No sooner had he parked in the circular driveway in front of the house than the front door opened and Carol and Robert Lockhart walked out.

They were a handsome couple in their early fifties. The denim-dress-clad social worker and her jeans wearing cowboy-husband bore the endless energy one would expect from a couple who had adopted eight siblings, aged three to fourteen, simultaneously.

It was also clear from the calm, relaxed expressions on their faces, they had absolutely no idea what was coming.

Mackenzie's parents hugged her and shook Griff's hand. "What a wonderful surprise!" Carol exclaimed.

"We've got an even better one," Mackenzie said, as they all walked inside and gathered on the twin sofas flanking the big white stone fireplace.

She looked directly at her mom and dad, then reached over and took Griff's hand in hers. Though not discernible to the eye, he felt the unusual dampness of her palm and the tremble of her fingers. She squeezed once, as if for courage, then let go. "Griff and I just eloped."

Her parents' glances cut to their left hands, and the matching gold bands. A long pause followed. "In Vegas?" her mom said.

"Actually, at J.P. Randall's," Mackenzie replied.

Another beat of silence fell. Her mom and dad reached for each other's hands, too. "Congratulations," they said in unison.

A pleat formed between Mackenzie's brows. She leaned forward earnestly. "You don't look surprised."

She seemed disappointed about that, Griff noted. Which made him wonder if she'd had another ulterior motive for wanting to wed him, aside from the desire to help him accelerate his career.

Carol and Robert exchanged glances. "We always knew there was something special between the two of you," her mom said finally.

"But we have to ask," Robert interjected, suddenly going all fatherly on them.

Carol's glance cut to her daughter's midriff. "Is there a reason you were in such a hurry?"

Mackenzie's mouth opened in a round O of surprise. She flushed, just like she had after he had kissed her. Griff couldn't help but be reminded of the way it had felt to hold her in his arms. Or how much he'd wanted, in that breath-stealing moment, to make her his.

He had always known he was attracted to her, on a basic male-female level. She was so damn gorgeous every man with even a glimmer of testosterone would be, too. But he hadn't ever been going to act on it. Wouldn't have if an end of ceremony kiss hadn't been required. But once he had tasted the sweetness of her lips and felt her against him, he had known it wasn't just a biological thing. No, what he had felt, what they had discovered, was more than that.

A hell of a lot more than that.

"Mom, Dad, for heaven's sake! Of course not!" Mackenzie vehemently discounted any possibility of pregnancy.

Carol and Robert shrugged, as if to say these things happen. And if they had, they were not going to judge.

Carol tilted her head. "Then why did you go to the bait and tackle shop?"

A pretty flush, that Griff knew emanated from guilt, filled Mackenzie's cheeks. He felt a little more of regret in that moment, too. "Ah...maybe it's a Laramie County tradition for anyone who doesn't want to wait?"

Apparently realizing her parents still weren't buying their story, she shifted in her seat, her knee pressing against his thigh. This time she seemed to be seeking courage from him. So Griff took it from there, explaining candidly, "We really wanted everything to be legal before we shared space."

"And since we're moving in together tomorrow," Mackenzie added, "we went ahead and got married today."

"Oh." Her parents murmured in unison, looking pleased about that much.

No surprise there, Griff noted. Most everyone his new in-laws' age liked formal commitment that ended in weddings.

"Well, there's no reason you still can't let us give you a proper wedding," her mom said.

Mackenzie paused. And he could see that she likely would have let her parents do just that had circumstances been otherwise.

Which in turn left him wondering if this was the right way to go, or a mistake. One that could still be undone.

"Thank you, but no," Mackenzie said stiffly. "Griff and I really don't want to deal with all that. Especially now when he is working so hard to make senior partner and I'm heading into my busy season with all the graduations and proms and weddings coming up."

She looked at her dad for support. "Weddings are certainly nice," Robert told them, "but it is the promises you make to each other, and the seriousness of your intentions that is most important, because you shouldn't get married unless it is for life."

Carol smiled in agreement. "I still think it is possible to have both," she demurred.

Mackenzie leaped to her feet. "And I think," she said with the evasiveness she showed whenever the talk got too close or too personal, "Griff and I really should be hitting the road."

Using the fact they both had movers coming the next day as her excuse, Mackenzie asked her parents to share the news with her siblings, and insisted they really had to leave. Although disappointed they weren't going to stay for dinner, Carol and Robert said they understood.

Short minutes later, she and Griff were on their way to Fort Worth, the packed picnic basket their mother had sent with them in tow. Once en route, life quickly went back to normal. Griff used his car phone to check in with his office, while she checked her messages on her cell, and texted instructions to her two part-time employees.

An hour into the trip, he suggested they stop at the rest area off the highway. She went into the concrete building to wash up. When she emerged, he was sitting down at a picnic table, thankfully one with the most privacy.

Wishing yet again she had Bliss with them, to comfort as well as distract, she joined him. He looked over at her. "You okay?"

Mackenzie opened the picnic hamper and began setting out the feast. "Why wouldn't I be?"

"You seem...upset...about the talk with your parents."

That was because she was, for reasons she couldn't begin to fathom. After all, the elopement and the conversation with her folks had gone pretty much as she ex-

pected. If you didn't consider the way Griff had kissed
her to seal their vows. Or her parents' questions about
the reasons behind their speedy elopement.

Pushing aside the memory of his hard body pressed
against hers, his lips ravishing hers, she deflected the
attention back onto him. "Are you telling me you're not
feeling a little bit annoyed or embarrassed by how pre-
sumptuous they were?"

"Because they jumped to the conclusion we were pregnant?"

We...

She liked the sound of that.

Too much.

"Well, that and the fact they always expected us to
get together, I mean," Mackenzie grumbled, feeling even
more emotional. Briefly, she met his eyes. "Where would
they even get an idea like that?" she asked hoarsely.

His gaze narrowed. In comparison, he seemed almost
too calm. He got out the silverware, too. "We have been
friends longer than either of us have had a relationship
with anyone else," he pointed out.

Mackenzie knew that was true. Part of it was that they
had been in foster care together, but she was closer to
Griff than she was to anyone else in her family. Still...

She harrumphed, hoping her parents' false assump-
tion hadn't made him anywhere near as uncomfortable
as it had made her. Because she didn't want anything
screwing up their friendship, especially now. When it
was about to get a lot more complicated.

She drew an invigorating breath. "That doesn't give
them the right to assume that we have had something romantic going on, ostensibly for years now."

Without warning, masculine satisfaction dominated

his expression. "Yet here we are," he said lazily. Mischief glimmered in his amber eyes. "Hitched."

Wondering if he were as ravenous as she was, given they hadn't eaten since midmorning, she unwrapped a luscious-looking brisket sandwich. And tried not to think how much she wanted to kiss him again. Just to see if it was as thrilling as she remembered. She forced herself back to the conversation and looked him right in the eye. "That's not my point."

Griff sobered, suddenly appearing as conflicted as she felt. "Then what is?" he asked, setting out the German potato salad.

Grateful for the tasks that diverted her attention from the mesmerizing depths of his eyes, she uncapped a bottle of peach iced tea and spread a paper napkin on her lap. "I just get irritated when people think they know me when they clearly don't," she finally admitted.

His regard gentled. "Go on."

Aware he could get her to fess up better than anyone, but there was still a lot even he didn't know, she divided a small cluster of red grapes in half. Deposited them on two picnic plates. "I'm just annoyed because I thought they would be stunned when we told them we had eloped."

"And yet they were okay with it."

More than okay. "They acted like they expected this to happen all along!" *Like they knew her better than she knew herself.* "And there was no way they could have predicted what we were going to do this week, because we didn't know what we were going to do until a few days ago!"

He set his half-eaten sandwich on his plate. "Would you have felt better if they had disapproved?" he asked, his expression deliberately mild. "Or told me I wasn't good enough for you?"

Darn it all, she had just hurt him without meaning to. Aware how many times he had been rejected at adoption fairs, when he was a foster kid, because he just didn't fit someone's preconceived notions about what an adoptive child should be, she said, "Of course not!"

His broad shoulders relaxed. He resumed eating. As did she. "Then I really don't see why you're so crabby," he told her. "I thought your parents were very gracious under the circumstances."

They had been. To a point anyway. "They asked if we were pregnant!"

Talking about sex with him made her heart do a little cartwheel in her chest.

"Others will probably jump to the same conclusion, Mack. Given how quickly we wed. Since that *is* usually the main reason behind shotgun weddings…" he continued, appearing both lawyerly and matter-of-fact.

"Not in our case!" Ignoring the telltale quiver in her tummy, Mackenzie tried—and failed—not to imagine what it would be like to actually make love with this handsome, sexy, funny and charming man.

One corner of his sensual lips quirked up. "So? They'll figure that out eventually. But if it bothers you…"

"It does." Mostly, because it made her first think and then yearn for something she might not ever have. A baby or babies of her own. Sired by Griff…

Her exasperated tone brought a provoking smile to his lips. "Then we'll just have to convince people we eloped for the *other* most popular reason," he countered.

Given the mischievous gleam in his eyes, she was almost afraid to ask. Fighting yet another self-conscious flush, she demanded, "Which is what?"

"That we've finally realized we're madly, passionately in love and we can't keep our hands off each other."

* * *

For a second, Mackenzie was so stunned she couldn't breathe. Up till now, she and Griff had always been equally matched. Or so she had thought. Now, she felt like she had a tiger by the tail. "And how would we do that?" she demanded, gathering up her trash.

"Well..." Finished with his meal, Griff followed suit. He walked languidly beside her, adapting his longer strides to hers. Then, sending her a teasing sidelong glance, reached over with his free hand to ruffle her hair the way he had when they were kids. "We could always talk about our quivering knees and wildly pounding hearts."

A jumble of emotions whirled through her. She elbowed him playfully in the side and rolled her eyes. "Like anyone would believe that, coming from you," she muttered. Although, since they had said their I do's, she was increasingly *feeling* that way. Which again, was crazy, given their long history of being nothing but friends. *Best friends.*

He elbowed her right back and flashed her a roguish smile. "You're right." Together, they emptied their trash into the bin. Then turned and headed back to the table. "Actions always do speak louder than words."

Trying not to notice how masculine and capable he was, Mackenzie turned to square off with him. She propped her hands on her hips and challenged him with a tilt of her chin. "Public displays of affection?"

He sauntered closer. Pausing to look down at her. "A well-timed touch of the hands or kiss can do a lot to reassure any doubters," he pointed out smoothly.

Mackenzie returned to the table and closed the lid of the picnic basket. "Is that why you really laid one on me at the end of our vows?" *When I really would have preferred that we not?* "Especially when a simple kiss would have sufficed?" Was that really all it had been? she wondered, disappointed.

For a moment, he paused. Then shrugged.

"Us kissing, rather passionately, was expected. Us not kissing...would have come across as strange and been re-marked upon, and once told, was a story that would have likely gathered steam with every consecutive revisiting."

So he really had been thinking ahead. "Kind of like the telephone game," Mackenzie said.

He sobered, too, his guard going right back up. "Right."

With a mixture of relief and dismay, she said slowly, "So you were just proactively heading off any untoward gossip."

"Exactly."

Which told her that the kiss hadn't meant what she'd thought. "Well, that's a relief," she fibbed.

He studied her, as protective as he always had been, in a big brother sort of way. "Feel better?"

Mackenzie told herself this was for the best. Espe-cially since adding sex to their relationship could mess up everything between them. And she did *not* want that. Forcing herself to be practical, she nodded. "Much."

"So back to our problem of allaying uncomfortable gossip about the reason behind our speedy nuptials..."

"We'll go the PDA route," she told him briskly.

"You sure you're going to be comfortable with that?" He studied her, his own expression inscrutable.

I can do this. I have *to do this.* Mackenzie nodded. "Like you said...wild, unbridled passion is a reason everyone will accept."

His shoulders flexed beneath his casual cotton shirt. "And the sooner our marriage is accepted, the better."

Mackenzie picked up the wicker basket and headed for his sports car. Once again, their steps meshed perfectly. "So how do you want to tell everyone else?" she asked casually.

Lifting one broad shoulder in an indolent shrug, he ventured, "Mass announcement via email?"

Glad to be talking about something other than their *feelings*, Mackenzie bantered back, "Works for me! As long as it's kind of lighthearted or humorous in some way." The Special Occasion Signs part of her brain went into overdrive. "What if we took a selfie of the two of us, showing off our wedding rings, and superimposed that over a photo of the back of your Porsche, with a Just Married sign in the license plate holder and some ribbons and tin cans tied to the bumper?"

The crinkles around his eyes deepened when he smiled. "Sounds great," he told her huskily.

Happy to be in business mode once again, knowing their friendship was secure, Mackenzie promised, "Great! Then we'll get it done and send it out tonight!"

Chapter Four

"I can get that for you," Griff said, after the movers had left, late the following afternoon.

Mackenzie picked up the box of cherished books from her pickup truck. This was something that never went on a moving truck. She always transported it herself. "Thanks. I've got it."

He glanced at the TVR scrawled in big block letters across the top. "Still collecting *The Velveteen Rabbit* editions?"

Warmth curled inside her. "Oh, yeah."

He accompanied her up the steps. "How many do you have now?"

"Thirty-two." All with different illustrations.

Their bodies brushed briefly as he held the door for her. "Nice."

She knew he meant that. Griff loved the classic children's story, too. Both their moms had read it to them when they were very young, before they passed. And they had read it to other small kids in foster care, when they had ended up in the system as adolescents. Although Griff had always wondered if the book's theme was really a good message to be giving to kids who had been either separated from their families, or permanently orphaned. That you had to be really and truly loved, to be real...

She knew he had a point. Since many of the kids, including him, would never end up with another permanent family, but would instead age out of the system... To venture out alone.

Except Griff was loved. And always had been. As a friend, as family, by *her*...

She set the box down in the foyer and looked around. He stood back and scrutinized the living room, too.

She saw his glance rest on the first two pieces of furniture he had bought after he had graduated from law school, a copy of the famous Resolute desk, and an equally stunning chair that went with it. Both had been placed against the wall and were now surrounded by stacks of unpacked moving boxes.

She sighed. "It sucks your desk was too big to go up the staircase."

He nodded in a way that indicated he didn't really want to talk about it. "A larger problem is...our furnishings don't really go together."

He was right. Her overstuffed English chintz love seat and sofa completely clashed with his oversize mahogany leather sofa and matching reading chair, and ottoman. Where his end tables were overtly masculine and traditional, hers were as cozy and feminine as her furniture. Their lamps were equally disproportionate.

Griff strolled closer and she greedily drank him in. His hair was clean and rumpled, and he looked relaxed and ruggedly masculine in jeans and an old law school sweatshirt. Without warning, Mackenzie felt the urge to kiss him again.

"We could move one set to the family room," he suggested.

She shook her head. "I don't want to do that until after we've had time to paint and refinish the floors in there." Activities that along with her work at Special Occasion Signs would keep her from fixating on the reality of intimately sharing space with him. Because no matter how drawn she was to Griff, she was determined *not* to give in to her carnal urges. But there was no reason to believe they were ever going to kiss again unless it was to demonstrate via PDA the reason behind their hasty marriage. And she doubted they would have to do that very often before word got out. Probably, a little hand-holding, or hugging, or simply sitting close together would suffice.

The doorbell rang and she turned to him. "Expecting anyone?"

"Probably just someone from the neighborhood."

Reminding herself to keep her guard up, lest they further complicate an already ridiculously complex situation, Mackenzie looked down at her ripped jeans and paint-splattered oversize man's shirt. "Well, whoever it is, I hope they don't stay long," she said.

Griff opened the door. Joe and Alice Carson stood on the threshold. Joe held a large gift-wrapped box, while his wife carried a bottle of champagne and a bouquet of four long-stemmed glasses.

Mackenzie wasn't surprised the couple had stopped by. Since Griff had started working at the firm, as an intern, while in law school, they had been sensitive to his lack of family, and had often stepped in to take the place of loved ones in milestone situations like this.

They had attended his law school graduation, along with her, and taken them out to a celebratory dinner afterward. Joe had guided him through the dos and don'ts of their mutual profession, and the purchase of his first car. Alice advised him on real estate and the right clothes.

And of course both had wanted to see him settled down, with a loving family of his own.

"We got your email announcement," Alice said, smiling broadly. "We're so thrilled for you two!"

"Thank you," Mackenzie said.

Griff ushered the handsome couple inside their home. He looked as embarrassed as Mackenzie about the moving mess, but Joe and Alice did not seem to mind. They also looked like they were headed for another more formal social engagement.

"We can't stay long," Alice said, "but we did want to offer our sincerest congratulations."

"And see when the two of you would like to schedule a firm party celebrating your new marriage," his boss said.

Mackenzie looked at Griff, beginning to feel a little panicky. This was suddenly getting a little too real. Worse, it made her feel dishonest. Joe and Alice were both very nice people. She did not want to mislead them. On the other hand, she and Griff were legally married. The fact their arrangement was half business and all friendship was no one's concern but their own.

Luckily, the look on Griff's face said he was feeling the same reticence about accepting. "That's really not necessary," he told the Carsons.

"Actually, it is," Joe countered in a tone not to be denied. "It's a company tradition to celebrate the milestone events of all our employees' lives."

"Your family and friends could be there, too," Alice

said. She looked at Mackenzie. "Unless…your family is planning a formal wedding or reception of their own?"

Mackenzie tensed. Doing her best to ease their way out of a sticky situation, she replied kindly, "We eloped because we did not want all that fuss."

Griff reached over and squeezed her hand. "We just wanted to get married as soon as possible. And it made sense to do it before we moved in together so…" Voice trailing off, he shrugged his broad shoulders amicably.

"Still," the older woman countered practically, "it must have been disappointing for your parents, Mackenzie. I know how Joe and I would feel if we had not been able to witness the weddings of our four sons."

A flash of guilt crossed Griff's face. He turned to Mackenzie, apology in his eyes. She knew that look. It said he would find a way to make this up to her. She gave him a look back that said it really wasn't necessary. After all, he hadn't talked her into this. She had been the one to coax *him* into it.

"My parents understand that it's the promises we make to each other that count," she said softly, still holding his eyes. "Griff has been there for me since the first day we met, and I have tried to do the same for him. The only difference is now it will be in an official capacity." She smiled.

"Well, I think we should toast to that!" Joe said. He opened the bottle of champagne, and Alice held the glasses while he poured. When he had finished, the four of them lifted their flutes. "To Griff and Mackenzie," Joe said, toasting them.

His wife turned misty. "May they live and laugh and love together for the rest of their lives," Alice said.

In that instant, Mackenzie did not have to feign joy; it flowed through every fiber of her being.

* * *

"And don't forget to check your work email," Joe told Griff short minutes later as he and his wife headed out the door.

"Will do," Griff promised. "Thanks again for the gift and the champagne and the well wishes."

"See you Monday!" Joe said.

Griff shut the door and turned back to Mackenzie. She had handled herself beautifully during the impromptu visit from his boss and his wife. But then, she always did rise to the occasion. That was one of the things he most admired about her.

Right now, however, she was busy gushing over their incredible wedding gift. "This is some espresso maker," she said. "I feel like I'm going to need barista training to be able to use it. Either that," she chuckled, "or another college degree!"

Griff pulled up the email on his phone. The inbox held a message from Joe. Contained within was an attachment that invited him and Mackenzie to The Heart of Texas retreat the first weekend in April.

For a moment, all he could do was stare at it, hardly believing that everything he had worked so hard for was finally coming to fruition.

A look of concern on her face, Mackenzie rose. She crossed to his side and touched his elbow lightly. "Is everything okay?"

Griff grinned and hugged her close, inhaling the sweet scent of her hair. Joy flowed through him. "Well, what do you know!" he whispered in her ear. "It finally happened."

She tilted her head at him quizzically.

He squeezed her close once again. "Thanks to you, Mack, it looks like we're finally going to the weekend event of my dreams."

Chapter Five

"I'm surprised to see you here this morning," Joe Carson said, four weeks later. Briefcase in hand, he was leaving the office building, while Griff was headed in.

"I needed to get a few things done before I leave," Griff said.

"Does Mackenzie...?"

"Suspect anything?" Griff guessed where this was going. "No, she doesn't."

The older man grinned. "She's really going to love you for this, you know."

Griff certainly hoped that was going to be the case.

"And so will her family," Joe continued affably.

Griff knew he needed to be in the good graces of the entire Lockhart clan if his relationship with his new wife were to be successful.

"It will also help make up for the fact you aren't taking a honeymoon, at least right now," Joe said.

Griff supposed that was true. Or at least he imagined that would look true to anyone who knew them.

Misunderstanding the reason behind Griff's tension, Joe patted him on the shoulder. His expression grew paternal. "You've got this," he said. "You and Mackenzie both do. Just don't be late for the retreat," his boss warned.

"I just have to sign two things, and then I'm heading home to pick up Mackenzie." Griff could only hope she would be ready. It seemed she was as nervous about the upcoming weekend as he was.

The home they were sharing was just as he had left it that morning. Furniture crowded among stacks of moving boxes and cleaning supplies and home repair materials. To his disappointment, the closeness and camaraderie Griff had hoped for had never materialized. In fact, during the month that they'd been cohabiting, he had seen less of her than when they had been residing in their own places.

Mornings he was usually out the door pretty quickly. He had to be. Meanwhile, Mackenzie went straight for the art studio she had set up in the carriage house. She painted signs all morning, made deliveries and took care of business in the afternoon, and by the time he got home late in the evening, she and Bliss were sound asleep behind her closed bedroom door.

Weekends were just as busy but this one would be different, he promised himself. They would have time alone together on the drive to the corporate retreat in the valley between Echols Mountain and Sanders Mountain in West Texas. Some quality time together at the actual retreat. And then one-on-one time again on the drive back home. But before that could happen, they had to get Bliss squared away.

Luckily, Mackenzie's sister Jillian, a botanist and antique rose specialist, had already arrived. She was going to house-sit and take care of the canine while they were at the weekend gathering.

Jillian's bags stood neatly in the foyer, next to Griff's. Whereas Mackenzie's suitcase and garment bag were wide open on the sofa. Clothing was scattered around every which way. And jewelry, shoes and lingerie— a bit sexier than he would've expected her to wear—was laid out on the coffee table. The thought of her in all that silk and lace had the blood rushing through his veins.

Ignoring the pressure building at the front of his pants, Griff quipped, "We're only going for three days."

Mackenzie sat down beside her pet and stroked Bliss's silky head. For a moment, looking as bleak as her Bernese mountain dog. "But there are multiple events on each day. Some with the other spouses. Some with the whole group. Not to mention the semiformal partners dinner this evening and the black-tie dinner on Saturday evening."

No stranger to being the odd person out, Griff looked Mackenzie in the eye and did his best to comfort her. He wasn't sure why she was stressing. Usually she was very confident when it came to deciding what to wear. "I'm sure you will look fine in whatever you put on," he said gently.

Mackenzie looked remarkably unconvinced. He glanced at his watch, knowing if they were going to make the welcome luncheon, they had to hit the road. "We just need to get going," he said, a little impatiently.

Abruptly Mackenzie looked as if she might burst into tears from the stress of it all. Another anomaly.

Noticing, Jillian looked over at him. "She'll look *fine*?" her sister echoed disapprovingly. Not so subtly telegraphing that he needed to step it up, romantically. Like the *newlyweds* they were.

Aware he had to get a lot better at this being wildly in love stuff if they wanted their ruse to be successful, Griff moved over to settle on the arm of the leather sofa next to Mackenzie. He put his arm about her shoulders.

"Obviously, I mean you'll look beautiful," Griff corrected himself hastily.

Understanding they both had a role to play, Mackenzie visibly pulled herself together. She hugged her dog. Stood. "You're right," she said, every barrier tightly back in place. "I am being silly. I need to stop second-guessing myself and just go."

"What you mean you don't have a room for us?" Mackenzie asked Callie McCabe Echols, the owner of the corporate retreat.

Callie smiled, as friendly now as she had been when she'd grown up in Laramie County. "Your reservation came in last. But not to worry." She continued typing something in the computer in front of her. "We were able to get you a really nice suite at The Double Knot Wedding Ranch on Sanders Mountain. That's the property just west of us. Your group will be taking the train up and congregating there…in Nature's Cathedral…at the very top of the mountain for dinner on Saturday evening."

"But everyone else will be housed here," Mackenzie said, upset. She couldn't understand why Griff wasn't more annoyed. The whole point of this weekend was the access he was going to have to the other high-ranking members of his firm.

Griff touched her arm. "It's okay, Mack. We will be fine." He looked at her steadily. "The important thing is that we're here." He paused to let his words sink in. "It's all going to work out."

Mackenzie sure hoped so. She hated seeing Griff shortchanged in any way.

They collected their bags and went back out to his Porsche. As Callie had promised, the drive next door was short. The Double Knot's hotel had a rustic yet elegant charm, as did the numerous cottages scattered around the property.

"Newlyweds, huh?" the bellhop said as he carried their bags upstairs to the comped room, which also happened to be the bridal suite.

Mackenzie's eyes widened. "How did you know?" she asked.

"Oh, we heard from Ms. Echols that you might be wanting some privacy." He looked at Griff and winked.

Of course, Mackenzie concluded. Callie was the daughter of Jackson and Lacey McCabe and therefore connected to all the Laramie County gossip. News of a Lockhart elopement at the bait and tackle shop definitely would have reached her. She just hoped it didn't reach any of Griff's colleagues. Because she doubted the high-powered attorneys or their spouses would understand. Right now, all anyone knew was what Griff had told them, that they had been married by a justice of the peace in Mackenzie's small rural hometown.

Oblivious to her worries, Griff handed the bellhop a folded bill and ushered him out the door. "Let us know when you're ready for your complimentary champagne," he said. "I'll bring it right up."

Griff deliberately averted his gaze. "Maybe later. A *lot* later," he grumbled.

As the bellhop left, Mackenzie turned to look at her husband. He was being deliberately aloof again. This was nothing new. He had been holding back a lot of what he had been thinking and feeling since they had gotten hitched. And while this was nothing new, it made her feel shut out. Like they were never going to recapture their former closeness.

"We should have fought harder for accommodations beside everyone else in the group," she said. "Even if it was in the maid's quarters or something."

Griff walked over to the window. Stood, looking out at the beautiful mountain scenery. He shoved his fists in the pockets of his slacks. It was almost like he had expected this all along, she noted. Still not looking at her, he shrugged his broad shoulders. "Maybe they think they are doing us a favor by giving us some privacy. A little bit of the honeymoon we were unable to take right now."

Mackenzie bit her lip. "Maybe," she allowed. Wishing she could put her arms around Griff and hold him close, she sauntered nearer. Then, positioning herself so he had no choice but to look at her, she confessed, "It still makes me sad to see you not have the same advantages as the other two people in the running for new senior partner."

Once again, he seemed curiously unperturbed. Given how often he had talked about the importance of access in the past. It was why he had face-to-face meetings with clients whenever possible.

"It shouldn't make a difference." Griff opened his garment bag and pulled out a fresh suit, shirt and tie.

Mackenzie retrieved a pretty spring dress and coordinating cardigan. She caught a whiff of his familiar masculine scent as they crossed paths. "But if it does…" she said, worrying out loud.

Griff turned to study her with sudden acuity. "Would it bother you," he asked finally, in his deceptively mild, cross-examination voice, "if I *don't* get the promotion, after all?"

It seemed like a loaded question. "What do you mean?" Suddenly feeling like she was on the witness stand, facing off with him, Mackenzie toed off her cowgirl boots. Her body tingling with awareness at his nearness, she sat down on the side of the big bed to take off her socks.

Griff tugged his sweater over his head. The T-shirt beneath clung to his sculpted abs and chest. He dropped down on the bed next to her. Looked deep into her eyes. "Would you be sorry," he asked soberly, more stranger now than best friend, "that you married me?"

Mackenzie had felt somewhat estranged from Griff for several weeks now. Part of that was her fault. Keeping her distance from him both emotionally and physically had been the only way to tamp down the secret desire she had harbored since their wedding kiss.

That defensive action had come with a price, though.

It had left her feeling lonely and vulnerable in a way she had never felt before. It had made her want Griff all the more.

Yet she knew what their deal was. This was a platonic business arrangement designed to give him career opportunity and her a chance to realize once and for all the many reasons why their relationship would never be more than it was right this very minute.

Because he didn't love her, and he never would, not in the way she would need him to for her to fall in love with him in return.

And without romantic love, there was no way their marriage would be viable for anything more than the very short term.

She tossed him a look. "Why would you think that I'd be sorry?" She grabbed her dress and slipped into the bathroom. Dispensed with her jeans and sweater. And shimmied into her dress. Sashaying back out, she reached behind her to zip up her dress. "Do you really think I'm that shallow?"

Griff shrugged, standing his ground. "It wouldn't be the first time that I...that a guy...got the boot for disappointing a lady."

"A guy like you?" Mackenzie asked. Suddenly, this was getting personal.

Griff removed his shirt from the dry-cleaning wrapping and tugged it on over his plain white T-shirt. Sensing she was onto something, Mackenzie glided near enough to look into his eyes. What was she missing here? "Is this what happened when you and Iris broke up?"

Griff frowned and went back to his bag for a different tie. "Not just Iris," he said roughly.

He had only had one other serious relationship. "Lynette, too?"

Griff looped the tie around his neck. Then strode over to the mirror. Although she was pretty sure he didn't need to see his reflection for the familiar task.

With a frown, he admitted, "They both had the same problem."

Mackenzie stood next to him and looked at his image in the mirror. She noted how handsome he was, how capable. "Neither knew a good man when they found one?" she guessed lightly.

Griff knotted his tie with quick economical movements. The brooding look was back on his face. "They didn't like my background. Or lack of one, I guess I should say. The fact I didn't have a normal respectable family history, but instead was the orphaned child of a working-class single mother."

Mackenzie gasped, taken aback. "You're kidding," she said, horrified and heartbroken all at once.

Griff turned to face her. For the first time she could remember in a very long time, he let down his guard. "I was good enough to date, to have a good time with, but when it came time to consider marriage, they just couldn't do it."

"They actually *said* that?" Mackenzie whispered.

Sorrow came and went in Griff's eyes. Replaced by cool acceptance. "They didn't have to," he replied, pulling his collar down over the knotted tie. His expression grew even more bleak. "The moment we started talking about weddings and traditions and family guest lists... and the fact that I wouldn't have anyone there on my side of the aisle except work colleagues—"

"And me," Mackenzie said fiercely.

"—they began pulling away," he continued bitterly. "Iris said she was too young to get married."

"Except she did get married a year later," Mackenzie remembered, upset.

He exhaled heavily. "Lynette wanted to concentrate on her career for a few more years."

"But then she got married, too," Mackenzie recalled.

Griff started to step past her. Unable, *unwilling*, to let him go without offering what comfort she could, she splayed both her hands across his chest. Beneath her fingertips, she felt the heat of his body and the steady thrumming of his heart.

Tilting her face up so he had no choice but to look into her eyes, she chided, "You should have told me this."

It hurt that he had not done so then. When she could have comforted him.

Griff's lip curled cynically. "And what would you have done? Or said?" he challenged, the barriers around his heart going right back up.

Mackenzie's eyes stung.

She hated the fact he was pushing her away after letting her get close enough to see what was in his heart.

Knowing that he needed her support, whether he acknowledged it or not, she gripped his arms to keep him from moving away. The hard curve of his biceps warmed beneath her fingertips. "I would have told you these women were fools." The depth of her emotion made her tremble. "I would have told you…"

Another flash of pain moved across his face. Then his head lowered, his mouth slanted across hers. He claimed her lips in another hot and tender, wickedly passionate kiss. Mackenzie's knees went weak even as her spirit soared. She wreathed her arms around his neck and molded her body close to his.

She couldn't believe they were doing this again! But she didn't want to stop. Not now, maybe not *ever*.

Chapter Six

Griff hadn't intended the kiss to do anything more than end the conversation he did not want to have. Especially when the information he had impulsively revealed caused Mackenzie to look at him with such tender empathy. It was bad enough when others privately pitied his lack of a loving, traditional family background. But it was unbearable when Mackenzie felt sorry for him, too.

So he had taken advantage of the compassionate sheen in her eyes and, ignoring her soft gasp of surprise, wrapped his arms around her waist and pulled her all the way against him. The sweet taste of her lips and the feel of her soft body pressed against his was all it had taken to make the blood pool fast and low.

Against his chest, he felt her heart quicken, too. She made a soft acquiescent sound, low in her throat, and parted her lips even more. Her tongue pressed against his ardently, stroking and enticing in a way he had never imagined.

She was soft and sweet and womanly. And in that moment of mutual vulnerability, she was all his. Which was why he could not let this happen. Not here. Not now. And especially not because she felt sorry for him or was trying in her own too-innocent way to comfort him.

He broke off the kiss. Lifted his head. Momentarily, gazing up at him, she seemed confused by what had just happened.

The sheer hell of it was, he was bewildered, too. Hadn't he promised himself no more? Because to make love with Mack, without being *in love* with her, or having her in love with him, was just not going to work. Not for either of them.

Pretty patches of pink color stained her cheeks.

Hand to his chest, she pushed him away and stepped back, wedging even more distance between them. "What are you doing?" she asked indignantly. "Practicing our PDAs?"

Griff wished he could say their clinch had been just that. But he knew now, after kissing her a second time, that the attraction between them was real and intense. And very dangerous to their long-standing friendship.

However, sensing casual attitude was what she needed from him now, given the weekend they had ahead of them, he flashed her a mischievous grin. "Well, we don't want it to look like we've never done that before if we are called upon to kiss."

The color in her cheeks deepened. She whirled away from him and strode, barefoot, to the suitcase. Rifling around, she eventually plucked out a pair of sexy ecru heels. She put a hand on the bed to steady herself, as she slipped on one shoe, then the other. Tossing her head, she turned back to him with a withering glare. "First of all, given the straitlaced nature of your law firm, I do not expect that to happen. Second, and most importantly, you need to know that we have had all the practice that we will *ever* need."

Griff reached out to ease up the zipper at the nape of her neck the last inch or so. "So noted," he said with lawyerly ease, aware that even though he knew what she wanted, it was all he could do not to bring her close and kiss her again.

As if sensing that, she lifted a censoring brow. "We're going to be late if we don't get a move on." She grabbed her phone and slid it into her purse.

Griff followed her to the door. Then out into the hotel hallway. "We wouldn't want that," he said.

"So, where and when are the two of you going to honeymoon?" Griff's rival for the senior partner slot asked.

Mackenzie turned to her husband. He gazed lovingly into her eyes like the newlywed husband he was supposed to be. "We haven't really decided," he said. "Although, Mackenzie has always wanted to go to Hawaii."

Which was true; she had.

She sent him an openly adoring look. "Griff has talked about going fly-fishing in Montana."

His other rival for the position joked, "Hold out for Hawaii, Mackenzie! Sounds like a better deal to me!"

Everyone laughed. Talk then segued into which of the Hawaiian Islands were best. After dessert was served, the four name partners rose. "Time to split up into groups," Joe Carson said. "Attorneys come with me. Spouses adjourn with my wife, Alice."

Mackenzie felt a momentary bolt of panic. The other attendees had already been giving her sly looks throughout the meal. Everyone seemed to be assessing the size and shape of her midriff. Wondering if pregnancy was the reason behind the speedy nuptials. Worse, when people did speak to her, they did so with great care, as if they wanted to be very sure they were saying the exact right thing. With Griff right beside her, she had been able to endure the extra scrutiny, but without him, she felt totally inept.

Griff leaned over to whisper in her ear. "You've got this," he murmured, brushing his lips just above her ear.

"Aw," one of the others said.

"Newlyweds!" another teased. Mackenzie flushed as Griff reached under the table and squeezed her hand. Then stood and pulled out her chair for her.

He looked down at her with the same tenderness and protectiveness he had evidenced when she first landed in foster care. "I'll see you in a bit," he said, before walking off to join the others gathered in one of the great rooms across the lobby.

Mackenzie followed the other spouses to the opposite great room. And although the two groups could see each other, they could not make out the general conversations.

The attorneys seemed to be speaking about business. The spouses were focused on preschools, colleges, and private children's sports leagues that some of them were coaching.

None of that involved her, of course, so Mackenzie was able to just sit back and listen. Which would have been easier had the phone she had tucked in the pocket of her spring dress not kept vibrating. It seemed like every five minutes it went off, and with her two college-age employees back in Fort Worth running her business, she had no choice but to discreetly check it out.

With a smile, she momentarily excused herself and

went off in the direction of the powder room. Easing past it, she went through the big French doors that overlooked the terrace, then headed down to the corner and stepped behind a tall ornamental evergreen shrub. She withdrew her phone. Groaned when she saw it was work.

She listened to the dilemma and the proposed solution. And while she admired their enthusiasm, she was not entirely sure such a task should be undertaken in her absence. Still, Luanne and Lenny persisted until finally she relented. "But call me if there are any problems!"

They said they would. She ended the call, closed her eyes and momentarily leaned back with her fingertips pressed against her lids.

Almost immediately there was movement to her left. The hint of a familiar masculine cologne and soap unique to only one man. Warm breath brushed her brow. "What are we doing?" he whispered playfully.

Mackenzie opened her eyes slowly. Griff stared down into the sea-blue depths that suddenly shimmered with guilt.

"I had to return a work call," she said.

Knowing it had to be important for her to have sneaked away, he moved intimately near. Inhaling the sweet, citrusy fragrance of her hair and skin, he asked in concern, "Everything okay?"

Briefly, she explained an opportunity had arisen in a suburb an hour outside of Fort Worth.

Content to remain out of sight of others for the moment, Griff lounged against the side of the building and tucked a strand of hair behind her ear. Damn, she was beautiful in the shimmering spring sunlight. More beautiful in fact than any woman he had ever met. "I didn't know you serviced that area," he murmured, thinking a quiet respite with her was just what he needed. What he had *always* needed to lessen work stress.

Mackenzie sighed. She pressed her lips together in a kissable pout. "I don't. And normally, I wouldn't even consider it, but the client is one of Luanne and Lenny's college professors. His mother just recovered from a devastating car accident and is going home tomorrow for the first time in months. He wants to provide a welcome home banner for his mom, in front of her home, commemorating the occasion, and a Heroes Work Here sign for the rehab facility, to thank everyone who helped her get better."

"I can see why you'd want to do that," Griff said, as something raw and elemental twisted in his gut.

He caught the brief, worried look in her eyes and knew she might want to talk about it.

She sighed, in no hurry to rejoin the others, either. "I just hope it's not too much for them to handle," she admitted, raking her teeth across the inviting curve of her lower lip. She gazed up at him beseechingly. "Because they are going to have to make the signs, not just deliver them."

It was all Griff could do not to pull her into a consoling hug. Advocating as best he could, he said, "They've helped you do that before, though, haven't they?"

Mackenzie drew in a breath that lifted and then lowered the luscious curves of her breasts. "I would just feel better if I were there to supervise. And speaking of supervision—" she looked up from beneath a fringe of thick blond eyelashes and speared him with a testy gaze "—what brings *you* out here?"

"I saw you get up and leave and I wanted to make sure everything was okay. But then you didn't come out of the ladies' room. So I asked someone if they had seen you go in. And they said they thought you'd gone outside to smoke. Which was news to me. Since I did not know that you smoked."

She choked out an abrupt laugh at the ludicrousness of it all. Then looked beside her and saw the concrete ashtray on the other side of the bushes. "Oh," she said, her fingertips flying to her throat, her wedding band glinting gold in the sun, just like his. "I guess we are in the smoking area." She paused, her delicate brow furrowing as she glanced around. "It's kind of secluded, though."

Yes, he thought, his hormones shifting into overdrive. It was. Aware her gaze was locked on his again, he joked, "Probably because they don't want people to be seen out here puffing away. That being so unpolitically correct and all."

She stifled another giggle. "Like that would stop you," she chided, rolling her eyes.

Reminded of how much he liked making her laugh, he angled a thumb at the center of his chest. "Hey, I am as upright a citizen as they come."

She shook her head, still holding his eyes.

He leaned in. Taunting softly, "Don't believe me?"

"I think when the opportunity presents itself you are as *mischievous* as they come."

Figuring as long as he was going to be damned if he did and damned if he didn't, he might as well get into some of that trouble she was talking about. Palms moving to her shoulders, he lowered his head and tilted his mouth over hers.

As expected, she went very, very still. "Griff Montgomery," she whispered, indignant, "don't you dare!"

Which was, of course, all the invitation he needed. His lips captured hers and they softened immediately against his, her response honest and passionate and uncompromising. He tasted coffee and chocolate and the sweet essence that was her. Loving the way she could open herself up to the moment, and the desire sizzling between them, he backed her up against the wall, sliding his hands low beneath her hips. Still kissing her deeply, he lifted her against him and finally felt her begin to surrender, just a little bit. Excitement roared through him; his body hardened all the more. With a soft mewl of pleasure, she brought her hands up to encircle his neck. Her tongue tangled with his and he deepened the kiss even more, his heart pounding and his body pulsing with need. Who knew what might have happened next had a throat not cleared.

Griff and Mackenzie broke apart. And turned to see the firm's four name partners standing there, unlit cigars in hand, a mixture of amusement and approval in their eyes. "Looks like that honeymoon can't come soon enough," Joe Carson said.

To Mackenzie's relief, the activities for the rest of Friday kept her and Griff very busy. There was no more time or opportunity for private conversation or hot, stolen kisses. No time to do much besides stay fully involved in the retreat.

By the time they got to the bridal suite late that evening, all she wanted was to go to sleep. Luckily, the room's king-size bed was big enough to accommodate both of them, even with the extra blanket that she rolled up and stuck in the center.

Griff stared at the hastily erected barrier, his expression as unreadable as his embrace had been passionate. "I could sleep on the sofa if you like," he said finally, going back to being the Texas gentleman she had known and loved for years.

"It's too short for you." Determined not to make things

any more complicated or crazy confusing between them than they already were, Mackenzie left her robe on over her pajamas and climbed into bed. Shoulders stiff, she turned her back to him. "This will be fine."

She felt Griff standing there behind her for several seconds. He seemed to be weighing his options. In the end, though, he just said gruffly, "Whatever you want," and climbed into bed after her, turning his back to her, too.

Although she'd been sure she would not be able to sleep, lying so close to him, especially after the two steamy kisses they'd shared that day, Mackenzie drifted off immediately. She woke only when the alarm went off at 7:00 a.m. Griff took the shower first. He had an early meeting with Joe and the other three name partners. Fifteen minutes later, he was out the door, as breathtakingly handsome as ever.

Telling herself she was one-third of the way through the weekend retreat, Mackenzie headed into the bathroom. Breakfast followed in the banquet hall, then the attorneys all headed for a nearby golf course, where firm business would be discussed on the links.

Mackenzie and the other spouses boarded a luxury tour bus that took them to a local artists' retreat, lunch and then a cooking class.

When they got back, there was one more stop and yet another surprise waiting for them.

"Wow," Griff said, as Mackenzie swept into the bridal suite at The Double Knot, shortly before 5:00 p.m.

He was standing in front of the windows. Already dressed for the biggest event of the entire weekend, the black-tie dinner that was going to take place atop Sanders Mountain, he looked incredibly handsome.

His glance roved her upswept hair, then her face, then

returned to her glamorous updo. "Your hair looks fantastic like that," he said.

Mackenzie flushed self-consciously. He looked amazing too in the black evening suit, snowy white shirt and black tie. "Thank you." She went to the closet and pulled out the garment bag containing her evening clothes. She laid it on the bed, unzipped it and brought out the shimmering cerulean gown she had bought for the occasion.

"Our last event was a stop at a very nice hair salon near here. All the women got their hair done for tonight, courtesy of the firm."

Griff sprawled in one of the club chairs in front of the window. "So you had a good time today?"

"Yes." Mackenzie paused to pull out her phone. She checked the screen, then laid her hand across her heart. "Oh, thank goodness!"

"What is it?"

Relief pouring through her, Mackenzie looked up. "Luanne and Lenny delivered the signs. They sent pictures to show me. It all looks great."

Griff grinned. "Glad to hear it."

Mackenzie grabbed her dress and disappeared into the bathroom. She dressed hurriedly and touched up her makeup, which had been done at the salon. Then came back out into the suite. "How was your day?" she asked, suddenly feeling a little too married for comfort.

"You mean did I let the partners win at golf?"

Mackenzie paused in the act of putting on an evening shoe. She sat down on the edge of the bed and slipped on the other. "Were you supposed to?"

Watching her every movement with lazy male interest, Griff shrugged. "I don't know. So I erred on the side of caution. Gave them a run for their money...until the very end...when I blew the last shot."

Mackenzie studied the mixture of excitement and triumph on his face. "On purpose?"

He shrugged his broad shoulders and stood. "Half-and-half," he said.

Mackenzie gazed at him, aware how much she was beginning to enjoy being with him like this... If she discounted the crazily confusing PDAs, of course.

It felt like they were partners in something important. Like they were forging unbreakable ties. And even though she knew they might be hitched only for the next year or so, when Griff had secured his promotion and his future at the firm, she relished the way it felt now. And that, she knew, could be a problem.

Hoping he had not made a mistake in agreeing to the plan his wife still knew nothing about, Griff escorted Mackenzie to the old-fashioned steam train that powered parties up the mountain.

They were among the last to arrive, so they took a seat near the rear of the open-air train. The wooden seats on the antique car barely sat two, and he draped his arm along the back of the seat. She cuddled against him in the cozy space, turning to gaze at the beautiful woods on either side of them, while he turned to gaze at her. It was funny. He had started out this weekend worrying about a potential promotion. And now, thirty-six hours later, he was chiefly concerned about how Mackenzie would react to what lay ahead.

And he wasn't the only one.

She turned her face into his shoulder, tipped her head up and whispered in his ear, "Is it my imagination? Or does everyone keep smiling at us like they know something we don't?"

Actually, they *all* knew something she didn't. But that

would be rectified soon. He would no longer have to hide what was really going on.

Unable to help but note how gorgeous she looked in her evening gown, he leaned over to whisper back at her. "Everyone smiles at newlyweds."

The train slowed and stopped. People rose. Griff and Mackenzie remained in their seats until the path was clear. He went first so he could help her down from the train.

Her hand clasped tightly in his, she stepped down onto the ground. They followed the smooth, paved path into the glorious clearing atop Sanders Mountain known as Nature's Cathedral. Rows of white chairs were set up on either side of a red velvet aisle way. A beautiful white arbor, decorated with flowers, served as an altar.

Perplexed, Mackenzie turned to him. "Is there a wedding going on here tonight?"

Carol and Robert Lockhart came around the corner of the catering building. They were accompanied by Joe and Alice Carson. Hearing her question, all smiled. "Yes," Alice said. Carol and Robert looked at their daughter in unison. "And it's yours!" they exclaimed.

Chapter Seven

Mackenzie was about to refuse when she saw Bliss coming toward her, her tail held high. Her beloved canine was accompanying her three sisters and four brothers, all of them grinning broadly and dressed in their wedding best. Griff's colleagues and their spouses looked similarly delighted.

Struggling to contain her shock, she knelt to pet Bliss then turned and looked at Griff. There was no doubt; he had been in on this. Reluctantly, maybe. But still… Shouldn't his first allegiance have been to her?

Griff turned and gave her a privately cajoling look that suddenly made it very difficult to blame him. Obviously, he'd been outnumbered.

Nevertheless, he should have alerted her to what was going on, she thought, aware just how easy it would be to feel swept away in an over-the-top-romantic setting like this.

With all their close friends and family there cheering them on.

And she couldn't afford to get swept away.

To let what had been a lifelong crush become something more.

Not when they had made a deal to stay just friends…

Of course no one else but Griff knew that.

Doing his best to hold up his end of the deal, he smiled. "I knew that you wished we'd had Bliss at our previous ceremony," he said, slipping his arm about her waist and giving her a brief companionable squeeze.

She had. "So now you will!" her sister Jillian said, handing the leash over to Griff and taking Mackenzie by the hand.

Their sister Faith fell into step beside them. A hopeless romantic, she was bubbling with excitement. "Wait until you see the dress we picked out for you!"

"And the evening sandals I made and brought all the way from Italy," Emma Lockhart, an apprentice shoe designer, chimed in.

Her sisters whisked her away to a white dressing tent near the edge of the clearing. They helped her get out of the blue evening dress and into an even more stunning white satin gown.

Tears misting her eyes, her mom slipped a diamond necklace around Mackenzie's neck. She recognized it as the gift her father had given her mother the previous Christmas. "This will be something borrowed," Carol said.

Jillian dangled a fancy garter to wear beneath her dress. "And something blue…"

Emma hugged her and added, "The shoes I made for you will be something new."

Faith handed over a diamond bracelet she'd worn at

her own wedding, to her Navy SEAL husband who was currently deployed. "Something old, for luck."

Her tiara and veil were added. The music outside started, signaling the ceremony was about to start. And then suddenly, for Mackenzie, this make-believe union got very real...

Griff stood beside the minister, watching as Bliss trotted happily up the aisle, a wreath of flowers adorning her neck.

Mackenzie followed on her father's arm. She looked breathtakingly beautiful in a high-necked long-sleeved white satin gown that clung to her torso and flared out at the waist. A glittering tiara was nestled in her upswept hair. And when her father paused to lift her veil, kiss her cheek and give her away, he couldn't help but notice the tears glittering in her eyes.

However, *whyever*, this had all started, Griff realized, his heart filling with an unfamiliar emotion, it was beginning to feel like a lot more than a bargain between friends.

It was beginning to feel...real.

To Mackenzie, too?

Aware there was no way he could ask her that, especially right now, Griff listened along with everyone else as the minister spoke about the sanctity of marriage. Then added, "In lieu of an exchange of rings and wedding vows, which Mackenzie and Griff have already taken in their previous marriage ceremony, they are going to read a poem by E. E. Cummings, to symbolize their love and abiding commitment to each other."

Appearing surprised that he had remembered that wish, too, Mackenzie drew in a quick breath, looking more achingly vulnerable than he had ever seen her.

Feeling a familiar surge of protectiveness, Griff pulled the printed page out of his suit pocket.

Mackenzie locked eyes with him. Her cheeks turned a delicate shade of pink and she released a soft, quavering breath. Then together, they began to read the poem, their voices blending in perfect harmony. "'I carry your heart with me.'" Their eyes met and then held once again as tenderness reverberated throughout the clearing. "'I carry it in my heart…'"

As they continued reading, the beautifully written words resounded through Nature's Cathedral, and found a way into Griff's soul, as well.

When they finished, there wasn't a dry eye among the people gathered there, including stunningly enough, Griff and Mackenzie.

"I now pronounce you husband and wife." The minister beamed. "Griff, you may kiss your bride!"

And glad to be at this part of the ceremony, Griff did.

As Griff's head lowered, Mackenzie braced herself for a knee buckling, completely over-the-top kiss. What she got instead was a soft, tender, incredibly chaste buss on the lips.

Griff lifted his head and, smiling gently down at her, looked deeply into her eyes.

She steeled herself again. Thinking here it comes. The public display of affection to end all PDAs.

Except to her stunned disappointment, that didn't happen, either. Her handsome groom merely wrapped his arms around her and pulled her in for a warm, all-encompassing, "gosh, we're the best of friends, aren't we?" kind of hug. He pressed another kiss against her temple, then leaned down to whisper in her ear, "Sorry about the surprise, but not to worry. When it comes to the rest of the evening, we've got this." Giving her no chance to respond, he squeezed her shoulders one more time, then drew away.

Bliss, obviously sensing something phenomenal had just happened, jumped out of her sit-stay position and trotted over to wedge herself between them. Tail wagging furiously, she gazed up at them adoringly and let out a cheerful woof.

The crowd erupted in hoots and hollers and Bliss let out another happy bark as if to say: "Look what my people have done! Don't you-all just love it!"

Moments later, the string quartet began to play the jubilant recessional. Griff took Mackenzie's hand, along with Bliss's leash, and the three of them swept down the aisle with the expected triumph.

After that, there was little time to think, never mind genuinely react. The next few hours were a blitz of constant activity as every tradition from dinner and champagne toasts, dancing and cake cutting, garter removal and bouquet toss were honored. Endless pictures were taken. Heartfelt congratulations accepted. Finally, around midnight, a stretch limo arrived to take them down the mountain. Bliss was once again handed off to Mackenzie's sister Jillian.

Making their way through the sea of sparklers held by the guests, Mackenzie and Griff ducked into the waiting car. She had no idea how he felt, but as soon as they were alone, exhaustion hit. For her, it had been a long weekend and an even longer evening. Griff was as quiet and reflective as she was during the ride down the mountain on the old logging road. And still silent as they headed for the privacy of the bridal suite.

But then the emotion she'd been suppressing bubbled up uncontrollably. She could hold back no longer. "Well, now I know why the firm had us stay here," Mackenzie said, gesturing at the sumptuously romantic surroundings.

She turned to face him, ready finally to have it out with him. She stepped closer, her satin skirt swirling around her, and tilted her face up to his. Hurt mixed with humiliation. "What I don't know is why you betrayed me and kept it a secret."

Easy, Griff thought, realizing all over again how incredibly beautiful she was. He surveyed her pink cheeks and softly pouting lips, glad to know he wasn't the only one conflicted about everything that had been going on. "I had no choice."

Irked, she narrowed her eyes at him. "Of course, you had a choice!" she shot back, ripping the tiara off her head. "People always have a choice!"

Exasperation rippled within him. She was acting like she was the only person under pressure.

Never one to let anyone else take the lead, he lowered his face until they were nose to nose. "Well, I didn't think so when your parents called me the day we eloped, and let me know just how disappointed they were in me for depriving you of what they were sure was your lifetime dream of a big beautiful family wedding."

Mackenzie huffed in indignation and stepped back in a drift of orange blossom perfume. "We told them that was what we both wanted!"

Griff scoffed and let his glance drift over the delicately sculpted lines of her face before returning to her sea-blue eyes. "Well, they didn't believe it and they expected me as your new husband to help set things right. And they weren't the only ones." He put up a hand before she could interrupt and began to pace.

"Joe and Alice understood our desire to make things legal before we moved in together, but they still wanted to honor law firm tradition and give us a reception. I tried to talk them out of it, at least for now, by saying your parents were already making plans."

Mackenzie blinked, listening.

"Alice called your mother to see if there was anything she and Joe could do, since they are the closest thing I have to family—" *except you* "—and then it somehow became a joint venture, planned to take place during the firm retreat."

Mackenzie stared at him with her usual fiery pride. "Why didn't you tell me this was going on?" she demanded.

Griff hooked his hands around his waist, pushing the edges of his dinner jacket back. He reached up to loosen his black tie and the first two buttons of his shirt. "Your parents asked me not to. They felt you'd object—"

Mackenzie glared at him. "I would have!"

"—and they really wanted to do this for you. I had already disappointed them. I didn't want to do anything else that would make things worse, and I knew if I told you that you would probably go ballistic and confront them and then it would've turned into a royal mess."

She crossed her arms in front of her, the action pushing up the soft globes of her breasts. Pacing back and forth, the satin folds of her skirt swishing as she moved, she finally swung back to face him. Her eyes glittered furiously. "So you took their side instead," she accused.

Griff pressed his fingers to his temples and grimaced. He hated feeling like a failure, but in these types of situations it was often inevitable. "I wasn't taking sides. I found myself between a rock and a hard place. And I did the best I knew how. But you're right," he admitted ruefully, wishing he hadn't disappointed her, too, "family dynamics...especially big family dynamics...are really not my forte."

Unable to disagree with that observation, Mackenzie squared her slender shoulders and took a deep breath. She walked over to the bottle of champagne, chilled and waiting on the bar. Plucked the bottle out of the ice, dried it with a towel and then poured two glasses.

Sensing a truce might be possible, he crossed to her side. She handed him a flute filled with bubbly golden liquid. Still regarding each other warily, they silently clinked glasses. Sipped.

"In any case," Griff concluded with biting sarcasm, irritated she hadn't appreciated any of his efforts to make things nice and meaningful for her, "it's over now."

Apparently *not* in her opinion. Her chin lifted in that all-too-familiar way. "Were you responsible for Bliss being there tonight?"

He nodded. "Your parents weren't sure it was the best idea, but I remembered what you said about how our wedding would have been perfect—if it were a real wedding, that is—if Bliss were there so I made sure it happened."

Although she was still holding herself apart aloofly, her blue eyes shimmered moistly. "And the E. E. Cummings poem?" Her tone turned throaty. "Was that your idea or one of my sisters'?"

He wished he could just kiss her and make this tension all go away. "I remembered what you said about that, too," Griff rasped.

She continued watching him steadily, an emotion he could not decipher in her expression. Aware she seemed to think he had let her down again, he explained, "We had to make it look real."

The firestorm of emotion she had been holding back

all evening suddenly sparked. She glowered at him. Then rolled her eyes and took another long, thirsty gulp of champagne. Setting her glass down with a thud, she swung back to face him. Ready to tango. "Oh, yeah," she retorted, letting her gaze rove his face, "that kiss... The one at the end of the ceremony? That was real all right!"

Clearly, she had her regrets. He had his, too. But it was too late to turn back so he focused on their end of ceremony kiss. "I was trying to be respectful," he said quietly. "To honor you in front of your folks."

Her eyes narrowed all the more. "Well, it couldn't have been more chaste," she claimed with an indignant huff, thrusting out her kissably soft lower lip. She paused to give him another long, debilitating look. Continuing sassily, "*Unlike* the ones you gave me when trying to demonstrate a PDA."

So, Griff thought triumphantly, she had been thinking about the other two times they had kissed, as well. "If you're talking about what happened yesterday afternoon..." he said.

When they had been caught making out.

"And at the bait and tackle shop..." she reminded him.

Both of which had been memorable, at least from his point of view. "Those were spur of the moment liplocks..."

"So...what? You're saying you planned that lack of passion at the end of the ceremony?" she asked incredulously.

"I restrained myself with effort," he admitted. And it had been hard as hell to hold back, too. Because all he had really wanted was to bend her backward from the waist and really plant one on her.

"Unlike the other times."

Griff wasn't sure what she wanted from him. Although

he knew what he wanted from her—to feel close again. But it felt good to be arguing with her. Maybe because it was the most honest thing they had done since they had moved in together.

"As I recall," he said, draining his glass and setting it down beside hers with an equally resounding thud, "you weren't happy with those kisses, either." Although it hadn't stopped her from returning them passionately.

She sashayed closer and continued throwing down the gauntlet. "Well, then, counselor, I guess that means I don't like the way you kiss!"

That would have been okay. If her declaration weren't so patently false. Feeling his own emotions begin to sky-rocket, Griff stepped toward her. "Is that so?" he taunted.

Her gaze narrowed. The tension that had been build-ing between them for weeks now boiled out of control. She scoffed at him. "I just said it, didn't I?"

Griff nodded, wrapping his arms about her waist and pulling her close. Then slanted his face over hers. "That doesn't mean it's true."

Before Mackenzie could draw a breath, Griff cupped her face in both hands, lowered his lips to hers and de-livered the most spectacular kiss she had ever received in her life. It was the kiss she had been waiting for since the ceremony. It was the kiss she had been dreaming of her entire life.

As unprepared as she always seemed to be when it came to her feelings for him, she moaned softly. Then found herself winding her arms around his shoulders, pressing her breasts against his chest and inviting him closer. He felt so big and warm and strong as he deepened the kiss, his tongue mingling with hers, the evocative ca-ress wreaking havoc with her carefully built defenses.

Mackenzie had always known how much she needed to be loved. She just wasn't sure it would ever happen for her. But she knew, even as she came close to surrendering every bit of her fast-dwindling independence, that this was most likely the nearest she would ever come to it.

Her insides melting like butter on a hot stove, she broke off the kiss and gazed up at him. His eyes were dark and unwavering on hers. She wasn't sure what he was feeling but she knew, same as her, it was a lot. Enough? But did it matter, when they both yearned to be together like this?

Their marriage was supposed to be a means to an end, nothing more. And yet their union felt all too real. He rubbed his thumb tenderly across her lower lip. Apology for hurting and shielding her warred with the desire in his eyes. Gallant as ever, he said, "If you want me to stop…"

She let her forehead rest on his shoulder, aware she felt far too vulnerable, too ripe for his taking. Her breath caught in her throat. "I don't."

He waited until she looked at him again, her heart racing erratically in her chest. His eyes blazing with want and need, he regarded her closely. "Our situation is already complicated," he warned.

Mackenzie took a deep breath. For once, following the courage of her convictions.

"Then maybe this will simplify things." She went up on tiptoe and kissed him again.

He kissed her back just as fiercely. Sensation swept through her, more potent than before. And suddenly, everything she had ever wanted from him rose to the surface.

Passion roared through her and she flattened her hands across his chest. She felt the solidity of his muscles, the rapid beating of his heart, and lower still, his hardness pressing against her. He kissed her again even more provocatively, slid his palms down her spine, rested them on her hips and pressed her lower half to his.

Mackenzie surged against him, the sensible part of her knowing this was reckless and shortsighted, but not caring. She needed to be close to him again. Not just as best friends. But in a way they had never been before. She needed to see if the red-hot lust they were feeling was as fulfilling as their convenient marriage could never be.

And still they kissed and kissed. Sweet, fiery need spiraled through her, arrowing straight from her brain to the depths of her soul. Long moments later, she finally wrenched her lips from his. Then looked up at him and said, with everything she felt in her heart, "Make love to me, Griff. Make love to me tonight."

Chapter Eight

Griff wasn't sure when he stopped thinking of Mackenzie as a kid sister. And best friend. Had it been the first time he kissed her? The second? Earlier, when she first suggested they get married? Or when she walked down the aisle on her father's arm?

All he knew for certain was that things had changed. And there was nothing ambiguous about the way he felt now. He wanted her more than he had ever wanted anyone. The fact she seemed to feel the same about him gave him license to continue. Still kissing her, he swept his hands down her back, pressing her as close as the voluminous folds of her dress would allow.

She made a low, acquiescent sound in the back of her throat and offered her mouth up to his. He thought the times they had kissed up to now had been incredibly sweet and satisfying, but he soon discovered those times were nothing compared to this. He kissed her long and hard and deep, and she kissed him back with a wildness beyond his most erotic dreams, her hand sliding beneath his suit coat, skimming over his back and shoulders, then down across his abs to his belt.

As much as he wanted her, he had to be certain this wasn't something she'd regret. Because they'd made a contract, the attorney in him knew. And making love would change that contract.

Forcing himself to protect and care for her the way he always had, he lifted his head and threaded his hands through her hair. "If we do this," he told her gruffly, "we're going to consummate a marriage that was supposed to be between friends only."

The irises of her eyes turned a darker blue. Mackenzie sucked in a tremulous breath, looking as protective of him as he had always felt of her. "So it will be a legal marriage in every sense," she murmured.

Aware what a good wife she would make if this were a traditional union, Griff paused to let his gaze rove over her face. His need to make love to her intensified. Yet due diligence needed to be carried out. Especially for her. "So the only way out, should one of us want one, will be divorce. And that could change things," he warned, his own body coming alive with desire. "And not necessarily for the better."

"That's just the thing." She curved her hands around his biceps and looked up at him sweetly. Undid his zipper. Moved her hand south. "It doesn't have to, Griff. Not if we don't want that." The feel of her hand closing in brought a new wave of heat. Groaning, he caught her wrist, not about to let her get that far ahead of him.

Hands on her shoulders, he kissed her temple.

"If that's what you want, then it's what I want, too." He spun her around. First order of business? "Let's get

you out of this dress." So they could make love the way
they were meant to, slowly, meaningfully.

He eased the zipper down. Then helped guide the dress
down her arms, past her waist. She held on to him with
one hand as she stepped out of the shimmering satin
gown, leaving her clad in a very sexy bustier and petti-
coat, and heels.

Her sumptuous breasts spilling out of her lingerie's
low-cut neckline, she turned back to face him and eased
off her organza half-slip, too.

As he surveyed the garter belt and satin panties and
stockings cloaking her long, silky legs, his entire body
hardened. He was so turned on, he couldn't help but wonder what had taken him so long to pursue her like this.

"Damn, you're beautiful," he rasped. Inside and out.

She grinned saucily, helped him out of his jacket, shirt
and tie. It was clear from the ardent look in her eyes that
she knew exactly what she wanted from him.

"So are you..."

Eager to ravish her, now that the decision had been
made, he slid a hand beneath her knees, lifted her against
his chest and carried her into the bedroom of their bridal
suite. Heart pounding, he set her down next to the bed
and disrobed her the rest of the way. Claiming her velvety
softness, caressing and weighing the feminine globes
and taut crowns.

And still, they kissed and kissed and kissed, her slender body swaying, even as his lower half throbbed. She
sighed with pleasure; her hands went to his fly, and this
time he let her find him. Until impatient, he broke off the
embrace long enough to lose the rest of his clothing, too.

Naked, they came together again, and for Griff, nothing had ever felt so right. Still kissing her thoroughly, he
tumbled her onto the bed. His entire body pulsing with

excitement, he slowly made his way down her body, kissing and caressing as he went.

She was ready for him then. But not about to accept anything less than her full surrender, he stroked her with the pad of his thumb until the air between them hummed with desire and she arched her back and strained against him, her whole body quaking. He held her till the storm passed, then let her go just long enough to find the protection he brought but had not expected to really need.

Mackenzie had time to come to her senses and call a halt to this, but when he returned to join her, foil packet in hand and still fully aroused, it was all she could do to catch her breath. She had always expected him to be magnificent. He was. She had always expected him to be kind and generous in bed, and he was that, too.

What she *hadn't* expected was for him to be so sensual. But when his lips fit over hers, all rational thought went out of her head. She moaned at the masculine taste of him, and the touch of his tongue sent her even further over the edge. Trembling with need, she shifted her body over top of him and nestled the softness of her breasts into the sinewy hardness of his chest. She kissed his cheek, the line of his jaw, his throat. Pulse pounding, emotions soaring, she made her way down his body. Stroking. Exploring. Until there was no more holding back.

They rolled on protection and came together. He slid between her thighs, cupped her bottom, lifted her toward him and took her slowly and tenderly. Sensation spread. And pleasure flooded her in hot, irresistible waves. Emotion overwhelming her, she wrapped her arms and legs around him, taking him deeper, urging him on. The fantasy crush she had held in her heart for years had suddenly and magically come true.

And even though she knew it wasn't a real marriage, and was never likely to be, this had still turned into the wedding-night-lovemaking of her dreams. So when their breathing slowed and he shifted onto his back, taking her with him, she put her normal reservations aside. Rested her head on his chest and fell asleep, listening to the steady beat of his heart.

Mackenzie woke to see Griff standing at the window in the living area of the bridal suite, staring out at the mountains beyond. He had the same battle-ready look on his face that he used to have when he was preparing to attend an adoption fair, and it broke her heart. Life shouldn't have to be this hard.

She slipped on a thick, terry-cloth robe and went to join him. "When will you find out the results?"

He turned toward her, hands stuffed in the pockets of his suit trousers. "You mean who gets promoted and who doesn't?"

She nodded and poured herself some of the coffee he'd made in the suite.

He picked up the cup he'd been drinking from and held it out. She topped his off, too. "My final Q and A with the nominating committee is at eight o'clock."

She looked at the clock, saw it was seven fifteen. "And the other two candidates?"

"Nine and ten."

She stirred in a double serving of cream. "Then what?"

"They meet, take a vote and let us know the results privately before they announce it at the luncheon." He quaffed his coffee and set the cup down, the brooding look once again etched on the handsome planes of his face.

They turned to each other in silence. Mackenzie wasn't sure what he wanted from her; she only knew she wanted to help alleviate whatever was bothering him. "You should feel confident."

The irises of his eyes turned a darker amber. "Why do you say that?"

She moved close enough to curve a hand over his biceps. "Everyone knows how hard you've worked."

He covered her caressing hand with his palm. Frowning, he pointed out, "The others have worked hard, too."

"True, but Joe Carson reveres you."

He tensed but his expression did not change. "I think he likes us all."

Mackenzie tried again. "But he and Alice helped my parents plan the wedding of our dreams and then gave us a reception…"

Griff lifted his shoulder in a hapless manner. "It's company tradition to throw a party when someone gets married."

Deciding he needed his physical space, Mackenzie backed away. "Some of the other spouses think it's a sign you're going to win."

He watched her perch on the arm of a sofa.

"Or a consolation prize."

She peered at him, not sure what he meant.

He gestured in frustration. "As I mentioned before, I don't have the solid family background the other two candidates have."

Mackenzie's middle tightened, the way it always did when she saw Griff suffering any kind of injustice. "But you're solid, through and through." Unable to stay away, she moved toward him once again, reiterating, "And you've had to overcome challenges other people haven't. That makes you strong, too."

His grin turned into a hearty chuckle. "Maybe you

should do this last interview on my behalf." He waggled his brows flirtatiously at her.

"I would if I could answer questions on property and eminent domain law, and ways to grow the business in those areas, but I can't." She went to the closet to get her last outfit. "So, I'll just have to do what the other spouses are doing this morning."

He put up a staying hand. His big body neared her, filling up the space. "Actually, you don't. This morning your mom is hosting a postwedding breakfast in a private dining room downstairs. Alice and Joe want you to attend that and just enjoy spending time with your parents and siblings." He wrapped his arms around her shoulders and gave her a brief, companionable squeeze. The kind a big brother gave a kid sister, she couldn't help but note.

Griff continued, "You can join us later over at the retreat for lunch."

Another brief silence fell. Mackenzie held the dress for that's day event in front of her like a shield. Wary of letting him down, the way almost everyone else in his life had, she asked, "Are you sure *you're* okay with that?"

He relaxed. "Yes." He leaned down to give her a chaste kiss on the cheek.

Once again, Mackenzie felt oddly disjointed.

Griff said a casual goodbye and was out the door.

And once again, she could not help but wonder how Griff would feel, having married her in order to get the promotion to senior partner and then end up not getting awarded it, after all.

Yes, he should get it.

But what if he *didn't*?

Chapter Nine

Carol Lockhart was setting out place cards and individual baskets of wedding favors when Mackenzie walked into the private dining room. She gave her mother a hug. "Where's Dad?"

"He and Jillian are taking Bliss for a walk."

Mackenzie missed her pooch. Aware she probably sounded like an overprotective dog mom, she asked, "Did she do okay last night?"

Carol smiled and reflected affectionately, "The little darling always does great with us. Question is, how did *you* do? Judging by the sparkle in your eyes and the pretty color in your cheeks, you had a very nice night."

The maternal teasing filled Mackenzie with happiness, even as she rolled her eyes, chiding, "Mom…"

Carol airily lifted a hand. "Yes, I know. You don't like to talk about things that are too personal."

So true.

"But...I am glad you and Griff finally admitted how you've been feeling all along and made it official."

Except they hadn't admitted anything, Mackenzie reflected anxiously. And now...if something untoward happened and Griff didn't get his promotion...would he regret marrying her?

"Honey," Carol said. "What is it?"

She realized she needed to confide in someone. At least part of the way. "I think I've got the postwedding jitters."

To her surprise, Carol wasn't the least bit concerned. She moved to the next table. "Well, of course you do. Everyone gets them."

"You and Dad, too?" They had a love for the ages! No one had a stronger, more durable relationship.

"I think we were...oh, three or four days in...when we had our first argument."

Mackenzie had a hard time envisioning that since her parents rarely disagreed about anything. "What was it about?" she asked curiously.

"Officially? I left all my beauty products on the bathroom counter next to the sink—to the point he barely had room for his toothbrush and razor. This irritated him almost as much as his refusal to measure the coffee and water when he was making a pot of coffee irked me. Because it was always too strong or too weak. And it didn't need to be that way if he would just follow the directions on the canister!"

"Those were pretty easy things to correct, though, right?" Mackenzie asked.

Her mother made a seesawing motion. And continued gently, "But it didn't feel that way when we were quarreling. In the moment, it felt like maybe we'd made a mistake, that a lifetime commitment was too much to make."

So her mother did understand, Mackenzie thought, relieved. She leaned in. "So what did you do to fix things?"

"We both went our separate ways and cooled off. When I came home that night, I was ready to make up. And so was your father. He promised to measure out the coffee from that point on, and I vowed to keep my mess off the bathroom counter. Because we knew that if something was important to one of us, it should be important to both of us."

Like Griff's promotion was important to both of them.

"The point is, we were of the same mindset even when we didn't think we were. We also realized we were both a little scared of the enormity of the vows we had taken. But that was okay. We knew if we took it day by day and talked openly and honestly about our problems, and respected each other's feelings, it all really would be okay. And it has been." Carol hugged her. "So all you and Griff have to do is keep those lines of communication open, and you'll be just fine."

Easier said than done, Mackenzie thought anxiously. Given Griff's penchant for holding back his innermost thoughts and feelings. And, coupled with that, her unwillingness to feel truly exposed or vulnerable, especially when it came to matters of the heart.

She had no more chance to discuss it. Her family started coming in. First were her doctor brother Gabe and his wife, Susannah. Maybe because it was one of the rare occasions when they did not have their quintuplets with them, they looked like they had been honeymooning.

Next were Cade and Allison. Brought together during a babysitting gig for mutual friends' quadruplets, the baseball coach and lifestyle blogger were newlyweds themselves with four-month-old twins currently being babysat by the very same mutual friends.

Her very single cowboy brother Travis accompanied her widowed executive brother Noah and his three elementary-school-aged daughters.

Her sisters Emma, Faith and Jillian came in last with her father Robert. Along with her dog Bliss who promptly came over to get petted.

"Great wedding," Gabe said.

"Surprisingly emotional," Cade agreed.

"Too bad Griff can't be here with us," Travis said, giving her a hug, too.

Noah shepherded his daughters forward to do the same. As always when the topic of marriage came up, he looked a little sad. As if he were still suffering his own loss. He forced a smile. "But we understand he has important business to attend."

Her dad embraced her and kissed the top of her head. He winked. "So Griff gets a pass this time," he declared.

"Same as my guy," Faith spoke adoringly of her Navy SEAL husband, who was currently serving their country overseas.

"Well, I for one understand not wanting to let an opportunity pass by," Emma—who yearned to start her own footwear company—said.

The once jilted Jillian smiled and handed Mackenzie a bouquet of beautiful pale pink antique roses. "Just as long as he doesn't forget the romance," she said. "It will all be fine."

Would it? Mackenzie wondered, her mind going back to the stellar lovemaking of the previous night. One thing was certain. She had never been swept up in desire like that before. All she could do was hope the passion would last.

Three hours later, Mackenzie said goodbye to the members of her family. Jillian, who was in charge of

Bliss, was the last to depart. "You're sure it's okay for me to take her to Laramie and then bring her to you-all in Fort Worth tomorrow?"

Mackenzie knelt to give her dog a chest rub. "Absolutely. I wish we could take her with us but there's no room in Griff's Porsche so..."

Jillian understood. "I love having her. You know that."

Mackenzie did.

"Mind giving me a ride to the retreat next door?"

Jillian agreed. "Moment of truth, hmm?"

It didn't take long for Mackenzie to figure out what had happened. One look at the grim countenances of the two colleagues who had been Griff's competitors and were now loading their bags in their cars, and another at the beaming expression on Griff's face, and she knew.

She walked across the lobby toward him. He held out his arms to her and hugged her tightly. Joe Carson, who was standing beside him, said, "Meet our new senior partner."

Tears of happiness blurred Mackenzie's eyes. "Congratulations!" she said thickly.

"Thanks," he rasped, giving her another squeeze. Together, they walked into the luncheon. And sat side by side as the festivities continued for the next hour.

Finally, it was time to depart. Griff thanked everyone on the nominating committee and he and Mackenzie took his Porsche back to The Double Knot Wedding Ranch, picked up their bags and were on their way home.

For the first half of the 120-mile journey, Griff said almost nothing. Wrung out from the nonstop festivities of the weekend, Mackenzie said little as well. Eventually, though, the silence began to get to her. "You must be really happy," she said.

Griff nodded.

He continued to drive, his focus on the lonely country road.

Mackenzie thought about what her mother had told her about communication being the key to a successful union. Of course, she and Griff weren't really married, at least not in the traditional sense, but they did have a long-standing relationship as friends, and last night anyway, they had been lovers. She needed to know. What lay ahead? Would the passion continue? Or merely be a one-off?

There was no way to tell from his current mood.

So maybe she needed to do what she always did when she was restless or upset, and forget her secret wishes, and concentrate on her work, too.

Chapter Ten

Half an hour later, Griff turned his Porsche into the subdivision and drove toward the home they shared. He wasn't sure what was going on with Special Occasion Signs, but it was clear Mackenzie wasn't happy as she sat beside him, talking to her employees on the phone.

"Well," she conceded, after listening some more, "there is that… No, I will call Mrs. Rawlins myself. And I will also follow up with the Forest Hills High School PTA… Yes… See you tomorrow. And nice job on the signs. I thought they were stunning." She ended the call with a sigh.

"Everything okay?" he asked, parking next to her pickup truck and cutting the ignition.

Mackenzie tilted her head back, shut her eyes and rubbed her temples with her fingertips. "Yes and no."

Heaving in another bolstering breath, she opened her eyes and sat forward. Slender shoulders squared as if for battle, she put her tablet and phone in her bag, unclasped her seat belt and emerged from the car.

Griff joined her at the trunk. She had been so fantastic the entire weekend. Rising to the challenge. Taking everything in stride. And that didn't even count the incredible way she had unexpectedly and definitively lowered her defenses and made love with him.

He brought out the garment bag containing her wedding gown and veil, and two more encompassing the rest of their business clothing. He draped both over the roof of his car, then reached in to bring out their two wheeled suitcases. She looked so stressed, his heart went out to her. "Anything I can do to help?"

He certainly owed her.

She took her wheeled suitcase while he carried the rest. "No. It was just a misunderstanding."

He lifted a brow. She punched in the security code on the panel next to the front door and led the way inside. The house had a faintly musty smell. Part of that was from some old carpeting still waiting to be taken up. The rest likely from the sea of moving boxes gathering dust.

Frowning at the side of her gown visible through the clear heavy plastic of the zippered bag, she walked to the front hall closet and hung it up inside and hastily closed the door behind her.

Out of sight? Out of mind?

Aware she seemed pretty upset for a simple misunderstanding, he left his luggage next to the stairs and followed her into the kitchen, which was only slightly more organized than the rest of their house. Which was to say, not at all. "What happened?" he asked.

She lifted her chin and speared him with a testy gaze. "My business got a bad review on social media."

He took up a station opposite her. "From whom?"

Color flooding her cheeks, she blew out a frustrated breath. "The woman who came home from the skilled nursing and rehab facility."

Griff blinked in surprise. "She didn't like her sign? Luanne and Lenny did a great job on that!"

Mackenzie pulled out her phone. She typed in several commands and then brought up a screenshot of a social media page for her business. The customer review, posted that afternoon, showed a picture of the sign in front of her home and said, "What a beautiful gift from my loving family. It's just too bad Special Occasion Signs messed up the colors and did it in green and lavender instead of my favorite yellow and pink. But it's the thought that counts, right?"

He let his glance shift over her, aware again how pretty she always looked. Even now in her distressed state. "Did the family ask for yellow and pink?"

"No." She turned away and drew another breath that lifted the soft swell of her breasts. "I saw the order invoice and instructions yesterday. They did ask for the mother's favorites," she allowed, as she reached into the cupboard for a clean glass, "but they listed them as green and lavender. Not yellow or pink." Because, frustratingly, their old-fashioned fridge had no water or ice dispenser, she filled it at the sink.

Thirsty, Griff helped himself to a glass of water, too. "So it was the family's mistake." He lounged next to her as they sipped.

Mackenzie studied him over the rim of her glass. "Right."

"What are you going to do?"

"Well," she continued holding her glass in front of her as she folded her arms beneath her breasts, "I will tell you what I am *not* going to do. And that is tell someone recovering from a very serious accident that her well-intentioned family, who went *all out* to try to welcome her home, also screwed up."

Griff looked at the post again. "She does sound like she might be a little difficult."

"Or just cranky because she's been ill for months." Her expression softened.

Another thing he liked about Mack. She had a heart as big as all Texas.

Still wanting to be able to help her, he focused on the practical. "Can you take this review off the SOS social media page? Or maybe just post a few other things and move it farther down so it won't be the first thing people see?"

Her blue eyes clouded. "That's not my policy."

O-kay. "Have you gotten negative reviews before?"

She stiffened. "A couple times in the very beginning. But whether it was my fault or not, I rectified any and all mistakes on the theory that the customer is always right even when they're *not*."

He followed the same principle in his law practice. Gently, he asked her, "Can you do the same thing here?"

Another sigh. "Already on it. Luanne and Lenny are working on a replacement as we speak. Hopefully, the customer will be so surprised and delighted by how we've gone the extra mile she will put something on the social media page proclaiming her happiness."

"And if she doesn't?"

"Then it's a lot of time and effort and money for a project done while I was out of town that is also outside of our normal service area. Luckily—" a smile lit up her face, from the inside out "—there is a silver lining to all this. The PTA president for Forest Hills High School is a neighbor. She saw the sign and loved it and wants to talk to me about making yard signs for all the graduating seniors, ASAP. Apparently they weren't happy with the vendor that did them last year. I was going to catch my breath and then call her this evening."

Griff nodded. "I was going to go for a run so I'll leave you to it. See you later?"

Her manner more aloof than it had been in weeks, Mackenzie turned away from him. Ready, it seemed, to resume her very independent life. "Sounds good," she said.

Hoping they would be able to retain at least some of the closeness they had been able to get back over the weekend, Griff went up to change, then did his usual six miles. As always, the exercise cleared his head. Left him feeling relaxed and happy.

When he came back in the house, the delicious smell of dinner underway filled the air. Now *this* was one of his fantasies!

Grinning, he headed toward the rear of the house. Mackenzie was in the kitchen. She had changed into a pair of soft, figure-hugging jeans, a navy-and-burgundy plaid shirt, and sneakers. Her hair was swept up into a ponytail.

She had a mesh bag of yellow onions, another bag of romaine lettuce and a cantaloupe on the counter. He saw she was busy checking the labels on all three items, against the screen on her phone.

"What's going on?" Griff helped himself to more water.

"I got an alert. There's been a listeria outbreak and recall. I'm checking to make sure we don't have any of the contaminated items in our possession, and…we don't." She smiled in relief.

"That's good. Listeria can really be serious." Griff recalled seeing a news story on an otherwise healthy man who became ill after eating contaminated produce and died after several days in intensive care.

"Yeah, I know." Mackenzie turned back to the fridge. Rummaging through it, she began pulling out several blocks of cheese, a carton of milk, some butter, a few tomatoes, a red onion, a jalapeño, a bunch of cilantro and a lime. She added those to the package of tortilla chips on the counter, then walked over to the stove and gave the sizzling crumbles of spicy ground beef another stir.

That must have been what he inhaled walking in! "Tex-Mex?" he asked excitedly.

"I feel like nachos," she said.

He opened the refrigerator and pulled out two beers.

"Then we *must* be celebrating," he murmured playfully, aware how quiet it was without Bliss in the kitchen with them.

A sudden smile lit up her gorgeous face. "We are," she reported. "I got the Forest Hills PTA gig. Three hundred eighty-six signs at twenty dollars each. And another big sign for two hundred fifty dollars, congratulating all the graduating seniors."

"Sounds like a lot of work." He opened both bottles and handed her one.

She toasted him wordlessly. "And it will bring in a lot of work."

Wondering why she was so eager to take on something today that she had almost turned down a few days ago, he said, "I thought Forest Hills was outside your usual service area."

She added several tablespoons of butter to a hot saucepan. "I changed my mind about that. Maybe it is time to expand."

Griff wanted her to be successful. He also knew the

steep personal cost of all work and no play. Nevertheless, he would support her the way she had bolstered him. "Well, then, congratulations!" He nodded at the dinner preparations. "Anything I can do to help?"

She replied merrily, "I was hoping you'd ask!" She handed him a box grater and two blocks of cheese. "Shred these for me, please."

Happy to see some of their old camaraderie returning, he smiled back. "Sure."

She drained and rinsed a can of spicy black beans. Cast him a glance. "Did the run make you feel better?"

So, she had noticed his unexpectedly black mood on the journey home, Griff thought as he began to grate the Monterey Jack. He had been trying to hide it. But he also sensed she wanted him to give some sort of explanation for it. Trouble was, he didn't really know why he'd suddenly been so cranky. He'd thought the victory would be the crowning achievement in his life. And it had been, yet after the initial elation had faded, he had been left feeling like the old song lyrics: *Is that all there is?*

But maybe all he really needed was a new goal. Like name partner of *his own* firm.

Or something else that would take years, and tons of effort and focus… Something that would make him forget about the absence of family in his life.

Aware Mackenzie was still waiting to hear his explanation, he said, "Yeah. The run helped. It always does."

"I feel the same way about my long walks with Bliss." She stirred equal parts milk and chicken stock into the roux of butter and flour. "So what were you grumpy about earlier?" she queried, assessing him with a head-to-toe look. "I mean, you got what you wanted. To be named the new senior partner at the firm."

"Normally, I'm all about winning, especially when it comes to the law, but I felt bad for my two competitors."

"I saw them when they were leaving. Grant and Ella were trying to hide it, but they were pretty dispirited."

He handed her the Monterey Jack. Their fingers touched as they made the exchange. He felt a surge of awareness.

"What do you think they're going to do?"

He started working on the block of longhorn cheddar. "Ella will hang on. Maybe use this window to have the baby she and her husband have been thinking about. Grant will probably do what I would in the same situation. Leave and get promoted elsewhere."

She turned. "You really would have done that?"

He had privately been working on a contingency plan all weekend—in the event he had turned up a loser. "Cut my losses and move on? Yeah," he said. "I really would have." Although he wouldn't have wanted to change anything about his arrangement with Mackenzie as a consequence, especially now, since they had made love and discovered the depth of passion between them.

No wonder Griff had been grim on the drive home. He'd been a razor's edge away from leaving the law firm he had dedicated his life to for the last ten years. "You would really do that?" When they had talked weeks ago, he had been on the fence.

Griff nodded. "As much as I love Joe, and his wife Alice, and lot of the other people who work there, sometimes you just have to accept you don't belong and you're not ever going to as much as you might wish otherwise. Had I not been promoted now," he confessed soberly, "that really would have been the reason."

"But you married me," Mackenzie protested. She

grinned, adding, in an attempt to lighten the mood, "*Twice!* So you could stay at the firm!"

He grinned back, flirtatiously now, and waggled his eyebrows at her. "I know!" He stopped what he was doing, took her by the hand and danced her around the galley kitchen, ending with a little spin and a dip that left her clinging to his broad shoulders. "They would have been nuts not to realize what a find you are!"

Except, Mackenzie thought, Griff didn't really feel that way. At least not in the I'm-so-in-love-with-you-I-have-to-marry-you way that she wanted her forever husband to someday have. And deep in her heart she knew that this marriage would not work over the long haul unless they were both really and truly, *hopelessly* in love with each other.

Sensing a shift in her mood, Griff slowly righted her.

Mackenzie worked to reconfigure her feelings, too. She wrinkled her nose at him. "Those dance lessons you made us take when we were in college really paid off," she teased.

"Yeah, well," Griff said, shrugging, "if there's a hole in your background…"

Like growing up without a dad and then later, without a mom, either, Mackenzie thought. Worse, having no one interested in adopting you.

Oblivious to the heart-rending nature of her thoughts, Griff continued, "…you have to fill it somehow. In my case—" he splayed his hands across his broad chest "—it was with dance and etiquette classes."

She put an index finger to her chin. "I always do look to you when I have a question about silverware."

He chuckled and the rich, masculine sound filled the kitchen. Their glances met, held. Mackenzie felt another shiver of awareness.

She really was close to falling in love with her best friend.

Not that she would ever let that happen. If he could never reciprocate...

As always, seeming to be on the same wavelength as her, Griff sobered slightly, too. "So what else can I do to help?" he asked in that low, gravelly voice that she loved.

Distraction. That was what they needed. "Help me put together the nachos?"

For the next few minutes, they spread a single layer of chips on a parchment-covered baking sheet, then sprinkled it with black beans, seasoned beef, queso, sliced jalapeños and shredded cheese. Several more layers followed. Mackenzie slid the tray into the oven and put the finishing touches on the pico de gallo and guacamole while Griff set the table in the mini breakfast nook next to the window.

"I miss Bliss," he said finally.

Mackenzie sighed. "Me, too. But she will be back tomorrow afternoon."

They divvied up the towering stack of nachos into two plates and then carried them over to the small round café table and two chairs Mackenzie had owned since her college days. They sat opposite each other. Their knees touched briefly as they got settled, and again Mackenzie felt another fierce surge of attraction.

Damn it all, if she didn't want to make love to him again.

Knowing, however, that decision wasn't just up to her, she focused on the reality of their current situation. "So what's up for you next?" she asked casually. "Do you move offices right away or does that wait a while?"

"They'll probably go ahead and move me up there tomorrow, but then I'll have to meet with the decorator and decide how I want it to look."

She bit into a crisp, delicious chip loaded with sump-tuous toppings. "And how's that?"

He paused to extricate a melty layer, and top it with pico and guac. "Classy."

She watched as he took his first bite, then smiled. "Masculine?"

"Definitely." He devoured another. "Wow, this is good."

Mackenzie giggled. Her sister Faith swore the way to a man's heart, or at least her man's heart, was through his stomach. She had always been skeptical. But now...was it possible there was something to it? Should she cook for Griff more often? Or hold back, the same way she was deliberately curtailing her feelings? "And it's got all the food groups, too," she teased.

He savored every bite with the same sensuality he made love. "Then we're going to have to have it for din-ner more often."

We. She liked the sound of that.

"So...what else?" she inquired as they both continued to chow down. "Are you going to get a new car?"

His sexy smile widened. "What makes you think that?"

She shrugged, aware his happiness was contagious. This was the kind of spirited emotional reaction she had expected from him, in the wake of his win. "The fact that you always get one when you celebrate another rung up the career ladder."

"True." The crinkles bracketing his golden-brown eyes deepened. He tilted his head, his gaze drifting over her. "And you're right," he murmured. "I have been thinking about my options. But I probably won't decide the specifics right away. I like to take my time picking something out, special order it."

She held his gaze, her pulse accelerating. "Another Porsche?"

He winked at her. "I'm going to surprise you. And Bliss. But—" he paused to give her a more serious look "—now that we're on the topic of money, I am getting a rather significant raise."

What did that have to do with her? Since they had decided not to comingle finances? She felt a little irritated, though she couldn't say why. "Good for you."

"So we can afford to do something about all this." He pointed to the orange flocked wallpaper and the very dated olive-green appliances in the kitchen, along with the mess of stacked moving boxes in the adjacent family room.

"I'm okay with it like this for now."

But he wasn't.

Recalling how neat and tidy and well-decorated his downtown loft had always been, she drew a deep breath. "I promise you I'll get to it or at least a lot of the reno by summer's end." Then they could fully unpack.

He sat back in his chair, his broad shoulders flexing beneath the fabric of his running shirt. His look gentled. "The point is you don't have to, Mack. We can afford to hire painters. And floor refinishers, or buy area rugs, at the very least. And then maybe *we* can both put all our stuff away?"

There he went with the "we" again.

Only this time it was in the sense of him telling her what to do, and how and when to do it!

Mackenzie held on to her temper with effort. She finished chewing. Dabbed the corners of her mouth with her napkin. Then took a deep breath and gave him her most politely sincere look. Reminding herself he was no doubt trying to be helpful.

"Thank you. It's very generous of you to offer to finance the labor. But I wouldn't feel right about it unless I could pay half and I can't afford that right now, not without dipping into my savings…"

His gaze narrowed. "The point is," he returned patiently, digging in, too, "I can."

She stared at him, hurt. "You really want to rub in the disparity of our incomes?"

He caught her hand before she could get up. "What I want is for us to tackle this problem we're facing—and it *is* a problem, Mack—and talk realistically," he said in what sounded suspiciously like a take-charge husband tone. "You're going to be awfully busy for the next few months."

But she was no obedient wife. She compressed her lips. "We'll get those signs for the high school PTA done."

He wasn't arguing that. "But there's also Mother's Day, and other graduations, and weddings. Then Father's Day and the Fourth of July…"

He really had been paying attention.

Somehow, that soothed her.

She sat back. "Okay. Point made. It's my busiest season."

He reached over to cover her hand with his. "So how about you let me help you?" He held up a staying palm before she could object. "You can pay me back by cooking for me on the weekends, or something."

She realized he meant it purely as a negotiating point. Because he knew she didn't like owing or depending on anyone else. Still, it rankled. Maybe because it reminded her of a past error in the relationship department. She let out a slow, indignant breath. "I'm not cleaning up after you, counselor."

"Wouldn't ask you to do that. *Ever*," he replied firmly, and somehow she knew that was true.

He studied her, his heart suddenly on his sleeve. "So, do we have a deal?" he asked softly.

She wanted to say yes. "Give me time to think about it," she hedged.

He nodded, not happy, but not necessarily unhappy, either. "Okay."

They continued eating, and his cell phone chimed. He looked at the screen. She lifted a brow.

"Work email." He thumbed through the messages, his face resigned and tense.

"What is it?" she asked before she could stop herself.

"I just got handed five big eminent domain cases from Ed Hale, the founding partner who is going to retire permanently next May."

"Is that good?"

He scrubbed a hand over his face. "Challenging. Given the stakes are always so high."

Mackenzie didn't envy him that kind of pressure. "Do you need to start working on them tonight?" she asked kindly.

He shook his head. Turned off his phone completely, then put it away. "Tomorrow is soon enough." He took her hand and pulled her to her feet. All the way into his arms.

She gripped him by the shoulders. "What are you doing?" she asked breathlessly.

He unbuttoned her shirt. Reached behind her to unclasp her bra. "What do you think I'm doing?"

Her nipples pearled against his palms. "Griff…"

He kissed her temple, cheek, the nape of her neck.

"You asked me to make love to you last night. Now, I'm asking you to make love with me."

She trembled as his hands scored her skin. "This could become a habit."

Desire flared in his amber eyes. "I certainly hope so," he murmured, his lips quirking into a sexy grin. "So... your bed or mine?"

His was bigger and more comfy. Plus she was feeling oddly territorial. "Yours."

"Then mine it is." He swept her up in his arms and strode down the hall.

She clung to him, her breath coming hard and fast in her chest. "The dishes..." she protested weakly.

He stopped to kiss her cheek. "I'll do them later." His lips gently traced hers. "Right now, I have serious business to attend to."

He carried her easily up the stairs and down the hall to his bedroom. To her surprise, the usually neatly made covers had already been turned down. He set her down next to the bed, his gaze intently locked with hers. Then he kissed her, slow and sweet, hard and deep, and every way in between. She felt his need and yearning, and it mirrored hers. Helpless to resist, she arched against him, both pursuing and surrendering.

Aware she had never felt sexier in her life, she let the sandpaper feel of his evening beard sensually abrade her face. Her nipples beaded and her breasts swelled as his lips made an unbearably sensual tour downward. The next thing she knew, her shirt and bra were all the way off, her pants unzipped, her panties whisked off.

She made short work of getting him naked, too, then ran her fingertips across his broad shoulders, the hard muscle of his chest and his satiny warm skin. Lower still, past his flat abs, he was even more masculine.

"Have I told you how gorgeous you are?" he whispered, guiding her down onto the center of the bed.

He certainly made her feel that way. She brought him down to stretch out beside her. They lay on their sides, her thigh draped across his hip, his hardness pressed against the apex of her thighs. Her body ignited, and she was so consumed with wanting him inside her she could barely breathe. His gaze traveled over her, causing her to quiver all the more. Moments later, he found her with his lips and hands, sending her to the brink. Needing to give as well as receive, she whispered back, "Let me…" She wanted to say "love you" but murmured, "…touch you…" instead.

Grinning devilishly, he held fast. "In due time." And then his mouth was on her in the most intimate of kisses, commanding total surrender. She slid into oblivion. Still devouring her, he held her while she quaked.

Moving back up her body, he reached for the condom beside the bed. Opened the pack and with her help, slid it on. Possessing her with one smooth sure stroke. Awash with feeling, she rose to meet him. Easing his hands beneath her, he lifted her, going deeper, slower, harder. Their bodies blended, merging in a way that was truly seismic. Until there was no more waiting, only feeling this hot, melting bliss.

Afterward, Mackenzie lay with her head on Griff's chest. She wasn't sure what any of this meant. If *any-thing*. So, the logical thing was to ask. Lifting her head, she rested her chin on her fist, hoping like heck their passion wasn't just a fling that would quickly fade away. Summoning her courage, she did her best to pretend an insouciance she really didn't feel. "Um, Griff?"

He stroked his hand through her hair. "Mmm-hmm?"

"Are we going to have to renegotiate our deal?"

For a moment, he went very still. Too late, she realized he hadn't seen this coming. But her question was out there. She couldn't take it back.

He squinted matter-of-factly, proposing, "To what?"

She spouted out the first thing that came to mind. "Friends with benefits...?"

"Who just also happened to be legally married now in every sense...*except*...the financial?"

Sometimes he was such a lawyer! But then, maybe that was good, to have it all out in the open. Certainly they'd been straightforward in terms of their desires for the last twenty-four hours, so...why pretend now? They'd had a deal. The original terms of no sex had definitely changed. Like it or not, they needed to discuss what came next so there would be no unpleasant or hurtful surprises. Aware he was still watching her carefully, she shrugged. "Something like that. Yes."

Griff gave her the look, the one that said he would never be able to get enough of her. He pulled her all the way on top of him and framed her face with both his hands. He kissed her thoroughly.

"Sounds good to me," he rasped with that gruff tenderness she adored. And then as if to prove it, made love to her all over again.

Chapter Eleven

July 7...

Luanne and Lenny put the last of the signs into the delivery van and shut the doors. Mackenzie closed the tailgate on her pickup truck and opened the door for Bliss, who jumped into the front seat.

"So what are you going to do for your anniversary?" Luanne asked, starry-eyed as ever.

Mackenzie stopped dead in her tracks. She faced off with her twenty-year-old employee. "What are you talking about?"

"You and Griff eloped four months ago today," Lenny reminded her.

She slid behind the wheel and, leaving the driver's door open, started the engine. Turning up the AC until cold air blasted out of the vents. "Oh, yeah. Right..."

"Aren't you going to celebrate?"

Mackenzie was pretty sure they'd make love. But for no other reason than they really liked making love with each other.

"Griff is working late tonight, too," she said. "But we'll probably do something special this weekend," she fibbed. "In the meantime, we better get these deliveries made. You-all got your list?"

They nodded. Waving, took off.

Mackenzie headed off in another direction. Three hours later, she had installed the last yard sign and headed for her own neighborhood.

Nine thirty; it was starting to get dark.

Griff likely wouldn't be home until very late. She thought about hitting a drive-through and getting something to eat, but the truth was she was a little nauseated from all the running around in the heat, so she drove straight home and pulled into the driveway. His side of the driveway was empty. The house was dark. And the lack of motion felt good. Bliss stood, stretched all four of her legs, and moved across the bench seat to plop down next to her and place her head on her lap. Mackenzie liked the song playing on the radio, so she sat there in the air-conditioning, petting her dog, listening to the music and reflecting on the last four months.

It had been an incredibly busy time, for both her and Griff. Thanks to the graduation sign gig, her business was expanding exponentially. And he was so slammed at work, she almost never saw him before 10:00 or 11:00 p.m. But they made love and slept together every night.

And that made up for the chaos in the rest of their personal life. The fact that neither had yet unpacked all their stuff or done any renovating. Or that any spare time they did have was spent tossing the ball for Bliss, or walking her.

But Mackenzie imagined that, too, would change, once things settled down. In the meantime, all she really wanted to do was sit here a few moments longer, with her eyes closed and her dog snuggling against her.

Although Griff didn't actually see Mackenzie turn her pickup truck into their driveway, it was obvious from her still-running engine and the dark house that she had just arrived home, too. He shut off his ignition, climbed out of the Porsche and circled around to the driver's door. To his surprise, his wife wasn't talking on the phone. Instead, she had her eyes closed and was slumped slightly to one side. Bliss was nestled beside her, with her head in Mackenzie's lap. But, seeing Griff, she sat up and wagged her tail, looked at Mackenzie in obvious concern and confusion, and then gave a short woof.

Griff understood. He was alarmed, too.

Unfortunately, the driver's door was locked. He rapped on the window sharply. "Mackenzie!" he shouted to be heard above her car radio. "Mackenzie! Are you okay?"

Bliss barked again. She pawed Mackenzie's shoulder and then her lap.

Mackenzie moaned and struggled to sit up. He called her name again, rapping on the glass. Rubbing her eyes, she turned to look at him sleepily.

"Unlock the door!" he ordered.

Frowning, she pushed the electronic button beneath the window. The lock clicked and he pulled open the door. Mackenzie rubbed her eyes again. "What's going on?" she asked in confusion.

"I just got home! Your truck engine was on. You were passed out behind the wheel."

She frowned. Sighed loudly. "No, I wasn't. I think I just fell asleep."

This was even less like her. He reached across her to turn off the truck engine. "For how long?"

She shoved her hands through her hair. Swiveled in the seat and stepped down onto the driveway beside him. "I don't know. Maybe half an hour." Yawning, she collected her handbag and keys. Then grabbed the leash and gestured for Bliss to follow her.

Aware how pale and off-kilter she looked, Griff asked, "Are you sure that's what happened?"

"I am sure I did not faint!" She glared at him beneath the fringe of thick blond eyelashes. "And I did not have anything alcoholic to drink so...what else could it have been, except me accidentally falling asleep?"

Thank God she had not been driving at the time.

Bliss headed for a patch of grass. When she finished, she turned and trotted toward the front door. Griff and Mackenzie followed behind her.

As they reached the front steps leading up to the door, Mackenzie swayed slightly and then stumbled. He reached out to steady her only to be pushed violently away, as she spun around and lurched toward the bushes.

Mackenzie thought the evening couldn't get any more humiliating. She was wrong. The last thing she wanted to do was throw up in front of anyone. Never mind Griff. But that was exactly what she had done, she realized with dismay as she sat down on the front porch steps and tried to regain her equilibrium.

"Well, this explains a lot," Griff remarked. He sat down beside her and put a consoling arm around her shoulders, regarding her gently. "How long have you been feeling under the weather?"

Not exactly sure—she had been dragging all day— Mackenzie shrugged and pushed to her feet once again.

Knees wobbling, she picked up her shoulder bag from where she dropped it and headed toward the front door. Bliss was on one side, Griff the other.

She hated any sign of weakness. And right now she felt shaky as a newborn kitten.

"Mack?" he prodded again.

Fighting a second wave of nausea, she punched in the security code and opened the front door. "Let's forget you just witnessed that, okay?" She motioned for Bliss to go in ahead of her and then followed, hitting the lights as she moved.

Clearly not about to honor her request, Griff accompanied her to the kitchen. "Why didn't you call me and let me know you were sick?" he persisted.

Mackenzie turned on the faucet and splashed cold water on her face. Then rinsed out her mouth. "Because I wasn't sick." She leaned back against the counter, hands braced on either side of her, feeling more miserable than ever. "At least I wasn't until just now."

"Do you think it could be food poisoning?"

"Doubtful. I haven't had anything to eat since lunch, and salmonella usually hits within a few hours of ingesting bad food."

He touched her forehead. "Doesn't feel like you have a fever."

Mackenzie shook her head to try to clear it as another wave of dizziness moved through her. "I—I probably should just go to…"

Bed, she started to say.

But couldn't.

Turning, she whirled back toward the sink and thoroughly humiliated herself in front of Griff for a second time.

This time when she finished, he brought a chair over to her where she stood and guided her onto the seat. Got a clean dish towel out of the drawer, wet it with cold water and put it around the back of her neck. Then he grabbed a second towel, dampened it and gave it to her to use on her face.

"We're taking you to the ER."

She gulped, terribly afraid she was going to be sick for the third time. She waved off the idea. "Can't get in a car right now." The motion would trigger another round of puking.

His concern intensifying, he knelt in front of her. "You want me to call an ambulance then?"

"Don't be ridiculous." Mackenzie drew in short, stabilizing breaths. "It's probably just some weird virus," she said vaguely.

"Or listeria. There's been three separate outbreaks since April. Roughly one every four to six weeks…"

"And I checked the fridge each time, remember? We didn't buy anything that was recalled."

"Which doesn't mean you didn't eat anything that was contaminated. Because you have had raw fruits and vegetables at restaurants."

"So have you."

"Except I'm not sick. You are."

"If it is listeria, and not just a wicked twenty-four-hour virus—" she pressed a hand to her lips as another wave threatened "—then we will know because I'll keep getting sick."

"Yes, and if it is listeria it can also be deadly." His handsome face grew even more determined. "We are not taking any chances with your health, Mack, so we're going to the ER."

He paused long enough to put fresh water in Bliss's drinking bowl. "Has she eaten her dinner?"

Appreciating his love for her beloved pooch, Mackenzie nodded. "Earlier."

He eased a hand beneath her elbow. "You want me to get a towel for you?"

"And maybe a bucket." Since the last thing they needed was anything messing up the pristine interior of his Porsche.

She put the window down as he drove to the hospital. The abundance of fresh air helped, and she managed not to get sick again but she was still very shaky and unbelievably nauseated as she signed in with the registration desk.

The clerk looked at Griff. "Are you her husband?"

Mackenzie said no at the same time Griff said yes. Which for some reason made Mackenzie blush and giggle in distress. How could she have forgotten that?

The clerk lifted a brow.

"Newlyweds," Griff explained.

Embarrassed, she waved off her mistake. "I'm just a little woozy," she said in way of explanation.

The clerk looked at Griff. "She confused about anything else?"

He paused, his worry evident. "Not sure. Maybe."

"I'll let Triage know. Luckily, we're not very busy right now."

They were advised to take a seat. She had left her bucket in the car but still had the towel in her hands just in case. Griff wrapped his arm about her shoulders. Even though it wasn't necessary, she felt comforted by his tenderness and compassion.

"Sorry about the marriage thing," she whispered. "I just forgot."

He nodded, for the briefest second showing a flash of

the hurt he had often evidenced on adoption fair days. Then it was gone. "Crazy night."

He seemed to have forgiven her lapse, and at least it hadn't been in front of anyone he worked with, she thought gratefully. She held his gaze, telegraphing her deepest apology. "It really has—"

They called her name. Griff didn't even ask if she wanted him to go or stay, and she was glad about that. She really wanted him to accompany her but didn't know if she should ask him to. In taking the decision out of her hands, he had made it easier on her.

And he continued supporting her as she answered all the admitting nurse's questions about what had brought them to the hospital emergency room. The nurse put an oximeter on Mackenzie's finger and a blood pressure cuff on her arm. As the cuff inflated, she stuck a thermometer under Mackenzie's tongue and asked, "When did you start feeling nauseated?"

"A few weeks ago. Off and on."

Griff did a double take, which forced Mackenzie to defend herself. "I never actually got sick. I thought it was from the heat."

"You are dehydrated," the nurse observed, pinching her skin.

"That why her complexion is so gray?" Griff asked.

The nurse nodded. She withdrew the thermometer. "Your temp is normal. Your blood pressure and heart rate are both elevated. Have you had any problems with either before?"

Well, her heart raced a lot whenever she was around Griff these days, but that probably wasn't what the nurse was referencing. Mackenzie quashed a smile, and Griff gave her another curious look. The nurse waited for her reply. "Um, no," she said. "No history of either."

"You said you were dizzy." The nurse gestured for Mackenzie to get in the wheelchair. When she did, she pushed her through the triage room doors and past the center circle of desks in the corridor, to one of the private exam rooms.

"Have you fainted?" She indicated Mackenzie should move to the bed. Griff gallantly assisted her.

Mackenzie leaned in to his masculine strength. When her cheek brushed his stubbled chin, a whiff of his sandalwood and leather scent set her heart to racing even more.

Figuring she had to be completely candid if she wanted an accurate diagnosis, she admitted ruefully, "No, but I've come close a couple of times."

Griff's brow knotted. He exhaled, still watching her intently. And remained close enough to reach out and help if she needed him.

"Again, I thought that it was the heat." Sneaker-clad feet dangling, Mackenzie perched on the side of the bed. She braced her hands on either side of her. "That can get to me sometimes, particularly when I am out in the sun."

Griff reached out to tenderly tuck a strand of hair behind her ear. "I didn't know that," he said.

Mackenzie imagined there was a lot they still didn't know about each other.

"You should have told me," he chided.

Except their marriage vows hadn't contained the in-sickness-and-in-health part.

The nurse seemed to agree with him. "Okay, everything off," she said, handing Mackenzie a hospital gown. "This ties in the back." Griff was given a blanket. "She can put that over her. It will help keep her warm."

It was cold in there, Mackenzie thought, beginning to shiver.

"Want some help?" he asked gently.

Figuring she had been humiliated enough for one night, Mackenzie shook her head and motioned for him to turn around. She stripped down quickly beneath the unforgiving fluorescent light, put the gown on and climbed onto the bed.

"Ready for the blanket?" he asked, with his back to her.

Mackenzie tied her gown at the neck and then the waist. And felt it gape uncomfortably in between. Shivering all the more, she said, "Y-y-yes."

He spread it over her and helped her adjust the pillow behind her head, making her realize what a good husband he was. Even if their union was not romantic in nature.

"How is the nausea?" he asked.

Mackenzie gulped back the acid rising in her throat. "Still there."

The nurse returned, an IV bag and antinausea medication in hand. "This will help," she said.

And it did.

By the time Dr. Phillips, a petite woman in her late forties, came in a few minutes later, Mackenzie no longer felt like she was going to upchuck again.

"So tell me what's going on," the ER physician said.

Mackenzie explained. Dr. Phillips examined her abdomen for tenderness, and they went over everything she had recently eaten.

Griff stood against the wall, arms crossed in front of him. "I'm worried about listeria," he said.

Dr. Phillips stepped to the computer in the room, logged in and began to type. "Understandable with the wave of outbreaks we've had this spring and summer. But not to worry. We'll check for that and other foodborne illnesses in the blood work we're going to run."

Finished making her initial notes, she turned back to Mackenzie. "Any history of GI problems?"

"No."

"Are you on the birth-control pill?"

Mackenzie flushed self-consciously. "No." She and Griff always used condoms.

Dr. Phillips squinted. "Any other kind of hormones?"

Now Griff and the nurse were watching her closely, too! Mackenzie shook her head.

Dr. Phillips checked off a box. "When was your last period?"

Good question. Had she even had one since she and Griff had hooked up? Heat gathered in Mackenzie's chest and moved into her throat. She felt herself flush bright red. "I'm not sure." She explained there had been one super light one, but she wasn't sure when that had been.

Dr. Phillips lifted a brow. "Is that normal?"

Mackenzie could no longer even look at Griff. She focused on a spot on the wall. "When I'm stressed, yes. Sometimes they stop altogether for a few months."

Dr. Phillips asked gently, "And have you been under pressure?"

Was the world round? Mackenzie swept both hands through her hair, or tried to—one was still attached to an IV line. She had no idea how to answer that. Luckily, Griff stepped in, taking her hand. He smiled over at Dr. Phillips and the nurse. "We got married a few months ago and moved into a new place. And—" he squeezed her palm "—we're both really busy with our jobs."

Dr. Phillips sympathized. "So, you've had a lot going on."

Mackenzie nodded. "Yes." Although a lot of it, especially the sex and the sleeping together, and the occasional shared meal or dog walk, had been good...

The ER doc tilted her head. "Any chance you could be pregnant?"

Mackenzie looked at Griff. They had taken such pains to safeguard against that! "No," they said in unison.

Dr. Phillips jotted something on the chart. "We'll run some blood work. See what turns up."

The nurse and doctor exited.

Neither Griff nor Mackenzie could think of much to say while they waited for the results. "We've used a condom every time," she said finally, as much to reassure herself as him.

"And they weren't expired, either," he added.

Mackenzie drew a deep, enervating breath. "So we can't be…"

Except, as it turned out, they were.

Griff stared at the ER doc, feeling every bit as stunned as Mackenzie looked. He had always wanted a family, but he had never been sure it would actually happen for him. And certainly not like this. "You're sure?" he rasped, torn between elation and shock.

Dr. Phillips beamed. "Yes."

Mackenzie reached for his hand. Realizing she was shaking outwardly the way he was shaking inside, he squeezed her fingers tightly. "When are we due?"

"Since we don't have the date of her last menses, the quickest way to pin it down would be to refer you to your ob-gyn and let them do an ultrasound."

Mackenzie didn't look like she could wait. She bit her lip. "Can we do one tonight?"

The doctor hesitated momentarily, but then she smiled. "Actually, we've got an intern working here tonight who could use some practice. Hang tight, and he will be right in."

Still appearing as if she were in shock, too, Mackenzie looked at Griff. "Unbelievable," she whispered. Tears of joy shimmered in her eyes.

He felt a lump of emotion tightening his throat. "Very much so," he whispered back, moving in to hug her close.

She was still clinging to him when the door opened. A young kid in scrubs and a short white coat wheeled in the machine. He barely looked old enough to drive. Griff wasn't sure he wanted "Doogie Howser" working on his wife, but Mackenzie seemed okay with it, so…

Still holding Mackenzie's hand, Griff watched as the machine was plugged in and turned on; gel was spread across her middle.

The intern explained what he was doing, as he moved the wand across Mackenzie's belly. The screen filled with shifting white waves and blurry images. He seemed to be squinting at the screen every bit as much as they were. Finally he stopped the wand and smiled. "And here we have a heartbeat. Nice and strong…and…" The intern moved the wand again. Then went very still, while the blurry white sound waves continued to move. "Um." He put the wand aside and stood abruptly. "I, ah…" He swallowed hard. "I'll be right back." He darted out of the room.

Mackenzie looked at Griff. "What was that all about?"

Griff forced himself to be the calm, reassuring husband Mackenzie needed him to be. "Maybe he needs to figure out how to get us a picture to take home…" he suggested.

Mackenzie did not look convinced. Which wasn't surprising. Griff wasn't, either.

The door opened.

The ER doctor and the intern came back in. "Okay," Dr. Phillips said, "show me what you found."

He resumed the test. "See…this is…"

"Definitely a baby. A good-looking, healthy baby," the ER doctor said, smiling.

"And then I found this..." the intern told them.

Dr. Phillips nodded approvingly. "Which is another good-looking, healthy baby."

"So there are *two*?" the intern asked, stunned.

"Yes." The ER doctor turned to them, her excitement evident. "Congratulations, you-all! In approximately six months, Mackenzie will be giving birth to a set of twins!"

Chapter Twelve

Mackenzie woke to sunlight streaming in through the blinds. For a moment, she wondered if it had all been a dream. Then she looked around and saw she was in Griff's bedroom. She remembered coming home exhausted at 4:00 a.m. and falling into bed. He had kissed her forehead and held her close. Now, he was gone. Her phone said it was 9:30 a.m., so she imagined he was already at work.

And she couldn't help but be a little disappointed about that. She had wanted to talk to him about their situation. Sooner rather than later.

But as she lay there looking around, she could hardly blame him for wanting to exit the premises.

The walls in his bedroom were an ugly shade of green instead of the sophisticated gray he preferred. The clothes in his closet were neatly arranged. Suits and ties and crisply dry-cleaned shirts on one side, weekend and work-

out clothes the other. Unlike her, he had unpacked everything that went in his bedroom. There were no stacked
moving boxes here. She could not say that about the rest
of the house.

Feeling guilty because she hadn't held up her end of
the bargain when it came to organizing and updating their
surroundings, she rose from the bed. Then she slowly
padded down the hall to her own bathroom, washed her
face, brushed her hair and teeth, and headed downstairs
still clad in a pink-and-white-striped thigh-length night-
shirt and snug-fitting white capri leggings.

The first thing that hit her was the smell of freshly
brewed espresso. Which smelled good, although, given
her recent bout of nausea, she couldn't say she actually
wanted any. Or should have anything but decaf, now that
she knew she was pregnant.

The second thing that registered was the sight of a
boxer-and-T-shirt-clad Griff struggling to work at the
small café table in the kitchen.

His chestnut-brown hair was rumpled and standing
on end in a tousled bedhead kind of way, and his handsome jaw was rimmed with a day's growth of beard.
Papers were stacked around him, along with a laptop,
phone, legal pad and pen. Bliss was curled up contentedly at his feet, sleeping soundly. The sight of the two
of them brought on an unexpected wave of tenderness
and contentment.

Looking equally satisfied, he glanced up and broke
out in a relieved smile. "Hey, you're up."

Filled with the urge to throw herself in his arms and
indulge in a lengthy, and let's face it, *needy* hug, she instead went to the fridge and got out the orange juice.
They had a deal to be friends and lovers, and nothing
more, she reminded herself. Expecting twins did not need

to change a situation that had been working out okay. Because change could bring on an awareness of unmet needs, and a breakup. And that she really did not want.

Smiling back at him as casually as possible she poured herself a glass. "What are you doing here?" She sipped the tart liquid, testing the state of her tummy, and thankfully finding it to be nausea-free. "Shouldn't you be at the office?" It was Thursday, after all. A workday.

He continued to watch her, with a deep affection that was as new and different as her pregnancy. His glance slid to her tummy. He rose languidly, being careful not to disturb the still snoozing Bliss, and moved to her side. Then reached past her to get a glass from the cabinet and poured himself a serving, too. Wordlessly, he clinked the rim of his glass against hers. Sipped. "I'm not leaving you when you're sick," he said quietly.

Recalling how she had humiliated herself with repeated vomiting the night before, she flushed. "But I'm not sick," she argued back just as quietly. "I'm just pregnant."

He nodded, his gaze darkening seriously, as they roved her, head to toe, before returning to her eyes. "And we need to talk about that."

For a moment, Griff thought Mackenzie was going to refuse, or at the very least put the discussion off. Apparently realizing avoidance would not make this situation any easier, she gave a brief nod. Then looked toward the table. "I can move all this." He gestured at his work.

"No." Mackenzie drank the rest of her juice, suddenly looking as if she were feeling boxed in. "Let's go outside." Her slender shoulders squared determinedly, she walked through the French doors leading to the covered patio and took a seat on the cushion glider she took with her from place to place. Guessing she needed her space, at least for the moment, he pulled up a cushion chair and set it opposite her.

He leaned toward her, hands clasped loosely between his knees, as he took in her tousled blond hair and pink cheeks. Guessing what might be behind her wary attitude, he said, "First of all, I want you to know I'm really happy about the pregnancy."

A dazzling smile broke out across her face, the shock they'd both felt the night before replaced with pure joy akin to his own. "I am, too." She looked deep into his eyes and lifted a delicate palm. Her plain gold wedding ring glimmered in the morning sunlight, along with his. "Even if it was unexpected."

He grinned ruefully, recollecting as he rubbed a hand across his jaw. "We were careful despite what the doctor seemed to think last night."

"So careful that…" she agreed, blushing, "it's pretty darn close to a miracle." Her eyes took on an emotional sheen. "And then, when you consider it's twins…!" She shook her head in renewed wonderment.

Again, shared excitement shimmered between them. Wishing they'd embarked on a traditional marriage from the get-go, if only because it would have made this situation so much easier to handle, Griff remarked, "It sort of seems like it's meant to be, doesn't it?"

She nodded, clasping her hands in front of her, abruptly looking as off guard as he felt. "The question is—what do we do next?"

Luckily for both of them, complicated situations were his specialty. Sensing she needed him to be exceedingly practical, at least for now, he went into lawyer mode and countered affably, "We negotiate another new deal."

She sucked in a breath. Wariness dominated her expression. "What kind of new deal?"

He moved to sit next to her on the glider, his bare leg pressing against her knit-clad thigh. "The kind that lets us stay married and bring up these kids together," he replied.

She raked her teeth across her lush lower lip. Then sent him a sidelong glance. "We could still do that if we eventually divorced like we originally planned."

Aware he had never met a woman who fascinated him as much as Mackenzie did, he asked, "Do you want to only have custody of the kids fifty percent of the time?"

She looked at him, her stubborn resistance to real, enduring commitment seeming to slip just a little bit. "No."

"I don't, either."

Silence fell. She used the toe of her moccasin to push the glider restlessly back and forth. "It still wouldn't be a real marriage."

It felt pretty real to him right about now, but he knew what she meant. They hadn't been in this for the long haul and still weren't. Unless things changed.

Exhaling, he wrapped an arm about her shoulders. When she turned to face him, he looked into her eyes, admitting gruffly, "I know this isn't the fairy-tale love that you probably dreamed about when you were growing up."

Sorrow clouded her eyes. "I never really thought I would get that."

Nor had he. "But what we have is pretty darn good," he conceded, pushing aside his wish for more. More closeness. More time together. Not to mention a love that would last a lifetime. "We're friends."

"Really *good* friends," she corrected.

Reminding himself it was slow and steady patience that would win out in the end, he said, "And lovers."

Her luscious lips curved into the contented smile she

wore whenever they were in bed. She wrinkled her nose at him, adding, "Pretty darn good lovers, too."

Savoring the feel of her soft body next to his, he stroked a hand through her hair and kissed her temple, continuing gently, "Who are now going to be parents to two babies that I already love very much."

"Me, too." Her low voice quavered happily once again, the excitement of parenthood bonding them in a way nothing else could.

Masculine satisfaction roaring through him, he drew her tighter into the curve of his body, then with his free hand, covered both her hands with his.

Candidly, he admitted, "I want our kids to have everything that it is possible for them to have." Everything he hadn't had from age twelve on. "A good loving home. A mom and a dad. A solid and secure financial future. And of course—" he thought of her Bernese mountain dog "—Bliss..."

She released a sentimental sigh, cuddling unusually close. She ran her hand idly over his thigh. "Pets are important."

Griff thought of the many foster homes he had been in. The unhappiness that came when you didn't belong any particular place or with any one person or family. But instead were always on the outside looking in. Feeling so damn alone.

Joe and Alice Carson had changed that, when he had first started working for the firm, as a college intern. Initially, by mentoring him, then by treating him not just as coworker, but a very dear family friend.

So had Mackenzie and Bliss...

"An extended family helps lend security, too," she said.

Which was of course the one thing he could not give, he realized sadly.

"As does any kind of continuity," he said.

Seeming to realize what she had said, she dropped her head to his shoulder and shut her eyes. When she looked up at him again, he saw her steady, quiet strength. "I agree we need to give the babies the most stable life possible. But…if we agreed to stay together at least until the twins are eighteen or maybe through college, then it's probably going to change things between the two of us. Make our arrangement more like a traditional marriage."

He could tell she thought that might not necessarily be a good thing. Hiding his disappointment, he shrugged. "I'm okay with that."

She frowned. "Having kids will change our relationship, too," she warned.

Make it even deeper and more long-lasting, he hoped. Sensing she wasn't ready to hear any impetuous declarations right now, however, Griff tucked an errant blond curl behind her ear and said cheerfully, "I'm fine with that, too."

She hesitated, raking her teeth across the inviting softness of her lower lip. Her eyes took on a troubled sheen. "If there are problems…"

Luckily, coming up with solutions was one of his strengths. He moved close enough to drink in the feminine scent of her hair and skin. Took her hand in his. "Then we will find ways to work them out together."

She rubbed the pad of her thumb over the gold band of his wedding ring. As she gazed up at him, she managed to look thrilled, stunned and terrified all at once. Which coincidentally happened to be exactly what he was feeling. "This is really happening, isn't it?" Her words came out in a breathy whisper.

Aware for the first time in his life that things were falling miraculously into place, he leaned forward to kiss her. Joy filled his heart. Lifting his head to stare into her eyes, he acknowledged softly, "It really is."

"What are you doing?" Griff asked, several hours later.

They'd had brunch. She'd showered while he'd gone back to work. And now she was downstairs again, her freshly shampooed hair in a bouncy ponytail on the back of her head. Standing with her hands on her hips, she surveyed their disorganized, overcrowded front rooms that still looked the way they had on moving day, four and a half months prior.

The chaos hadn't seemed to bother her before.

Now, vibrating with fresh energy, she turned toward him. Even without makeup, her skin had a special glow. Ditto her eyes. Was that the pregnancy? *Already?* All he knew was how he felt. Happier than he had ever been. And hell, for all he knew, he was glowing, too!

"What would you think about clearing out the formal dining room and turning it into your study?" She held up a delicate palm before he could interject. "I know the plan was to put your office upstairs, but since your desk was too wide to be carried up the stairs, and we're going to need at least one of the extra bedrooms if not both for the twins' nursery…"

He moved closer, loving the way she looked in the sleeveless white button-up shirt with the notch collar, rose-colored skort that stopped at midthigh and sneakers. He realized her breasts were fuller, now that he took a good look at them, but her waist and hips seemed to be the same svelte size.

Narrowing her eyes at him, she was awaiting his opinion.

Griff rubbed at the tension building in the back of his neck. "I agree it would take an awful lot to turn this into the family home the twins should have when they are born. So, I've been thinking, too." Especially at the hospital the night before. "Maybe we should pay the penalty and break the lease."

Her lips opened in a round O of surprise. Clearly, this was not what she wanted. She stared at him unhappily. "You want to *move again*?"

He captured her wrist before she could whirl away. "I want to buy a house that's move-in ready," he admitted with a shrug, liking the way her silky skin warmed beneath his touch. "But yeah, that's the idea."

She extricated herself from his grip and threw her hands up in frustration. "I thought you liked this house!"

He gave a ragged sigh. "I liked what you said it could become." He had enjoyed the idea of living here with her and Bliss. Discovering what suburban utopia was all about. "But we have to face it, with both of us so busy with our work, and now two babies on the way, it might be time to cut our losses."

She let out a slow breath and sat down on a nearby moving box marked Books. Her shoulders slumped even as her chin jerked up. "You think I've let you down?" Abruptly, she looked near tears.

"No. Of course not!" Aware this might be his first glimpse of pregnancy hormones, he knelt in front of her, like a knight addressing his queen. Then, covering her hands with his, he squeezed them reassuringly. "I just think it's time to renegotiate where and how we're going to live."

She drew in a quavering breath. His gaze moved over her silky-soft lips before returning to focus on the tumult in her pretty blue eyes. Before she could tell him what she thought they should do, the silence was broken by the insistent buzzing of his phone. Work. Exhaling roughly, he got to his feet. "Sorry."

He listened as his paralegal explained. Then asked to be sent the details immediately.

"Problem?" Her gentle gaze traversed his face.

The warm understanding in her eyes was a balm to his soul. Keeping his gaze meshed with hers, he confided ruefully, "An eminent domain case I've been working on has just been given a court date in Houston. The trial is probably going to last several days to a week." Torn between wanting to protect the four-generation cattleman from having his ranch seized by the government and the encroaching entity, or stay here in Fort Worth and watch over his family, he sighed again and shoved a hand through his hair.

"Then you have to go."

Not without you, he yearned to say. "I don't suppose you and Bliss would want to go with me? Stay in the hotel?"

She shook her head. "No."

Griff felt a stab of disappointment. "I can't leave you alone."

Color filling her cheeks, she sent him a knowing glance. "You could. You just don't want to." She rose gracefully and moved toward him in a drift of orange blossom perfume. "But that's okay because my sisters have been wanting to come for a visit. And this would be the perfect time."

He supposed she did need familial support to help her handle the surprise pregnancy.

"So, counselor." Stepping even closer, she drew a breath that raised and lowered the shapely lines of her breasts. "When do you need to leave?"

Aware if they stood there much longer talking intimately while she looked so sexy and beautiful he'd end up kissing her again, instead of coming up with a plan that would simultaneously protect her and help him meet his work obligations, he said, "Tomorrow morning, first thing."

"Then I'll call them and see if I can get at least one of them here tonight."

As it turned out, Faith and Jillian both agreed to come.

"Are you sure you're going to be all right?" Griff asked at the crack of dawn the next morning, garment bag, suitcase and briefcase in tow.

She walked with him toward his Porsche. Bliss accompanied them, her tail wagging.

The summer morning was warm and humid. The tree-lined street quiet, except for an occasional car or pedestrian. She knew he was worried about her, and she couldn't blame him after the way she'd been sick earlier in the week. But she was fine now. "It's going to be a total girls' week."

He gave her a thoughtful once-over. "They'll take care of you and the babies?"

"Are you kidding?" She glanced up at the ruggedly handsome contours of his face, appreciating his kindness and strength, the way he made her feel like the luckiest girl in the world. "They are worse mother hens than you!"

Worried if they let this goodbye go on too long, they'd slip out of friend-and-lover mode and into something far riskier, she stood on tiptoe and bussed his cheek.

They had a deal, she reminded herself. Theirs was a marriage of convenience that now just happened to have produced twins.

"Seriously, we'll be fine," she reiterated with a bracing smile.

"If you need me, call me."

Her heartbeat quickened at the unexpected compassion in his low tone. He promised, "I'll get one of the other partners to step in."

Confident as ever, he put his belongings in the trunk, then shut the lid and reached down to give Bliss a pat on the head. "You watch out for Mack, okay girl?" he said. As if she understood, Bliss wagged harder.

One goodbye said, he turned back to Mackenzie, his dark gaze skimming her intently. Then pulled her close and bent his head, indulging in a long, hot kiss that quickly had passion sweeping through her. She had only to feel his hardness to know he wanted to take her to bed again to make hot, wild, wonderful love. She had only to think about the times they had made love to realize how quickly and thoroughly he had rocked her world. And always would...

Unfortunately, they had no time to explore their passion further. He had to leave. And she was going to stay behind.

"I'm really going to miss you," he rasped, when they finally broke apart.

Regret pouring through her, she wreathed her arms about his neck and kissed him again. He felt more like a husband than a lover and friend, she his wife. A mixture of excitement and tenderness sifted through her. "I'm going to miss you, too."

Aware though that if they stayed there like that any longer she might get all misty, she forced herself to release him and step back. Feign a casual attitude she couldn't begin to really feel. "Call me if you get a chance."

Griff lifted her wrist to his lips and kissed the inside of it.

Oblivious to the tingling his brief caress engendered, her own growing need, he said, "Oh, I'll get a chance."

He flashed a wicked smile, kissing her temple, her cheeks, her lips, then warned softly, "Although it could be really late."

Another flurry of emotion swirled through her. Wondering where her legendary independence had gone, she hugged him back, for a moment burying her head against the solid warmth of his chest. "Late is fine."

He nodded slowly, deliberately, and let her go. Then gave Bliss another affectionate pat on the head, climbed in the car and seconds later drove off, taking a tiny bit of her heart along with him.

Chapter Thirteen

"Ah, that was so sweet," Jillian teased, as Mackenzie and Bliss went back inside.

Mackenzie looked at the silly grins on her sisters' faces. "Were you watching?" Dumb question since she already knew the answer.

Faith chuckled. "Of course!"

The three indulged in a sisterly hug.

Faith linked arms with her. "We were going to ask how the marriage is going but after that kiss…"

"Not to mention your pregnancy!" Jillian added, sharing in the joy.

"I don't think we have to inquire," Faith said even more sentimentally.

Their erroneous perception sent a wave of guilt flooding through Mackenzie. Her entire family was under the impression she and Griff were madly in love. Instead of just friends and lovers who also happened to be married. And pregnant.

She had never lied to her sisters before, even by omission. It felt wrong to be deliberately misleading them now. But she couldn't tell them the truth. Not without making them think less of Griff for ever agreeing to her cockeyed idea. This wasn't something she would ever want their twins to know about, either.

Jillian squinted at her. "What is it?" she asked. "What's wrong?"

Mackenzie led her sisters into the woefully outdated kitchen for lattes. She confessed what had been bothering her since the previous day. "I just don't think I've been a very good friend—I mean, wife," she corrected hastily, "to Griff."

Faith frowned. "Why would you say that?"

Mackenzie gestured at their highly disorganized surroundings. "Look at this place. I wouldn't let him unpack most of his stuff, because I wanted to take care of the updates first, and I haven't done a darn thing. I mean, it's hard to even find a place to sit down."

"We'll help you get the place organized while we're here," Faith said soothingly. "That is, if you'll let us."

"You have a rep for being a tad independent," Jillian teased.

"Takes one to know one," Mackenzie teased. Jillian hadn't let herself lean on anyone since her failed elopement when she was eighteen. In fact, she still hadn't forgiven cowboy Cooper Maitland for blowing the whistle on her and her fiancé. Thereby allowing Carol and Robert to intervene and end the ill-begotten romance.

"Hey, I'm not criticizing you." Jillian went into the other room and after a few loud thumps, and crashes, eventually came back with a third chair to pull up to the little café table. Sobering, she announced, "I admire both you-all's independence. I don't think any person should rely on anyone else for their happiness, and that goes double for husband and wife."

Faith made a dissenting face. "Of course, a wife's happiness is dependent upon her husband!"

"It does not have to be," Mackenzie countered. And she was not going to let it be. She didn't want things like money and expectations coming between her and Griff, especially now that they had twin babies to raise. Squaring her shoulders, she put a paint deck onto the table. It held the full rainbow of color possibilities. "Which is why I'm doing this without his input."

Jillian tilted her head. "Decorating?"

Mackenzie made a seesawing motion with her hand while the milk steamed and frothed. Carefully, she corrected, "Making this into a comfortable home instead of a storage locker."

Everyone chuckled at the apt description. Mackenzie was used to living in renovation chaos. Most others, including Griff, were not.

"Speaking of mess..." Jillian smiled, pragmatic as ever. "I don't understand why you didn't take Griff up on his offer to just find another place that is move-in ready, now that you are expecting."

Good question. Mackenzie wasn't sure why she was so attached to this place, either. Since she'd lost her childhood home in a fire that also took her parents' lives, and left her and her seven siblings orphaned, she hadn't allowed herself to get emotionally connected to any residence, including the Laramie County ranch where she'd lived after being adopted by Carol and Robert Lockhart.

She usually just fixed up places to her liking, then moved on to the next challenge.

But something about this house was still calling to her. She did not know whether it was the fact that Griff had

picked it out as the first place they should live together.
The idea she had not yet done anything to help the property realize its full potential. Or that the two of them
had made love here so many times. She only knew that
even though things weren't perfect, she'd still been happier here than she could ever remember being. And that
was before she realized she was carrying twins! Hence,
she could not bring herself to leave this house. Not now.
Not yet...

Aware her sisters were still waiting for an explanation, she said, "I like the neighborhood. It's perfect for
long dog walks, and it's got a great yard for Bliss. And
it's convenient both to my business and Griff's office
downtown."

She set vanilla lattes in front of her sisters, before
turning back to the state-of-the-art espresso maker. "Plus
we're both so busy with work and it's such a hassle to
do all the address changes, and utility turnoffs and turn-
ons, and so on."

"Well, I'm sure Griff will go along with whatever you
want, which is nice," Faith said on a wistful sigh.

Abruptly, Mackenzie had the feeling they were no longer talking about *her* situation. She measured out decaf
coffee grounds. "How is Harm?" she asked. Faith's Navy
SEAL husband was currently deployed, and she knew
communication between the two could be sporadic.

Faith exhaled. "I imagine he's enjoying his last few
assignments."

"So he's still planning to get out of the military by
year's end?"

Her sister nodded. "He knows if we want to have a
big family, and he does, we have to get started soon."

Jillian spooned sliced mango onto a plate. "Has he

decided what he wants to do when he gets out of the military?"

Faith sipped her latte. "He has a construction job lined up in Laramie County."

Mackenzie made herself a decaf, heavy on the steamed milk, light on the coffee, and sat down to join them, aware the table was barely big enough to accommodate the three of them. There was no way it was also going to fit two adults and two high chairs. Nor would the mini breakfast nook accommodate a bigger table. "I didn't know Harm had any experience in that field," she said.

Faith sat up straighter. "He doesn't, but he's a quick learner. And it's physical, and outdoors, so I am sure he's going to like it," she concluded on a burst of enthusiasm.

There was a little too much cheerleading going on there, Mackenzie noted.

"So what's the problem?" Jillian picked up a scone. "Because you look like something is bothering you."

Faith traced the edge of her plate. "I guess I'm just a little worried that Harm is going to miss the military more than he even realizes right now."

Just like Griff, who would have been privately heart-broken had he not made senior partner… Which was why, Mackenzie assured herself, she'd had to marry him…so he could achieve his life's dream. Maybe for the future harmony of her love life, her sister should do the same…

"Harm could stay in the service and still be a parent," Mackenzie pointed out, taking a bite of pastry. It wouldn't be as if Faith would be on her own. She lived in Laramie County and had plenty of Lockharts around to help out.

Faith toyed with a strawberry. Mackenzie noticed she still hadn't eaten anything. "We talked about that. Harm doesn't want to miss out on any part of parenthood. Including and especially my pregnancy. We've already put off starting a family for six years. So we are both making a compromise."

Jillian, who was every bit as independent as Mackenzie, squinted. "What's your compromise?"

Momentarily, sadness filled Faith's eyes. Bliss ambled toward her and, sensing canine comfort was needed, rested her head on Faith's thigh. She smiled down at the Bernese mountain dog and stroked her silky head. Taking comfort in the spirit that was given, she looked up at her sisters with a heartfelt sigh, admitting, "I didn't become a foster mother because Harm didn't want me getting too attached to a child that I wouldn't be able to keep."

Mackenzie had not realized Faith wanted to foster, but it should have been no surprise. Fostering was what had led Carol and Robert to adopt them.

"So instead," she continued, squaring her shoulders matter-of-factly, "I started volunteering at the elementary school with Tinkerbell—" her Canine Good Citizen–trained Norwich terrier "—and helping out with the reading program. So I would have an outlet for my need to nurture."

They all knew how much her volunteering meant to her. The kids she helped tutor adored her and her therapy dog, too. But, Mackenzie thought, Faith probably should have fostered a child or two, as well. Although, on the flip side, her heart-on-her-sleeve sister might well have become too attached. And had a hard time letting go emotionally when it was time for the kids to leave her care. Harm might have had a point about that…

"Well, I think you should have done what you needed to do for you," Jillian said, "and to heck with what your husband wants. But then I'm not married and have no intention of ever getting hitched." Her expression turned disgruntled as she addressed Faith. "You are married so it's probably good that you honored Harm's wishes. Because I know from bitter experience that if you disappoint your man in any truly significant way, you may very well lose him…"

Was that true? Mackenzie wondered in alarm. Did both of her sisters have a point? About the need to both compromise and please…?

Eight very long days later, Griff turned onto the street where he and Mackenzie lived, and then parked in the driveway. As he got out of his vehicle, he saw his wife round the corner, Bliss trotting along proudly beside her.

Mack looked absolutely gorgeous in the dusky light, and her eyes lit up when she saw him standing there. "Hey! You're home! Welcome back, stranger."

He pulled her into a hug. Dipped his head and kissed her thoroughly. "Happy to be here," he murmured back when he finally lifted his head.

Mackenzie grinned up at him, making no effort to pull away. "I can tell!" She looked at the Cadillac Escalade parked next to her pickup in the driveway. "Where is your Porsche?"

Wanting attention, Bliss ambled up next to him. Still holding on to Mackenzie, and enjoying the way she felt snuggled up against him, he petted her dog with his free hand. Damn, he had missed her. Missed them both.

He turned to glance at the black luxury SUV with the tinted windows and every possible upgrade. "I traded in the Porsche while I was in Houston."

Mackenzie frowned, looking upset. "Why? You loved that car! I thought when you gifted yourself a new vehicle, that it would still be another Porsche!"

Griff inclined his head in mute acknowledgment. At one point he had imagined he would have that vehicle forever even if he no longer drove it, but circumstances had changed. He pressed a kiss into her sweet-smelling hair. "I needed something more family friendly."

Mack regarded him skeptically. "Porsche has SUVs."

Griff knew. He had spent the last few months looking. Although in the beginning, he had just been worried about accommodating the two of them and a dog. So the three of them wouldn't always have to take Mack's truck if they went somewhere together. He hadn't yet known about the twins. "Yes, but those SUVs are not big enough to fit two car seats, a big dog and everything we are going to need if we do take a road trip."

Happy color flooded her cheeks. "Where are we planning to go?" she asked, smiling.

He opened the door to the spacious cargo area. "Laramie County, to see your family. Unless…" He paused at the sudden hesitant look on her face. "I am not invited, too?" It wouldn't be the first time.

Mackenzie playfully tapped the center of his chest. "Of course you're invited! You're family now, and you always will be!"

Was he? Then why had Mackenzie seemed so wary of going on a trip with him? To Houston?

She linked her arm through his and, leash still in hand, stepped back to let him get his gear out of the SUV. As he carried it to the house, she asked, "So how did the trial go?"

Client confidentiality had kept him from sharing details during the case. Now that it was concluded, the results were a matter of public record, so he could talk freely. "The jury sided with our clients, which meant he and his wife got to keep their ranch."

"That's wonderful!" Mackenzie held the door for him,

and she and Bliss waited as he led the way inside. "Your clients must have been so happy."

"They were." Griff set down his briefcase and garment bag in the foyer, not sure he was in the right house. When he had left, it had been a terrible mess. Now it was a home. And a pretty damn beautiful one at that.

For a moment, "wow" was all he could say.

The former formal dining room had been set up as his study. And painted the exact same shade of dove gray his loft had been. New French doors framed the entry. Bookcases with both shelves and cabinets flanked one entire wall. His heavy wooden desk and work chair sat on a beautiful Persian rug, in the center of the room. Even his printer and scanner had been set up.

On the other side of the foyer, which had been painted a creamy ivory, was the formal living room. The walls there were also ivory but the long drapes framing the windows were a coordinating dove gray and ivory print. A darker gray, brown, tan and ivory rug covered the center of the now gleaming hardwood floor. His oversize leather sofa, reading chair, ottoman, end tables and lamps completed the masculine lair.

Gone were all the boxes. The mess.

He turned to her.

No one had ever done anything like this for him. And clearly, it *had* all been done for him.

She clasped her hands in front of her and gazed up at him. "Do you like it?"

There were no words to say how much. He gathered her in his arms and squeezed her tight. Dropping his head, he buried his face in her hair, drinking in the familiar citrus and woman scent of her. "Love it," he rasped finally.

Beaming and taking him by the hand, she urged excitedly, "Come and see the rest!"

The family room was as cozy and feminine as the front of the house was sophisticated and masculine. Her chintz sofa and matching wing chairs sat atop a pastel rug. The walls there had been painted the same ivory, while the long drapes framing the windows sported the sage green found in both the fabric and the rug. There were bookshelves in the room, too. They contained her cookbooks and many how-to guides.

The galley kitchen and mudroom had been tidied up and painted a pastel yellow, but little else had been done. The appliances and Corian countertops were still woefully out of date. Even so, it was amazing what she had done.

"I can't believe you managed all this in a little more than a week." He reached into the refrigerator and brought out a beer.

"My sisters helped me with all the decorating stuff. And I hired painters."

"Let me pay half."

She shook her head.

He couldn't say why; suddenly he felt she was working up to something she wasn't sure he was going to like.

"No," she said, lounging against the counter opposite him, "this is my responsibility. Because—" she pushed on before he could object "—I am buying this house."

Chapter Fourteen

Silence fell as Griff stared at Mackenzie in shock. "You mean you want to *purchase* this house?"

Granted, the orange flocked wallpaper in the kitchen was gone, but the solid oak cabinets were really ugly.

She drew a breath. "What I mean is, I've already talked to our landlords and put an offer in on this house." Contentment flowed through her low tone. "They accepted. The mortgage company approved me yesterday. I'll close on the property before the end of August."

Talk about moving fast! Still, if this was what would make her happy… He shifted his gaze to her lips. "I can buy it with you if that's what you want to do."

Her smile widened. "Remember our vows?" She winked flirtatiously. "What's mine is mine, and what is yours is yours?"

There was no way he could forget their elopement ceremony at the bait and tackle shop in Laramie County.

He had thought having the twins together changed every-thing. Or would change everything. Apparently not.

At least not yet.

"Right," he said finally, leery of scaring her away by going all Neanderthal on her. She had always been ex-ceedingly independent. Twins or not, she was apparently not going to start leaning on him now. At least not in all the ways that he desired.

Seeming to understand she had touched a nerve, she promised, "We can still share the utilities, if you like."

"I do."

"But the property will be mine."

He moved closer. The lawyer in him had to ask. "Would you feel better if we did a postnuptial agree-ment that spelled everything out?"

She lifted an airy hand. "We don't need one."

Really? She was behaving like they did.

"I'm not going to go after any of your property or income." She paused to let her words sink in. "You're not going to go after mine. So there's no point in going through all that."

He couldn't disagree. He trusted her. Working on a postnup now would also create questions at the firm if word were to get out. And word *always* got out.

Her gaze drifted over him. "Did you eat dinner?" she asked.

"On the drive back. You?"

"With my sisters before they headed back to Laramie."

He reached into the refrigerator and started to get out two beers. Then realizing she couldn't drink, put one back. He turned to her. "Do you want anything?"

"Maybe a glass of milk."

He handed her the carton and she took a glass from a cupboard.

As they stood there, sipping their beverages, he couldn't help but look around again. The café table was really too small. They would have to do something about that eventually. But it meant a lot, what she had done to make this a home instead of a house where two room-mates lived. The effort she had gone to on his behalf made him want to do more for her, too.

He moved so they were lounging against the counter, hip to hip, her shoulder to his chest. Noticing all over again how truly lovely she was, he said, "You want me to hire an architect? Come up with a plan and renovate the kitchen?"

"Eventually, I will do that." She smiled as if the matter were settled. "For now, it is fine."

He tried again. "At least let me give you new appliances as a housewarming slash wedding gift."

At last. A chink in her considerable armor. She tilted her head, considering. "What am I going to give you then?"

"You already did." He spread his hands wide, his gesture encompassing the downstairs. "This is fantastic. I never imagined this house could look this way."

She drained her milk and set the glass down. Taking him by the hand, she gave him a sultry glance and said, "If you really feel that way, then you should probably see the upstairs…"

Sensing she might have made a mistake, putting an offer in on the house without at least talking to him first, Mackenzie kept her grip on Griff's hand and led him up the stairs.

He took in every detail as they moved. The ivory walls. The newly painted ceilings and trim. The absence of a single moving box. The two bathrooms were still outdated, but each had been painted and freshened up with new towels and accessories.

His bedroom was painted the same dove gray as his loft had been. The sleek masculine linens for his king-size bed were the ones he'd brought with him.

Her home office was tidy. The room next to the master, bare of anything but a new coat of sunny yellow paint. "This going to be the nursery?" he asked.

Unexpectedly, a lump rose in her throat. "Yes. Since we don't know the sex of either twin, I figured yellow was a good choice."

His fingers tightened on hers. "Nice."

The low, gruff compliment warmed her through and through. She had wanted to find a way to please him, and apparently she had.

Feeling herself begin to tremble slightly, she moved on to her bedroom. Her white cottage-style queen-size bed was covered with a sky-blue comforter and stack of cozy pillows that matched the color on the walls. She'd set up her mirrored vanity, and added a long cushion-topped bench at the foot of the bed. Making her private sanctum a feminine counterpoint.

He used his grip to guide her around to face him. Gazing down at her, he caressed her cheek with his open palm. "I love it all…" he said, and then his lips were on hers. Her arms were around his neck. The kiss was more incredible than the homecoming clinch had been. With a low moan, she snuggled against him, soaking in the thrilling heat of his hard, masculine physique. Their tongues tangled as surely as their hearts. Her knees went weak and her lips opened even more to the dizzying pressure of his.

Sliding her hands over his chest, she unbuttoned his shirt and pulled it off, admiring his glowing, golden skin and smooth muscle. She traced the enticing tufts of curly chestnut-brown hair that spread across his chest and arrowed downward, delineating the goodie trail.

Damn, but he was gorgeous, with his nice broad shoulders, long, powerful legs and strong arms. She could stand here admiring him all night long. As he noticed the depth of her enjoyment, his own pleasure grew.

He eased off her skort, pushing it down her slender hips. Then reached for the buttons on her blouse. "Missed me, hmm?"

More than she had ever imagined possible.

But, remembering their deal, to be married in name only, she smiled and lightly teased back, "Missed this…"

Determined to have all of him, she divested him of his pants and boxers, capturing the male essence of him with both hands, sculpting and caressing the hard, velvety-hot length.

"Whoa…" He groaned as she kissed him again then knelt and touched him with lips and tongue and teeth. "Getting a little ahead of you here…"

She caught her breath. "That's all right…" Especially if it meant he would soon be buried deep inside her.

He chuckled low and deep. "No, it's not." Finished unbuttoning her blouse, he eased that off. Then her bra and panties. "But it soon will be…"

She gasped as her lips fused with his once again and his mouth locked on hers in a slow, sexy caress that made her tingle from head to toe. He tasted so good. So dark and male. And he felt even better with his thighs and chest pressed intimately against her. She could feel the hard evidence of his desire as he swept his hands over her hips, sliding low, cupping her against him.

And still he kissed her deeply and irrevocably, possessing her heart and soul until she thought she would melt from the inside out.

The next thing she knew he was easing her back onto the bed. He lay down beside her, pulling her over top of him. Her nipples tingled and ached, and the damp throbbing between her thighs intensified.

It was crazy, but she felt so much like his wife in that moment, she could almost believe they were truly meant for each other.

Griff had been thinking about making love to Mackenzie again for days now. This was the only time she really let her guard down. Or let them be more than just lovers and friends. Every time they held each other, pleasured one another, the barriers around her heart—and his—slipped just a little bit. And while he didn't believe in the happily-ever-after, he knew they could get closer. He wanted that more than anything. More than senior partner. More than career success. More than money or legal acclaim.

Desire flowed through him, fueling a want and need that matched her own. As she wrapped her arms around him and offered her mouth—her body—up to his, all his good, gentlemanly intentions went by the wayside.

He had planned to spend the evening talking. Catching up. Savoring their time together. But as soon as he tasted the sweetness that was uniquely hers once again, his hands took on a life of their own. He kissed and stroked her breasts and explored the silky smoothness of her inner thighs, cupping her buttocks, guiding her against him, as her legs opened wider. She pressed herself down, rocking against him, leaving him with absolutely no doubt about what she wanted, what they *both* wanted.

Her soft cry echoed in the room, and then they were

one. She was climaxing, opening herself up, inviting him deeper still.

That swiftly, he catapulted over the edge, too. Shuddering, their breath noisy and rough, they clung together. And still he wanted more. Much more.

When or if he would get it was another question entirely. Although if things kept going in the direction they had been, he noted as Mackenzie snuggled close and drifted off to sleep, it was looking more and more likely every day.

In the meantime, he had been out of the office for eight days while the trial was going on. He had four other eminent domain cases to catch up on. As senior partner, he had to hit the ground running on those tomorrow.

Reluctantly, he leaned over and kissed Mackenzie's forehead. She sighed contentedly and slept on. Wishing he could stay, yet knowing he couldn't, he quietly eased from the bed, grabbed his clothes and headed for the comfortable study she had set up for him.

Chapter Fifteen

"What a beautiful mural," Alice Carson said on the first Wednesday of November.

She stood back to admire Mackenzie's floor-to-ceiling take on *The Velveteen Rabbit*. It was a collage of the Boy's playroom, a wildflower-strewn meadow, and forest. The stuffed bunny watched over the collection of expensive toys, a family of real rabbits and a magical fairy.

"I'm not quite finished with it yet," Mackenzie told her. She was still adding details here and there. "But I will be before the twins are born."

"Joe said that Griff has been raving about it at the office nonstop." Alice shook her head in wonderment. "Now I see why…"

"Really?" Mackenzie blushed. It wasn't like her husband to divulge details about his personal life.

Alice headed downstairs with Mackenzie. "He said it was your favorite book growing up, and that you collect different editions."

"Actually, it was the favorite book for both of us. Our moms read it to us when we were young. And then we read it to other foster kids after we were orphaned."

"I imagine you will read it to the twins, too."

Actually…"But…speaking of babies…" Alice said, as they reached the first floor again. And surveyed the after-party mess. "I guess a surprise baby shower wasn't such a good idea, after all."

The guests had all been either partners or female spouses of partners from the law firm. "It was lovely. Thank you for thinking of me."

"But…?" Alice prodded, beginning to be as intuitive of Mackenzie as she was of Griff.

Mackenzie gathered up some dishes and headed for the kitchen. "It's a little embarrassing for me—" *or rather Griff*"—to have everyone see our home while we are still in the process of getting it completely fixed up."

Alice carried dishes over to the sink and began loading the new state-of-the-art dishwasher. "First of all," she said with motherly concern, "what you and Griff have managed to do in the last seven months that you've lived here is nothing short of amazing. The house is beautifully decorated."

"Except for the kitchen and baths."

"Well," Alice said, shrugging, "it's an older home in an established neighborhood and modernizing it takes time."

And money, Mackenzie thought, aware she had spent a hefty chunk of her savings on the down payment, closing and updates thus far. And although Griff had offered more than once to put in a whole new kitchen for her, she had refused, since that would mean comingling their finances and their interest in the property more than they had initially agreed upon.

"Plus kitchens are a big project," Alice commiserated.

"Which is why I haven't actually tackled it yet," Mackenzie fibbed.

"The appliances all look brand-new, though!"

"They are a present from Griff."

"He is such a great guy, isn't he?"

"He is." Unfortunately, Mackenzie had the feeling that she had embarrassed him today in front of his colleagues, albeit unwittingly, because she had seen the shocked and disapproving looks on some of the women's faces as they walked into the kitchen to help themselves from the buffet that had been set up there.

Alice covered serving dishes with plastic wrap and slid the leftover tea sandwiches into the fridge. She paused to survey the layout, then turned back to Mackenzie. "The babies are due in mid-January, right?"

"The fifteenth," she confirmed.

"It's November 6, so you have a little over two months if you wanted to get this finished up now."

Mackenzie needed to get off her feet. She plucked her idea folder from the kitchen drawer and poured herself a fresh cup of decaf tea from one of the pots on the warmer. Then sat down at the café table. A second later Alice joined her, cup of regular green tea in hand.

"This is what I was thinking." She showed the older woman samples. "I don't need new cabinets. The boxes are all solid wood. Just new doors and hardware."

Alice nodded approvingly. "That would be gorgeous in here," she said. "Your hardwood floors look fine."

"I think so, too. But I'm going to need new countertops and backsplash."

Alice perused the samples. "Those are heavenly, too.

And really, if you did all that, which wouldn't take long at all, the kitchen would be wonderful."

"The problem is contractors. Everyone is really busy right now helping customers get their homes ready for the holidays. January is no problem of course. Because that's their slow time."

"But you'll have new babies."

"Right." Mackenzie sighed. "And the last thing I want is a house under construction even a little bit with newborns."

Alice got out her phone. "Luckily, I can help. I will just call my guy, explain the situation. He will make it all happen for you. I promise. In the meantime, how long of a maternity leave are you taking and when will it start? Or…are you going back?"

When Griff got home that evening, Mackenzie met him at the door. The living room still bore the remnants of the baby shower that had happened earlier in the day. But she was wearing her painting clothes. Which these days meant fuzzy slippers, a multisplattered man's shirt and maternity jeans. Her golden hair was swept into a clip on the back of her head. Tendrils escaped to frame her face and the nape of her neck. Her skin held that pregnancy glow. Making her look prettier and more womanly than ever.

She sent him a level look and put one hand on her hip. "Did you tell Alice and Joe Carson you wanted me to stay home after the babies were born?"

Griff set his briefcase down. Aware this was a minefield he did not want to enter, he replied, "No, but they asked me about it."

"Well, they asked me, too!"

He shrugged out of his suit jacket. Loosened his tie. "What did you say?"

She scowled, moving toward him indignantly. "What did you say?"

Hormones heightened her emotions these days. He didn't mind. In fact, he thought it was kind of cute when she overreacted because when she did that she always let her guard down.

Wondering if he would ever get tired of gazing into the deep blue depths of her eyes, he reached down and captured her free hand in his. Squeezed it briefly. "I say... what I always say. That I want you to be happy."

Taken off guard, and realizing she had nothing to be upset about, she wrinkled her nose. Her shoulders slumped. "Oh."

Seeming to think it now safe to intervene, Bliss came up to greet him, wagging her tail. He petted her then turned back to face his wife. Taking her by the hand, he guided her past a towering stack of elegant baby gifts, to sit down on his big leather sofa. He'd had to work through lunch and he was starving, but this couldn't wait. If she had been accusing him of something, he needed to know what it was. "What did you think I said?"

"Alice seemed to think you had reservations about me not really actually taking a leave, at least not much of one."

He regarded her protectively. "She knows you stopped delivering the signs yourself when you hit the five-month mark? And now just manage the business?"

"Yes! I explained that I had rented another work space and hired three more part-time college students to help with painting, construction and deliveries. But she acted like even that was probably going to be too much."

And it could very well be the case, Griff thought. But that would be up to Mackenzie to determine. He pulled her into the curve of his arm and kissed the top of her head. "I'll support you in whatever you want to do. You know that."

She leaned into him, enveloping him with her citrusy orange blossom perfume. "I do."

He stroked his hand down her arm and asked gently, "So what else is going on?"

"I'm also going to finish the updates on the kitchen."

She leaned back, waiting for his reaction.

And again, he wasn't sure what he should say. Except... "Okay."

She peered at him closely. "You won't mind living in a construction zone for about two to three weeks?"

That sounded optimistic. He forced himself to remain casual. "Is that all it's going to take?"

"Apparently." She explained what she was arranging to have done.

"Do you want help with the financing of the project?"

"No." She sighed again, looking even unhappier.

"Then...?" Griff knew something else was bothering his wife. He wanted her to just say it.

She bit her lip. "I think I might have embarrassed you today."

He found that hard to believe. "How?"

"I've been in Joe and Alice's home. I know the luxury of their surroundings, and I think most of the other partners live that way, too."

"So?" He shrugged uncaringly. "They all know we are just getting started. That we're working on things." He grinned at her playfully. "It's part of *adulting*."

Mackenzie made a great show of rolling her eyes at him. "Did you really just use that word on me?"

"*Us.* And yeah. I did." He tugged her even closer. "Got a problem with that, Mrs. Montgomery?"

She blushed prettily. Shook her head. Then rose and headed for the kitchen, her fuzzy slippers shuffling across the floor.

He followed, enjoying the view from behind as much as the front. "How did your doctor's appointment go this morning?" She'd texted "fine" but that hadn't revealed much.

She whirled to face him. "Baby B was head down."

"Just like he was supposed to be."

Another sigh. This one discouraged. "But Baby A was transverse again."

He tried not to worry. She had excellent medical care. "They still have time and room to move around?"

"Yes. And in fact Dr. Connelly thinks they will. But even if one or both of them is breech on delivery day…"

"They'll be able to be delivered safely via C-section," Griff reminded her.

"Yes, I know that." Worry clouded her eyes. "Although I really would prefer them to be born without surgical intervention."

Griff regarded her solemnly. "I'll let them know." He bent down to her waist level and shouted into her tummy. "Kids! Mommy wants you to come out the old-fashioned way! Hear that?" He cupped his hands around his mouth to further concentrate the sound. "So be sure when the time comes you're in the right position!"

Beneath her shirt, he saw her tummy bulge in one place, then another.

"See?" He straightened, grinning. Even as he rubbed

his hand lovingly over her baby bump. "They kicked in response! That means they are listening."

Now she was grinning, too. "That probably means an extra bedtime story for them tonight."

"You may scoff," he told her seriously, "but reading *The Velveteen Rabbit* to them in the womb gets them off to a great start."

"I agree." It also brought back many pleasurable childhood memories for the two of them. She opened the fridge. "Mind having baby shower leftovers for dinner?"

"Sounds good."

Together, they got out tea sandwiches, petits fours and various canapés. "So how was your day?" she asked kindly.

"Still working on that settlement," he admitted.

She nodded understandingly, even though all he had really been able to tell her was that it was another eminent domain case. Client confidentiality kept him from giving her any other details. Still, it helped, knowing she cared, that she had his back. And that it was okay with her when he went back to work right after dinner, or had to get up right after they made love, and go back to work in the study…often into the wee hours of the night. Which was why the partners wanted everyone married. Because otherwise this life would be one hell of a lonely existence.

Mackenzie misunderstood the reasons behind his frown. She smiled, layering an assortment of finger sandwiches and very fancy canapés on two plates. "You'll get them to an agreement eventually."

He brought two glasses to the table. One filled with water for him, the other with milk for her. His mind on his work again, he shrugged. "Or we'll all end up in court." Jury trials were unpredictable.

She gave him a confident look. "Either way, you'll prevail."

He hoped so. Because it wasn't just his client's property or his career he had to worry about now. He was supporting Mackenzie and their twins. And *they* needed him to succeed.

Chapter Sixteen

A few weeks later, Joe Carson stopped by Griff's door on his way out. He was wearing a raincoat to ward off the November rain and had a monogrammed leather satchel in hand. "How are things going with the Cabot case?" he asked.

"The brief should be ready to submit to the court tomorrow morning." Even if it meant pulling another all-nighter.

Joe moved all the way into Griff's office. He looked at the city lights sparkling against the evening darkness. Then at the time on his watch. Eight p.m. "You know if you want to work remote as much as possible, now that Mackenzie is in her last trimester," he pointed out kindly, "you can."

Griff stood. His boss was right. It was time for him to be heading home.

Joe continued, "You could probably work at home most days."

Griff shut down his laptop and put it in his bag. He grabbed his phone and his coat. "Actually, I can't." The two men walked down the hall toward the elevator. "Because of the construction in the kitchen."

Joe squinted.

"Alice didn't tell you?"

His boss shook his head.

"She's been helping Mackenzie find contractors to update the kitchen. And they are trying to have it all done in the next couple weeks." Although every time they turned around there was another delay or hitch of some sort. The cabinets doors had all been taken off, the contents put into boxes temporarily. So, half of their downstairs was back to looking and feeling like a storage locker again. Thankfully, not his half. His study and the formal living room were still in good shape.

"Ah, nesting." Joe accepted the chaos as a matter of course.

Which in turn made Griff think maybe he shouldn't worry so much about the upheaval. Or take it as a sign of Mack's discontent. With *him*.

Sympathetically, Joe asked, "How are the birthing classes going?"

"Good." It was the one time—the only time—that she leaned on him just a little. Otherwise, it seemed like she was more independent than ever and while part of him appreciated that, part of him felt surprisingly shut out.

Joe shook his head, as if not envying all Griff currently had on his agenda. "Well, whatever you do," he advised seriously, "don't forget the push present."

Aware his mentor was also the closest thing he would ever have to a dad, Griff turned to Joe, not afraid to ask for help when it came to something like this. "Any idea what that should be?"

Joe grinned with the expertise of a longtime husband and father. "You can never go wrong with diamonds." He pushed the down button on the exterior elevator panel. "Got the nursery set up?"

Unable to contain his enthusiasm, Griff smiled. "We're doing that in a few weeks—as soon as the furniture comes in. But the mural is done, the room is painted and ready to go, and we have purchased safety seats for each car, a twin stroller, a couple of bassinets and two glider rockers." One for her and a larger size one for him.

He couldn't wait for the times when they would sit together, each cuddling a child... If that wasn't family, what was?

The steel doors slid open. They stepped in. The door shut. "What about a baby nurse?" Joe asked.

Griff hit the button that would take them to the parking garage belowground. He leaned against the wall as they descended. "Mackenzie hasn't mentioned bringing in outside help." Up till now, he hadn't considered it, either. Now, given the skeptical way his friend and mentor was looking at him, he wondered if that was a mistake.

They stepped out into the mostly empty garage, their footsteps echoing on the concrete floor. Together they headed for the assigned parking slots for senior partners.

Casually, Joe advised, "I know you and Mackenzie are hands-on. But still...you might want to hire a baby nurse for the first few months, at the very least. She is having twins, after all, and she only has one set of hands."

Griff knew Joe had left most of the child-rearing and domestic duties to his wife, Alice.

The older man paused next to his Bentley. "We had someone in to help out after the birth of each of our four boys, and we found the assistance invaluable."

Griff stalled. He was sure that was so, but he wanted to be more involved with his own children.

"I'll be around to help in the evenings and on the weekends." In fact, he was looking forward to it, dirty diapers, colicky moments and all.

Joe nodded as if he had heard this all before. Sternly, he reminded him, "You also have a number of important trials coming up." He gave Griff a paternal clap on the shoulder. "And we were also hoping that you would take on even more…"

"Well, don't you look like you just lost your best friend," Mackenzie remarked the moment Griff walked in the door to her painting studio in the carriage house.

"Work."

She squinted. "Did you lose a trial?" Given how hard he worked, and what a talented lawyer he was, it seemed really unlikely.

"The opposite."

She put down the brush filled with paint she had mixed herself, made with natural earth pigments and walnut oil, and waited for him to go on.

"I have been so successful in the last six or seven months that now the firm is getting requests for my services in other states. Consequently, the four name partners would like me to get licensed in Oklahoma, New Mexico and Colorado."

"You have to take the bar exam in all those states?" she asked, aghast, knowing that took months of preparation and several days of testing for each.

"No, there is reciprocity for all three because I have been a practicing lawyer for more than five years. But—" Griff sighed, explaining further "—I will have to apply to and get accepted by each of those three state bars."

Mackenzie recalled what she could about his original licensure process. "That's pretty arduous and complicated on its own."

Griff shoved his hands through his rain-dampened hair. "Twenty-five pages of personal information. Dozens of references."

"And when is this all supposed to happen?"

"ASAP."

"Oh, Griff." She moved toward him, taking him in her arms and getting as close as her big belly would allow. "I am so sorry."

He flashed a lopsided grin. "The price of success."

"I guess." Aware her painting shirt was now nearly as damp as his raincoat, Mackenzie stepped back.

His gaze fell to her damp breasts. "Sorry."

"No worries."

He looked behind her at her latest project. "What's this?"

She turned and took in the nearly finished three-foot-high plywood bird. "A turkey."

"I can see that. What's it for?"

"A local cafeteria."

She brought out a second finished sign with the words: "We're feasting all weekend! Join us Thursday through Sunday for the best holiday buffet ever!"

Turning back to Griff, she explained, "They don't think they have been getting as many customers as they could, so they are putting these signs out tomorrow."

"Which is why you're painting tonight."

"Yes. Plus it's a fun project." And would help pay for her kitchen update. So she wouldn't have to keep diminishing her savings.

He gave the two commercial signs another admiring glance. "Well, it's really eye-catching."

Mackenzie beamed. "Thanks."

He looked at her questioningly. "And speaking of holidays… What exactly are our plans?"

She paused, proceeding carefully. "What do you usually do?"

"Hit a cafeteria for a meal and then spend the entire weekend in the office, working, because it is so quiet."

She imagined that way, he didn't really have to think about all that had been lacking in his life. But now that he was married to her, by extension, he had family, too. Or at least in-laws!

She picked up her brush and added the finishing touches with deft, sure strokes. Then turned back to him. "Is that what you want to do this year?"

Holiday plans could cause stress in a marriage. That much she knew. She really didn't want any stress in their arrangement.

He looked at her steadily, walking on eggshells, too. "What do you want to do?"

Finished, she put the brush in a container filled with Murphy's wood oil soap and water to soak and wiped her hands on a cloth. Then figuring she might as well go for it, said, "Well, my parents want us to come to their ranch in Laramie County for dinner on Thursday. Maybe spend the night."

His gaze narrowed. "What does your ob-gyn say?"

"Dr. Connelly says that it is okay for me to travel as long as I have someone with me. She doesn't want me driving alone."

His amber eyes never left hers. "Nor do I."

Her heart skittered in her chest. "Would you be okay doing a family thing with me this year?"

She had asked him to come by, on previous holidays, when she knew he was going to be alone, and he had always refused. And she had known why. Because he thought it would be far too uncomfortable, to be an outsider looking in.

This time, he merely shrugged and ambled closer, shoving a hand through his hair. "It's probably expected, don't you think?" He cupped her cheek and lifted her face to his. "Given we're married."

Which wasn't really an answer. Especially considering what he had just confided to her about the overwhelming pressure he was feeling at work. "But...if you need to stay here and fill out state bar applications, I will. We could probably throw something together or go to a cafeteria." She put the lids on the jars of nontoxic, all-natural paint.

He stepped in to help. "I don't want you to miss your time with your family on account of me."

"So you'll go?" Finished, they set the colors on the shelf. "We can drive out Thursday morning, return Friday morning?"

Griff nodded. "Sounds good to me."

Silence fell. She had the feeling he wanted to ask her something else. Something he wasn't sure she would like. So, she waited...

"One more thing..." he said eventually.

She lifted a brow and sat down on a stool. "I'm listening."

Griff rubbed the flat of his hand across his forehead. "Joe and Alice Carson gave me the name of the baby nurse agency they used when their kids were born."

It took a moment for that to sink in. Mackenzie stared at him. "You're kidding." He *wasn't* kidding. "Why would we need a baby nurse?" she asked, not sure if she felt insulted or just stunned.

He picked up the umbrella she'd brought out to the carriage house and opened it up just outside the door.

"Because there are going to be two of them, instead of just one, and I won't be here all the time And it's not fair for you to have to take it all on yourself the majority of the day."

She locked up behind her, then stepped beneath the nylon cover. Their bodies brushed as they walked across the backyard. Around them, the rain sluiced down in heavy sheets. "I told you my mom is coming to stay with us for a week or so after the babies are born, and my sisters Faith and Jillian have offered to pitch in too if I need them."

"I'm talking about after that," he said.

It hurt to realize he did not think she was capable of mothering their babies on her own. "After that," she promised, stepping inside their mudroom, "I won't need help."

He set the umbrella next to the door, on the rubber boot tray, to drain. Continued, just as stubbornly, "Look, it can't hurt to at least interview someone now…"

Sure it could. "I'd be wasting their time." She glared at him, the tenderness she'd felt for him earlier fading as her pregnancy-fueled emotions rose. "And speaking of time, I have paperwork for my business to complete in my office upstairs. So…" She gestured at the door.

He gave her another long, thoughtful look, then stepped aside to let her exit.

"Well, that didn't go over well, did it?" Griff asked Bliss. He snapped a leash to her collar and headed out the door. It was still raining lightly but steadily. He didn't mind. He needed the exercise. So did their pet. "Not that I expected her to welcome the suggestion."

Bliss trotted happily at his side, listening and gazing up at him. "I mean, I know how independent she is. But

I was between a rock and a hard place. Because I knew if Joe mentioned it to me, it wasn't going to be long before Alice mentioned it to Mack, and I didn't want her to be blindsided."

Bliss's tail wagged more slowly.

"Of course," Griff lamented as they rounded the corner and stepped onto the next block, "now she is just ticked off at me. And I didn't want that, either. So maybe I should just apologize…"

Even though he hadn't done anything wrong.

Was that a good precedent to set?

Griff wasn't sure.

And he was still thinking about it when he came back in the house, stopped in the mudroom and toweled Bliss off. She headed for her water dish. He hung his soggy raincoat on a hook to dry, took off his equally damp loafers and walked into the kitchen.

Mackenzie was waiting for him.

She looked like she had been crying.

"What's going on?" he asked in alarm.

She threw up her hands in frustration. "I don't want to fight with you."

Was that what they had been doing? He didn't know enough about family life to be able to tell. "I don't want to fight with you, either," he said quietly. But they would disagree, and they would have to figure out how to handle that.

"Then can we just not discuss this again?" She sniffed.

He wasn't sure that was a good idea, either. Ignoring a situation did not necessarily make it go away. On the other hand, peaceful families were happy families. And if she thought she could handle two babies and working all on her own, who was he to judge? She had always managed a heck of a lot on her own. And like she had said, her mom and her sisters were ready and willing to pitch in. Maybe he should just leave it at that. Not go borrowing trouble ahead of the twins' arrival.

"Sure," he said.

She released a quavering breath. "Good." And as they stood there, in the torn-apart kitchen, looking at each other, there really was nothing more to be said.

Griff changed clothes, grabbed some dinner out of the leftovers in the fridge and went into the study to work shortly after that. Meanwhile, Mackenzie emailed the invoice for the Thanksgiving buffet sign to the customer. Luanne and Lenny would collect payment when they delivered the sign early the next day. Then, checked the social media sites for Special Occasion Signs, found nothing amiss and went to bed.

She figured Griff would sleep in his own room that night, given how crabby they had been with each other. But when she woke up around two in the morning, he was cuddled up next to her, his arms and legs wrapped around her. And the next morning, it was almost as if nothing had happened.

She was incredibly relieved.

Mostly because she feared delving too deeply into the intricacies of their practical marriage would create problems that would not be easy to solve.

Luckily, the next two days were busy ones. And their next dilemma did not appear until very early Thanksgiving morning when Griff asked her to come into his bedroom for a minute.

Fresh out of the shower, Mackenzie tightened her robe around her and complied. His overnight bag was open but held only his shaving kit, clean underwear and socks. Which also happened to be the only clothing items he had put on after showering. "What is the dress code for today?"

This was new. "Relaxed and casual."

His expression remained inscrutable. "Not helping."

Was it possible? The ultraconfident Griff was nervous about his first holiday with her family?

"The men will all be wearing cords or jeans and nice button-downs or sweaters." Mackenzie unwrapped the towel around her head and rubbed it through her just-shampooed strands. "The women will be wearing dresses, skirts and sweaters."

He walked over to his closet. The majority of his wardrobe was courtroom-ready business attire.

He tossed her a look over his shoulder. "What are you wearing?"

Mackenzie admired the way his broad shoulders tapered down to his waist. He had nice buttocks, too. Although if she started thinking about that, they would never hit the road.

She swallowed around the sudden dryness of her throat. He turned to give her another look. Now unable to help but admire his underwear-clad front, she shrugged. "Don't know yet." Depended on what she could get around her that would not leave her looking and feeling like a beached whale.

Griff grabbed a couple shirts, and business casual slacks. "We will be there tomorrow for breakfast, right?"

She nodded.

"What's the dress code then?"

"Whatever you want to travel in," she said, wishing they had time to make love, knowing they didn't. Not that he was thinking about a roll in the hay. "I plan to wear jeans."

"Okay." He grabbed some, too. "Got it."

Aware they were already running late and she hadn't begun to pack yet, Mackenzie turned and headed for the door. "It might not be a bad idea to bring an extra set of clothes, though, just in case." She wrinkled her nose. "Gabe and Susannah's quintuplets can be a little messy, and they are also very affectionate."

He squinted. "Meaning?"

She grinned, thinking of the last time she had babysat them. "Peanut butter and jelly hands."

He laughed. "Message received." He went back to packing, and she went down the hall to finish getting ready.

Thirty minutes later, Bliss had been fed and walked, and situated on a dog bed in the middle row seat, and their suitcases loaded in the back of his Escalade.

They grabbed to-go breakfast sandwiches from a coffee shop drive-through on the way out of town. And hit the road. The drive to Laramie was uneventful. Bliss quickly fell asleep, and so did Mackenzie. The next thing she knew, the vehicle was stopping and Griff had his hand on her cheek, as he whispered in her ear, gently waking her.

She opened her eyes to the view of her parents' sprawling Circle L Ranch house, and the sight of family pouring out to greet them. She sighed, wondering if either of them were ready for this. Especially Griff. "And here we go…" she said.

"So, no gender reveal party?" Faith asked several hours later, when the holiday meal preparation was well underway. The men were simultaneously watching football and entertaining Gabe and Susannah's quintuplets, as well as Cade and Allison's one-year-old twins. Meanwhile, the women set the long tables and cooked in the kitchen.

Happy to be home again, happier still to be there with Griff, Mackenzie sat on a stool and trimmed the green beans. "We elected not to find out the sexes. We both wanted to be surprised."

"What about names?" Carol crumbled cornbread for the stuffing.

"Still deciding," she admitted, inhaling the delicious scents of fresh sage and roasting turkey.

"How are you feeling, though?" Susannah diced big piles of celery and onion.

"Pretty good most of the time," Mackenzie replied, pausing momentarily to stand and stretch out her over-burdened muscles. "Except for the backaches."

"Oh," Susannah said in sympathy, adding diced veggies to the butter sizzling in a pan. "I had that trouble when I was carrying the quintuplets."

Finished with the green beans, Mackenzie moved on to help her baby sister Emma put together the sweet potato casserole. "What did you do?"

Susannah gave the sautéing veggies a stir. "Prenatal Pilates. In fact, I still have all the workout recordings and gear. I would be happy to lend it to you."

"I don't know." Mackenzie rubbed a hand over her tummy, which felt enormous to her, even six weeks out from her due date. "I stopped doing yoga several years ago, and I've been getting pretty unwieldy lately." It could be hard to get up or down. Never mind gracefully!

"This will help, I promise," Susannah said.

Mackenzie regarded her sister-in-law dubiously. Unlike her pro-baseball-playing-brother Cade, she had never been very athletic. The thought of anyone seeing her attempt such a thing was very embarrassing. On the other hand, she would be in the privacy of her own home. She had done yoga once, at least the really easy poses. Plus she could try it out when the contractors weren't around and Griff was at work… So, she accepted Susannah's generous offer. "Thank you." Mackenzie released a breath.

"I'll bring them by in the morning before you head back to Fort Worth," Susannah promised.

"Well, pregnancy problems or no…" Faith peeled potatoes with the patience of the military wife she was. "I envy you all your children."

Mackenzie paused to give her sister a consoling hug. She knew how much Faith wanted a baby, too. How long she had waited. She felt guilty for complaining. "When is Harm going to be discharged from the navy?" she asked sympathetically.

Faith smiled. "He's supposed to come home for good in two weeks."

"And then—" Jillian predicted merrily, giving the cranberries a stir in the pot on Carol's big six-burner stove "—Faith will be pregnant, too, and I'll have all the advantages of being a beloved aunt with none of the daunting day-to-day responsibilities of parenthood!"

Faith flushed but did not deny that was what she wanted fervently, too.

"And speaking of the men in our lives," Emma, just in from Italy, said, while looking out the window onto the sprawling backyard. "What are Dad and Griff talking about so seriously?"

Griff had known the moment that Robert Lockhart asked him to help bring in some wood for the fire that it wasn't a simple errand.

Their man-to-man "talk" began as soon as they were out of earshot of the ranch house.

"Although Carol and I suspected that the two of you would always end up together eventually, and we gave you our blessing when you announced your elopement," Robert said candidly, after a few private words of welcome, "I have to admit I wasn't sure your hasty nuptials were a good idea at the time."

Griff thrust his hands in his pockets as they continued walking toward the woodpile. "And now?"

Robert sent him an approving glance. "I've never seen her look so happy. Neither has her mother."

Except, he thought guiltily, that glow she had was not due to him. "She is really excited about the twins," he admitted honestly. "As am I."

"It's more than that." Robert held out the canvas sling, while Griff put logs in, stacking them one on top of another. "Mackenzie hasn't wanted to open up her heart, or really embrace the idea of family, since she lost her folks in the fire."

Griff remembered how shut down the grief-stricken Mackenzie had been when she had been separated from her siblings and landed in foster care. He nodded grimly and looked her dad in the eye. "I know she's had a hard time believing in happily-ever-after." So had he. Gruffly, he continued, "And that there is a part of her—" *just as there is a part of me* "—that really doesn't expect any good times to last." Each of them was continually waiting for the next hitch to occur.

Robert clapped him on the shoulder. "You've changed all that for her, son."

Had he?

"Your *marriage* has changed all that."

Except theirs wasn't a real marriage, Griff thought reluctantly to himself. Not yet anyway, and it might never be, given the careful parameters they had set up. But they were friends and lovers and expectant parents now. Soon they would bring their two babies into the world. And the love and concern they felt for their children would connect them for the rest of their lives. Of that he was very sure. That was just going to have to be enough.

Chapter Seventeen

Late Thanksgiving evening, Griff set their overnight bags just inside the door and looked around. "So this is your childhood bedroom."

She swung around to face him, the fatigue of a long day showing on her pretty face. "Is it what you expected?"

Yes and no. The patchwork comforter on her double bed had the pretty pastel pinks, greens, blues, creams and yellow hues that she favored. There was an easel set up in one corner, a comfy reading chair in another. The small bookshelf was full. Without a vintage or new *The Velveteen Rabbit* in sight. All the titles seem to be Nancy Drew. Glad to be alone with her at long last, Griff shut the door behind them. "I didn't know you were such a fan of mysteries."

"I used to be." She sighed and toed off her shoes.

"How come?" He reached around behind her to undo the clasp on her necklace.

She tilted her head to allow him better access. "Good question." She pressed her lips together, thinking. "I guess it's because everything in them is so clear-cut. There are no loose ends. Each clue has meaning. And there's always justice and peace at the end."

He reclasped the necklace and set it aside. "Unlike real life."

She eased off the knit dark brown maternity dress she had been wearing. Her breasts spilled out of the cups of her ecru silk bra. "Well, you know how random this world can be."

He did. His glance dropped to her rounded belly. The knowledge it was his children she was carrying filled him with pride and love.

She took a white nightgown out of her suitcase and pulled it on over her head, and pushed her arms through the long sleeves. "What was your childhood home like?"

This was the kind of thing he did not like to think about. Forget discuss… The kind of thing she had always known better than to ask him about. But she had shared so much with him he supposed he owed it to her to answer her question.

He took off his shoes, too. Walked over to close their blinds. "We lived in a small one-bedroom apartment on the wrong side of town. My mom insisted I have the bedroom because I always went to sleep earlier. She slept on a pullout sofa in the living room and kitchen area. And while we didn't have much in terms of material belongings, we took really good care of what we did have. Our home was always neat and clean."

"A trait you carry through to today." She smiled and went into the Jack and Jill bathroom to wash her face. "What was in your room?"

He stood in front of the other sink and layered toothpaste onto a brush. "A twin bed." Moving the washcloth over her face, she slanted him an inquisitive glance. "What kind of covers did you have on it?"

Trying not to think how familiar and good this all felt, he said, "A plaid bedspread."

She squinted, as if imagining. "Color?"

Now he had to think. He watched as she bent and rinsed the cleanser from her face. "Red and blue," he said eventually.

She brushed her teeth, too. Wiping her face on a towel, she brushed past him and headed for the bed. She slid beneath the covers, turning onto her side. Her head propped on her elbow, she watched as he undressed. "What else was in your room?"

He folded his slacks and sweater over the back of her reading chair, pulled out his pajama pants, and put them on. Finished, he joined her in the bed and turned out the light. He drew her into the curve of his body. She felt so warm and womanly. So his. As she laid her head on his chest, he felt his heart expand. "There was a desk and a chair, so I could do my homework. And have a place to keep my library books."

She snuggled closer, draping one knee across his thigh. "That sounds nice," she murmured approvingly.

It had gotten him off to a solid start, that was for certain. He wrapped one arm around her, used his other hand to stroke her hair, loving the way the soft, silky strands felt beneath his palm.

"My mom was big on education." He swallowed as a knot gathered in his throat. "She really wanted me to go to college and make something of myself."

He wished she were here now. That she could meet Mackenzie. Get to know her. Love their twins.

Aware Mackenzie was listening, waiting for him to

go on, he confided emotionally, "She really didn't want me to be stuck in a low-paying job, the way she was."

Mackenzie splayed a gentle hand across his chest, cuddling as close as her blossoming belly would allow. Tenderly, she whispered, "She would be so proud of you."

Griff liked to think so. "Your family is awfully proud of you, too."

"True. Although—" she rolled onto her back, easing a hand beneath her to rub her lower spine "—I am aware that all together we can be a bit much."

With gentle hands, he guided her onto her other side, eased a pillow beneath her knees, just the way they'd been taught to do in Lamaze class, and massaged his way down her spine. "What do you mean?"

She moaned in ecstasy as her tense muscles began to relax. And cast a look at him over her shoulder. "The endless stories. All the picture albums that we looked at after dinner."

He continued working his way up the other side of her spine. "I thought it was nice." But she was right. He had tried his best to hide it. And thought he had from everyone but her maybe. But seeing all those family events, with everyone gathered around. The barbecues, the graduations, athletic competitions and music performances, even the other weddings…made him realize how much he had been missing, not having a family history of his own. At least not one that existed after his mother had died.

With a relaxed sigh, Mackenzie rolled onto her back. She took his hand and put it on her belly, where he could feel the nightly athletic activity of their twins, as they bounced around inside her.

He smiled as he felt the new life.

Mackenzie curved her hand around his jaw. "It reminded me, though," she said softly, "that I've never seen any of your family pictures."

He knew all of her early family photos had been destroyed in the fire that took her parents. Some had been gathered since from various sources. He was not as lucky. "That's because I don't have any."

She paused. "Not even one?"

He shrugged, unwilling to admit just how tight things had been on a waitress's salary. "I don't remember her having a camera or ever really taking any pictures."

"Surely you have school photos?"

He didn't recall her ever having the money to purchase those, either. "If I did, they were lost at the time of her death."

Compassion reverberated in her low tone. "I'm sorry."

He went back to holding her. "It is what it is."

She snuggled close, their babies still rodeoing in her tummy. "But now I really feel bad about putting you through all that Lockhart family history."

"Don't." He stroked a hand lovingly up and down her arm and shoulder. Leaned over to kiss the nape of her neck. "I'm glad things have worked out for you the way they have and that you ended up having a good life."

He brought her close, and kissed her as if she were as vital to his survival as the air that they breathed. Because really, when it came right down to it, she was.

When they finally drew apart, she studied him. "So your first holiday with the in-laws wasn't all that bad?"

"It was great." Best he had enjoyed in forever.

Her delicate blond brows rose. She reached over and turned on the bedside lamp. "Even the talk with my dad?"

She looked gorgeously tousled, just kissed, in the low light. "What do you know about that?"

She raked in a tremulous breath, surveying him seriously. "Just that it looked, um, kind of important, I guess."

Having never seen her this nosy, and/or protective of him, he grinned. "You were spying on us?"

She stiffened. "My sisters were. So naturally—" she waved an airy hand "—I had to take a gander, too."

They had never spent a lot of time on pillow talk, up to now. When they were in bed together, it was for sex and sleep. Suddenly, he saw the allure. There was an intimacy to this…

"So, counselor, what was that discussion the two of you had all about?"

Griff pushed aside the guilt he felt, about the false assumptions that had been made by Robert Lockhart. Just because theirs wasn't a traditional marriage did not mean it wasn't a good one. "He's glad you're happy and thinks I'm taking good care of you and our babies."

Mackenzie smiled in relief. "You are! And for the record, I plan to take good care of you-all, too," she promised.

Clearly satisfied that all was well, that their first holiday trip home as husband and wife had been an undisputed success, Mackenzie reached over and turned out the beside lamp.

Once again, she slid into his arms, snuggling close. As Griff held her, he couldn't help but hope this day was just a preview of the happy family holidays to come.

"I guess we have run out of excuses, haven't we?" Mackenzie asked her dog several days later.

The work on her galley kitchen had finally been completed, and now the black quartz countertops and newly painted cream cabinets fit in nicely with their luxurious stainless appliances and warm wood floors. And though the café table was still too small for company, it did fit the mini breakfast nook quite nicely.

All in all, Mackenzie thought, admiring the updated kitchen for the umpteenth time that day, their house—well, really *her* house if you wanted to be technical about the ownership—was shaping up nicely. It might not be as swanky as the homes of Griff's colleagues, but it was definitely improving, and would be a great home to bring their babies to from the hospital. And she knew he was happy about that.

What wasn't getting any better was her lower back discomfort. And though she had managed not to try her sister-in-law's prenatal Pilates routine after nearly two weeks had gone by, she knew the time for excuses had come to an end.

Griff was still massaging her back to ease the stiffness, but it was no longer working. She had barely slept the night before, and her tossing and turning had kept Griff awake. She could not let that keep happening when he was working so hard, so she had ordered a maternity leotard online in a size up. Which was a good thing! She needed the extra stretch, she discovered as she put it on. DVD and cell phone in one hand, workout mat in the other, she marched into the living room. Bliss trailed along behind her, her tail wagging cautiously. As if she weren't sure this was a good thing or a bad thing. Mackenzie sympathized; she wasn't certain, either.

But she had to try.

Besides, it couldn't be all that much different from the Lamaze breathing exercises she and Griff did every evening to prepare for the delivery, could it?

"First order of business." Mackenzie set her phone on the coffee table, then using the furniture mover disks Griff had put under the table's legs, pushed the now-feeling-light-as-a-feather table out of the way. She laid the mat in the long rectangular space between that and the sofa, slid the DVD in the player and turned on Griff's large screen TV.

The instructor appeared. She looked to be about six months pregnant, and supple in the way Pilates devotees were. "You're going to need a sturdy footstool or a work-out wedge to lean against…" she said.

Luckily, Griff had a big leather ottoman that went with his reading chair. Using more of the disk-shaped furniture movers, Mackenzie brought that over, too, and following the picture on the screen, set it up against one end of the long narrow mat. Because she was going to need the furniture movers later, to move everything back where it had been, she left them under the feet of the ottoman. Bliss lay well out of the way, watching. She seemed to be questioning whether this was something Mackenzie should be doing if Griff weren't home. But there was no way she was letting him see her in this leotard. No way…

Bliss's eyebrows went up and down.

"I know," Mackenzie panted. "I'm out of breath and we haven't even started yet. But this is supposed to help, so…"

She settled on the mat. Turned the video back on. As directed, she sat with her back to the stool, feet flat, knees up. She leaned her spine against the stool, just the way the lady on the screen was doing.

The instructor lifted one leg and slid her ankle across the opposite knee. "We want to move gently and hold that position," she said soothingly. "Feel the stretch…"

"Oh," Mackenzie said, as the tense muscles in her lower back started ever so slightly to relax. "This is…" *heavenly*, she thought, as she leaned even farther back.

Without warning, the unanchored ottoman went flying. With a *whoomph*, Mackenzie landed flat on her back on the mat. For a moment, too stunned to speak.

Bliss leaped to her feet. Clearly concerned.

Mackenzie tested her left hand. She was able to lift it, no problem. She turned her head and looked her dog in the eye. "I'm good."

Bliss hesitated then sighed and lay down again, front paws stretched out in front of her.

"Okay. I guess I should have removed those sliding disks under the ottoman before I got started, but not to worry, I'll just get up and…"

Mackenzie tried to roll into a sitting position. Nothing happened. She was trapped by the giant weight and bulk of her pregnant middle.

With a grunt, she rolled to one side. Or tried to—but that didn't work, either. She took a deep breath. "I just have to give it a minute," she said to Bliss, as much as herself.

Unfortunately, a minute didn't help. Nor did anything else. Like a whale washed up on a beach, she was trapped by her unwieldly girth and the furniture on either side of her.

Worse, every time she tried to pull herself up, on either side, her lower back spasmed. So she lay where she was, relaxing as much as possible, while she tried to figure a way out of this.

Meanwhile, Bliss scooted forward on her tummy, an inch or two at a time. Wanting to help. And that gave Mackenzie an idea. "Bliss," she said, pointing to the other end of the coffee table. "Get my phone for me. Bring it here."

Bliss looked at her, seeming to frown in confusion.

"The phone." She pointed again.

Ready to come to the rescue, Bliss crawled even closer.

She went nose to nose with her owner, staring soulfully into her eyes. Mackenzie didn't know whether to laugh or cry, so she did a little of both.

Griff had started coming home early since Thanksgiving, making sure he had dinner with Mackenzie and walked and fed Bliss, before heading back to his study.

Tonight, though, they had plans to get a Christmas tree. She had promised to have food ready for them when he arrived.

But when he pulled up in the driveway at 5:00 p.m., he noted that despite the fact it was beginning to get dark outside, the lights in the house were still off. Except for the glow of the TV in the living room. And... what was that heap on the floor? he wondered in alarm as he walked in.

"Don't. Overreact," a grumpy voice warned.

"Mackenzie?" He dropped his briefcase where he stood and rushed to her side, pausing only to turn on a light as he moved. She lay on her back, in some sort of pale pink spandex workout gear that cloaked her body from neck to ankle, with Bliss snuggled up to her protectively. Her forearm was across her closed eyes. She could not hide the mortified flush encompassing her entire face.

"I'm fine," she said in a low, strangled voice that was thick with unshed tears. "I was trying to do some Pilates, and it didn't work out the way it was supposed to."

Only slightly less worried, he said, "Are you hurt?"

"No." She blew out a gusty breath. "I don't think so. I just need help getting up. So, if you can give me some support from behind..."

"Sure." He knelt behind her and gently slid his hands beneath her spine and shoulders. She winced once, as he brought her slowly and carefully to a sitting position.

Then, with additional help, she was able to stand. To his surprise, she appeared even more distressed. "What can I do?"

She burst into tears.

He wrapped his arms around her and pulled her close. And still she cried. "Are you in pain?"

"No! I'm just humiliated!"

"This has to happen all the time," he said, stroking a hand through her hair.

"Really?" She shoved him away and marched off. "Because I haven't heard about it!"

Trying not to grin at the fetching sight she made when she was in a temper, he followed her up the stairs and toward her bedroom. Pregnancy hormones were certainly keeping him on his toes. "That's probably only because people don't want to talk about it."

She spun on him. "If they did, if women knew this could happen to them, they would never get pregnant." She started to peel off her leotard, then abruptly seemed to think better of it. With an indignant huff, she stepped into the walk-in closet and slammed the door behind her.

Relieved it only seemed to be her pride that was hurt, he perched on the edge of her bed. They rarely slept in it now, because it was a queen, and they were far more comfortable on his king-size mattress and box spring. "That's probably why they don't know these things can happen to you!" he shouted, loud enough to be heard through the closed closet door.

Bliss came upstairs, took in the landscape, and then went promptly down again.

The door swung open. Mackenzie was wearing a plaid flannel maternity shirt that came just to the tops of her luscious thighs. She had a pair of elastic-front jeans in one hand and the offending pink leotard in the other.

After throwing the leotard in the hamper, she sat down on the other side of him.

Deciding a change of subject was in order, he asked, "Does this mean you want to go Christmas tree shopping?"

"I don't know!"

Damn, but she was cute when she was in a snit. He knew better than to tell her that, though.

Better to just show her how he felt. He shifted on the bed, closing in on her, then fell backward onto the mattress, pulling her with him. He slid one leg over her knee, pinning her to the covers, then moved one hand to the curve of her rear end and the other to her breast. She caught her breath. Her gaze was hot when she looked at him. "You can't possibly want me now, not after what you just saw."

He stood and ripped off his tie, tugged his shirt over his head and chucked off his pants, leaving his boxers on. And then he was stretching out next to her again, guiding her toward him, so they were lying on their sides, facing each other. He ran his hand down her body, and she gave a little moan and arched into him, making him so damn hard he had no idea how he was going to last long enough to give her what she needed.

"You have no idea how much I want you. How much I always want you," he rasped, unbuttoning her shirt and releasing the front clasp on her bra. He bent his head and kissed the full silky curves of her breasts, the valley in between, one nipple and then the other. "But I will show you," he said as she huffed out a breath.

Tears glistened in her eyes. She looked at him pleadingly. Then whispered, "Griff, you don't have to do this."

"Oh yes, darlin', I do," he whispered back. He took her lips again, kissing her passionately and thoroughly.

Ran one hand over the silky mound of her belly letting his thumb circle her navel, then easing lower, between her legs.

She moaned again, arching her hips into Griff's hand. She was silky, wet, so close. He could feel the desire building in her, and then he moved his lips down her body with one goal in mind. She arched again, fisting her hands in his hair, pulling him close. He kissed her again, there, his mouth intimating what the rest of his body wanted to do to her. And just like that, her entire body convulsed, and she let out the sexiest cry, the one that let him know she was and always would be his.

Mackenzie's heart was pounding in her chest, her whole body quaking. She had convinced herself that the only thing that really connected her and Griff besides friendship and the babies was physical lust.

Hence, she had expected the attraction between them to fade as she got more and more pregnant. In reality, just the opposite seemed to be true. As he folded her into his embrace and slid into her, she could not help but yield to him. He had a claim on her now—a claim on her heart, and her life, a claim on her future. And she wanted that. So much. Just as she wanted to savor the feel of his heart pounding in strong sure beats as he made her his yet again.

Chapter Eighteen

"So what's the urgent problem?" Mackenzie's mom asked later the next week, when they finally had a chance to FaceTime.

Mackenzie sighed. Putting down her paintbrush, she stepped back to admire the mural she was painting on the nursery wall. She had been working on this, off and on for weeks now, trying to perfect it. The Velveteen Rabbit was incredibly accurate and eye-catching, but he also looked a little lonely.

Just like herself. Griff had been working such long hours this month, as he tried to get ahead enough to be able to take a few weeks off when the twins were born in January. And while she knew that came with the territory with his high-powered job, she missed him.

Terribly.

"Honey?" her mom prompted gently again.

Mackenzie sat in the mommy-sized glider rocker. She

set her phone in front of her, so her mom could see her, too. "I'm having trouble figuring out what to get Griff for Christmas. And you're married, and know what husbands like from their wives, so I thought I would ask you."

Her mom settled back in her chair. "What do you usually get him?"

"That's just it." Mackenzie rubbed her hand over her ever-enlarging belly. Admitting reluctantly, "We've never actually exchanged gifts."

Her mom did a double take. *"Never?"*

Reminded once again how precarious her relationship was with her husband, she let out a breath. "It was a sore subject when he was in foster care."

"Because the only gifts you got were the generic, donated ones."

"Right." Mackenzie frowned sadly. "And once he was out of the system, he said they were pointless."

Her mother nodded. "Because he still really had no one to gift or be gifted by in return."

Except her, and he hadn't wanted to do that. "Correct. So…knowing that…we have always just celebrated special occasions by doing something like going out to eat or seeing a movie or a play."

"Then why don't you do that now if it's your tradition?"

"Because I heard from Alice Carson that Griff was talking with Joe about presents, and she thinks from the way it sounded that Griff might be getting me something pretty special."

"Have you asked him?"

Mackenzie ran her hand over her tummy again. "Well, no."

"Why not?" Carol pressed.

The heat of embarrassment moved into Mackenzie's

face. "Because I don't want to ruin his surprise," she said defensively. *And I don't want to put him on the spot if Alice misunderstood what was really going on with Griff. Which could actually be the case since Alice didn't know how he felt about gift-giving. Up to now anyway.*

Her mom asked gently, "So what do you think you should do?"

"I was thinking maybe I should start a new tradition for him…for us…by gifting him with something. I mean, I know we will be giving gifts to our children next Christmas. He's already talked about what Santa might bring them next year. And how at some point he wants to get them both stuffed bunnies. Pink or blue, depending on their sex, of course." She gathered all her courage. "So why not start that tradition now? Whether he gives me a gift or not. Shouldn't I show him how much I appreciate everything he has done for me this year, especially since I've been pregnant?" She got choked up, just thinking about it. "I mean, isn't Christmas all about giving, not receiving?"

Her mother regarded her proudly. "It is."

Now, the real dilemma. "So…then…what should I give Griff?" Mackenzie asked desperately.

Her mother shook her head as if that would clear it. "You're asking me?"

Of course! If there was any woman on this earth who understood how to make her husband happy, it was her mom. Mackenzie nodded in confirmation. "What kind of things did you give Dad when you were newlyweds? For your first Christmas or birthdays together?"

Her mom was at a loss. "Honestly, honey, I'm not sure I remember."

How was that even possible? Mackenzie wondered.

"We didn't have a lot of money when we were first

starting out. So, whatever it was, it couldn't have been much. It was more about the feeling. Me letting him know that what was important to him, was important to me, and vice versa. So, all you have to do," Carol concluded, "is ask yourself, what means most to Griff in this life? And then get him something connected to that."

It took a few days of researching gifts, but Mackenzie finally came up with something appropriate. Which was good because about the time she had it wrapped and tucked away, the rest of the furniture they had ordered for the nursery finally came in.

On the evening of December 23, she and Griff were upstairs, putting the room together. He was assembling both cribs. She had been washing the new baby linens and clothing all day, and was now folding every soft little item and putting it neatly away in one of the two changing table slash bureaus.

"Do you think we should have found out the sexes of our babies?" she said. Inside her, the babies romped.

Looking remarkably content, the way he did most of the time now, Griff slanted her a glance. "Why do you ask?"

Mackenzie surveyed the sea of linens and clothing. "We have so much yellow and green and white."

"No pink and blue."

"Right."

He fit a side of the crib to an end then screwed it in. "Dr. Connelly must know. It's got to be in the records from the ultrasounds and so on." He squinted at her as if he knew where this was going. "We could just call her. Ask."

"I know." Mackenzie sighed, her spirits already beginning to deflate.

He fit another side to a crib end board. "But…?"

She gestured uncertainly. "We wanted to be surprised."

Finished, he stood and came over to embrace her. "We will be surprised whenever we find out." He buried his face in her hair. Kissed her temple.

She leaned against him, as much as her pregnant belly would allow. "I know." She drank in the wonderful manly scent of him and listened to the steady thrumming of his heart. "I'm just being silly."

He released her and went back to working on the crib. "You still having trouble sleeping?" he inquired gently.

She shrugged. "It's hard to get comfortable the last few weeks of pregnancy. At least that's what I've read."

His sensual lips curved in a half smile. "The babies will be here soon."

In nine days, to be precise. Since their check-in date at the hospital was on January 2. A good thirteen days ahead of her due date.

Twins, Mackenzie had also learned, often were scheduled to be born a little early, or somewhere around the thirty-eight-week mark, as that was the ideal time.

She folded a stack of baby T-shirts and slid them into the drawer of the changing table, next to the newborn-size diapers. "Yes. They will be here before we know it." She turned back to Griff, trying to do what he was doing and look only on the bright side. Not sweat the small stuff so much. "And then everyone says all I will want to do is sleep and I won't be able to because I'll be so busy taking care of them."

He continued working on the cribs as if he'd been born to do just that. "In the meantime, I actually have the next two days off," he announced cheerfully, looking over at her. "So, what do you want to do?"

Go home to Laramie for the holidays and be with my entire family, the way I always do, Mackenzie thought. But she couldn't. Dr. Connelly had said she could not travel now. Couldn't do anything taxing that might bring on the birth of the twins earlier than scheduled.

Griff fit the baby mattress into the frame. "Tomorrow is Christmas Eve, you know."

And except for the gift she had gone to great pains to get for him, she had made no plans. Partly because she didn't know what he might or might not want to do. Since generally he felt the same way about holidays as he did about gifts in general. And partly because she felt so much pressure these days to get it all right.

To not do anything to upset their peaceful existence or drive him away. She drew a calming breath and smiled over at him, marveling yet again at how wonderfully masculine and capable he looked no matter what he was doing. She shrugged. "I don't know." Recalling they had already done what she wanted to do on Thanksgiving, and now it was his turn to choose, she asked quietly, "What do you want to do?"

He turned back to her, his expression shuttered. "Alice and Joe have an open house on Christmas night for their close family and friends." He paused, as if to let that sink in. "You and I are invited this year."

She was unsure whether that was cause for celebration. So, she replied, just as casually, "Are you usually?"

The moment the words were out, she regretted them. Unwittingly, she had pointed out one of the glaring absences in his life. The fact on holidays he'd had nowhere to go, no one to spend them with. Up to now anyway.

For a moment, he went very still. She sensed she had hurt him. Or at the very least embarrassed him.

Something flickered in his expression, then disappeared.

"This is a first," he said matter-of-factly.

What that invitation meant to him, however, was hard to discern. He revered the Carsons. Did that mean he wanted to attend? His inscrutable expression gave no clue. Figuring he wouldn't have mentioned it had he not wanted to go, though, she put her own preferences aside and said, "Sure."

Finally, a smile. "Great." He pulled his phone out of his pocket and began to text. "I'll let them know."

And just like that, their two-day reprieve from the rest of the world went from a very personal, very private holiday, back to business as usual.

Even though their kitchen was finished, Griff didn't want to cook, so they went out to dinner on Christmas Eve. When they came home, they drank mulled nonalcoholic wine and watched the Bill Murray movie *Scrooged*.

The classic slapstick comedy had them giggling non-stop, and they were both happy and relaxed as they headed for bed.

Mackenzie felt the same way when she woke the next morning, to see Griff sitting beside her. He was wearing a robe and slippers—a first!—with his pajama pants.

He took her hand and kissed the back of it. "Come downstairs."

Her heart kicked against her ribs. "Why?"

"You'll see." He kissed her hand again, then disappeared.

Hurriedly, she combed her hair and brushed her teeth, found her own robe and slippers. He was waiting for her at the bottom of the stairs. When she joined him, she saw why.

Presents were piled around the bottom of the tree. He held up his phone. "I promised your folks I would get a photo and send it to them." Which he promptly did. "They want to see you opening your gifts. Hence, they suggested we FaceTime with them now, if you like, or later."

It was all she could do to keep her smile from faltering as much as her mood. For a second, she had thought Griff had played Santa and done all this for them! Which would have been a huge change indeed!

Her smile frozen in place, she reminded herself that hadn't exactly been their agreement. Nowhere in their deal had they discussed making their holidays real. Yes, the previous night had been fun but they always had a good time when they shared a meal and/or hung out together.

"Um...how about later?" she said, not sure she was up to dealing with her family just yet.

Nodding to let her know that was okay with him, he led her over to the sofa and waited while she settled with a cushion behind her back. He winked. "In the meantime, we can look at what Santa brought."

Okay, now he was killing her. Because this did seem as real as the stuffed bunny in *The Velveteen Rabbit*.

The emotion inside her built. "Santa?" she croaked.

He nodded, looking very pleased with himself, then went to the tree and brought back two gaily wrapped packages. There were no tags.

Beginning to get in the spirit, Mackenzie demanded playfully, "How do you know these are for me?"

Mischief sparkled in his eyes. "Call it an educated guess."

While he watched, she undid the bow on the first gift and gently removed the paper. Inside were two gorgeous but not identical pink coming-home-from-the-hospital outfits, in newborn size. "We're having twin girls?" She gaped.

He lifted his palms. "Who knows? Open the other one."

She did. Inside, were two very handsome but not identical newborn outfits in blue.

"I don't understand."

"The other night, you said you lamented all the white, and wished you had more pinks and blues. Depending on what we're having. Girls or boys. So here you go."

This was the silliest thing! And also the *sweetest*! She laid a hand over her heart. "So you don't know what we're having."

"No. But now we're prepared, either way. And one more thing…" he said, before she could find the words to thank him. He pulled a long narrow gift from the pocket of his robe. She undid the ribbon. Inside was a velvet jewelry box containing a diamond-studded tennis bracelet. It was the kind she had seen the other senior partners' wives all wear. It was beautiful. And so unlike him, so unlike *her*, for a moment she didn't know what to say.

"Want to put it on?" he asked.

Trying not to cry for so many reasons she did not understand, she nodded. "Yes," she finally managed to say hoarsely. "Thank you. It's beautiful, Griff." She watched as he fastened it on her wrist. "I'll wear it later, too," she promised, "when we go to Joe and Alice's home for the party. And…" Knowing she needed a moment to compose herself, she used her free hand and pushed to a standing position. Then turned to him with a wink. "Santa just may have bought you something, too."

She went to the laundry room and came back with a gaily wrapped box that had been stashed in a cupboard there. Hers did have a tag. It said: *From Mackenzie, To Griff.* "For you."

He took the present. "It's heavy."

And expensive. Though probably not as much as her diamond bracelet. But who was counting? Christmas, she reminded herself, was all about the giving...

He opened it up and saw the handcrafted leather briefcase with his initials. The kind of gift, her research had told her, every attorney would covet.

"For court," she said. "For luck."

For a long moment he stared at it. Looking as stunned and overcome as she just had been.

"Thank you," he said finally. "This is really, really nice."

The trouble was, she had the feeling that nice was not what he had been angling for. Any more than she had been angling for diamonds.

"Thanks for meeting with me after hours," Griff told the jewelry store owner several days later.

"It was my pleasure to make an appointment with you," Allen Cabot said. He ushered him toward the customer table in the luxurious store. "But first...how did your lovely wife like the bracelet?"

Griff sat down where directed, then paused, not sure how to phrase it. "She wore it that same day."

Allen lowered his reading glasses on the bridge of his nose. "But...?"

"I think I may have misinterpreted what kind of woman she is when it comes to jewelry." Griff got out the two push presents he had selected at the same time as the bracelet. Both still bore the store gift wrap. He set them on the table. "Mackenzie is set to deliver in another week..."

Allen saw where this was going. "You'd like to exchange what you purchased, perhaps pick out something else, before the twins are born?"

"Yes," Griff said, relieved.

"No problem. We want all the wives at *Carson, Hale, Shelton and Strickland* to be happy." He templed his fingers. "So, what kind of woman is your wife...?"

It took a while, and some back and forth with the jeweler, but Griff finally figured out what he thought his wife would want. And she was his wife, even if she wasn't so in the traditional sense.

"You understand this will be a custom piece?" the jeweler said as he processed the return and wrote up a new sales ticket.

He nodded. "She will like having something that is unique."

Allen smiled. "I think so, too."

"Can it be ready in a few days?" Griff asked nervously, aware timing could sometimes be everything.

The older man smiled. "I'm sure under the circumstances, our artist can make it happen."

Griff stood. "Thank you."

"You're welcome." They shook hands and Griff headed home.

Bliss greeted him at the door, leash in her mouth, tail wagging. Mackenzie appeared soon after. She looked restless, impatient and physically uncomfortable.

Immediately, he wondered if she were having any sign of oncoming labor. "What is it?" he asked.

She waved a desultory hand. "The usual. I'm tired of being so unwieldy. Tired of being pregnant. Tired of wondering if these two babies are ever going to come." From the foyer closet she grabbed her wrap-style winter coat that no longer had a prayer of closing at her waist. He set his briefcase down, stepped behind her and helped her ease it on. Tenderness sweeping through him, he kissed her cheek. "It's just a few more days…"

She turned to face him, her pretty face suffused with the soft maternal glow he had come to love. "I hope so, Griff, because I really don't know how much longer I can wait."

He understood her impatience. He was impatient, too.

"You don't have anything at work to distract you?"

Her lower lip slid out in a delectable pout. "It's really slow right now. Which is typical. We never get a lot of business in December and January. Then of course it always starts picking up around Valentine's Day." She squinted. "What about you? How is your work going? Is it slower than usual, too?"

He wished. Between the three bar applications, his current clients and new cases, he was swamped. To the point he didn't know how he was going to take as much time as he wanted to take off when the babies were born. But figuring she didn't need to worry about that, too, he wrapped a comforting arm about her shoulders. "Downtime can be good." He nuzzled her ear. "You should enjoy it while it lasts…"

She swung around to face him, resting her hands on his chest. "I wish I could, but I can't," she lamented. "Not when every hour of every day is going by at a snail's pace."

No doubt about it. Her hormones were in overdrive again. Could her moodiness also mean the birth was nearer than they knew?

His protective instincts surged. "I'll walk Bliss with you."

She looked at his suit and tie. "Do you want to change clothes first?"

It did not appear like she could wait. He divested himself of his jacket, grabbed a coat from the closet and put that on. Although jeans would have been more comfortable, he said, "I'll go like this."

Mackenzie calmed down as they walked Bliss around the neighborhood. When they arrived back home, she threw together something for dinner and went to bed early.

She knew she was being overwrought. Up one minute, down the next. She also knew the babies were going to be born when they were ready, and not a second before.

She supposed it was their first Christmas together that was bothering her. She couldn't say why exactly. She just knew that somehow, someway, it had fallen flat at the end. And she still felt disappointed, somehow. Like the happiness she wanted, the happiness Griff had always deserved, was still just out of reach. And for the life of her, she wasn't sure how to rectify that.

Chapter Nineteen

"It's time."

Griff glanced up from his computer screen. It was 4:00 a.m., and Mackenzie was standing in the doorway. Not in her maternity pajamas or one of those old-fashioned nightgowns she had taken to wearing during the last trimester, but a cranberry-red sweater and maternity jeans.

She came all the way into his study in a drift of feminine perfume. With her hair freshly washed and blown out, she had never looked lovelier.

"Time for what?" he asked dumbly. Her ob-gyn appointment had been yesterday. On December 30. Check-in at the hospital was scheduled for January 2.

"The babies to be born."

Griff jumped up so fast, he nearly knocked his chair over. "You're in labor?"

"No contractions. But my water broke about an hour ago."

Good Lord, he was in a panic. "You didn't tell me!"

She shrugged and pointed in the direction of bed. "You weren't there."

Griff stared at her, wondering why she wasn't more distraught. Weren't women who were about to deliver supposed to be distraught?

"I was here!" he reminded her.

Mackenzie got even calmer. "I called the doctor." She spoke slowly and looked him right in the eye. "Dr. Connelly said this is my first delivery. I was barely dilated yesterday. The babies were both in the right position. So there is no reason to worry. There's plenty of time. I just need to be at the hospital in the next hour. Sooner, if I feel any contractions. But…I don't…so…" She waved an airy hand.

Griff rushed by her. "I'll get my keys!"

She followed, waddling slowly. "You have time for a shower."

What was she talking about? It was bad enough she had taken her sweet time!

She followed him into the foyer, then stood there, calm as could be, watching him as he sprinted up the stairs. "Definitely, you should get dressed," she called after him.

She probably was right about that.

Griff rushed into his bedroom. He pulled on jeans and a clean sweater, brushed his teeth, and grabbed his phone and keys from the bedtime table. Shoes on, he raced back down the stairs.

And momentarily, could not find her. He dashed around the first floor. Nothing. "Mackenzie?" he called. *"Mackenzie!"* She wasn't in the bathroom, either.

He was about to have a heart attack when the back door opened. She came in out of the dark, with Bliss beside her. Belatedly, he realized the switch that controlled the motion-detector lights outside was in the Off position.

He turned it back on. "What were you doing out there in the dark?" he demanded, upset.

Mackenzie turned to him with an unperturbed smile. "I fed Bliss and put out fresh water for her." She pointed to the bowls in the laundry room. "And I wanted her to have a chance to do her thing before we left for the hospital.

"Plus," she added with her usual resourcefulness, "I had to text the dog walker we hired to take care of Bliss and let her know we are headed for the hospital. She will be coming by three times a day to care for Bliss, until I get home."

Okay. That made sense. But...

He looked at the completely dark backyard. "Why didn't you turn the floodlights on?"

She showed him the flashlight in her hand. "I didn't want to wake—or alarm—the neighbors."

Good point, too, Griff thought, calming slightly as Mackenzie unsnapped the dog's leash.

Bliss curled up on her cushion in the family room with a yawn. Looking beautiful and maternal and ready to pop, Mackenzie knelt to pet her beloved dog one last time. "Next time I see you," she murmured, "our family is going to be a whole lot bigger."

"Not how you thought we would be spending our first New Year's Eve as a married couple, is it?" Mackenzie asked, as she paced back and forth in the private labor room. She had been at this for fourteen hours now and was still only three centimeters dilated. Her contractions were five to ten minutes apart.

"I can think of worse ways. But, yeah it will definitely be a story to tell our kids."

"Speaking of kids." Looking alternately frustrated

and bored by the slow progress, she perched on the birthing ball and bounced lightly up and down. "We haven't settled on names."

Griff knew what they said in Lamaze class, but he didn't think any type of motion was going to shake those two babies loose until they were good and ready to come out. "No Griff Junior."

"Sure?" Mackenzie bounced some more.

"Positive," he said firmly. "No boy needs to be saddled with Junior as a surname."

Mackenzie slanted him a loving glance. He gave her one back.

"What about you?" he asked. "Do you want a girl to be named after…" He stopped in midsentence as she gasped and turned completely red in the face. Everything in him went completely still, too. "Problem?"

Seemingly unable to speak, she motioned him closer, then took his hand and put it on her belly. It was hard as a rock. This, Griff knew, was the kind of powerful contraction their birthing class had taught them about. And they just kept coming.

Two minutes apart, at first. Then closer still. And so fast they almost seemed to run one into the next.

Dr. Connelly had them moved into the delivery operating room just in case a C-section was needed. It was crowded with several nurses, two pediatricians, a respiratory therapist, an anesthesiologist and, of course, her ob-gyn.

Griff was near Mackenzie's head, aware, now that it was finally happening, all the preparation they'd made was paying off. He coached her the way they'd been taught, and she held on to his hand. And together, he and the doctor encouraged her to push through each contraction. On the third, the head of Baby A was crowning. Griff had never seen anything as miraculous in his life!

"Push, Mackenzie!" Dr. Connelly said.

She did. Their first child was born with a quiet little sob while Griff and Mackenzie both cried with joy. Griff had the privilege of cutting the cord. And Mackenzie had a chance to see their gorgeous little girl. Then their firstborn daughter was whisked away to a corner of the room for postbirth care while Mackenzie concentrated on delivering Baby B, and Griff focused on helping her.

This time she needed only one powerful contraction for the baby to crown, and another to come all the way into the world. The birth of their second child was every bit as miraculous as their first.

"It's a boy!" Griff said, his voice catching with emotion. "A beautiful, healthy little boy!"

Their son let out a lusty, indignant cry. His sister joined in. And this time Mackenzie and Griff cried freely and joyfully, too.

"You should go home and get some sleep," Mackenzie urged Griff, several hours later. She looked gorgeous and elated after nursing both twins for the first time. "The babies are in the nursery. There's nothing for you to do."

Except take care of you.

He didn't want to leave.

Didn't want to be anywhere but where she and their kids were, but he also knew he needed a shower and shave.

And her family was coming in, first thing the next morning. He clasped her hand and lifted it to his lips. "You sure?"

She smiled as he bussed her fingers. "Positive."

Suddenly, he realized how tired she looked, too. If he

were here, they'd be tempted to talk. Replay everything that had happened. Neither of them would get any sleep.

"I'll be back first thing," he promised. He made sure she had her cell phone within reach. "Sooner, if you need me."

She took his hand and pressed the back of it to her lips. "I promise, I'll call if I do." She brushed her lips across his knuckles again. "Now go. Take care of Bliss. And get some sleep."

"Ohhhh," Emma Lockhart whispered early the next morning when she caught sight of the twins. "They are soooo cuuuute!"

Mackenzie had just finished nursing them both, one on each breast, the way the nurse had showed her. She handed Jake to Emma, who perched on the side of the bed and rocked him in her arms. While Mackenzie cradled Jenny.

"How much did they weigh?"

"Jake was six pounds, seven ounces. Jenny was six pounds, three ounces," Mackenzie recalled proudly.

"Griff must be over the moon."

"He is."

Her sister sighed wistfully. The youngest girl, and baby of the family, she had been the least affected by their biological parents' deaths since she had just been an infant at the time. She was also the most stubbornly impractical of all of them.

She looked at Mackenzie admiringly. "You really do just have the best love story of all time. I mean to go from friends to wildly in love to married to twins…!" She shook her head and mugged comically at the sleepy infant in her arms. "I'll tell you, little fella, what I wouldn't give to experience just a little of that kind of lightning in a bottle myself!"

"Oh, come on," Mackenzie steered the conversation in another direction. "You've had love."

Emma pouted. "You are not talking about Tom Reid!"

Her childhood sweetheart. Everyone had thought they would get married after college. But Tom had gone back to Laramie County to run his family's ranch. While Emma struck out for a career with international roots.

Mackenzie lifted a brow. "Just the fact that you immediately jump to that conclusion says you still have a thing for him!"

Emma scowled. "It wouldn't matter if I did. He is not the man for me. And speaking of men...what did Griff give you for a push present?"

Presents, like holidays, were definitely not her and Griff's forte. In fact, after they kind of seemed to give each other the wrong things at Christmas, she was wondering if the two of them should ever even attempt it again.

Although she did have one more thing to give him. When they finally got home with the babies and were celebrating the birth of the twins. But that gift was going to be private. And she didn't want her nosy little sister worming anything out of her.

Mackenzie waved off the subject. "That's not the kind of relationship that we have," she said cautiously.

Emma's eyes widened. "You really don't want him to give you any more diamonds?"

That was easy. "No."

"Why ever not?" she demanded.

Because it made her feel like it was all a charade again, that she was playing the role of the senior partner's wife who just happened to have accidentally gotten pregnant.

Unable to say that, however, without getting into the whole in-name-only marriage deal, Mackenzie shrugged. "It is just not who we are." *Or who I want to be.*

Her sister tilted her head to one side. "I don't understand. Do you not think you deserve it? I mean, why wouldn't you want your husband to give you diamonds for every important occasion if he could afford it and obviously now Griff can!"

"Of course, I like nice things. Everyone does. But I don't lie awake at night plotting how I'm going to get my husband to give me the next piece of expensive jewelry. If I want something, I'd rather provide it for myself."

Emma, who had always been all about being adored, did not get that. Not at all. "Then what *do* you want from Griff?"

Noting both newborns had fallen asleep again, Mackenzie rose to put them back in their Plexiglas infant beds. "Nothing more than what we have right now," she stated firmly as she settled her babies on their backs. "And nothing less."

"Love and romance..." Emma guessed enthusiastically.

If only, she thought. Although the sex between them had been very good since they'd said "I do" and become lovers.

"Friendship," Mackenzie countered, knowing that was something she and Griff did have.

"And what else?"

"I want him to be a good co-parent." Which he already was.

"And provider," Emma added.

That was a lot less important, since she could support herself and their kids monetarily. But figuring that would be too hard to explain to her sister who aspired to be extremely rich and world famous, Mackenzie simply said, "Yes. Having Griff make a ton of money obviously helps make him an enviably good life partner."

It was the things that were less tangible that mattered most, however. The way he understood her, even when she was so hormonal and grumpy she barely recognized herself. The manner in which he kept his promises. And never gave up. But at the same time was not afraid to give in to her, if he saw the issue meant something to her. Like their...er, actually *her* house...

"We just have a good deal going," she said matter-of-factly. "One that works on all the important practical levels."

So what if she still wished deep down that she'd gotten what she had always wanted, from the time she was a little girl? And that Griff had seen her as the woman she had become and fallen head over heels in love with her?

The point is, they were married now.

And thanks to the birth of the twins, they were going to stay married.

And raise their children together...

Emma wrinkled her nose. "If you say this...arrangement...you have with Griff is a good deal, it's a good deal. Myself, I think I'd rather have a man who buys me lots and lots of diamonds."

Deciding it might be time for her to tidy up, Mackenzie padded over to the mirror above the sink. Heavens! Her hair needed taming. Wondering if she had looked this bad when Griff left, she reached for the brush in her toiletries bag and set about restoring order to the thick blond strands. "Well, you're not me," she muttered back.

"Obviously. Since I know how to receive a truly elegant gift in the spirit in which it is given." Arms folded, Emma lounged nearby. "Although...as long as we are on the subject of gift-giving, haven't you heard? It's usually best not to look a gift horse in the mouth?"

Mackenzie brushed her teeth, rinsed, spit. Regarding her sister with mock indignation, she lectured, "First of all. Money is not and will never be the way to my heart."

"Meaning what?" Emma challenged. "There isn't one?"

Mackenzie stuck out her tongue. Waving a finger, she continued fiercely, "Second. Just because you like to make ranch metaphors and still have a thing for cowboys like Tom Reid..."

It was her sister's turn to make a mortified face.

"...does not mean you should compare my husband to a ranch animal!" Even though he was quite the stud, she mused contentedly.

"Why?" Emma teased as their conversation took an even more lighthearted turn. "Are you saying Griff is *not* a stallion? Because those twins there..." She pointed to the dual bassinets. "They speak to a man who's got it going on!"

Mackenzie moaned, sorry she had started this game of sisterly one-upmanship and ridiculously bad repartee. "Of course Griff is sexy!" Duh!

A rap sounded on the mostly closed door. A nurse poked her head around and then breezed in. "Guess who I found in the hallway?" She grinned.

Griff sauntered in. He looked remarkably better than the last time she had seen him. Freshly showered and shaved, in a clean set of clothing. He still appeared tired around the eyes but she imagined so did she.

He nodded at Emma, and then bent and kissed Mackenzie's cheek.

"How long were you out there?" she asked warily. Or in other words, how much, if anything, had he heard?

He shrugged, still poker-faced. "Just a second. I wasn't sure I had the right room, and then Nurse Hazel came along and set me right."

"New dad delirium, we call it," Hazel teased. "They are all so slaphappy once their babies are born they can barely remember their own names."

"Well, I better get going." Emma paused to give Griff a familial hug. She inclined her head at Mackenzie, advising him, "You've got one in a million there. Take care of her. In fact, take care of all four of them!"

Griff hugged Emma back as warmly as if he had always been one of their family. "I will."

"So how are things at home?" Joe Carson asked a week later when Griff finally made it back to the office.

Wishing he had been able to take another week off, the way he had planned, Griff set his briefcase down and removed his winter coat. He had been trying to keep up as best he could, but the mail in his inbox was still overflowing. "Good."

"Mackenzie's family in town?"

"Her parents are here for the full week." Which was really the only reason he was back at the office, no matter what was going on. "Then her sisters are coming in, one at a time, for one week each."

All would be sleeping in Mackenzie's former bedroom, which was now their guest room. She had moved in with him, since his room was closer to the nursery. Hence, there was no musical beds. She was sleeping with him, in his king-size bed, every single night. And while they wouldn't be able to have sex for another five weeks, he was able to hold her in his arms every night as they fell asleep. Be there with her, to assist in whatever way she needed, in the middle of the night when she nursed.

Joe smiled. "So, lots of help."

"Yes." And while he was grateful for that, it also meant a lot less privacy for him and Mackenzie and their babies, and he could have used more of that.

But he had to be practical. He'd taken off more time than his partners had wanted him to take, and they had twin newborns and needed help.

Her family was giving it. So, if the price for that was less intimacy…

"And after that? Is she hiring someone to come in?"

He tried not to think how exhausted Mackenzie already was. "We're still figuring that out."

His boss frowned, but let it go. "Did she like her push present or presents, whatever the case may be?"

It was one present. "I didn't give it to her yet."

Joe lifted a brow.

"She's not really into big, expensive presents, as it turns out."

Not really understanding, the older man nodded, and delivered this parting shot before heading off. "Just make sure that she feels appreciated no matter what."

Griff was trying.

How successful he was being was debatable. He'd thought they were doing great. As friends, co-parents, even as a "casually married" couple. He had even started to hope they were finally getting that happily-ever-after they had never figured on. Until he had walked up and overheard Mackenzie and her sister Emma bantering, just hours after the twins' birth.

Not wanting to interrupt what had sounded like a private Lockhart family conversation, he had paused outside the slightly ajar hospital room door. Heard them joking about his stallion-like sexiness. Talking about the "arrangement." And the fact Mackenzie's heart wasn't really invested in him. Although he thought that might have changed with the twins. She was head over heels in love with their babies. As was he.

She had talked about appreciating the fact he was a good provider, while still owning up to not caring anything about money beyond what it would take to live comfortably. Or wanting to lean on him financially. And most definitely she hadn't wished for any gifts from him.

So he had stood there, feeling a little like a combination man toy and prolific baby maker, who was never going to be any more than a friend and co-parent and husband-in-name-only to her. The push present he'd gone to so much trouble to get for her burning a hole in his pocket.

It was clear *she* hadn't wanted it then. But it was custom and couldn't be returned. So he had taken it home. And put it in his sock drawer, where it still resided. Waiting for…well, he wasn't sure what.

In the meantime, he was working hard to keep his own expectations about their future reasonable. Yes, they'd just been through a pregnancy and that had been a romantic, magical time. But now that was over. The twins were here. And she clearly wanted their relationship to remain exactly as it had been before the birth of the twins. With "nothing more, nothing less."

And while that might be what she wanted from their marriage bargain, he knew he was beginning to want more. *Much* more.

Whether that was going to be possible, however, he mused as he tackled his overflowing inbox, was anyone's guess.

Chapter Twenty

Four months later, Mackenzie sighed in heartfelt frustration. "Let's face it," she muttered, as she measured powdered formula and filtered water in half a dozen baby bottles. Then looked around her unbelievably untidy kitchen while Bliss lounged close by. "I'm a failure on so many levels."

Griff paced around the kitchen, a swaddled infant in each strong arm. Still in the suit and tie he'd worn to work—and the doctor's office—he looked handsome and relaxed.

Pausing to give her a scolding look, he countered with lawyerly precision, "That's not what the pediatrician said, Mack."

She screwed on the bottle tops and covers. Then shook them all vigorously. "The goal is to nurse exclusively for six to twelve months."

Griff swayed back and forth and soothed their hungry babies with ease. His gaze scanned her, head to toe while their children looked up at him adoringly. "But nursing along with supplemental feeding for six months is fine, too. The important thing is for the babies to get the proper nutrition."

Mackenzie put the bottles in the warmers. "And I haven't been making enough milk for the last few days to give them that."

They had been hungry constantly. To the point she had gone through all her reserved breast milk in the fridge and freezer.

"Which is why we are going on to plan B." Griff watched her test the liquid in both bottles. She found it to be just right. "And starting them on the baby formula the pediatrician recommended, in addition to your breast milk. To make sure they have the necessary nutrition."

Griff followed her into the family room. They sat down on the sofa, side by side. She took Jenny. He held Jake. They began to feed.

She had heard that sometimes babies rejected the taste of formula, at least on the first couple of tries.

Her children loved it.

And while that soothed her somewhat, she was still disappointed in herself for not being able to give them everything they needed, when they needed it. And that went for Griff, too.

It seemed she was always letting him down, too, in some way or another.

She exhaled again, as Jenny wrapped her hands around the bottle, little milk bubbles appearing at the corners of her rosy lips. Looking over, she saw Jake beaming up at Griff, too. Felt herself smile. "I know they're going to be fine."

He leaned over and kissed her temple.

"In two months, they will start on solid food." Mackenzie reflected on the schedule the pediatrician had laid out for them.

Griff nodded, and she could tell from his expression that he was looking forward to that as much as he did every milestone. He gazed into her eyes. "Which will make things even easier. At least as far as feeding them goes."

She knew that.

So then why was she so on edge?

Her cell phone rang.

With one hand, she fished it out of her pocket. Saw the caller ID. "I have to take this."

She hit the button on the Bluetooth speaker-receiver looped over her ear and answered, "Special Occasion Signs, Mackenzie speaking..."

For the next few minutes, she listened, apologized, promised to make it all right and apologized again.

"Problem?" Griff said, when the call ended.

Mackenzie settled the now-sleeping Jenny into her bassinet. "Yes. Can you keep an eye on things while I call Luanne and Lenny and straighten this all out?"

"Sure."

When she returned fifteen minutes later, Jake was sleeping in his bassinet, too, and Griff was in the kitchen, tie off, collar unbuttoned, sleeves rolled up. He had put all the clean dishes away and was loading the dishwasher again. It was nearly full, and there were still items on the countertops and in the sink. Guilt flooded through her.

Mackenzie stepped around a basket of clean, unfolded laundry that had made it only as far as the kitchen and picked up another basket of soiled baby items. She carried it into the adjacent laundry room. They were all pastels, so she emptied them into the machine, added laundry detergent formulated especially for babies and turned the machine on.

Going back out, she saw Griff had poured her a cold glass of milk. Which she needed, to help up her own production. Their fingers brushed as he handed it to her. Tingles swept through her. She wondered how long it had been since they had actually made love. One week? Two? Impossible as it seemed, she could tell he still desired her, just as she lusted after him, but they were always so tired, or so busy with the babies...

She cleared her throat. "Thanks."

He smiled down at her tenderly. "You're welcome."

A new flood of regret washed through her. She wasn't the only one who was tired. Griff had been running on three, four hours of sleep a day for months now, too. Mackenzie leaned against the counter and took a couple of long, thirsty gulps. "You didn't have to do this. It was my mess."

"I don't mind." He fit in as much as he could, then added a cleaning pod to the dishwasher soap dispenser, turned it on and filled one side of the double sink with soapy water.

"So." He sized her up. "Everything okay at work now?"

Mackenzie planted the flat of her palm against her forehead. "It will be," she lamented, "as soon as Luanne and Lenny swap the signs they delivered this morning."

"They made a mistake," Griff guessed.

She set down the empty glass and grabbed a dish towel, aware how good it felt to be talking with him like this in the middle of the day instead of so late at night neither of them could keep their eyes open.

"At my behest. I don't know how I did it, but I checked

the instructions I emailed to them, and I had them send a graveyard gag fortieth birthday set meant for a really big jokester, to a very prim and proper Southern belle celebrating her bridal week."

"Oh. Wow."

"Yeah. The jokester thought all the pink and white roses were a hoot, but the bride-to-be did not appreciate the graveyard humor. Anyway, Luanne and Lenny had already explained to both customers that I had just had twins and was really sleep-deprived, and I waived all charges for both customers, since it was our error, and everyone is happy now. Well, sort of. The bride didn't really appear to have a sense of humor or empathy. But the guy was fine."

"Special Occasion Signs," he quipped. "Never a dull moment."

She laughed, despite herself. Leave it to Griff to help her see the humor in what otherwise might have been a dreadful situation. "I could do without moments like that." Shaking her head, she put a stack of dishes in the cupboard. "Although I don't know how I made such a mistake." She sighed heavily. "It was really clear on the invoices."

He regarded her sympathetically. "You have been working really hard, just taking care of the twins."

"It's still no excuse. Speaking of work, though—" Mackenzie glanced at the time and saw it was still only three thirty in the afternoon "—shouldn't you be going back to work?"

He shrugged. "It's Friday. Besides, I thought I should be here when your parents arrived."

Mackenzie blinked. She was sure she was not confused about this! "What are you talking about? They're not coming until *next* weekend."

"Today," he corrected. "The first weekend in May. They're going to babysit for us while we go to Ed Hale's retirement dinner, downtown."

"That's *tonight*?" Mackenzie croaked in complete dismay.

"Cocktails start at seven. So if you want to go lie down for a while and take a nap or do whatever it is gals do before they go out on the town since the twins are asleep…" he offered, as their doorbell rang.

OMG. It was her parents!

Completely frazzled, she hugged them and ushered them in. But breathed a sigh of relief that Griff had thought to tidy up. After all the hellos had been said, she turned back to her husband. "About tonight. I'm not sure I even have anything to wear…"

He remained as unperturbed as ever. "Then run out and get something, or call a store and have them send something appropriate out," he suggested kindly.

Money wasn't an issue now, thanks to his huge bump up in salary; they both knew that.

"I could go," her mom offered.

Now it was Carol who was missing the point.

Mackenzie swallowed. "I'm just not sure I'm up to going," she said honestly.

Her mom and dad exchanged glances, then turned to Griff. Everyone seemed of one mind except her. "Which is why you should definitely go," her parents said, in perfect agreement.

Mackenzie looked imploringly at Griff.

His patience with her was abruptly at an end. "I agree. Ed Hale is a name partner at the firm. It would be incredibly rude and disrespectful for us both not to go."

And that, it seemed, was that.

* * *

Tears of defeat pricking her eyes, Mackenzie whirled and headed up the stairs. This wasn't like her, to not want to be there when Griff needed her. But then lately, nothing was as it should be.

In the distance, she heard her mother say, "You men take care of the babies. I'll handle this."

Mackenzie moved blindly into her bedroom, not bothering to hide her tears now.

Her mother came in behind her. "Oh! Honey…" She gestured at the heaps of dirty laundry, towels crumpled on the floor of what was now their guest quarters, and her dressing area. "What is all this?" Carol asked, aghast.

A huge, horrible, disorganized mess. Mackenzie sat down on the edge of her unmade bed. "I've got twin four-month-old babies, Mom, as well as a business to run! I barely have time to shower and brush my teeth, never mind sleep. There's no time for laundry or cleaning."

Carol put her arms around her and held her close. "And you're exhausted," she said soothingly.

"Yes." Still feeling like an alien had taken over her body, Mackenzie cried silently. Horrible, shaking tears. The kind she hadn't had since she had watched as the house collapsed on her biological parents, killing them instantly. She felt the same way now, like her whole world was on the edge of imploding.

Her social worker mother had never birthed a baby of her own, but she had been a mother of eight adopted children. She understood the bone-deep-fatigue that could come from being a parent. She understood sometimes falling short of expectations, despite your best effort.

And yet, instead of the permission to retreat and go take a nap until she felt better that Mackenzie yearned to receive, Carol straightened and stepped back. Hands still on her shoulders, she looked deep into her daughter's eyes. "Listen to me, honey. Griff needs you tonight. And you need to be with him, too. So, you are going to do this for him, just as he has done so much for you during the past year."

She threw up her hands. "Mom, if I go tonight, everyone is going to see how horrible I look and what an emotional wreck I have become, and I'm going to embarrass him." And that, in Mackenzie's opinion, would be worse. *Much* worse.

Carol whipped out her phone. "Do you want me to see if I can get you a shampoo and blowout somewhere?"

"Mom, I can wash my hair."

Carol shrugged. "Okay."

"The problem is, I don't have anything to wear."

Carol lifted a skeptical brow and headed into Mackenzie's closet. She came out with a cap-sleeved black cocktail dress with a sexy flounced hem. "How about this?"

It was the best of her current options, but still far from suitable. Too tired to argue, Mackenzie lifted a staying palm. "I'll just show you." She stepped into the closet, stripped down and came back out. The once figure-hugging dress now hung on her like a potato sack. "All my dresses are like this."

Carol studied Mackenzie's visibly too-thin arms. Her brow knit. "How much weight have you lost in the past six weeks, since we saw you last?"

"I don't know. Twenty, thirty pounds."

"Are you dieting?"

"Heavens, no, Mom, I'm nursing twins! I'm eating like a truck driver and gulping glasses of milk every chance I get! I just can't seem to take in as many calories as I am expending."

Carol looked thoughtful, but again, not all that sur-

prised. "Understood." She checked the size on Mackenzie's dress. "Okay, here is what we are going to do. You're
going to hop in the shower and wash your hair, and I'm
going to go to that mall that is ten minutes away and pick
up some options. When I get back, you can decide what
you are going to wear, and finish getting ready."

Tears pricked her eyes again.

"Griff needs you, honey. And you need him. So buck
up." She patted her shoulder. "You're going."

On that note, Carol turned and headed out the door.

While her mom was gone, Mackenzie took the longest
shower she'd had in months. She put deep conditioner
in her hair, and let it sit, while she sat on the teak bench
and shaved her underarms and legs. She had to admit,
that felt good. So when she got out, she slathered herself
with lotion and rubbed it in, then set about blow-drying
her sleek butterscotch-blond waves. When she had finished that, she examined herself in the bathroom mirror.

There were bluish-gray circles under her eyes. Big
circles. A tightness around her mouth. Wrinkles framing her eyes.

Part of it was due to weight loss.

The rest, lack of sleep, fatigue.

But makeup could cover a lot of it.

A knock sounded on her bedroom door. Wrapped in a
thick robe, Mackenzie said, "You can come in."

Her mom breezed in, triumphant.

She had four dresses on hangers, all in a size Mackenzie had never even aspired to wear. "I don't think those
are going to work, either."

Her mom countered, "We'll see."

With a beleaguered sigh, Mackenzie tried them on,
one after another. Finally, she paused in front of the full-
length mirror on the inside of her closet door. Admitting

reluctantly that she might have overreacted about going out on the town. "In the right size clothing, I don't look half-bad." She swung back to her mother. "But what is going to happen when the evening goes on and my breasts start to fill up with milk?" The way they should fill up with milk anyway, she thought.

"I think you will be okay if you just pump right before you and Griff leave. In any case, the gala is being held at a very nice hotel. If you would need to express milk while you're there, I am sure they would have place for you to go."

Or maybe, she thought, already tired just anticipating the hours of small talk and very long evening, it would give her a chance to leave before midnight. Surely no one would fault her if she slipped out early to go home and nurse.

As it happened, Mack had very little breast milk to express before they left for the evening. Determined not to worry about that—she had supplemental formula now, after all—she put what she had aside, and then finished getting ready.

Heels and handbag in one hand, bottled breast milk the other, she started down the stairs.

And that was when she heard the voices coming from the kitchen. Griff said, "I don't want her to know we've been talking…"

Robert replied, "We won't tell her."

Tell me what? Mackenzie wondered, freezing where she was.

Griff countered in a low, worried tone, "But you agree with me…this has to happen…"

Carol spoke in her no-nonsense, social worker voice. "Under the circumstances, there is no other choice."

A long pause followed. Finally, Griff said, "I don't want her to be hurt."

Hurt? What were they talking about? Her heart beating rapidly, Mackenzie edged closer. She heard her mom say, "I am not sure you can avoid that, at least initially, but in time I am sure Mackenzie will come to understand what you want to do here really is for the best. For all of you. And anyway, given the overall situation, what choice do you really have?"

What choice indeed, Mackenzie wondered, as Bliss suddenly became aware she was in the vicinity, and leaped up out of the kitchen, toward her.

Mackenzie plastered a smile on her face. She transferred everything to one hand and bent to pet her dog, just as Griff rounded the corner, too.

He smiled at her, as if he hadn't just been scheming against her, and let out a low wolf whistle. "Wow, you're gorgeous!" he said. His eyes slid over her fancy cerulean cocktail dress.

He looked fantastic, too, in a black suit, snowy white shirt and sleek gray silk tie.

Stung by the fact he had apparently been talking about her behind her back, she smiled up at him once again. Her mom and dad came out to relieve her of her dog and the container of breast milk. They looked approvingly at her and Griff, and not the least bit guilty.

Which made her wonder just what was going on.

"You're awfully quiet," Griff observed, as he navigated the traffic in downtown Fort Worth. The bar and restaurant scene were always busy on Friday evenings. Not that he and Mackenzie had spent any time here in months and months. Tonight was no exception. It was stop-and-go traffic all the way.

She shrugged and continued looking out the window, her evening bag clutched in both hands. The fragrance of her perfume tantalized his senses. "I just realized I forgot to tell my folks what the twins' schedule is now."

He caught a glimpse of silky thigh, where her skirt had ridden up. "I wrote everything out for them before we left. Including all the emergency numbers. The hotel where we're going to be. Everything."

She regarded him in an aloof, thoughtful manner that made him wonder if she suspected something was up. But that was impossible, wasn't it? He had been so careful in his planning. There was no way she could know.

Reassuring himself that his efforts were going to make things better, he reached over to squeeze her forearm. "I'm really glad you came with me tonight," he said.

She nodded and looked out the window again. Clearly not as happy to be spending the evening with him as he had hoped.

Traffic inched forward.

Finally, he was able to turn into the entrance of the hotel. He stopped beneath the portico; the valet took his SUV. Together, he and Mackenzie swept inside.

"Mackenzie, darling, it's so nice to see you here tonight!" Ed Hale's wife Cynthia said, hugging her hello.

Reminded how kind and welcoming the other spouses were, Mackenzie smiled. To her surprise, she realized she really had missed the socialization with Griff's friends and colleagues. "I'm happy you-all invited us," she replied.

Joining them, Alice Carson beamed. "Isn't it wonderful?" She gazed around at the three hundred–plus people in the elegantly appointed ballroom. "The whole firm is here to honor Ed!" Paralegals, secretaries and recepti onists, the tech crew, plus all the attorneys, and every employee's plus one, as well, Mackenzie noted.

"We missed you at the annual retreat, though," Cynthia continued.

Mackenzie nodded. Guilt flooded her anew. "I missed you-all, too. But I was nursing and still in new-mom phase."

The other women smiled.

"Next year," Alice proposed.

"Next year," Mackenzie promised airily. *If there was even a next year with her and Griff.* She shook her head, as if to clear it. Where had that thought come from?

The conversation between him and her folks had unnerved her more than she knew.

Alice Carson linked arms with Mackenzie and steered her in the direction of the bar. "Let's get something to drink, shall we?"

"Do they have milk?" Mackenzie asked, only half-joking.

Alice laughed. "We'll see. In the meantime, I wanted to tell you how happy everyone is about Griff's licensure by the Colorado bar. He's already been asked to represent a client in a really big case, one that will bring national prominence to him and the firm." The older woman squeezed her waist. "I'm telling you, that husband of yours is really going places!"

Places he had yet to tell her about? Mackenzie wondered. Was that what he had been talking with her parents about? And why had he told them, and not her? Why was he suddenly shutting her out and plotting behind her back in a way he never had before? Even more puzzling yet, why were her parents going along with it?

Mackenzie had no answers. But this was not the time or place for these kind of questions. So, she did what he seemed to want and mingled with as many people from the firm as possible. Until finally, the cocktail hour had ended and it was time for everyone to take their seats.

A sumptuous dinner of all Ed Hale's favorites followed. Filet mignon and lobster. Potatoes au gratin, baked in heavy cream. Tender spring vegetables. All followed by a tasting flight of luscious desserts.

By the time they got to coffee, which she had to refuse because of the caffeine, Mackenzie was incredibly full and sleepy.

Griff put his arm around the back of her chair and pushed in a little closer as the ballroom darkened even more and the laudatory speeches began.

One after another, people got up and told how Ed Hale had positively affected their life. As Mackenzie listened, her eyes...indeed her entire body...got heavier still.

Doing her best to stifle a yawn, she breathed in deeply, letting her eyes shut just a little bit. The voices at the podium faded, growing quieter and quieter still.

Chapter Twenty-One

Mackenzie woke to thunderous clapping, and the horrifying knowledge that she had fallen asleep during the speeches!

Everyone around her was rising to give Ed Hale the standing ovation he deserved upon his retirement. Including Griff.

Mortified, she pushed to her feet, too, and began to clap. There was no way to tell how long she had been snoozing but the tense set of Griff's shoulders, the way he wasn't looking at her directly at all, told her he was not happy with her.

When the cheering finally subsided, and the lights in the ballroom began to come back on, Griff finally turned and looked at her.

She drew a breath. Ready to apologize.

He gave her no chance. Taking her by the hand, his amber eyes unreadable, he leaned down to whisper in her ear, "Let's get out of here."

She supposed he was right. This wasn't the time or place for a mea culpa. She nodded, swallowing around the growing knot of emotion in her throat. "Sure."

Realizing that Griff had never once lost his patience with her, in all the time they had been married, she moved with him as they threaded their way through the crowd still headed for the podium, to offer more personal congratulations and goodbyes to Ed and his wife. Her heart racing, still trying to formulate what she could say to make this up to him, she followed him out of the ballroom, her hand still clasped tightly in his.

Instead of heading for the bank of elevators that would take them to the lobby, he led her to the ones that led to the hotel rooms. He still looked intense. Not angry, exactly. Just…like a lot was at stake.

She gave his hand a little tug. "Shouldn't we be going the other way?"

"Nope." The doors slid open, and he guided her inside. Hitting the button for 22. The top floor of the hotel.

Wondering if maybe there was a bar up there, overlooking the city lights, she shrugged. It was only eleven o'clock. The twins were asleep… Her parents were babysitting. Why not take the time for a private chat?

But when the doors opened, all she saw were rooms. Griff led her to one halfway down the hall. Extracting a key card from his pocket, he opened the door, then guided her into a sumptuous suite with a sitting room, bedroom and spa bath.

A huge bouquet of her favorite pastel roses sat on a room service table. Next to it was a platter of chocolate-covered strawberries and a bottle of nonalcoholic champagne on ice.

Two fluffy spa robes were laid out on the king-size bed, which had already been turned down. In the closet, she saw two overnight bags, and the case that contained her breast pump. She stared at him in stunned amazement. *"What is all this?"* Except the most wonderful kind of romantic surprise!

He gave her a smile as big as all Texas. "I thought we'd get a jump on the holiday, after the dinner. So happy first Mother's Day." He glanced at his watch. "Approximately twenty-five hours early…"

"Oh, Griff," she murmured on a tsunami of emotions.

The next thing she knew, she was all the way in his arms. He was kissing her like there was no tomorrow, no yesterday, only today. And she was kissing him back with the same pent-up fervor.

Damn, she had missed this. Missed *him*.

They broke apart long enough to gaze into each other's eyes. "You like it then?"

"Oh, yes…"

He jerked in a breath, as if trying to push whatever emotion he was feeling deep into the depths of his heart, where it could reside without her ever seeing it. "Glad to hear it," he said gruffly.

And suddenly, despite the deal they had made to keep their relationship simple, easy, she did not want that.

What she wanted was to see all the complicated, messy sides of his personality, the way he had seen hers. Moreover, she wanted to do away with all the rules they'd put in place, to ensure their independence, and start all over again.

Griff, however, seemed more interested in possessing her the way she had always secretly wanted to be possessed. "Now where were we?" he growled, kissing the shell of her ear, the nape of her neck, her lips.

He moved one hand up and down her back, and the other sifted lovingly through her hair, from crown to ends.

And still he kissed her and kissed her. Wooing and seducing. Adoring and desiring. Each new touch of his lips and sweep of his tongue against hers bringing her closer and closer still, infusing her with a deep longing to become part of him, and have him become part of her.

She melted into him as he pulled her so tight against him she could feel the heat and hardness of him pressing through their clothes.

"Bed," she demanded hoarsely, feeling lusty and happy, excited and desired.

"Ladies first," he teased. Stripping her down, piece by piece. Until she stood naked before him. And even though she knew she was too thin, he looked at her like she was the most glorious woman on earth.

"Gentlemen, too." Quivering with need, she unwrapped him like the unexpected, incredible present he had become to her.

They clung together, dancing in the quiet of the suite. Swaying back and forth, and side to side. Kissing amorously.

Until there was no more waiting.

They were tumbling down onto the silky-smooth sheets. Their hands were full of each other, touching, tormenting. She was right there and he was, too. Together, they climbed the summit. She groaned and arched and felt the magic that only happened when she was with him. He slid deeper still. Moving slowly, evocatively. Her entire body convulsed. And then, in tandem, they catapulted into the most passionate, satisfying pleasure either of them had ever known.

Mackenzie snuggled against Griff, filling his arms and warming his body the way she had infiltrated every aspect of his life. She fit so perfectly against him. As if she were made for him, and he was made for her. Only her… Making him want to believe that happily ever after could be possible, after all…

"How much longer do we have?" Mackenzie asked drowsily.

He savored the warm, womanly feel of her. "Sunday morning."

She lifted her head, stunned. Her makeup had faded a little during the evening. He could see a trace of the deep bluish shadows beneath her eyes. "We're booked here until then?"

He nodded, glad to see she was as delighted as he had hoped she would be. "Your parents understood that we needed the time." He and Mackenzie would have to make good use of it. Because once they went home again, unless things changed, it would be back to the chaos that was beginning to take a toll on Mackenzie, their relationship and, in a roundabout way, their twin infants…

"My folks knew we needed to reconnect," she guessed in the soft feminine voice he loved.

"And work out a lot of other things, too," he told her gently. Wishing he knew what was most important to her going forward. To not feel so overscheduled and over-stressed? Or to continue to build on the career and resulting financial success they had both worked so hard to achieve? Or like him, did she really just want to do whatever was necessary to ensure that the two of them could actually stop and smell the roses and enjoy life again? Instead of rushing from one moment to the next?

All he knew for sure was that the intimacy they had just felt while making love was almost never there anymore. And that stung. More than he had expected that it could.

"Like what we are going to do about better managing

our work and home balance." Because right now it was a disaster. He figured she had to know that.

And he guessed she did, given the resentment suddenly on her face. She stiffened against him and splayed one hand across the center of his chest. It did not exactly feel warm and loving.

She glared at him from beneath the thick fringe of her lashes. Frustration welled between them. "As long as we're on the subject of work and schedules," she said sweetly, "when exactly were you going to tell me about the hugely important eminent domain case in Colorado that you have been asked to take?"

Damn. He had been hoping to work his way around to that, after everything else had been settled. He squared his shoulders as the romantic afterglow they'd been feeling earlier fled from the room. He moved to sit against the headboard. "Who told you about that?"

Mackenzie looked starkly angry in the beautifully muted light of the bedroom. "Alice Carson mentioned it tonight. And—" she sat up against the headboard, too, dragging the sheet up over her breasts "—I have to admit I was stunned to find out you were going to be leaving Texas to try a case elsewhere right now, with our babies so young…" Briefly, hurt glimmered in her eyes.

A muscle ticked in his jaw. "I haven't agreed."

She swiveled toward him, one arm still holding the sheet against her like a shield, and tucked her legs beneath her. Hair spilling in glorious waves over her shoulders, she gave him a long, knowing look. "But you will." Her soft lips tightened with resignation, turning as serious as her blue eyes. "Because a win would lead to national prominence in your field. And probably a ton more money. And basically everything you ever wanted."

In the past it had meant a lot to him to have her understand the depth and cost of his ambition. Now, he wanted her to know what was in his heart, too. He traced his fingers over her sheet-covered knee. Wishing he knew how to best care for and protect her. So he wouldn't make a mistake that would have her pulling even farther away than they had felt from each other recently. "It would also mean opening up a satellite office in Denver for *Carson, Hale, Shelton and Strickland.*"

For a moment, she was silent. Her feelings shuttered from view. "Would you have to live there?" she asked cautiously at last, peering at him from beneath her lashes.

Did she want him to stay or go? He couldn't tell. "Would *you* want to live there?" he asked, just as cautiously.

She rose and found her way into one of the sumptuous spa robes. Barefoot, she bypassed the nonalcoholic champagne on ice and grabbed a couple of bottles of water from the mini fridge. She came back, all capable businesswoman now. "Griff, my business is here." She perched on the edge of the bed. Their fingers brushed as she handed him the drink.

"You're running it remotely now." Luanne and Lenny and the other part-timers were doing almost all the work, from the creation of the actual signs to delivery. Mackenzie was mostly just taking orders, giving instructions, dealing with customers on the phone. And even that seemed to overwhelm her. Which was why he thought, if one of them should dial back on their career right now, it should be her.

She uncapped the bottle, tilted her head back and drank deeply. "Right." She rested the bottle on her terry-cloth-covered thigh. "And as you saw from the mix-up today, the current strategy is not working out all that great."

It seemed she was implying had she not been so hands-off recently, and distracted by everything going on in their lives, she wouldn't have issued incorrect delivery instructions to her SOS employees.

He didn't agree. In fact, he failed to see how her stretching herself even thinner than she was now would solve anything. "You could hire a manager."

She took another long thirsty gulp, then shook her head adamantly. "And hence bring my profits…aka my salary…down to near zero?" she countered. "If I did that, I would have no way to pay the mortgage on my home."

Yet another problem. One that also needed to be addressed *now*: her legendary independence. He rose slowly and put on a robe, too. Aware what was supposed to be a "spa weekend" was fast turning into something far less satisfying. "I could pay the mortgage."

"No."

She couldn't pay her mortgage without ongoing income or substantial savings. Which led to the next idea. Systemically working through all the options, he asked with lawyerly calm, "Have you considered selling your business then?"

Color flooded her high, sculpted cheeks. She drew in an indignant breath and held up a delicate hand. "Please tell me you're joking," she said grimly.

This was never going to be an easy conversation. He had known that. It was why he had reserved a whole weekend to come to a consensus. Because like it or not, changes had to be made if their life together was not going to turn into a complete disaster.

"Then would you like to hire a baby nurse to help out with the twins so you can spend more time running Special Occasion Signs?" he asked patiently. Because if that was what she wanted, he was ready to make concessions, too. More than ready.

Sorrow clouded her eyes. "I don't want someone else raising our babies."

Griff didn't, either. Yet they were running out of options.

"Then what do you want?" he asked her kindly, knowing that between the two of them they had the resources to make nearly any plan work, as long as they labored toward their agreed-upon goals together. "A cook? A housekeeper? An assistant at work or at home or both?" It was clear they had to do *something* to lessen the chaos in their lives.

Oblivious to the depth of his concern, she narrowed her eyes at him. "Is that what this is about?" She finished her water and tossed the plastic bottle in the bin. She whirled on him, hands planted on her hips. "Look, I know the house has been a mess since the babies were born."

He lifted a hand in exasperation, not about to let her derail their conversation with a detour into personal accusations. "It's more than dirty laundry and dishes that are piled in the sink. It's your *health*, Mackenzie. The fact you're so completely exhausted sometimes you can barely eat and you never have time to sleep—"

"And can't produce enough milk to breastfeed our children?" she interrupted him pointedly.

He said nothing, because he knew whatever came out of his mouth on that subject was going to be received in the wrong way. And the last thing he wanted to do was make things worse between them…

"Or stay awake," Mackenzie continued sardonically, "during the speeches in what was an admittedly very nice but very long evening?"

He closed the distance between them. "That's not it." He gently cupped her shoulders between his palms.

She extricated herself from his light, staying grip and stepped back. Chin up, she stared at him, determined to take offense, no matter what he said or did.

"Then what is it?" she asked like the long-suffering wife she apparently aspired to be. "Are you angry because I didn't go to the law firm retreat in April this year?"

It had been a long lonely weekend for him, Griff admitted to himself reluctantly. But he hadn't had a choice; as a senior partner he'd had to go. He had really missed her and the twins; however, whenever he had called home, she had been too busy and preoccupied to talk to him. Which in turn had made him think long and hard about the potential pitfalls of him doing anything work-wise, where they had to be apart.

She was waiting for his reply. And would likely jump to her own erroneous conclusions if he did not tell her. He took another sip of water, to ease the tightness in his throat. "I'm disappointed," he stated quietly, forcing himself to look her in the eye and see the unvarnished truth of her reaction, "because you no longer seem to want to do anything with me."

She recoiled. "That's not true," she countered, stung. But even as she denied it, he knew it was sadly accurate.

He stepped toward her, this once not about to let her run away without revealing what was—or maybe, more accurately, was *not*—in her heart. "Really?" He took her in slowly, head to toe, then returned his gaze to her eyes and spoke to her the way he would a hostile witness on the stand.

"Answer this then," he said impatiently. "If I had told you I wanted to stay in the hotel for the weekend, just the two of us, while your parents watched the kids, so we could figure out how to retake control of our lives, would you have said yes?"

She flinched. Clearly he had hit the bull's-eye.

"That's not fair." Her eyes were fierce. Her lips compressed in a tight, thin line.

"So, in other words," he concluded sadly, feeling like maybe he didn't have the innate skills for a successful family, after all, "no, you would not have."

Silence stretched between them. She paced away, looking guilty and distressed. She ran a hand through her tousled hair. The shadows beneath her eyes showed even darker. "You know how tired I've been…"

How reluctant to spend time or make love with me…

"I know you are making excuses," he replied brusquely. It hurt like hell to keep being pushed away. Made him wish he had stuck to his resolve, after his mom had died, to not ever let anyone really close again.

She swallowed hard, then spoke in the ultra conciliatory tone she used with her most difficult customers. "We had an agreement not to make unnecessary demands on each other." She held out her hands beseechingly. "To be friends and lovers. Co-parents."

He waited for her to add something more. Something deep and personal. She didn't. The center of his chest ached, in the region of his heart.

"Just not husband and wife." His vision blurred with grief.

She wet her lips, looking like she were about to cry, too. With effort, she held back her emotions. Her chin set. "Not traditionally. No."

So once again he wasn't good enough to be really and truly welcomed into the heart of a family. It didn't matter what success he had achieved. Or how much money he made. Or what sacrifices he stood ready and willing to make.

At the end of the first year of marriage, he obviously wasn't what Mackenzie wanted when it came to the next twenty years, while they raised the twins, never mind the rest of her life. Like his previous two serious girlfriends, she just hadn't figured out how to tell him yet.

"But we can still have a nontraditional relationship, even if we don't live in the same place!" she promised.

So she was ready to ask him to move out and move on? Although he probably should have realized this was coming when she insisted on purchasing the house on her own. "Actually, we can't," he said bitterly.

He walked back into the bedroom and started to get dressed.

She followed him, a hurt and panicky look on her face. "Griff? Are you nixing our agreement?" She stared at him in disbelief. "Now? *Tonight*?"

Did she really think he wanted it this way? That he had moved heaven and earth to arrange this weekend for them, if he hadn't been willing to put it all on the line? The trouble was, he had mistakenly thought that they were both all-in their hopelessly misguided union. That they *both* desperately wanted something more.

Enough to question what they had already decided. Enough to change.

But she had made it clear that any change that was coming was going to be completely one-sided. And successful families didn't work that way. That, he knew.

"Over one silly disagreement?" she asked, aghast.

"Actually," he said bitterly, "it was a whole string of disagreements that were never voiced because I didn't want to rock the boat."

"I don't…"

"You buying the house without consulting me, or letting me participate in the purchase? *After* you knew you were pregnant and we had agreed we would raise the twins together?"

She flushed guiltily.

"Refusing to line up a baby nurse in advance of the birth, even though it was suggested to us and we knew it could be helpful?

"You deciding you no longer needed to attend any law firm functions with me. Or support me in any way. Even though I was getting by on three, four hours sleep and bending over backward to support you and the twins."

He shook his head sadly. Their glances meshed, held for an interminable minute. He exhaled wearily. "The list goes on."

Finally she seemed to realize where this was going. Where it had to go. He watched her go very still. Tears the likes of which he had never seen welled in her eyes and rolled down her cheeks.

And suddenly he knew he had to do the tough thing, the only *honest* thing, and put them out of their misery before they completely destroyed each other's lives. He reached out and took her hands in his, laying his entire heart on the line. "I thought this situation was an opportunity for something more."

He felt her go as arctic as his tone.

"I thought you and I and the twins could be a real family," he admitted hoarsely, forcing himself to give up on the only deeply personal dream he had ever allowed himself. Reluctantly, he let her go, stepped back. "I was wrong."

Tears of sorrow continued to stream down her face. In that instant, he knew they had wounded each other enough.

"And that being the case…?" she choked out.

What choice did they have? Heartache reverberated between them. He looked her in the eye and did what had to be done. "I think we should call it quits," he said bluntly.

Chapter Twenty-Two

Griff watched as Mackenzie shut the hotel room door very quietly behind her. He had wanted to drive her home, so she could be with her parents and the twins, since that was what she wanted, but she had insisted on calling an Uber to transport her instead. And now at one thirty in the morning, he was alone. He finished getting dressed in the clothes he had worn earlier in the evening, save the tie, and headed down to the bar off the lobby.

He didn't really want a drink. He just couldn't bear to be in the luxurious suite that he had hoped would help them reconnect, and then sort things out.

Shoulders slumped in defeat, he walked in and took a seat at the bar. The bartender nodded toward a booth behind him. "Do you know them?"

Griff turned. Joe and Alice Carson were sitting close in a back booth of the cozy, intimately lit establishment, looking as happy and head over heels in love as ever. And they were waving at him to come over.

With a sigh, he rose and walked over. He did his best to put on his game face, but Alice took one look at him and knew something was very wrong. She motioned for him to sit. "What's going on?"

With a grimace, he slid into the U-shaped booth opposite them.

"Where's Mackenzie?" Joe asked.

Griff knew he could do what he always did when it felt like his world was crashing down around him and pretend everything was fine. Tell them Mackenzie was sleeping in a suite upstairs and he was restless and had come down so he wouldn't wake her.

This time, the words wouldn't come.

He had spent far too many years putting up a good front. He needed to unburden himself. Joe and Alice were the closest he had to family, outside of Mackenzie and the twins. Over the years, they had parented him in so many ways. Stepping in to be there for him, when needed. Offering advice, and/or a listening ear. Up till now, as with everyone else, he'd only let their closeness go so far. But he saw now that had been a mistake.

Before he could stop himself, the whole story came tumbling out. "You don't look shocked," he said, when he had finally finished.

They exchanged meaningful looks. Alice signaled the bartender and then ordered coffee for the table. Turning back to Griff, she said, "It was pretty clear why you were getting married when you eloped, Griff. But we had seen how you and Mackenzie were around each other..."

"We didn't think it was a mistake," Joe added kindly.

"Well, it was." Griff shoved his hands through his hair. "Our life is a mess. And she won't meet me halfway on anything."

The bartender brought three mugs of freshly brewed

coffee and silver containers of sugar and cream. She set them on the table, then discreetly moved away.

"And you've been good about articulating your needs to her?" Alice prodded.

Griff tensed. "Our deal was to be independent. To come together when it was good, and when we couldn't, to let it go. Just do our own thing."

"Which is why you didn't tell her about the Colorado opportunity," she guessed.

"I was waiting to bring it up tonight. After the party," he said, defending himself grimly.

"And how did that go?" Alice asked.

Griff exhaled. "Not good."

"She doesn't want to move there?" Joe seemed surprised.

"Worse." He chugged half his coffee in a single gulp. "She wants me to go."

"While she stays here in Texas," Alice concluded.

Griff shrugged. "She has a business to run."

Joe studied him, more father figure than boss mentor now. "What do *you* want her to do?"

Sorrow filled Griff's chest. "Honestly?" He forced himself to lay it all on the line. "I don't think it matters. She's going to do what she is going to do."

Alice regarded him soberly. "So you haven't told Mackenzie what is in your heart."

He had gone one better. He had shown her, every time he'd been there for her, held her, made love to her and claimed her as his. "Again," he repeated staunchly, not about to let her break him all over again, "I don't think it matters."

Empathy filled the older woman's eyes. She reached across the table to squeeze his hand with maternal warmth. "That's the funny thing about feelings," she disagreed softly. "You can board them up and fence them in, and do your level best to squash them down, but they're still there. Waiting to catch you by the heart when you least expect it."

A tiny spark of hope flickered. Only to disappear just as swiftly. "You're saying I should ask her to go with me, again."

"I'm saying the two of you might be more connected than you want to admit right now." Alice paused to text him something. "And there's a reason why, for both of you, your favorite childhood story—" *The Velveteen Rabbit* "—is the same."

Bliss greeted Mackenzie as she eased in the front door of her house. Her parents followed soon after. "How are the twins?" she asked, setting her evening clutch on the foyer table.

"Their midnight feeding went well, so they are sleeping." Her parents belted the robes they had thrown on over their pajamas. "What are you doing here? And where is Griff?"

Misery engulfed her heart. "He's, um, still at the hotel," she said finally. Her parents continued to stare at her tearstained cheeks, forcing her to admit, "I think we're taking a break."

Their expressions softened sympathetically. "What does that mean?"

I don't know exactly. He hadn't said divorce, but it seemed like that was the next logical step. Especially for an attorney.

"It means we aren't getting along as well as we should be." She drew a deep breath and pushed on with difficulty. "The truth is I am not helpful enough to Griff right now." First, she had forgotten all about their "night out," then she hadn't wanted to go, and then she'd fallen asleep during Ed Hale's retirement bash. Talk about disappointing and embarrassing your husband! No wonder he wanted to do some kind of marriage reset. Or at least he had, before he had decided they should just call it quits instead.

Her parents waited for the rest.

"There isn't enough of me to go around," she explained, thinking how stressed out and incompetent she had been lately. Messing up everything from her ability to nurse the twins, run her business and keep an organized, comfortable home. Never mind not being available to give Griff the kind of familial support he needed in a job at his level…

"Because there isn't?" her mother prodded gently. "Or because you don't want there to be?"

Up until now, Mackenzie had only been on the receiving end of devastating disappointment. It stunned her to realize she had dished it out, too. When that was the last thing she had ever intended when she proposed marriage to Griff.

Carol led Mackenzie into the family room. She guided her to sit between her and her dad. "When you care about someone, you don't give up no matter how hard it gets."

Was that what she had done once the twins were born? Mackenzie wondered in dismay. Because she was afraid she was beginning to care too much for Griff? When he was still casual about her?

Carol patted the back of Mackenzie's hand. "For instance, I could have abandoned your dad when he wanted to leave his job as a junior exec and buy a broken down ranch and turn it into one of the best cattle ranches in West Texas. Or he could have left me when he found out I couldn't ever have children."

Her dad nodded. In his low, gravelly voice he said, "We also could have quit fighting the system when family court said there was no way one formerly childless couple could handle eight traumatized kids."

But they had started with as many as they could... which happened to be three...and kept adding one more until they had all eight back together again, Mackenzie remembered.

Her mom smiled. "And we certainly could have quit on you. Remember what you said to us when the judge said we were officially adopting you?"

Mackenzie shook her head. She knew she should recall the moment when she was reunited with her family and was blessed with a new mom and dad to fill the void of the beloved parents she'd lost, but that time of her life was still such an unhappy blur.

Carol told her, "When it was announced that the adoption was official, you just shrugged and said, 'Whatever.'"

Tears blurred her eyes as it all began to come back.

Her dad wrapped his arm around her shoulders. "You weren't going to let us in no matter what because you didn't trust us not to leave you the way your first parents did."

Mackenzie wiped the tears from her face. Her anger and rebellion all seemed so foolish and self-defeating now. With an ache in her throat, she reminded them, "My first mom and dad didn't leave me voluntarily. They died in the fire caused by the lightning strike. When the gas water heater exploded and the house collapsed on top of them."

"You were twelve," her mom noted gently. "You had been in foster care for two years. You didn't see it that way."

Carol was right; she had felt abandoned. Angry. Mackenzie swallowed and wrapped her fingers in her mom's. "I'm sorry I gave you such a hard time." *Sorry a part of her was still so closed off.*

Her dad patted her shoulder. "We were tough enough to take it, sweetheart, and we understood how badly you and the rest of your brothers and sisters were hurting back then." He looked her in the eye, and continued even more seriously, "And we also knew that being with family... your *whole* family...was what you-all really needed. So we didn't quit on you when you made it clear you did not want to leave foster care to come be with us."

That's because Griff was there, and I didn't want to leave him.

"Just like your family—you, Griff, the twins—need to be together now," Carol said gently.

"The difference between our two situations is that when you were in the process of rescuing and adopting us, you two already had a rock-solid relationship," Mackenzie pointed out stiffly. "Griff and I are great friends." *Or, we were. Great lovers, too.* "But husband and wife?" she continued, admitting brokenly, "We don't seem to be doing so well in that department."

Her parents weren't surprised to hear there was trouble on the home front. "Griff talked to you about the changes he thinks you-all need to make?"

Reminded that her parents had been in on the Mother's Day weekend gift, Mackenzie nodded. "He suggested I quit working and/or sell my business so he would be free to move on to greater things. Or, I don't know. Maybe he just wants to move on," she said in frustration. "Go to Denver by himself. Leave the chaos of our current life behind and return to his serene, totally work-oriented bachelor life."

Because if he had wanted her and the twins to accompany him, surely he would have mentioned it when he first found out about the opportunity, instead of keeping it a secret from her.

Her parents looked stunned by the heartrending conclusions she'd drawn. "And that's it? That's all Griff said?" her dad asked.

"What else could there have been?" Except maybe, she thought even more miserably, *I want custody of the kids...*

Her parents looked at each other and shook their heads in remonstration. Her dad concluded with an unhappy frown, "She didn't hear him out."

Her mom looked really disappointed in her, too. Enough to go into full social worker–mom mode. "I think you need to ask yourself why you're running away, Mackenzie. And why, after all these years of being there for Griff *so completely*, you are suddenly so willing to quit on him."

Griff waited as long as he could. But at nine thirty the next morning, he checked his pockets to make sure he had everything he needed, and started to call hotel services to have his SUV brought around.

Before he could connect with the valet, however, the suite to the door opened quietly. Mackenzie walked in.

She was the most welcome sight he had ever had in his entire life. She didn't look as if she had slept any more than he had. In fact, she looked like she had been through the wringer, too. But like him, she had also done her best to clean up. Her wavy blond hair fell in a fluffy cloud to her shoulders. She'd put on makeup that emphasized her gorgeous sea-blue eyes, and lipstick that softly outlined her bow-shaped lips. Black leggings clung to her slim hips and long, sexy legs. A slouchy gray cashmere sweater covered her luscious breasts and fell off one shoulder, revealing the formfitting tank top beneath.

He set down the phone, unable to take his eyes off her. His chest filled with an emotion he could now identify. "Hey…" he said in relief. She didn't look as if she were there to ask for a divorce.

She shut the door behind her and walked toward him, the heels of her sexy shoes sinking into the carpet. "Hey."

She stopped an arm's length away. For a moment, all they could do was drink each other in. Without warning, moisture shimmered in her eyes. His throat ached with the effort to hold back his feelings, too.

For the first time, he noticed she was carrying a masculine gift bag, with tissue paper peeking out over the top. Her eyes remaining locked with his, she set it down. Then came a little closer. "I have a lot I want to say, but first—" she took both his hands in hers "—I want to apologize for falling asleep last night during the speeches."

Griff pressed his fingertip to her lips to keep her from continuing. "There's something you should see." He reached into his pocket and pulled out his cell phone. He hit Texts, and brought up the one from Alice Carson. Turned it so she could see the screen.

The caption read "A picture is worth a thousand words," and the photo was of the two of them at the party. Both were sound asleep. He had his chair pulled close to hers, his arm around her shoulders. Mackenzie had her head on his shoulder, and he had his head nestled against the top of hers.

The tears she had been holding back brimmed. "We look so ridiculously sweet and perfect together," she said.

"So maybe that's a clue that we need to take a step back and do a reset," he rasped.

"I agree." Taking him by the hand, she led him toward the sofa.

He exhaled roughly. "I should never have asked you to move in with me."

She turned so they were sitting knee to knee. "I could have said no," she countered, her chin held high, her expression so resolute it set his heart to pounding.

Clasping her soft hands in his, he said, "I knew you wouldn't."

Her cheeks pinkening, she regarded him intently. "How?"

He squeezed her fingers. "Because since we were in foster care together, you were the one person who was always there for me."

Tears of happiness misted her eyes, and the relief inside him built. "You were there for me, too," she pointed out softly.

He swallowed hard around the knot in his throat. And figured as long as they were opening up, he might as well tell her the rest. "The thing is, Mack, I was always attracted to you. And I always had to fight it because you were four years younger, and while the age difference might not matter now, when you were ten and I was fourteen, it was way too much."

"It's a good thing you did fight it," she replied tremulously, "because I had the wildest crush on you, Griff Montgomery, and if those emotions had been allowed free rein, we would have been separated and put in different homes straight away."

He drank in the sight of her. "Luckily, we were both smarter than that."

She nodded. "So we became best friends instead."

"Which worked for a long time," he remembered fondly.

"But then when we eloped for social and professional reasons and started living together, everything changed," she said ruefully.

Griff lifted her hand and kissed the back of it. "And then it changed again when we became pregnant with the twins."

Mackenzie gazed down at his lips on her skin. "And then again after they were born…" she said, ruminating. "Because as close as we were, I could feel you pulling away from me."

Griff exhaled, aware she wasn't the only one with a lot to confess. "Yeah, well, there's a reason for that. When I came back to the hospital that next morning, I had something I wanted to give you. And then I heard you and Emma joking around about push presents, and my stallion-like sexiness…"

Mackenzie moaned and covered her face with her hands.

"She was teasing you about getting more diamonds for push presents, and you told her we weren't like that…"

"Oh, Griff. I didn't really mean that," Mackenzie cried, upset. "I was just trying to protect our privacy. Because everything was still so new and uncertain."

He nodded, understanding. He had been playing it cool, too. "Anyway, after that, I realized that my feelings were starting to get out of hand, and I was starting to break our agreement to keep things casual. And I really didn't want to disappoint you that way. So I backed off, and tried to stick to the friend and lover and daddy roles and not let it go beyond that."

Regret clouded her eyes. "I did, too."

"So instead of us continuing to get closer the way most couples do after their babies are born…" Griff said.

"I dug into my independence. And focused on trying to do everything at once."

He grimaced, lamenting all the time they had wasted. "And I worked harder than ever at the firm, trying to be the good provider you and the kids needed me to be."

Her lips softened. "And that's when our lives began to fall apart."

He threaded his hands through her hair, turning her face up to his. "I think we can still have everything we both want, Mack."

"Just not everything all at once." She flushed beneath his tender scrutiny.

"Right." He shifted her over onto his lap. "Which is why I booked the hotel this weekend. I wanted to celebrate what an incredible mother you are," he told her huskily, holding her close. "And I wanted us to really put our heads together and come up with a plan together that would allow us to have the kind of family life we wanted. One that would have us sacrificing and benefiting *equally*."

She splayed a hand across the center of his chest. Then hitched in an uneven breath, suddenly looking as hopeful and apprehensive as he felt. "Denver...?"

"I didn't tell you because it was never really on the table," he admitted gruffly. "I was getting a lot of pressure to do it, but I let Joe and the other managing partners know definitively last night I would not be the one opening up a satellite office in Colorado. My life—my wife and kids and her family—are all here in Texas, and Texas is where we're going to stay."

"Oh, Griff." She thrust herself against him and hugged him tight. "I love you so much."

He kissed her softly, deeply. "I love you, too, Mack, more than I ever thought possible."

When at last they drew apart, she clasped his hands, and said, "For the record, you're not the only one who has come to the conclusion it's time for change." She paused, then went on, laying bare her soul, too. "I realize now I don't have to do everything on my own. That my whole world won't come crashing down…that I won't lose everything again…if I allow myself to lean on you and open up my heart to you."

They kissed again, sweetly and tenderly this time.

"So…gift time." Griff reached into his pocket and brought out the small square jewelry box. "This is the push present I had commissioned that I have been carrying around for months now. And just so you know—" he winked at her playfully, recalling what a bust his last gift had been, because he had gotten her what he thought she had deserved to have, not what she really wanted or valued "—this time it's not diamonds, because I realize you're not a luxury-jewelry kind of woman. That what you want is a present from the heart." *My heart…*

Fingers trembling, Mackenzie opened the box. Inside was a pendant made of five interlocking solid gold hearts. The clasp opened to reveal the inside of the locket, which contained photos of her and Griff, the twins and Bliss. "And the good thing about it is," Griff said, continuing his sales pitch happily, "is we can add to it, if we ever add to our family."

She looked dazzled. "I love it! Can you put it on?"

Tenderly, he did.

Mackenzie beamed. "And now, something for you." She went to retrieve the gift bag she had brought in with her. Griff placed a hand in the center of his chest and struck a girlish pose. "A Mother's Day gift, for me?"

Mackenzie's beautiful laugh filled the room.

"It's your push present, actually. I had bought it for

you, because I thought if I was going to get a gift it was only fair you be surprised with a present, too. Then I didn't give it to you, because I thought it might be foolish. And then last night, I realized even if we didn't exchange presents on that occasion that I really should have gone ahead and given it to you, because sometimes an action can speak louder than anything a person says. And maybe if you had seen this you would have known how I felt and we might have talked a whole lot sooner."

"Well, now I'm curious…" He dug through the tissue paper. And brought out a custom leather-bound album with the words Our Family on the front. Inside were photos of their time together. Dog-eared pictures of them as foster kids. Hanging out with Bliss. The elopement… the real wedding in Nature's Cathedral. Photos from Lamaze classes and their first Thanksgiving and Christmas as husband and wife. And then in the hospital, with the twins. Coming home. Watching their babies thrive…

"Naturally, we have a lot more to go," she said thickly, her eyes brimming with love. "We're probably going to need more albums, too."

"I love it." He hugged her close, his heart fuller than it had ever been. "I love *you*." He kissed her again, drinking in the feminine smell and taste of her.

Looking like she could never say it enough either now, Mackenzie hugged him back. "Oh, Griff," she whispered emotionally, squeezing him tightly, "I love you, too."

Epilogue

The real estate agent put the For Sale sign in the front yard, promised to have the online listing up in an hour and departed.

Griff turned to Mackenzie. She was holding Jenny in her arms. He had little Jake in his. Bliss was standing beside them. "Ready to go inside for one last look?" he asked.

Mackenzie nodded and bussed his chin. "Let's do it."

Inside, the home that had housed them for the past two and a half years was strangely quiet. All the furniture and belongings had been removed.

Together, they moved through the foyer and the room that had been Griff's study. On through the living room that had held his big leather furniture to the cozy family room that had held hers, and the kitchen that had been updated with its mini breakfast nook that was always going to be too small. Especially for a couple with two growing toddlers.

"Bunny!" Jenny demanded exuberantly.

"Bunny!" Jake echoed, waving his plump little hands.

They mounted the stairs to the second floor, went down the hall to the nursery. There, in the sunshine, was the wall mural that Mackenzie had painted when she was pregnant with the twins. They signaled they wanted to get down, so Griff and Mackenzie set them on the floor. Smiling, they toddled over to the floor-to-ceiling painting that featured Mackenzie's vision of The Velveteen Rabbit, and all his woodland friends.

They babbled nonsensically, running their fingertips over the blades of grass, gorgeous flowers and rough-barked trees, and the assortment of real rabbits, big and small, that mingled with Skin Horse, stuffed lion and of course The Velveteen Rabbit.

Jenny toddled back to Griff. She tugged on her daddy's pant leg and looked up with her toothy grin. He grinned back down at her, evidencing the same adoration he had for his entire family. "Bunny!" she said. Jake followed suit.

"Hang on, little ones!" Mackenzie opened the baby bag she had slung over her shoulder. She brought out the pink bunny for Jenny, and Jake's blue bunny, too. They clutched their adored stuffed animals to their chests and continued toddling around the big empty room.

"I'm going to miss this most of all," Griff said, touching the part of the mural that had the magical fairy, the one that took the old and unloved toys and turned them into Real.

Mackenzie smiled. "Not to worry. I'll paint another one in the new house."

He gave her an adoring look. "The kids will love it as much as I will."

"Well," she acknowledged flirtatiously, "it is our story. Finding out the only way to be Real is to be Loved."

"That, we are," he whispered, bringing her in close for a kiss and a hug.

Bliss, who had followed them upstairs, and the kids clamored to be included. A group hug followed, and then an exploration of the rest of the now-vacant upstairs.

"Sad about leaving the first home you ever owned?" Griff asked later, when they were on the way to the house they had selected and bought together, a few miles away.

"No," Mackenzie said, as he parked in front of the rambling two-story abode with the cottagey feel. "This is a better setup for all of us." The two children's bedrooms shared a Jack and Jill bath. It had a big kitchen with enough room for a breakfast table, a formal dining room for meals with the extended family, a big backyard for Bliss. A study for each adult, and a really nice master suite for the two of them.

She caught his glance, knew what he was thinking. "And no, I don't regret selling Special Occasion Signs to Luanne and Lenny and their parents," she said with her newfound serenity. "Any more than you regret giving up your senior partnership to take an of counsel position with the firm." Which, while still allowing for a handsome salary, also let him have much more control over his hours and the cases he took. They had weekends together now. Most evenings, too. That couldn't have happened had they not downshifted their careers. For now, for both of them, their family took priority.

"Well, then…" Griff unsnapped his seat belt and leaned over to gather her into his arms. He bent his head to hers. "I guess there is only one thing to say." He kissed her slowly, sweetly. "Welcome home."

* * * * *

MILLS & BOON

Coming next month

THE PRINCESS AND THE REBEL BILLIONAIRE
Sophie Pembroke

Isabella had to admit to herself that she was just postponing the inevitable. She had the whole rest of the week here in this glorious villa, beside this beautiful lake, with Matteo. Not making the most of it would be a terrible waste.

Throwing open the doors to the shared balcony that joined their bedrooms, Isabella let the morning air rush in, and felt her own breath rush out.

Once again, Matteo was already sitting at the table on the balcony. There were shadows under his eyes that suggested his sleep might have been as disturbed as her own. But he looked up as she appeared, and a slow smile spread across his face at the sight of her, making him look instantly younger. More free.

Was he remembering that moment last night, too? The one when he'd been close enough for her to kiss, if she'd moved her head just ever-so-slightly? Was he thinking about the suggestion he'd made to her?

The smirk on his face suggested he probably was.

"Good morning," he said, his voice low and warm. "Sleep well?"

She took her seat. "Like a baby." It wasn't a lie. Babies were notoriously bad sleepers, weren't they?

"Me too." The smirk hadn't gone anywhere. "So, how are we going to spend our second day in secluded paradise? Chess? Poker?"

He was teasing her now, but she didn't rise to it. Instead, she looked out over the lake, the balcony suddenly claustrophobic, despite all the fresh air. This villa was huge, and she knew that if she asked for space Matteo would give it to her. He wasn't the kind of man to press where he wasn't wanted, she could tell that already from the way he'd backed off last night after the merest suggestion of more.

The problem was, she wasn't at all sure she wanted him to keep backing off. But she wasn't certain enough to let him in, either.

She wanted him; she wasn't lying to herself about that anymore. But it was so against The Rules. And beyond anything she'd let herself want for so long—ever since Nate. The desire she felt for Matteo…it was overwhelming, and terrifying.

And it felt amazing, all the same.

She stared out over the water and the mountains in the distance. The June air was warm and welcoming, but the breeze from the water kept things fresh in the shady trees that surrounded the villa.

She didn't want to be trapped inside today—otherwise, this villa was no better than the palace in Augusta that she'd escaped from.

Maybe she wasn't ready to take the risk of letting Matteo in quite yet. But perhaps she could take the tiny risk of letting herself out. Just a little bit.

One small first step towards where she was almost ready to admit she really wanted to go.

To bed, with Matteo.

Isabella placed her empty coffee cup down on her saucer. "I'm going for a walk, down by the lake," she said, before she could change her mind. That would give her time and space to keep figuring out what she wanted from this week. Time away from the allure of Matteo's smile, or those green eyes that pulled her in whenever she caught them.

Matteo grinned. "Great! I'll come with you."

Continue reading
THE PRINCESS AND THE REBEL BILLIONAIRE
Sophie Pembroke

Available next month
www.millsandboon.co.uk

COMING SOON!

We really hope you enjoyed reading this book. If you're looking for more romance, be sure to head to the shops when new books are available on

Thursday 27th May

LET'S TALK

Romance

For exclusive extracts, competitions
and special offers, find us online:

 facebook.com/millsandboon

@MillsandBoon

@MillsandBoonUK

Get in touch on 01413 063232

For all the latest titles coming soon, visit
millsandboon.co.uk/nextmonth

MILLS & BOON

THE HEART OF ROMANCE

A ROMANCE FOR EVERY READER

MODERN

Prepare to be swept off your feet by sophisticated, sexy and seductive heroes, in some of the world's most glamourous and romantic locations, where power and passion collide.

HISTORICAL

Escape with historical heroes from time gone by. Whether your passion for wicked Regency Rakes, muscled Vikings or rugged Highlanders, aw the romance of the past.

MEDICAL

Set your pulse racing with dedicated, delectable doctors in the high-pressure world of medicine, where emotions run high and passion, comfort love are the best medicine.

True Love

Celebrate true love with tender stories of heartfelt romance, from the rush of falling in love to the joy a new baby can bring, and a focus on emotional heart of a relationship.

Desire

Indulge in secrets and scandal, intense drama and plenty of sizzling hot action with powerful and passionate heroes who have it all: wealth, statu good looks…everything but the right woman.

HEROES

Experience all the excitement of a gripping thriller, with an intense romance at its heart. Resourceful, true-to-life women and strong, fearless face danger and desire - a killer combination!

To see which titles are coming soon, please visit

millsandboon.co.uk/nextmonth

JOIN US ON SOCIAL MEDIA!

Stay up to date with our latest releases, author news and gossip, special offers and discounts, and all the behind-the-scenes action from Mills & Boon...

 millsandboon

 millsandboonuk

millsandboon

MILLS & BOON
MEDICAL
Pulse-Racing Passion

Set your pulse racing with dedicated, delectable doctors in the high-pressure world of medicine, where emotions run high and passion, comfort and love are the best medicine.